RAVES FOR
THE SIDEKICK SQUAD SERIES

"'The Best Superheroes Right Now Aren't on Screens. They're in Books'... *Not Your Sidekick* by C.B. Lee is a coming-of-age tale about Jessica Tran, the powerless daughter of two superheroes who gets a job at a tech company—and discovers that the world of heroes and villains is more complicated than she realized."

—*WIRED*

Lambda Literary Award Finalist for LGBTQ Children's/Young Adult | "*Not Your Sidekick* is an exciting story full of twists and heart."

—*Lambda Literary*

"Lee offers up a fast-paced, engaging tale set in a quasi-dystopian 22nd-century America where the line between hero and villain is often blurred. With a diverse cast of characters, both in terms of sexuality and ethnic background, and a wholly adorable romance for Jess, it's a lively exploration of morality in a superpowered age."

—*Publishers Weekly* on *Not Your Sidekick*

"Lee crams a lot of themes into a small package here, including LGBTQ relationships, a dystopian society, realizing your heroes have flaws, the importance of family and more... Jess and Abby are delightful characters and superhero fans like this reviewer will especially enjoy Lee's take on how superpowers work. I'm ready for the sequel!"

—*RT Book Reviews* on *Not Your Sidekick*

"This is a light romp of a middle grade adventure/romance, but the real strength is in its matter-of-fact representation of LGBTQ and first-generation American identities. While the meanings of these identities are explored, they are not the focus of the book and are simply part of the character- and world-building. Coming out has already happened, friendships based on immigrant identity are complicated, and there are many primary and secondary characters who fall into these categories so that no single character has to stand for everyone."

—*School Library Journal* on *Not Your Sidekick*

"*Not Your Sidekick* is a much-needed contribution for those of us who for whatever reason just don't tend to read comics very often and want superhero stories anyway… the whole thing shines with authenticity and verisimilitude… It's that kind of SFF so many people crave, where these marginalized kids get to battle evil forces and root out conspiracies as if–gasp–kids from marginalized cultures or sexualities have other enemies besides racism and queerphobia."

—Shira Glassman for *The Lesbrary*

2019 American Library Association GLBT Rainbow Book List | *Not Your Villain*

"The Sidekick Squad are back and better than ever in *Not Your Villain*."

—Hypable

"*Not Your Villain* shows just how meaningful superheroes (and supervillains) can still be. C.B. Lee has invented a world where the greatest power comes from friendship, love and becoming your truest self, and it's the heroic story we need right now."

—Charlie Jane Anders, author of *All the Birds in the Sky*

"A heartwarming bunch of friends, a fast-paced plot, this is the kind of book you open to page 1 and come up for air only when you've reached the end."

— 8Asians.com on *Not Your Villain*

"C.B. Lee's utterly charming Sidekick Squad series has it all—swoony romance, thought-provoking deconstructions of superhero tropes, and the cutest robots ever. But best of all are her very human, very relatable characters—vibrant personalities you just can't help but root for as they make their way in the world. If you're a fan of superheroes, thoughtful sci-fi, and/or general awesomeness, you need these books in your life."

—Sarah Kuhn, author of *Heroine Complex*

"I'm looking forward to spending more time with this incredibly engaging group of characters. The books are fast-moving, with fun action scenes and clever uses of superpowers."

—Smart Bitches, Classy Books on the Sidekick Squad series

NOT YOUR BACKUP

C. B. LEE

interlude **press** • new york

ISBN 13: 978-1-945053-78-8 (trade)

ISBN 13: 978-1-945053-79-5 (ebook)

Published by Duet, an imprint of Interlude Press

www.duetbooks.com

Book Design and Illustrations by CB Messer

10 9 8 7 6 5 4 3 2 1

interlude press • new york

For everyone finding their own way.

For content advisory, see end notes.

CH. 1...

The car rumbles into the turn, tipping precariously to the right as it careens just a little too close to the edge. The movement threatens to send the creaky vehicle off the cliff along with the headstrong driver and nervous passengers. Someone much more practical wouldn't have taken the turn so wide, wouldn't have been going downhill at such a terrifying speed, wouldn't have dared defy the law of gravity. A cautious, responsible driver and citizen educated by the Manual Driving Authority of the North American Collective would have never risked it.

Emma Robledo is neither cautious nor responsible.

She laughs, whooping wildly and pumping her fist into the air. Her stomach drops as the car flies down the dirt trail, and she speeds through the next few turns. The road is all downhill from here. Dust flies in the wind, and the kiss of adventure is in the air. She pushes her heart-shaped sunglasses to the top of her head; excitement pulses through her as steadily as the rhythm of her beating heart. Today is the day. Today, the Resistance will take action against the League. Their little contingent is small, but they're ready. Emma's more than ready. She's been planning this for weeks.

The steering wheel is warm under her calloused hands. She steps on the accelerator, pushing the car to go even faster, and jerks the steering wheel sharply, pulling the car out of the turn. The sun beams on the desolate wilds of the Unmaintained lands ahead of her; the desert seems wide open with possibility. Ahead of them, wavering in the heat, a single, shining, maglev track reflects the afternoon light. It seems out of place in the expanse of the desert as it cuts through the red and gold sandstone and the endless scatter of cacti and creosote bushes. The high-speed hovertrains that connect the otherwise-isolated cities of the North American Collective are lifelines, carrying everything from travelers to food to supplies across the barren wastes.

Today's manifest? Three-hundred-forty-seven MonRobots, all of them from the new MR-D4R series, right off the factory line.

Emma shudders, trying to block the memory of running for her life from the cold, silvery gleam of the relentless robots. Unlike the earlier chore-assistant series from Monroe Industries, the MR-D4Rs are fully furnished with a "security" program. Emma's seen firsthand what harm the new bots can do. Now there's one in almost every household— a sleeping robotic force that could awaken anytime and be used against anyone the League deems a problem.

A gleam flashes on the horizon. The train is approaching. They have mere minutes.

Everything is going according to plan.

"We'll be there right on schedule!" Emma announces.

"Slow down!" Ricky screeches. "Why did we have to drive? We could have just had Tanya teleport us right onto the train."

"How many times did I explain that I can only teleport things to places I've been be-*fooore*—"

Tanya's voice trails off as Emma jerks the wheel sharply again to pull the car out of another curve just before it veers into the canyon.

"Sorry, I meant Sasha could teleport us, but you've both totally been on a hovertrain before," Ricky says.

"Oh, yeah, Mr. Invisibility, let's just teleport to any random hovertrain, *sure*—"

"Robledo, slow down; you're gonna get us all killed!" Ricky's high-pitched shriek is muffled as Cal elbows him.

Emma rolls her eyes. She's driven down this canyon road from their hideout so many times during the practices for this mission, with weights substituting for passengers, that she could drive it in her sleep.

Emma steps on the pedal, pushing the car to accelerate even faster, deftly turning the wheel with each twist in the road. The little solar-powered car isn't built for this speed, or to be driven manually, but with enough modifications it's become the perfect mission vehicle.

Ricky's voice carries so loudly that Emma thinks people could hear them in Vegas. "Why are we going even *faster*? Honestly, there's no need. If *I* were driving..."

In the mirror, Emma can see Ricky tossing back his dusty brown hair and grinning as he launches into a story involving a car and a slow chicken while Sasha and Tanya give him identical, unimpressed looks. The two Black girls are dressed for the mission in comfortable clothing, but took Emma's suggestions in entirely different directions: Tanya's wearing formfitting athletic gear that manages to convey her eclectic, colorful style, and Sasha's outfit echoes her punk music taste with band logos and geometric symbols scattered all over her shirt and pants. Neither outfit is inconspicuous, but Emma did say to focus on comfort.

"I believe Emma is using the momentum of the vehicle and accelerating during turns to get us to our destination as quickly as possible," Cal says, adjusting their goggles on their face. The goggles leave little round depressions on their dark-olive-toned cheeks, which dimple when they smile at Emma. "You're doing great, Emma. Don't listen to Ricky."

Doubt seeps in, dulling Emma's adrenaline rush. Was her plan too ambitious? *No,* she assures herself. *The plan is foolproof.* This part had gone perfectly in her practices. Then again, the weights didn't talk. She'd imagined their first mission would flow like clockwork with all of them on the same page and no one questioning her plans. But Emma also imagined it differently: Jess giggling with delight at every turn, Abby's steady voice encouraging Emma, and Bells— Bells would touch her shoulder and give her that small smile, the one that's just for her.

Emma tightens her grip on the wheel. Her old friends wouldn't question her; they'd support her. But Jess and Abby are still at the Villain's Guild hideout, trying to sort out the next course of action with the adults. But most of them were content to hide and did not want to challenge the Heroes' League of Heroes or do anything about the militarized MR-D4Rs being sold across the country.

Part of Emma's plan is to build the Resistance into a force to be reckoned with, whether or not the Villain's Guild and the other meta-humans in hiding were ready. Emma didn't ask for permission to begin fighting back; she just did what she did best— led the way.

It's taken a grueling few weeks to convert the old movie-watching club's hideout into a true base of operations, but every moment has been worth it, from bringing in Bells' friends from Meta-Human Training to the recruits drawn in by coded clues left on message boards and conspiracy forums to the original members of the pre-Collective-film enthusiasts group.

Emma misses Jess and Abby fiercely, but they all have jobs to do, Bells especially. His part in this mission is the most dangerous, and if they don't get there in time...

Ricky's nasal whine continues. "My plan was great. We don't even need to use any cars or bikes, just get Sasha to teleport us there—"

"*I'm* Sasha. You clearly can't tell us apart or understand how our powers work. Since neither of us has touched any of those new robots before, we can't—"

"Right, but, uh— Tanya could have easily gotten us onto the train—"

"The one that's moving two-hundred miles per hour? The one that's changing location every second, also that, might I remind you, *I've never been on?*"

"Can everyone just shut up and let me concentrate?" Emma grips the wheel. The conversation stops immediately.

A gust of wind—no, not wind, Emma *knows* that flicker— rushes up to the car. A slight green-blue gleam—holographic cam-foil—fades to reveal Bells on his motorcycle. He waves and then slides up his helmet's panel to smile at Emma.

That smile— that's what settles her nerves and quells the doubt rising in her. Emma takes a deep breath.

"This is going to be awesome!" Bells calls out, pumping his fist in the air. "I'll see you down there!" He rolls the motorcycle backward and pops a wheelie, making Emma laugh. Her stomach drops as the car flies down the dirt trail, and she speeds through the next few turns after Bells.

Bells flicks at his shoulder to reactivate his cam-foil, then fades into the desert air. Emma does the same for the car as Bells races ahead of them. Emma can tell he's gaining speed from the cloud of dust kicking up behind the glimmer until he's just a streak of dust alongside the maglev track. She revs the car and looks over her shoulder, past Ricky's anxious face, past Sasha and Tanya whispering softly to one another, past Cal's earnest gaze. The track is still empty, but any second now—

There! A flash of silver. The train streaks across the desert; its shadow is barely a blur as it rushes along its magnetic track. The air between the train and the track glitters and hums, and soon Emma is racing alongside it. She's going as fast as she can, but there's no way a solarcar can catch up to a hovertrain. The whole length of the train zooms past her in a few seconds.

Bells and his motorcycle suddenly *pop* into visibility where the track curves before heading north to Middleton. In this visible moment, he's in disguise for the benefit of the cameras mounted on the outside of the train. The man whose shape he's shifted into is no one, really, a very carefully crafted "no one," designed to be forgettable and unplaceable.

Bells scrambles off his bike and grabs the track just before the train reaches him.

His eyes shut, and he disappears.

The gleam of activated cam-foil merely hides someone from view by mimicking the light refracted around them. But this is very different. Bells isn't gone or in disguise. He *is* the track now. Bell's shapeshifting abilities can affect not only himself, but anything he touches. At this moment he's changing the entire nature of this section of the track, removing its magnetic properties. It's amazing, what Bells can do; they haven't tapped the limit of his potential.

The train creaks and comes to a stop, hovering in place where the maglev tech is still live. Bells must have engaged the brakes.

Emma slows down. "Radios on," she says, double-checking that hers is working.

Ricky makes a face. "You don't have to remind us of every little detail."

"Yours isn't on," Sasha says, flicking the small device clipped to his sleeve.

"Get going!" Emma jerks her head at the train.

Ricky shrugs, flips his screwdriver in the air, and catches it. "I *was* going to turn it on. You can't do this part without me, anyway." He winks at everyone and then turns invisible. His footprints are barely perceptible as he runs toward the train.

This is the most dangerous part of the plan, when the cameras inside and outside the train are still active. They only have six minutes total; that's how long Bells can hold a shift of this magnitude.

Emma, Cal, and the twins wait with bated breath. The side door opens; Ricky's inside. Emma watches the seconds count down. Ricky should be going through each car now, turning off the cameras—

"Cars one and two are out," Ricky says over the radio.

"Go, go, go!" Emma doesn't realize she's shouting until Cal and the twins are both out of the car and racing toward the train.

"We'll see you at the end of the train, Emma," Tanya shouts, then disappears inside with the others.

The train is short, only five cars, each of them filled with MR-D4Rs. Through the windows, Emma can see Cal give her a thumbs up as they sprint to the next car in the train. Abby's program takes forty seconds to rewrite the code of each MonRobot within range— twenty feet, roughly the length of a freight car. They've practiced this over and over again. The plan was simple enough: In each car, invisible Ricky would shut down the camera while Cal, Sasha, and Tanya would follow, running the program and then racing ahead to the next car to do it again. It'd taken Emma several tries to come up with the most time-efficient plan, but she's still worried. Even their fastest time during practice—five minutes and fifty-six seconds—was cutting it close.

Driving beside the train, Emma revs the engine and listens intently for updates. The wind whistles past her, and the next forty seconds crawl by in excruciating silence.

"One down," Cal says, and Emma can see them running forward, past Sasha toward the end of the train, as Tanya is running for her next car.

"Two down."

In every car, they leave another batch of MR-D4Rs without the sleeper program. Emma makes it to the end of the train in no time and swerves to park across the track. She grips the steering wheel, watches the clock, and replays her plan in her head. Now they just have to get in the car and away before the track activates again. If any of them are still on the train, there will be a lot of questions when it arrives in Middleton. Tanya can only teleport one thing at a time, and that's going to be Bells. He'll be exhausted and when he lets go of the shift, he'll just be lying there on the track when the train comes back to life. Tanya will have a split second to teleport him out of danger.

Emma doesn't want to think about what might happen if they miss that second.

Emma glances at the magnetic track as her anxiety spikes. The metal has a faint, iridescent green glimmer. That must be Bells, completely incorporated into the track. Bells, risking his life for her plan.

It's going to work.

"Okay, okay." Emma listens for each update. Seconds seem to stretch into hours, and all Emma knows is the frantic beating of her heart while she thinks about Bells. She second-guesses herself. Maybe rushing into this was a bad idea. Maybe they should have waited until Jess and Abby were able to get the rest of the meta-humans at the Villain's Guild to help—

"Four down," says Tanya.

No time to think about that now. They're almost finished.

Ricky pops into visibility in the last car and smirks at her. "See? We totally didn't need ten practice runs. I had this down. All the cameras in all five cars, done. They didn't know what hit them. I mean, literally. Anyone watching those feeds would be suuuper confused." He saunters out of the train and hops into the seat next to Emma. "Did we bring any snacks?"

Watching the train fervently, Emma elbows him. They're almost out of time. She glances at the track. It's still glimmering green, but it's definitely flickering.

"Last one," Cal says as they enter the last car. Through the broken door, Emma can see them fumbling with the transponder, one person standing amidst rows of MR-D4Rs, waiting silently with their chrome bodies reflecting each other like mirrors. Their rectangular edges shine with a hard, sharp glint. Emma shudders, thinking of the stark difference between this new design and the rounded bodies of all previous MonRobots.

A terrifyingly loud clatter rattles over the radio.

"What was that!?" Emma yells.

"Dropped the transponder! I'm resetting it, but the light isn't turning on—"

Emma curses, glancing at the timer mounted on the car's dashboard. "We don't have enough time. Bells is about to lose the shift! We'll have to leave *now* and get Bells— let's go! Get off the train!"

A sharp electronic whir starts—the noise that haunts Emma's recurring nightmares—and she freezes.

Tanya screams. "One of the bots turned on! Cal!"

Next to her, Ricky is cursing, yelling wildly, but Emma doesn't hear. All she can see are rows and rows of MR-D4Rs lighting up, and one of them buzzes as it scans—

It's as if she's underwater and she can't move, but she has to. Her friends are in danger; *Bells* is in danger—

The world comes back in a roar of noise and confusion, and Ricky is gone, rushing into the car and holding aloft another device that Emma vaguely recognizes from an earlier, scrapped plan— the bomb. It was one of the initial ideas about destroying the robots, but they'd decided to reprogram instead. *Why did Ricky bring it?*

The MR-D4Rs are activating one by one in that unsettling whirr and Emma knows what's coming next when the first one intones, "Sasha Pierce, you are in violation of the Meta-Human Restriction Act…"

Emma doesn't wait to hear the rest. She knows they're all fugitives.

"Get off the train! We've got thirty seconds!" Ricky is yelling, pushing the others, and they're running, running—

Emma sees the three of them running right for her and the open car door and realizes: Ricky's explosive will stop the bots but not the *train*—

Bells doesn't *have* thirty seconds.

She jerks the wheel sharply, turns around, and accelerates, speeding the car through the last bit of distance between the last train car and Bells' section of the track.

Emma's aware of shouting behind her and she calls out, "Just run!" through the radio. All she can think is, *Bells is in danger, Bells is going to come back from his shift, vulnerable, with a train heading right toward him*—

"Tanya! Now!" Emma pleads over the radio. If she can teleport Bells—

Tanya voice is high pitched. "I can't concentrate! You have to *get out of the way*! We *all* have to get off the train before—"

The track rapidly loses its green color, and then there's a little *pop* and Bells' form is lying prone on the track. Emma doesn't think, just throws herself out of the car and races toward Bells. Her feet barely find purchase in the parched earth, but she runs as fast as she can.

Too late. The train roars to life—

Emma wraps her arms around Bells' torso, trying to drag him free. He makes a noise of protest. "Come on, Bells, we gotta—" Emma mutters, but she's not strong enough.

The lights of the train are on. There is no time.

Emma gives up trying to lift Bells and grabs him by the side and rolls both of them off the track into the dirt just as the train whips past them. The wind knocks Emma backward, and then there's the roar of an explosion.

Emma's ears are flooded with the noise, and for a seemingly infinite moment she can only hear a sharp, ringing sound and then it's all gone. There's nothing but the lingering heat and the smoke trailing behind the speeding train and its wrecked car, racing toward the horizon, leaving behind six stunned teenagers.

Sasha coughs, rubbing her eyes. Next to her, Tanya shakes dirt out of her braids, and Cal's goggles are all askew. Ricky is half buried in the sand.

Emma exhales, then coughs. "Well, that went well."

"That was great," Ricky says with biting sarcasm. "Look at my leg!" He winces, pointing at the tear in his jeans.

"Barely a scratch." Sasha rolls her eyes.

"I'm totally bleeding."

"We've got medi-gel back at the hideout," Emma says wearily as she watches the train disappear over the horizon. It'll arrive in Middleton soon, damaged car and all, and it's going to be all over the news. She sighs. The plan had been for a quiet, unnoticeable reprogramming of all the MR-D4Rs on that train. Now the Authorities are going to be on the lookout for any further tampering. "Why did you bring the explosives?"

"Oh, it was a good thing I did," Ricky snaps. "Otherwise all those MonRobots would have woken up, and we would have been toast!"

Sasha stands up, spits dust, and coughs. She glares at Ricky. "That was overkill. All we needed to do was get off the train and then get Bells free—"

Emma's adrenaline is fading, and her heart rate is returning to normal, but the cold, uneasy feeling of failure only grows. It seemed that everything that could go wrong, did. They're lucky no one got seriously hurt. "We need to go," she says. "The Authorities will be here once that train arrives in Middleton and they start investigating. Cal, you're still good to bring back Bells' motorcycle?"

Cal pulls their goggles down, gives her a thumbs up, and waddles over to the fallen motorcycle.

"Tanya, Sasha—"

"On it," Tanya says, with a quick nod at her twin. She doesn't bother with finger snaps, just jerks her head. Sasha disappears first, then Ricky. "Ready, Bells? I can aim for you to land right on the couch."

Bells gives her a weak smile. "Thanks, but I'll ride back with Emma. Can you help me to the car?"

He appears to be lightheaded, but otherwise awake and oriented. Emma isn't sure how long he'll need to recover. Bells' energy exhaustion once left him unconscious for three harrowing days. Emma won't easily forget going wild with worry, checking and double-checking every few minutes to see if he was still breathing, keeping him comfortable. He doesn't seem nearly as exhausted as the last time Emma saw him use his power to this extent. He even cracks a smile as Emma and Tanya help him to his feet, and they all wobble to the car together.

Waving goodbye, Cal speeds off on the bike.

"I'll see you back there," Tanya says. "And don't worry about what Ricky said. It was a good plan. You couldn't have known that the MR-D4Rs would wake up." She smiles, pats Emma on the arm, and disappears.

Now it's just Emma and Bells and the vast, open desert.

Emma turns on the engine and pauses to look at Bells. "You didn't have to ride with me, you know. It would have been much faster to just have Tanya teleport you."

Bells shrugs. "Sitting on the couch resting or sitting in the car resting with you— come on, it's not even a contest." His hand finds hers.

The simple touch reassures Emma and some of her nervousness melts away. "That was awful, though." The failure still weighs upon her, heavy and suffocating. "You could have almost—" Emma doesn't even want to think about losing Bells.

"It's okay, Em. Like Tanya said, you couldn't have predicted that." Bells gives her a puzzled look. "I don't know what happened, but we're all okay, and you all definitely reprogrammed a bunch of those robots, so it all worked out. Four out of five cars. Eighty percent. High marks!"

Bells grins at her, as if the mission was a test she passed. Thinking of it as a test is even worse. Emma gets full marks on all her tests! She's an honors student and in college prep and is going to bring back the space program so she needs fantastic grades. It's definitely *not* good enough for Emma's perfectionist standards. And the whole thing was supposed to be under the radar. Emma wants to bang her head against the steering wheel. *How did this go so wrong so fast?* Her very first mission as a Resistance leader, and everyone was counting on her, and it all failed.

"Hey. Look at me. C'mon, Em."

Emma glances up at him; his warm brown eyes meet her own. Today he's wearing his hair in short dreadlocks that sweep over a side-shave. Even without the dramatic hair colors, his style is still so very Bells— Bells, her best friend, whom she's known since she was five and today almost lost.

"You're doing that thing in your head again. It's fine," Bells cajoles.

"You're just saying that because you love me."

She's teasing, but Bells only gives her a sincere look.

"I do," he says and leans over, and here's the kiss she was expecting, soft and sweet on her lips. Bells kisses her again on her forehead, and then wraps his arms around her.

Emma closes her eyes, takes a deep breath, and inhales deeply, pressing her face into Bells' neck. She can still smell the acridity of burnt metal and chemicals, but here, close, is the light clean scent of Bells' skin and coconut soap. Emma wants to hang on to this moment forever, nestled in the warmth of his arms.

"You okay?"

"Yeah."

Bells grins at her again, and this time Emma smiles back.

"My girlfriend is obviously the best mastermind of all plans. This one just went a little sideways, but it all worked out."

"Thanks," Emma says. The word *girlfriend* feels heavy with expectation; it seems to hang in the air, like a pressure she doesn't quite understand. Emma pushes the thought to the back of her mind and focuses on the warm sunlight on her face and the way the car jitters on the dirt road as they drive to the hideout.

Lines of cracked asphalt and melted tar cross the desert, and occasional buildings stand like ships in a wide, desolate ocean of orange and red rock and parched earth. They haven't been in use for at least a hundred years, maybe longer. Emma wonders if these places were abandoned long before the Disasters; she knows from her history that there wasn't much here besides Vegas and a long-forgotten park. The area wasn't developed enough to have its own nuclear power station, which made the Nevada region one of the ideal places for the Collective to rebuild after the X29 solar flare of 2128 caused many nuclear power stations all over the country to fail.

"Do you think the people who made this road thought it would survive this long?" Emma asks.

"I don't think they thought about it." Bells gazes out the window. The fading afternoon sunlight dances across his dark skin. "This road, at least."

Emma agrees. The roads are just trails now, used by foxes and other animals roaming the Unmaintained lands. Did those people think that the road would fade from memory as cities rose and fell in the distance? Did they, as Bells suggested, simply go about their lives, not knowing that the footprints of their fossil-fuel-burning vehicles would remain until the desert slowly swallowed them?

Beyond the glimmer of the maglev track, the buildings of Andover appear. The city was founded far from its namesake in a desperate attempt by those who moved here to give their new home a sense of familiarity. The lone highway from Andover to the sparkling hub of Las Vegas stands out in stark contrast against the scatter of desert scrub. It's neatly lined and painted; advertisements and billboards block all view of the Unmaintained lands. There's no reason to leave the road when you can go from Andover to Vegas on a single solar charge, and from there, the rest of the country is just a train ride away.

Emma is hit with a pang of longing. She feels every bump and rock in the trail, driving this rusty, salvaged vehicle. She misses her old car, her first car, the cherry-red color, her custom programming, and all the high-tech features that came with it. Mama offered to buy her another one, even another red one, but Emma didn't see the point of getting attached to another car. The crash is still vivid:

the rogue MonRobots chasing them, her friends screaming for her to run, her beloved car tangled and wrecked beyond repair.

She shudders, trying not to let the memory take over. She inhales. Exhales. Looks at the bright blue sky. Concentrates on the feel of the stiff seat under her, on the car shaking as they move along.

"Hey." Bells looks at her. "You're making the face."

"What face? I'm not making any face. This is my driving face."

"*This* is your driving face." Bells stares out the window in intense concentration and scrunches his eyebrows together. "Okay, I feel like that joke would have landed better if I actually did have the energy to shift my face, but you know what I mean. You're overthinking something. Come on, there's no point in worrying about that right now."

Emma takes a deep breath. He knows her too well.

"Maybe we aren't cut out for this." Maybe *I'm* not cut out for this, she doesn't say. But there is no Resistance except what they've started, and they have to be *everything.* And Emma understands that in the vast history of civilization there have been many revolutions, but that's all pre-Collective history. Sure, they're taught some of it at school—a sanitized, bare-bones summary of the people who came before—but the histories and details of the wars fought before the country was forged anew are all gone— lost, banned, destroyed. Some records survive, few and scattered, but what lasts are collections of old books and movies, and, even then, that selection depends on the tastes of those who preserved them. All Emma knows about resistance are the stories they've seen in the banned films— ragtag groups of lone rebels fighting against huge, impossible empires and bringing them down with nothing more than hope and a mentor to guide the way.

Maybe that's what they're lacking, someone who's done this before, who's been fighting since the beginning. But all the adults at the Villain's Guild seem content to hide and even when they finally were spurred to action, it took weeks and weeks of arguing and fighting to agree on a single item.

The Sidekick Squad did a lot of trawling the Net and looking for secret algorithms, clues and crumbs of a hidden organization that was only rumored to exist. It took forever to find what they thought was the Resistance but actually was just a group of people who loved watching pre-Collective films. It was worth it, though, since those members became their first recruits into the new Resistance once they learned the truth. It made Emma realize why the films are banned; the themes of fighting against corruption, of a small group defeating the odds against a large one, all spur hope and change. The films and shows that the Collective produces share open-and-shut plotlines: superheroes saving people from villains, families in their day-to-day life, teenagers at school, but never a government, never questioning or changing the system.

Emma grips the wheel. They have to succeed. There's too much at stake.

"We're still learning," Bells says. "You're being too hard on yourself."

"I just feel like we should be doing more, taking the League head-on, like my plan that no one wants to do: showing up in the middle of a live broadcast and telling everyone what's going on! That's what we need."

"That would make us targets immediately." Bells gives her a contemplative look. "But it's a good idea."

Emma sighs. "Maybe not. We can see how well my last idea turned out."

It's almost dark by the time they get back. Bells has fallen asleep; Emma's eyelids drag. The uphill drive entails coaxing the car on the last of its charge to push way up the canyon and onto the plateau. Here, there are no longer any roads at all. The sandstone is so compacted that the car doesn't leave any tracks. Emma snorts, remembering when they parked so far away and hiked hours just to get to the cavern entrance, hoping to find the Resistance.

They've come a long way since then.

There's a gnarled and burnt Joshua tree right in their path, but Emma keeps charging ahead, clipping a particularly large rock with a loud *smack*.

Bells jolts awake, blinks at the tree in their path, and yawns as they plow through it, distorting the hologram and scattering pixels of light everywhere. "Cool, it didn't even flicker," he murmurs. "That's gotten so much better since we started." He stretches and smiles at her. "I wanna eat, like, a mountain of french fries."

Emma laughs. "Thomas and Kyle said they'd have dinner ready by the time we get back. I think french fries *might* be on the menu."

"Might" was a severe understatement. Emma made sure they were in today's dinner plans. Thomas loves cooking; he jumped at the idea of using the oven they just installed for the french fries. Emma requested them for today, when she knew Bells would need calories to recover properly. Thomas and Kyle, the original leaders of the illicit ring of pre-Collective media enthusiasts, had been more than happy to work with Emma's vision for them to become the hub of the new Resistance. The hideout is a lot cozier since the older married couple moved in to maintain it full time, giving it an air of domesticity it badly needed. Emma still thinks it's not quite her idea of a bustling headquarters, but it's come a long way from being a humble hideout for watching banned media. There's an entire new section for Thomas and Kyle's living quarters, rooms for the twins and Ricky, guest rooms in case anyone needs to crash overnight, a kitchen, and even a little underground herb and vegetable garden, courtesy of technology from Bells' family.

The past three weeks were a nonstop whirlwind what with retrofitting the hideout and trying to recruit new members. It was difficult at first, when no one knew where to start.

Emma's first plan was extremely ambitious: a nation-wide exposé of the League's true nature. They'd start small, with graffiti declaring "THE LEAGUE IS A LIE" to ignite the sparks of the Resistance movement and then spread the story by word of mouth, city by city. It would become an unstoppable piece of knowledge, growing and growing until everyone was questioning the Collective and the League they stood behind.

The plan, however, once Emma got it started, seemed meek compared to what they needed to do. The newest members bring them to fifteen here in Nevada. Their contacts in the Colorado region say that their group is up to eight, and they haven't connected with any other chapters yet.

Things are moving too slowly for Emma. They should already be seeing measurable, significant results. But the so-called "heroes" of the League are still celebrated across the nation; their staged, costumed antics with the League's designated villains dominate the news. They still sponsor countless products; their every hairstyle or fashion statement is the newest topic for every message board. Chatter about them consumes every moment of the entire Collective. And Emma knows why: to distract the public and keep them occupied with meaningless, contrived nonsense while the real crimes happened right under their noses. Captain Orion, the Commander of the League, the nation's most famous and revered hero captured on live video kidnapping and experimenting on meta-humans— that damning evidence should be enough to change the public's mind, but the League easily spun the story, making Orion out to be a villain with her own evil plot. With Lowell Kingston in power—and determined to keep the League under his thumb, keep the country involved in overseas conflict and the public eye away from his corruption—the Collective is a far cry from the egalitarian, peaceful society that it claims to be, the herald of a new age rising from war and disaster.

Emma sighs and parks the rust-bucket of a car. She knows there's no easy solution, yet she can't help but feel frustrated. So far all they've done is paint the words "THE LEAGUE IS A LIE" on various walls downtown. The new members are really into the graffiti, but Emma wants to do more. Her brain buzzes with the need for action. Emma's plans range from the extremely practical (shopping lists and supplies for the hideout) to the very ambitious (stop the production of the MR-D4Rs), but the mission that would really kickstart their fight only came together after Bells convinced his friends from Meta-Human Training to join their cause. Emma's plans went from vague to concrete once she had an idea of what they could do together, and she came up with the mission to reprogram the MonRobots on the supply train. She thought this would be their big moment, their first huge successful mission, with Emma at the lead.

Instead, she's a huge failure.

Emma pulls the sheet of cam-foil from the trunk with more force than necessary while Bells clambers out. He doesn't say anything, but she can feel his eyes on her as she drapes the foil over the car, tucking it carefully so the elements won't displace it. She pats her pocket and is confused when she can't feel the tablet she'd stuffed in there before the mission. *Oh no! What if it fell out at the track? Or worse, on the train now stopped in Middleton?* Brendan's clever design would be immediately recognized as contraband or unregulated tech, and if they searched the hard drive—

"I got it." Bells holds up the tablet. He taps the old-school touch screen and activates the camouflage program. The cam-foil flickers to life, bending the light around the car until, at a passing glance, it could be mistaken for boulders and cacti.

They've been using tablets instead of the data exchange devices that are issued to every citizen in the Collective. Sometimes Emma misses the ease of using the communication device and connecting to the Net, but the DEDs were a homing beacon, tracking their identification and location all the time. They can't use that tracked system anymore. With Brendan's design and Abby's programming, the clunky tablets work well enough, as long as they're within range, to send simple messages and operate custom programs like the cam-foil.

Emma and Bells walk the familiar trail until she hears the barely discernible echo under their feet. Emma sweeps aside the dust, uncovers the keypad, and presses her hand to it. It clicks, and a door swivels open to reveal quiet darkness.

The rickety ladder is something that Emma didn't factor into her plan for Bells-in-recovery to handle, because in every version of the plan, he is teleported to the safety of the hideout, where he can wrap himself in blankets and eat fries while he watches his favorite detective show. Bells takes his time climbing down the ladder, and Emma holds him steady.

"Tanya should have teleported you back," Emma grumbles as they slowly make their way down the tunnel.

Bells doesn't respond immediately; there's nothing but the dry whisper of air sweeping past them and the crunch of their feet on the dirt. "I could have gone that way," Bells says slowly. "I'm fine, really."

"Uh huh," Emma says, awkwardly attempting to hold him up. She's not as tall as Bells' shoulder, so it's difficult for him to lean on her, but she tries anyway. "So where on the scale of, like, from changing your hair to turning into a giant bulletproof rock person, which *took you out for three days*—"

"And I won't forget that," Bells says solemnly. "But I've gotten so much stronger, you know? And yeah, I could only hold the shift for the track for six minutes, but a month ago I wouldn't have been able to walk around like this after." He grins at her. "Maybe I just wanted to hold your hand."

Emma snorts but relaxes, and they walk the length of the tunnel hand in hand. Emma knows every dip and bend in the stone halls by heart, knows this walk should only take a few minutes at this speed, but she stretches it out. Those feelings of doubt and insecurity, her failure as a leader— those are all waiting for her once they rejoin the others. But for now, she's content, holding Bells' hand and walking forward with him. The future can wait, just a bit.

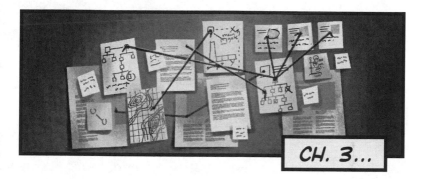

The usual chaos and excitement in the hideout is gone; a sour mood hangs in the air like a heavy cloud. The mission team is scattered about the sloping cavernous room that functions as the living room and the hub of the hideout. Sasha is flicking through feeds on the modified holoprojector, making expressive hand gestures and talking about the news while Tanya listens, her head tilted. Ricky has his leg propped up; the gash is neatly bandaged. Eyebrows knitted, he's staring at the twins. He probably forgot who was who again, which is absurd since Ricky's spent years going to classes with them at Meta-Human Training. Emma's only known them a few weeks, but she can't imagine confusing the two.

Behind them, an intricate map of the twenty-four regions of the North American Collective covers the entire wall; it's marked up with bits of colored string and notes and sketches. On a cluttered table along the far wall are their ancient computers, the radio setup, and other bits of cobbled-together tech.

In the background, a reporter's tinny voice echoes from the holoprojector; every so often the signal causes it to blip. "Preparations for the P019 event are well underway... New Bright City in the Hopestar Region is leading the charge in building a state-of-the-art repulsion shield... new technology... protect the entire city and its constituents from the impact… many other Regions are following suit, constructing shelters… travel advisory warnings will go into effect on November…"

Emma tunes out the report and focuses on helping Bells inside.

Thomas in the kitchen catches her eye and points to a tray of granola bars, sliced apples, and other snacks. Emma shakes her head, mouths "no thanks," and gestures at her own chin hoping Thomas realizes that there's red sauce flecked in his salt-and-pepper beard. He doesn't catch on.

Kyle appears from the doorway of his quarters with his arms piled so high with soft, fleecy blankets that only his tousled brown hair is visible. "Dinner's ready in ten," Kyle says, adding the blankets to the considerable heap already on the couch.

Despite Bells' protests that he's fine, he lets Emma lead him to the couch and wrap him in a soft cocoon of blankets. He gives her a bemused look as Emma fluffs up the pillows behind him and props his feet up. She can't help but blush when he presses a quick kiss to her cheek, and the room erupts into whistles and whoops.

"Hi," Bells says. One of his dreadlocks turns purple as he looks up at her.

"Hi." Emma reaches out. She's not sure if she should kiss him back— *on the cheek too? On the lips?* She touches his face instead, and Bells closes his eyes and leans into the touch. Emma tries to enjoy it without over-analyzing, but her brain is already on hyperspeed. *What does it mean? This is nice, right?* It feels nice, not entirely different from cuddling or hugging before— before everything changed. And now she doesn't know what this means, now that she and Bells are— *What are they? Boyfriend-girlfriend?* They haven't talked about this much since that fevered kiss in the

Rockies and they've been so busy with the mission plans that they have had only a few stolen moments. Emma's done the dating thing, but never with anyone she knew so well, not with her best friend.

They stare at each other, and Emma can't help but grin wildly. This *is* nice, she decides.

Ricky whistles. "Benefits of dating the president."

"I'm not the president of the Resistance," Emma says, rolling her eyes at him. "We're not doing that. See how well that worked out for the Collective?"

Sasha hums. "Eh, we're too small to have, like, a council or something like that. But we should."

"The Council system isn't terrible," Thomas says. "Although I hear a lot of people complaining, and then when it comes time to vote for a new Council member to represent their Region, they don't."

"I mean, you do give a lot of speeches, Em," Bells teases. "I feel like that makes you president."

"Aren't the presidents of the Collective just figureheads?" Cal asks, entering the main cavern from one of the adjoining tunnels. "I'm done fixing the radio, by the way! All ready for our call with the Rocky Mountains headquarters." They plop down on the beanbags between Tanya and Sasha, sniffing the air. "It smells great. Why are we talking about presidents again?"

"The three presidents—technically the Northern regions call theirs the prime minister—embody a cultural role rather than political. They serve on the Council with the rest of the representatives from each region, and each of the twenty-four have just as much power as anyone else," Thomas says.

Kyle nods. "Emma, your mom is the rep for the Nevada region. Would you say she and Kingston have the same amount of power?"

Emma laughs. "Not at all."

Lowell Kingston, President of the Central Regions of the North American Collective, has long been pushing his own agenda. Only recently they discovered how closely he's invested in the League's scam to make sure no one is paying attention to his involving the Collective in conflict overseas. *Remove Kingston from power*—one of the end goals of the Resistance—seems daunting, impossible even, especially in the face of today's disaster.

"Anything about the train yet?" Emma asks.

Sasha changes the channel; the feed flickers wildly. It's the only connection to the outside world in the hideout and is made of scrap pieces of pre-Collective tech cobbled together with an old DED that's modified with a burner citizen ID.

"Nothing yet," Tanya says. "Just the usual warnings about P019. Oh, and there was another report about rogue meta-humans unaffiliated with the League. Go back to the news from the Hopestar region, maybe—"

A mild-mannered reporter stands in front of a brand-new factory. "Monroe Industries insists that the features of the MR-D4R series are completely safe and are only to protect—"

Flick.

"And while Starscream says he and Aerodraft aren't quite dating, we spotted the two heroes looking *quite* cozy—"

Flick. Flick. Flick.

"Wait! Right there! Go back." Cal gestures at the projection.

"The Collective provides." Kingston stands at the podium. His holo flicks in and out, but his voice carries clearly. The Northern

Prime Minister and the Southern President stand beside him, nodding in agreement. Emma's seen plenty of announcements over the past few years with the three leaders of the North American Collecting standing side by side, announcing new economic policies, ensuring the public of their safety from radiation, and the like. Less familiar are the rows of rectangular MR-D4Rs flanking them.

Kingston's smiling, but it doesn't reach his cold, unwavering eyes. "I am happy to once again thank my fellow leaders Priscilla Gobal and Hector Martinez for their support in my campaign for President of the Central Regions of the North American Collective. Our nation was born out of cooperation between the three countries on this grand continent when it was besieged by the Disasters. Our innovativeness continues to move our great country forward…"

The speech is met with polite applause from the studio audience and groans and boos from everyone in the room. A few apple slices and crackers are thrown at the projection.

Emma flicks through channels and shakes her head as she skims through several shows and a few commercials, looking for some news about Middleton and the damaged train.

"Do you think the other members of the Council know what he's done with the League?" Cal asks.

"No," Emma says. "I mean, my mom knew he was corrupt in other ways; she didn't how far he was taking the hero-villain system of the League until I told her."

She flicks through several news broadcasts about Starscream fighting with Dynamite in New Bright City and is annoyed that the League is continuing to stage these fights.

"Middleton! There we go."

A reporter in a maroon headscarf is finishing a weather segment, and it seems she's about to pass to another newscaster. But she continues, clutching her microphone tighter.

Bells snaps his fingers. "Oh! I've seen her before. Rao, I think her last name is. She does the weather for Middleton and a few other Central Regions, but she seems honest, for a reporter."

Emma manipulates the feed for more information: Farha Rao. A quick search on the Net shows only a few credits in the last few months for news and weather segments; she must be a new reporter.

"In other news, a supply train from Vegas with a new order of MonRobots seems to be damaged. Thirty brand-new MonRobots, class MR-D4R, appear to have been destroyed in an accident. Monroe Industries assures that the rest of the robots are in pristine condition, and customers who have been awaiting their orders will all be able to pick up their robots at the normal time. The train did not malfunction, and whether this is the work of a new villain remains to be seen…"

Ricky rolls his eyes and turns down the volume with a wave of his hand. "What new villain! It was us! The Resistance!"

"A new villain," Emma muses. "Well, that's not the worst thing they could have thought. Maybe we should have left a note, like…"

"Signing as a new villain? Or what about just spreading the word that the League is a lie?" Sasha cocks her head.

"Shhh, wait." Emma turns the volume back up, trying to focus on what Farha is saying. The reporter keeps shifting her eyes, as if she's afraid that she'll be shut down at any moment.

"The Heroes' League of Heroes declined to comment on this situation here in Middleton, and I have to wonder— if this was the work of a new villain, why didn't Middleton's own hero, Fireheart, appear on the scene immediately? I'm not one of the Authorities, but even I can see that the damage was clearly done en-route as the train was traveling through the Nevada and Utah regions. Smasher and Shockwave may have retired, but clearly, if a hero sees danger, they would rush to be on the scene. Why didn't Salt Lake City's Bellevue apprehend the culprits?" The reporter's face is grim; her jawline is set. "I'm Farha Rao, reporting live from Middleton and I wonder—"

The news host cuts her off. "Thank you, Miss Rao! And now we're going to Wilton Lysander over in New Bright City for the latest in fashion and hair in this fall's trends with Aerodraft and Starscream—"

Emma sighs and turns off the feed.

Cal readjusts their goggles. "I mean, what impact are we really having on the League by reprogramming these MonRobots?"

"We're preventing people from having militarized spies in their homes," Emma says, but even as she speaks, she hears how hollow she sounds. "It's something. It's better than nothing."

"How about we go after the meta-humans imprisoned in Corrections? Wouldn't we have some badasses like Plasmaman and then we could just— kapow!" Ricky punches his fist into his hand.

"Plasmaman already escaped," Emma says dully. "We met him. He's at the Villain's Guild hideout and is very strongly in the camp of 'let's stay here and not do anything.'"

"What about finding other meta-humans?"

Emma sighs. "That's what Jess and Abby are working on. The adults at the Villain's Guild and the other meta-humans that they've rescued from Orion's experiments…"

Ricky glances from Bells to Emma. "Wasn't there a list? Like a directory of every single meta-human ever registered?"

"Yep," Bells says, almost amused. "Found it. Destroyed it. You know the story."

"I mean, that sounds pretty useful," Cal muses.

Bells shrugs. "The point of destroying it was so Captain Orion couldn't get it. She was planning to kidnap everyone for her experiments, you know, to make her own powers last longer."

"Wouldn't taking it have had the same effect of getting it out of her hands?" Sasha asks.

Emma gives them both pointed looks. They've gone over this, but somehow there's a strong disconnect between those who were there, staring at the massive collection of printed files and no possible way to carry them out of there with rogue MonRobots on their tail. "It's no use quibbling over what we could have or should have done," she says. "What we need to do now is focus on what we need to do next."

Everyone turns to look at her. Emma's heart pounds; she's got nothing. The train mission was her big plan, and the next mission would have built upon the success of this one, but now her brain is a blank slate.

Thomas brings out a heaping platter of chili cheese fries, and everyone is distracted by food. Bells sighs contentedly, shoving fries into his mouth. He looks better already; there are streaks of purple and blue in his short dreadlocks. His energy must be recovering quickly if he's able to change his hair already. Around them, the former members of the film club and the meta-humans recruited from the League's training center eat and chat about a new game Ricky installed on one of the computers. It seems that everyone is avoiding discussing the failed mission, probably to spare Emma's feelings.

She scrapes the leftovers on her plate into the compost bin, then looks at the clock. It's almost time for their scheduled check-in with Jess and Abby. Dread settles in her stomach; she doesn't want to share the bad news just yet.

Footsteps sound down the tunnel. After a shared look of shock, everyone springs into action. Thomas brandishes his spatula. Sasha and Tanya stand up, Ricky disappears, and Cal pulls their goggles down over their eyes. Bells raises an eyebrow at Emma as if to say, *really?*

Emma nods. They aren't expecting anyone else in the hideout today, but it could be one of the newer members who forgot to message ahead. Emma stands up, prepared just in case; she's actually quite proud of everyone's vigilance.

The door opens and shut— Ricky's scouting out the tunnel.

Several shrieks of surprise, and then: "Ricky! Why do you always have to scare me like that!"

Ricky enters the room again with Michelle and Anita, two Vegas locals Cal recruited a few weeks ago. Of all the new members, they've been most enthusiastic about Emma's directives, also the most forgetful about protocols.

"The mission was a huge success!" Michelle announces with a flourish, grinning at everyone. Her braces catch the light as she bounces on her feet.

"We told twelve people, and they were like *whoa*, and they definitely are passing the information on! My cousin Joan says she's going to tell three…" Anita blinks owlishly behind her thick gold frames. "Thomas, what are you doing with that spatula?"

Thomas sets his spatula down. "I thought we were under attack!"

"It could have been MR-D4Rs," Cal offers.

"We wouldn't have heard them," Emma says, gritting her teeth.

"They can fly." Bells' gaze hardens. Some of the purple disappears from his hair.

"Hovertech," Emma clarifies to the confused looks in the room. It's hard, with her and Bells the only ones here with firsthand experience of what those bots can do. That was supposed to be the point of the outreach mission, spread the truth by word of mouth— but it all seems like baby steps.

Anita shrugs. "Well, if they come back, we can just fight them off! The physical training has been going great!"

"Come on, it's time for the call." Bells stands up with the blanket trailing from his shoulders like a cape.

Emma doesn't think she can bear to hear any more talk about how successful that mission was— a mission that is literally just *talking to other people. Who came up with that?* Right, Emma did. *Ugh.* What a mastermind she is. She feels like such a fake.

DUCKING THROUGH THE LOW DOORWAY, Emma follows Bells into the next room. The radio, as Cal promised, is actually fixed. It'd been glitching, not receiving properly, but that had been due to a broken antenna. It took a while to set up all the repeaters from the Nevada region to the high Rockies. Ever since the last repeater was installed at the top of nearby Turtlehead Peak they've been able to check in regularly.

Bells is already tuning to the correct channel. They switched it last week after testing to see if anyone else was transmitting, but so far they haven't heard anything but static. Even with this ancient method of communication, it's important to be careful since anyone could stumble upon their frequency. It's not the most secure system, but it's so old Emma thinks no government official or the League would think of it.

Bells bites his lip and listens to the static as he turns the dial, and then there's the faint tinkling sound of dramatic music and a man talking in a gruff voice.

"So Meeks faked his own death?" This is definitely the correct frequency. Emma decided it was best to blend in with the other hobbyists and play something innocuous, just in case someone was to tune in. It's an episode from *The Gentleman Detective*, looping over and over again.

"Meeks has been lying to us this whole time," Styx Kipling, the wisecracking detective, says in a familiar drawl. "Don't you worry, sweetheart, I'm on the case. Soon everyone will know the truth."

Bells hums to himself. "Such a good episode."

Emma rolls her eyes. "You've seen this one so many times, you've got it memorized."

Bells shrugs, listening intently to the scene. He taps on the microphone. "Hello?"

The episode plays a jangly tune as Kipling finds a clue. "We should change this loop, I swear, every time we call them it's playing this episode," Emma says.

"It's one of the best ones," Bells insists.

Emma rolls her eyes but smiles all the same.

"Hello, hello!" Jess' voice comes on the line, and the sound of the episode cuts out.

"Jess!" Bells and Emma say in unison, and then they both launch into questions.

"Did you guys find any more meta-humans?"

"What's the update on Dynamite?"

Jess laughs. "One a time, one at a time. Not much to report over here. Getting them to decide on anything takes forever."

"Really?"

Jess makes a *hmm* noise. "I think my mom has almost convinced the others that it's time to make a stand against the League, but I don't think they're quite ready to do something public. They keep going back and forth about how staying put is the safest. Numbers are the same. We've got a total of five who are ready for action and seven who are strongly against it, and everyone else keeps arguing about what to do first. I think I've made progress with Tree Frog, though. She definitely is coming around."

"Okay." Bells sighs and taps on the desk.

Emma shakes her head. It's been almost a month since they got back. They should have made more progress by now, but she guesses something is better than nothing. "Okay, Abby, what about rescuing your dad?"

The line is silent for so long that Emma thinks there's something wrong with the signal. "Abby's in the research room right now. Uh… Mr. Monroe… Phillip… his location keeps changing," Jess says. "I can't get a read on where he is. If we go after him, by the time we to wherever he is, he'll probably be somewhere else. And I don't have a way of knowing distance; I can only still tell direction."

Emma sighs. Their plan to take down the League seemed so solid. But, not being at the Guild's headquarters and only getting updates once a week leaves her feeling that they're not making any progress at all. Splitting up seemed like a good idea at the time. Abby wanted to stay with her mom, Jess and her brother wanted to stay with their parents, and the Broussards had to come back to Andover to run their business. It made sense for Emma to come back with them; she missed her moms, and it was time to clue them in on what was happening. But after a month apart and such slow progress, Emma regrets coming back to Nevada.

"I know you wanted to ask me all the boring stuff first because you probably were just being nice about your big news!" Jess crows. "Tell me all about it. How'd it go?"

"Great," Bells says brightly, glancing at Emma. "The plan was great. We reprogrammed all the MR-D4Rs on the train."

Technically that is all true.

"Oh, cool! I wonder if we'd be able to pull something like that off—"

"It was a disaster," Emma says. She crosses her arms.

"No, it wasn't," Bells insists. "Our goal was to reprogram all the bots. We did that."

"And activated a whole car full of MR-D4Rs," Emma mutters.

"Wait, what happened?" Jess' face is probably scrunched up in confusion. Emma can see it clear as day in her head. She's probably got her chin in her hands too.

"We're all fine," Bells says. "No one got hurt, and we definitely accomplished the goal. But, uh, a bunch of bots on the last car woke up and started their capture-the-fugitives protocol or whatever, so Ricky decided to just explode everything."

"I should have had more contingency plans," Emma grumbles. She should have thought to make extra transponders in case any of them were dropped, but they didn't have enough parts.

"Emma! Bells!" Abby's voice crackles over the line. "So excited to hear from you! How'd it go?"

"We only have a minute or so left," Jess says. "What were you doing?"

"Important research!" Abby says breezily. "So, did you save me a MonRobot?"

"What?" Emma wracks her brain. Did she forget a crucial part of the plan? No, no, if the goal was to retrieve a MR-D4R she would have built the plan around it. *What is Abby talking about?*

"No, a bunch of—"

"I want to see if my dad left me any messages in the programming," Abby says eagerly.

"Like in the code?" Jess asks.

"Yes! We used to—"

Bells cuts in. "Hey, we have just enough power for another minute or so. Jess, can you catch Abby up later?"

"Sure," Jess says. Her voice sounds strained, as though something's been bothering her.

Bells goes through updates, and Jess does the same on their end: how many new members, progress on training, supplies needed, and the time and date for the next check-in. Emma wishes they had more than just a few minutes each week, but it's so difficult to coordinate, what with taking care of the repeaters and keeping the signal going. She wants to ask if Jess and Abby are really okay, if things are going as well as they say they are.

"Take care," Emma says.

"We will," Jess and Abby chorus. There's a crinkle of static, and *The Gentleman Detective* episode starts playing again.

"Hey, it's August twenty-eighth," Emma says, distractedly.

"What?"

"It's the first day of school." Emma shakes her head. "It'd be our senior year."

Bells laughs. "Right. School. I don't miss it."

Emma gives him a weak smile. "I do." She misses the structure, the simple routine of going about her day from class to class. She even misses stressing out about class assignments and doing piles of homework. This year they'd be working on their college applications: Bells picking art schools, Emma persuading Jess to join her at the University of Nevada.

"Well, school or not, we're being productive. Hey, and if this all wraps up soon, we can even think about finishing senior year. If you want to."

Emma shrugs. "Technically, I'm done. I finished all my credits this year." It feels strange to think of being finished when her classmates still have another year to go.

Bells whistles. "Really? Why are you still taking classes?"

"It's part of the experience," Emma insists. "Spending time with you and Jess, playing volleyball—we were gonna go to Regionals this year, I'm sure—and, you know, dances and stuff."

"Dances." Bells waggles his eyebrows at her. "Like prom?"

"Yeah," Emma says. She's not sure how she feels about missing the supposedly penultimate high school experience. She went to Homecoming and Spring Fling the past two years, and Carlos asked her to his prom before they broke up. Dances always came with dates; that was part of the package, part of what was expected.

Emma's own high school experience was carefully curated with everything she wanted: all the top classes, sports, college prep, extracurriculars, a healthy social life with friends, regular dates with an attractive and interesting person for the acceptable high school two-month-long relationship-lifespan. But here in the hideout, with the reality of the Resistance, it seems far away, and all the little things Emma did seem trivial now, as if she was playing a part.

Bells throws an arm around her shoulder, and Emma snuggles into his neck. "If you really want a prom, I can make it happen," he announces gallantly.

Emma laughs. Appreciating the moment, she closes her eyes. She imagines the over-the-top outfits, dancing with her friends, and enjoying the party. That always seemed fun and appealing, but she hated all the social pressure those kind of dates brought. Bells looks at her and gives her a soft smile, and then it hits her— she's in a *relationship* with Bells now. Emma has no idea what she's doing. *How is this going to work?*

"ALL RIGHT, MASTERMIND, WHAT'S NEXT?" Ricky asks. He's the only one who uses the names they came up with for the Sidekick Squad, and Emma's pretty sure he's only using hers because he thinks it's funny.

"Same agenda from last week," Emma says, glum. She glances at the clock. It's late; everyone who doesn't live in the hideout will be leaving soon.

"What about the communication plan?" Tanya asks. "Keep spreading the truth about the League?"

Anita nods. "That's good, and we've already started on that."

Michelle's already got her coat on and is gesturing for Anita to join her at the door. "And my friends are telling their friends in Crystal Springs, and they're spreading the word."

Emma clenches her fists. They've been doing this for *weeks*. "How long is it gonna take for the word to spread across the country? What's it gonna take for the people of the Collective do anything about the League?"

"There's the upcoming election," Cal says. "Vote Kingston out. He's the one in the League's pocket, right?"

"The other way around," Bells says. "He's totally in control of the League and supports what they do, experiments and all. Thinks it helps run the country better."

Kyle taps his chin. "More like run a smokescreen over all the shady stuff he's doing overseas."

Emma glances at the cluster of sketches and drawings they have pinned on the wall that confirm everything they've uncovered: the Collective's military presence in tantalum-rich Constavia, Orion's experiments and the connection to the disappearing meta-humans, the cover-up about the true nature of the League.

The map also details the whereabouts of the other members of the growing Resistance. Each chapter started from the network of pre-Collective film enthusiasts. But communication is proving difficult because of all the backchannels and encryptions.

Then there are the plans to nullify the new MonRobot threat. *But look how well that turned out with the first mission.* Maybe better to focus on the exposé.

"It's the network," Emma says. "The problem is that we don't have a way of communicating effectively with the parts of the

Resistance or of reaching potential members. Everything on the Net is monitored, so the current encryption you all had—"

"It's a long process," Cal says. "I agree. It's designed to make us hard to find in the first place, and then only for those who were looking in the right places. But do we really need every chapter to get radios right now? I mean, what's the plan?"

The question hangs over Emma. For the first time, she doesn't have a plan. She doesn't know what to do, doesn't know the best course of action.

"What about the old pre-Collective information networks? Even wireless routers were connected to something. There were tons of, like, steel cables underground carrying information, right? Can we tap into those?" Sasha asks.

Emma nods. "That's a good idea." The idea is solid, but she has no idea where to start. From the beginning, she guesses, with research. "But it would be like finding a needle in a haystack. Because of the ban on pre-Collective tech."

Bells raises his hand. "What if there was already an active network?"

Ricky laughs. "Really? Right under our noses the whole time?"

Bells shrugs. "I mean, last year we spent months looking for the Resistance, and you all were here the whole time, so I don't see why not. Think about it. We wouldn't have to try and create something that already exists."

Emma nods. *Another faction complete with their own efficient means of communication?* That would be great.

"Something to think about," Bells says.

"Look, I've been organizing this thing with Thomas and Kyle for years," Cal says, steepling their fingers. "If there was such a group, we would have found them by now. I mean, it's a great idea, Bells, but I don't think they exist."

BELLS IS QUIET ON THE ride to his motorcycle, and Emma is lost in her own thoughts, trying to figure out the next step. The explosion keeps replaying in her head with all of them barely getting to safety.

"I'll call you later." Bells gives her a quick kiss. "You did great today, okay? We all tried our best."

"Thanks," Emma says. They're nice words, but she doesn't think they're true.

CH. 4...

Emma dreams of fire and stars exploding. She awakes with a cold shock and catches her breath. Warm golden light streams into her room. How long did she sleep?

Doors open and close; the sounds echo through the house. Emma can hear people walking around in the kitchen; there's a clang of something falling, some cursing, and laughing. Voices echo through the hallways: her aunt's laugh, grandmother's grumbling, and even the shrieks of her five-year-old cousins.

She's not used to having her whole extended family living with her, let alone in the house built for Abby and her mom. The house, despite being built into the canyon, feels almost devoid of natural touches. It's all edges and sleek metal and cold laboratories. It's lovely, though the Jones' tastes are more austere than what Emma likes. But it's safe, safe from the League and from the prying eyes of the Collective. She's glad they're all here now.

Emma's stomach grumbles, so she dashes downstairs; her stockinged feet skid on the smooth concrete floors. For a moment she longs for the soft coziness of their old house. Her moms still drop by every few days to change cars to keep up the appearance of living there. Timed lights turn on and off in various rooms and loops of idle conversations in Spanish play intermittently throughout the house. They found a few bugs during Emma's very thorough sweep. She didn't destroy them; she figured being aware of the bugs would keep them one step ahead. They didn't know who was monitoring them— the League? Kinsgton? But either way it was safer to be careful.

Emma wanders into the kitchen, blinking wearily as she reads the projected time on the wall. Nine-thirty. "Mom? Mama?"

People can completely change the atmosphere of a room. The kitchen Emma once thought of as a cold, metallic place is filled now with soft, warm light, and her mothers are laughing. Emma can't help but smile at the way Mama gently rests her hand on Mom's elbow while she sets down a mug of steaming coffee for her wife. Josephine Gutierrez chuckles; there's a stain on her doctor's coat that she hasn't noticed, and Samantha Robledo is softly murmuring in her ear. It's an easy, comfortable dance Emma's seen a million times.

On autopilot, Emma pours herself a cup of coffee, then adds three spoons of sugar and a generous splash of milk.

"Mija! You shouldn't be drinking so much coffee; you'll stunt your growth," Mama says.

"I'm already short." Emma takes a large sip. "I might as well have the coffee."

Mom kisses her on the forehead. "Coffee has no effect on height; you all know this."

"Josephine," Mama says, rolling her eyes.

"Bye, loves!" Mom says, lingering in the doorway.

Her mothers exchange a look and glance at Emma, but don't say anything. Emma resists rolling her eyes. If they have something to say to her, they should just say it, but she knows her mothers.

"Have a good day at work," Emma says. Whatever it is, it'll come up, she's sure.

She grabs a pan dulce and bites into it with glee. With her mothers both juggling busy work schedules, Emma's breakfasts always were pretty simple: protein bar or instant oatmeal or fruit. Abuela must have gotten the sweet pastries from the market.

"Did Bells figure out the other alternate identity for you? For the hovertrain ticket back to the Rockies?"

"Yeah, it's all covered," Emma says. The new DED is on her desk somewhere. Bells gave it to her last week; the same person who made Bells' ID when he was pretending to be "Barry" created a new identity for her. It's a bit more sophisticated than the simple ones Brendan made when they were at the Villain's Guild and just needed it to pass muster for one train ride to Aerial City.

The new DED is nice, but after so long without wearing one Emma can't bring herself to put it on just yet.

"I'm not going to ask too many questions about it, but I do wonder what Bells and his family are involved in that they know someone who could make this," Mama says.

Emma snorts. Her mother can't turn off her Councilmember brain for one minute. "You know that it's because they didn't want Bells in the Meta-Human Registry," she says. "Since he's a mutant and all."

"Is that it, though? I mean, sure it's a curiosity, but Bells did say he turned down the offers for experimentation, which is great, considering what we know now of the League and their experiments."

Emma takes another sip of her coffee. "Do you have any meetings today? You're not traveling this week, right?"

Mama gives her a careful look and pushes the plate of pan dulces at her. "Abuela picked out your favorites but remember this one is for your cousin."

"Mama," Emma says warily. "What's going on?"

"I think I'm going to withdraw from the campaign," she says. "I'm perfectly happy being a Councilmember, and all this trouble with those MR-D4Rs— It's because Kingston wanted to get to me, to use you as leverage."

Emma drops her pastry. Samantha Robledo is the only other serious contender in the next Central presidential campaign. If she drops out, Kingston will win *again*. "But Kingston is *corrupt*. Our country deserves better. You *have* to run! What about everything we've been fighting for? I can't believe you would just give up like this!"

Mama gives her a stern look. "He's already tried to kidnap you once, sending us that new MonRobot under the guise of a present? What's to stop him from trying again?"

"But obviously if his plan didn't succeed—"

"But what's to stop Kingston from sending more? The only way you can be safe and be able to just be free to walk about the city is to give Kingston no reason to harm you."

Emma's stomach sinks. "That's not the answer! Please don't drop out of the race. I've already done so much to stay safe. I've been careful. I haven't been back in town. I even dropped out of school."

Her mother looks at her own cup of coffee. "Yes, that's another thing we wanted to talk to you about. We know it's a huge sacrifice and, honestly, you don't have to do it. I know you've had a lot of fun planning your protest escapades with your friends—"

Escapades? Emma stands up, anger rising inside her. "I'm not going back to school. Look, I've already passed the equivalency test—"

"But how will that look to colleges—"

"We've got more important things going on right now, like dismantling the entire Heroes' League of Heroes!"

"But what about after? I'm not disagreeing with you, mija, but once we've gotten that handled *then* what? What are you going to do?"

"I can always go back to school," Emma mutters.

"What about your dream to go to space?"

"I can always come back to that," Emma says. "There might not be space to go to if we keep on this path!"

Emma looks up at her mother. It's like looking into an equally stubborn mirror.

"Mija, we're just worried this whole thing is taking you away from your path." Samantha Robledo gives her a kind and understanding look that Emma *knows* is a well-practiced one.

"Don't— don't treat me like I'm one of your constituents! I'm your kid! And this is what I want to do. I'm ready to be a hero, even if you aren't."

Not waiting for a reply, she storms out of the kitchen.

EMMA KICKS A STRAY PIECE of tumbleweed, then glares at it when it catches on her shoe. She scowls, shaking her leg and finally yanking it free.

She paces in the shade behind the house. She's through packing, she's got no more plans to work on, and her moms still won't see reason about dropping out of the presidential race. And Bells sent her an ominous message an hour ago: just the line *we need to talk.*

Emma's gone over many possibilities; in all of them Bells breaks up with her for some reason or another. *We're better as friends. I don't think this is working out. Kissing you is terrible. Let's just focus on the Resistance.* Just imagining Bells saying these words fills her with dread. She didn't think the end would come so soon. The old insecurities flare up, the fears—why Emma learned it was always better to be the dump-er, not the dump-ee. But this is *Bells.* She doesn't know how to process her feelings; she loves him, but there's that feeling that's always been in her heart, that maybe the way she loves someone might not be the same way they want to love her.

Bells approaches on his motorcycle. It's a salvage that he and Kyle put together a few weeks ago. It's miles away from that gaudy beast the League outfitted him with to match his old Chameleon supersuit.

Bells pulls off his helmet and shakes his hair out. He's changed his hair: a fresh fade under short curls styled close to his head. Confident and cool as ever, he strides over to her, and Emma's heart beats quicker.

"Hey," Emma says. He seems to be in a good mood. *So maybe it's not a breakup talk?*

Bells beams, and then his face settles into a more solemn expression, and Emma's heart pounds on.

"Look, I came over to tell you something," Bells says.

"What? What is it?" Emma takes a deep breath and prepares her response: *Yes, we* are *better as friends. No, of course this won't be awkward. I don't want to lose you.*

Bells takes her hands and lowers his voice to a steady tone. "You know how we've been looking for a way to communicate effectively with people all over the Collective? In a way that is encrypted and isn't as complicated as Thomas and Kyle's version?"

Emma's internal emotional roller coaster suddenly stops, and her brain takes a moment to reprocess. *Right. Communication. The Resistance. Nothing about their relationship at all.* She tries not to look too relieved.

"Yeah, we've been talking about building—"

"We don't have to do that," Bells says. "It already exists."

"What are you saying?"

"What I'm saying…" Bells lifts his eyebrows. "…is that we don't need to create a whole new encrypted communication network."

Emma stares at him, at the dancing mischief in his eyes; it's almost the same look he gave her when he first told her he had powers. He'd been hiding a huge part of himself. *Is this like that? What else has he been hiding?*

"Come on. I'll tell you everything at the farm." Bells holds out her helmet.

Emma is filled with questions as she climbs on behind him. The Broussard's family farm is one of her favorite places, filled with memories: playing games with Bells, running about in the vegetable patches, dancing in the irrigation system. It's a good, comfortable place for both of them; that must be why he wants to go there to tell her about this new network.

She holds on tight as they race off into the canyons, and Emma soon realizes they're not headed to the Broussard farms outside of town.

"I thought we were going to your farm?" Emma shouts against the wind.

"We have another farm," Bells shouts back; it's barely audible. Emma holds on tight as they drive through the Unmaintained lands, past the turnoff for the hideout, going higher and higher into the mountains. Emma tightens her grip on Bells' waist as the air gets colder.

Bells stops the motorcycle and squeezes her hands. Enjoying their closeness, Emma rests her head on his. She and Bells have always shared an easy affection. Assuring and comforting touches are such a part of their routine that Emma isn't used to seeing what those touches could mean now.

She pushes the doubt to the back of her head and tries not to think about what touching means for their friendship now, their relationship, whatever it is between her and Bells. Instead, she focuses on the question at hand. "Since when do you have another farm?"

"Since always." Bells shifts. "It's a family secret. *I* didn't even know where Clairborne was until recently. The fewer people who know the better, since Grassroots is a huge secret."

"Grassroots," Emma says, turning the name over in her mouth. "I've never heard of it."

Bells laughs. "Exactly." He walks to a huge pile of rocks and then pushes one aside as if it's nothing. "It's fake," he says in response to Emma's stunned expression. "I didn't suddenly get super-strength or anything."

Emma laughs. "So that's where you got the idea for the camouflage for our hideout!"

"Yup!" He wheels the motorcycle through the opening and motions for Emma to walk through before he obscures the path again. "Come on. We've got a long way to go."

THEY DRIVE THROUGH THE UNMAINTAINED lands for another hour. The late afternoon sun barely beckons across the tops of the canyons, and the air feels thinner. Emma loses track of time, but the sun is dipping lower toward the horizon, and the bright blue sky is giving way to streaks of violet, heralding the evening ahead. The sun hasn't set, but up here in the mountains, long shadows are cast across the high desert as the wind whistles through the junipers and ponderosa pines. "How high are we going?"

"All the way up into these mountains," Bells says.

"There's a farm here?" Emma doesn't see anything. The junipers rustle in the wind, their blue berries shake, and all she can see is the mountain greenery.

"Just here, beyond the gate."

Emma doesn't see a gate. She looks around and then at the ground. "Is the farm underground? How are you getting sunlight down there? Artificial light? Mirrors?" She knows the Broussards have that tech, but it's only good for small vegetable gardens, like the one the Broussards made for the Villain's Guild.

"Nope, it's all above ground. I mean, we have the tech for that, but we don't have to use those resources here." Bells sweeps aside a small area of dirt to reveal a keypad and keys in a code.

The air in front of them shimmers. Something beyond Emma's field of vision is moving, sinking into the ground.

"Come on," Bells says in an excited voice.

They get on the cycle and drive through the "gate" and what looked like just a trick of light, and it's as if a whole hidden world has been uncovered. "Camouflage tech," Bells explains. "The gate operates the same way as cam-foil, but it goes up twenty feet around the whole property. If anyone was out here, they'd just see the forest."

Emma shivers; she hadn't expected this cold. In the Rockies, she'd been prepared; the white flurries warned of the cold, but here the desert looks exactly the same as it does in summer.

Clairborne is at least three times as large as the official Broussard farm, and Emma can see rows and rows of fruit trees and produce: lettuce and cauliflower and spinach and other vegetables she cannot name.

"Come on, it's warmer in the greenhouse," Bells says.

Inside the domed glass building, rows and rows of plants fill every spare inch; revolving tiers climb toward the ceiling. A fine mist is coming down, and Emma shrieks in delight. "You made it rain?"

Bells laughs. "There's a natural water cycle in here; condensation builds, then falls down as precipitation."

Emma shoulders him playfully. "That's awesome!"

He leads her down a row of trellises with plump little red tomatoes. "These will be picked soon, but for now, try some!"

Emma's had the Broussard family's fresh fruit before, but never like this, plucked right off the vine. She picks another one, and another, popping them into her mouth. "It's so good." She sighs. "Oh, no, I'm sorry, I'll pay you back. That must have been like twenty credits worth of tomatoes."

"It's all good, Emma. We've got plenty. I mean, Sean is the one who is the stickler for every credit, but you're family. My parents would be happy to feed you."

"So why the secret farm? What are you guys doing with all this produce?" Emma asks.

"Well, you know how we're required to sell directly to the Collective, and they turn around and ship the produce all over the country with a flat price?"

Emma nods. She knows it well. She feels guilty, remembering Jess complaining at lunchtime about the stale, processed food served at the school, especially the sad salads with wilted and browning lettuce. Vegetables were available, of course, and there's plenty of food, but it's not fresh. She always brought food from home to share with her friends, and Bells did, too, but it bothered her that some people couldn't afford fresh vegetables.

"Yeah, the Collective's Food and Distribution Regulations are supposed to make it possible for everyone to be able to get food and share those resources, but— I don't know, I think it makes it harder," Emma says.

Bells nods. "Take this tomato." He plucks the rosy red fruit and tosses it at her. "We grow this here. But we can't sell it here. We have to sell all our produce directly to the Collective, which then ships our fruits and vegetables all over, so that this same tomato, by the time it comes back here and you get it in a grocery store, a bag of them could cost twenty credits, when it should only cost five. So that's what Grassroots does: We give local farmers the support and the opportunities to sell directly to people in their area and the technology to operate farms under the Collective's nose."

Emma looks the tomato over, thinking about all the times Bells has shared his food with her since the first time they met over snacks in kindergarten. She looks at the rows and rows of vegetables in this greenhouse alone, food enough to feed a small town, food grown with care and love in a region where it was once thought impossible to grow food even before the Disasters. The lack of food, the lack of arable land to grow it on— that was what truly devastated the world, not the environmental catastrophes or the X29 flare, but the wars fought over dwindling resources. Here, Grassroots has been working on a solution all this time. "That's amazing. You do this for the Nevada region?"

Bells shakes his head. "Nope! Grassroots is all over the Collective! It's a multi-region operation, and we're also loosely affiliated with similar organizations around the world."

Emma's heart swells with pride at what Bells' family has accomplished. "We should tell my mom, I mean, she'd think it was awesome that you're helping feed people directly."

"No," Bells says immediately. "The Council can't know. I'm sorry. It's been such a huge secret and part of our lives—"

"I understand, but she's been trying to work from within Regulations for years, trying to fix the laws. And she's been on our side about the whole League thing; I'm sure that she'd understand."

"Right, but Grassroots isn't just *my* organization. Tons of people depend on us for affordable produce all over the country. And not just us, there's a whole secret network of farmers and people working to make food available."

Emma nods, watching a few older robots—MR-399's, she thinks—with long, slender arms, wheeling along the aisles in the greenhouse, meticulously watering and pruning plants. "So Grassroots is everywhere?"

"All twenty-four regions," Bells says proudly. "My parents are just a part of this."

Emma looks up. "I love it. If you talk to your parents, I think they should talk to my mom because she introduced this produce bill last year. I don't know the specifics of it, but I think she definitely wanted to give local farmers the option to sell directly to markets in their region if they want to." She tilts her head, taking in Bells' proud smile as he regards the rows and rows of crops. She's seeing the Broussards in a new light. The anti-government paranoia and all those family quirks were actually hiding this huge project right under the noses of the Collective. It's a great cause, and Emma can see why they do it, but they shouldn't *have* to do it this way.

"That would be cool," Bells says. "Grassroots has been so secretive for so long— even I didn't know the location of Clairborne until last week." He stands up a little taller, shoulders squaring with pride. "My parents figured I was ready for the responsibility. And then the first time I talked to them about bringing you and the Resistance in— they're all for it. You know, while we meet with the rest of the Resistance in the old Villain's Guild hideout, we can ask my dad to set up a meeting with the Grassroots leadership. And then you can tell them the plan and ask to use their communication network and everything."

Emma nods. This is the best idea they've had in forever. She's only a little bit jealous that it's not *her* idea.

Returning to the Rockies hideout takes planning, especially since all the new members of their fledgling Resistance chapter want to come with them. Bells hasn't heard from his dad, who's in the Louisiana region on Grassroots business, but Emma's itching for action anyway, so the timing works for their trip north. Thomas and Kyle offer to maintain the headquarters, and everyone is excited at the prospect of new missions. Emma convinces everyone there's no reason to risk Cal and Michelle or any new members since their identities haven't been compromised and they should continue to go about their regular lives while carrying out the original mission—spreading the word.

Emma hugs her mothers, rolls her eyes as they press kisses to her cheeks, and then hugs her abuelas and all her aunties and cousins and everyone gathered in front of the house to say goodbye.

"Call us every day," Abuela Isabella insists, patting her hands.

"You know that I can't," Emma says.

"I know," Mom says, hugging her again. "I hate it." She gestures to her wife to come forward. Emma wonders if they've talked about Emma's plans for the Resistance, about their reluctance to let her go.

"I know that this is important to you," Mama says, kissing her forehead. "And I'm happy to see you so passionate about fighting back against this corruption. Just promise me that you remember why you're fighting, and that we're fighting too. Maybe not in ways you understand, or as fast as you would like, but believe me, we're doing the work."

"I know," Emma says, hugging her close. "So remember, when I check in, it'll probably be brief and it won't be secure—"

"Got it," Mom says. "We'll be really obvious and in code."

Mama frowns. "Are you sure you'll be done before P019? I'm not sure about all of these shelters and claims that these shields will actually work protecting the cities. It would be best if you just got out of the impact zone."

"We'll be fine; we're traveling well ahead of the P019 impact event," Emma says, hugging her mothers goodbye.

Tia Rosa sniffs. "Are you sure? I hear that the shield constructions for those Regions impacted will create travel restrictions—"

Emma kisses her on both cheeks and then continues with Abuela Isabella and Abuela Carmen.

"Impact zone," Abuela Carmen scoffs. "What's a few meteors falling to earth?"

Mama shakes her head "P019 is a serious threat. Those meteors will knock pre-Collective military satellites to Earth; it's a good thing Emma planned to travel well before it even begins."

"Meteors! I've survived a World War and the Disasters! I'm not scared of any space rock. Emma, do you believe this nonsense?"

Emma laughs; she loves her family so much, especially her stubborn great-grandmother. An entire swath of the North American Collective is preparing for potential impact, and here is Abuela Carmen laughing in the face of it. Emma's pretty sure a lot of the danger is hyped up, since most of the impact zone is Unmaintained land. Like Hopestar, which has been boasting about New Bright City's repulsion shields, many Regions in the zone are adopting protections to brace for the falling space debris.

The impact has been predicted for November; now, on the cusp of summer's end, it seems so far away. It seems ridiculous to plan to stay in one safe place for the months to come, as so many Collective citizens are doing, forgoing out-of-Region travel long before any meteors crash to Earth. Emma's sure she and her friends can accomplish their goals and bring the Resistance together well before then. There's no need to worry about shelter right now; they've got too much to do. The new plan with Grassroots will work. Emma is sure of it.

Everything on Emma's preparation list has been checked and double-checked, and they're just about ready to join everyone at the Villain's Guild Rocky Mountain headquarters.

Ricky is nervous; Tanya and Sasha are curious. Emma guesses having grown up on stories of villains and then having to shift their entire worldview takes some getting used to.

Emma watches as the 3D printer churns out the last DED-lookalike. The slim wristlet mimics the look of a data exchange device and carries out a few basic functions, such as storing credits so they can purchase things without drawing suspicion.

"Did we just hack money?" Ricky asks, his eyes gleaming. He turns his wrist back and forth so the device catches in the light. "How many credits are on here? Can I get more?"

"No, it's real money." Emma rolls her eyes. "I rerouted it from my account. It should be enough for disguises, food, and the train tickets."

Sasha suggested using punk makeup to avoid being spotted by facial recognition software. It's music festival season, and there are plenty of punks on the train with their faces already painted in geometric designs. The alternative movement sprung up around music and found a growing audience in the past few years, and it's not uncommon to see people, especially teenagers, adopt the look.

"I think we look awesome. Very punk," Bells says, smiling at his reflection in the train window. Against his dark skin, the makeup looks great: a few triangles and pixelated square blocks all dusted with glitter that complements the bold colors of the makeup like an abstract cubist painting.

Emma nods. "We look like we're going to a concert. Sasha, what band did you say was our cover again?"

"The Limitless is on tour right now, which is perfect," Sasha says. "It's all in the write-up."

Sasha prepared an overview of the punk movement for everyone to review. Emma isn't sure anyone will question them about which singer left which band when, but it might be good to know, just in case. And, the punk fans might be good recruits for the Resistance; the music is all about questioning authority. It's funny that the Collective so strict about regulating movies and books and shows and popular pop artists, but they don't pay attention at all to indie musicians and the movements around them. Emma's already crafting an outreach plan.

"It's kinda weird, but whatever works," Ricky says. He's done the minimum necessary to confuse the software with a few pixels scattered across his cheek; he flatly refused glitter.

The landscape flies by. The North American Collective disappears into a vague, seamless blur as they continue north to Middleton, where the car they used on their run from Andover is hidden just outside of town. Emma still has vivid nightmares about that run. She remembers everything: the whirr of the pursuing MR-D4Rs, the cold intonation of the bots as they demanded surrender, the constant fear spiking her veins, Bells saving them and falling unconscious for three days. When Genevieve found them and led them to the hideout, Emma thought nothing of abandoning the vehicle, figuring the Villain's Guild would have plenty of resources. She wasn't entirely wrong; they were set up with food and shelter, but no one was prepared to make any change outside of their bubble.

Bells and Tanya are already asleep. Ricky is looking for the snack cart, and Sasha is in her own world listening to music. Emma settles into her seat, listening to the conversation flowing around her. The commuter train is filled with people traveling between Vegas and Middleton and talking about the usual: work and families and businesses and, of course, the Heroes' League of Heroes.

"Sublimate's powers are awesome—"

"Yeah, I'm so excited Aerial City finally has a new hero. Tree Frog was terrible..."

Emma doesn't know any of the heroes they're gossiping about. *Sublimate? Medusa? Stoic? I've never heard of them. Where did they come from?*

Without a connection to the Net, Emma can't do any research. She tries to sleep, but her mind is spinning: thinking of plans, thinking about the Resistance, thinking about Bells.

Bells' arm is wrapped securely around her, and she fits perfectly into the crook of his neck. It's familiar and new at the same time: the solid weight of him holding her. They've fallen asleep together before, at sleepovers and on that wild journey to find the Registry. That seemed so long ago, when they slept under the soft canopy of trees. Then she didn't think anything of sharing space and warmth by curling around each other. She's not sure what it means now that they're in a relationship.

Bells presses a kiss to her forehead, and Emma stirs. She thought he was asleep. Afraid to break the spell that's fallen over them, she keeps her breathing even and her eyes closed.

"I'm so happy we're together," Bells whispers. "I love you."

And then, slowly, his breaths take on a soft, easy rhythm, and Emma opens her eyes to watch him sleep. "I love you too," she says. The words hang in the air, as if they're waiting to sink into Bells' skin, waiting for recognition.

Emma's said it before, sure— to her moms, to her abuela and everyone in her family, and, of course, to her friends. She's certainly said it to Bells before, many times. But she wonders if it's all changed: the way he thinks about her, what he's expecting from her, and the way he loves her now. Emma *does* love Bells, too, but she knows it might be different. She thinks about love and relationships and thinks about Bells' love for her and wonders if there's another direction for them to grow into.

THEY SCATTER AT THE MIDDLETON hoverstation and find places to change their disguises. Emma dabs at her cheeks, scrubbing furiously while Tanya pulls wigs from her bag.

"You want the pink or the purple?"

Emma snorts; Bells probably picked out all these wigs.

"Purple," she says.

They transform themselves again, and then Emma hits the bathroom before their hike out of town. Something is scribbled on the back of the bathroom stall.

"No way," Emma gasps, when she realizes what the graffiti says.

MISCHIEF LIVES
THE LEAGUE IS A LIE
ORION IS STILL OUT THERE WATCH OUT

"Tanya, come look!"

"Oh, cool! Do we have a Resistance chapter here working on the communication project?"

"No!" Emma gasps. Here they are, hundreds of miles from any of their own efforts, and a complete stranger wrote this.

Emma traces her fingers over the words MISCHIEF LIVES. She didn't do this. Someone else did, someone who still believes Master Mischief is still alive, even though no one's heard from him for a year.

UNEARTHING THE CAR, EMMA IS exhilarated for what's to come. They let the solar panels charge while they eat, and the car is ready by late afternoon. Emma takes the wheel.

The long, winding stretches of the dirt trail through the forest are relaxing, and Emma is ready for something new, a new plan to focus on. The forest thins, and the trail meets another long-forgotten road, which stretches out in a long, flat line of packed earth.

Bells insists she take a break, and they switch. The road continues through endless, open fields, where grasses wave gently in the wind.

"There's so much land here," Bells says. "I wonder why the Regions never expanded."

"People are afraid of the unknown," Emma says. "Plus, we've been warned of all the dangers in the Unmaintained lands. No one wants to get radiation poisoning."

"What radiation?" Sasha mutters, looking outside. The grass seems to be flourishing.

Emma has a theory. "We know that X29 knocked out a number of nuclear power plants, but it's never been recorded which ones, aside from the major cities that required evacuation. I don't think the number of meltdowns was as high as the Collective reported."

Bells taps the steering wheel. "Yeah, after the Disasters and the war, people just accepted that everything outside of their cities was wasteland."

"Who's to say what is Unmaintained and what isn't?" Tanya murmurs.

They settle into a thoughtful silence, and the only sound is the soft rustle of the grass and the slow rumble of the car.

"THERE'S SOMEONE ELSE ON THE road," Bells says, gripping the wheel tightly.

"There shouldn't be." Emma frowns.

"Oh, but there is." Bells jerks his head at the road ahead of them.

Emma squints. Streaks of purple and pink race across the sky as the sun disappears from the horizon and night settles in around them. All she can see is the cracked gray asphalt of the road stretching to the horizon and the fading golden fields around them.

Wait. That big shadow— another car is moving toward them.

Emma sits upright, trying to formulate a plan for escape. She's never seen the Authorities this far past a city's limits, but one could never be sure.

"Turn off the lights," Tanya says. She elbows her sister and Ricky, who both startle awake.

"What's happening?"

"Shh!"

Bells fumbles on the dashboard and flicks a switch, but the lights brighten, illuminating the road and the approaching car. There are people inside— at least two. They're not dressed like the Authorities, though, and the vehicle is definitely not a sleek government-issued solarcar, but a rickety salvage like their own.

"It's fine," Emma says. "Whoever it is, they're out in the Unmaintained lands too. They know the risks they're taking and they probably won't talk to us." Emma flips the correct switch, and they're shrouded in darkness. "Pull over. They should pass us soon."

Bells swerves, jerking nervously, and the car dives into the roadside weeds.

"Turn it off!" Emma hisses.

"Got it," Bells says, turning off the engine. The computer hums, and then the only sounds are the wind and the other car.

Without the headlights, it's easy to let imagination turn every movement, every shadow, into a monster. In the distance, a huge shape looms, and Emma's logical mind knows that it's the mountain, but she can't help but see a hulking beast watching them pass by, waiting for the right moment to snatch them off the road.

An unnerving howl echoes in the distance.

Bells grabs her hand as the other car comes closer. Emma squeezes back, and they wait for the other vehicle to drive past their hiding place.

The sound of wheels crunching on the road comes to a halt.

Bells' eyes widen, and he looks at Emma.

Footfalls. Whoever it is— they're walking right toward them, as though they know exactly *where* they are in the dark.

Emma screams at the shadow outside her door.

"Emma? Bells?"

Wait! She knows that voice.

"Jess!" Emma cries out in relief.

CH. 6...

Emma can't get out of the car fast enough. Jess and Abby are really *here*! She seizes Jess in a hug. Jess squeals in delight, picks up Emma, and spins her around so fast that Emma's feet fly off the ground.

Next to her, Bells and Abby are hugging too. Emma laughs and hugs Abby as well. Bells pulls Jess in, and it's everything Emma's been missing.

"It's so good to have the Sidekick Squad together again," says a solemn voice next to Bells joining the group hug.

"Hi, Brendan," Emma says, laughing.

Jess' fourteen-year-old brother waves hello from where he's trying to squeeze between Bells and Emma. "We thought it prudent to come meet you as the security details for the Rockies base have changed." He pushes his glasses up on his nose and squints at them.

Jess laughs. "Well, I knew you were scheduled to come in sometime tomorrow, but I figured with how fast you drive you might be early. And arriving in the middle of the night wouldn't have worked, especially with finding the carport."

Abby grins, eyes sparkling. "I'm so excited you're all here! And hello! Are these the new recruits?" She peers into the car.

Ricky shrinks back, as if he's intimidated by Abby's energy. "Hi," he offers.

Sasha and Tanya climb out of the car, and Ricky follows, and soon they're all exchanging names and pronouns.

Emma smiles; the Resistance is moving forward with the communication plan, Bells' parents are setting up that meeting with Grassroots, and now they can proceed to help the members of the former Villain's Guild take on the League.

"Let's do this," she says, cracking her knuckles.

EMMA IMAGINED MORE OF A response: Applause, maybe, acknowledgment. She just gave a whole twenty-minute presentation to the Villain's Guild. It's a simple plan. The adult meta-humans, dressed in their recognizable supersuits as heroes or villains, would interrupt the staged battles put on by the League across the country. Then, with the cameras on them, they would expose the entire situation as a setup and initiate a call to action, to oppose the League and Kingston. With public opinion behind them, they could easily vote Kingston out of office.

And yet, silence.

After arriving at the headquarters last night and being shown their guest rooms, Emma stayed up late working on her speech. She examined every possible angle and laid out all the benefits of executing the plan. Jess said there's a meeting every morning, and Emma imagined a busy, productive Council-like gathering, where people would discuss current missions and plan for the future.

Emma instead finds herself awkwardly standing on a chair during breakfast.

Victor, Jess' dad nods at her. Emma still is amazed that the unassuming, quiet man she's known forever is also the outspoken B-class hero Shockwave. "That's a great idea, Emma!"

"Thanks for sharing!" Genevieve, Abby's mom, says. "I think we should get started right away."

Emma exhales in relief. She knows the opinion of Mistress Mischief is valued here. Emma's also pleased to see she looks much better than she did when they rescued her from the building where Captain Orion held her captive; her face is full and vibrant once more. Abby, standing next to her, on the other hand, looks pale and wan, like a sickly shadow. Emma frowns; she thought Abby looked tired last night, but thought it was just a trick of the light. She'll ask her if she's okay later. Maybe she's stressed and hasn't been eating well.

A woman with fair hair swooped into a delicate updo stands up. Emma vaguely remembers her from their last stay here— Deirdre, that's her name.

"That does sound like a wonderful idea," Deirdre says, smiling sweetly. "I think it fits right in with our current plans. I think we can plan at least five successful confrontations before the P019 impact shuts down safe travel between Regions."

"Yes!" Emma whoops. "I just think it's time we do something out in the open, you know?"

"Absolutely." Li Hua, Jess' mom, stands up and claps. She looks so much like Jess: the same stubborn jaw, dark hair, and brown skin and the way her mouth quirks upward and her face seems full of hope. Her support spurs a smattering of polite applause, which is better than nothing.

Chloe claps enthusiastically. In front of her, a vase of shoots and buds blossoms into full, colorful flowers, complementing Chloe's elegant aesthetic. Emma wonders if, like Bells, spikes in mood can turn on her powers.

"Let's get started!" Deirdre says. "Let's see, I think Li Hua, Genevieve, Cass, Chloe, let's think of a good place to get our powers into shape for confrontation—"

"I need to go work on the farms, but go ahead," Chloe says, waving them on. She clears her breakfast plate and bustles out of the cavern, but not before smiling warmly at Emma and giving her an encouraging pat on the shoulder.

Genevieve nods. "Cavern Six is empty and would be great for practice. I'll go ahead and start shifting some of the stored stuff out of the way so we have room to work."

Li Hua grins. "Great! I can help."

Jess is bouncing on the edge of her toes. "This is awesome! Remember when we were trying to train on our own? We'll have so much help, and one of the new meta-humans has a directional power! I could see if he could give me some tips."

Abby smiles. "Yeah, it is a great idea, Emma. I'm glad you brought it up."

Bells laughs. "Well, I'm still the only shapeshifter, but I guess Steven's pink-spot-on-the-wall kinda falls into my realm. We can train together."

The mood has changed entirely, people are laughing and grinning and excited and hopeful. Emma tucks her hair behind her ear and grins. She's great at this. She's a mastermind. She organized their campaigns in the Sidekick Squad and now here at the Villain's Guild they're forming a valid and capable faction to fight the League.

Jess is already giggling and following Abby toward Cavern Six. Emma jokes with Bells about possible exercises, remembering how they tried to scare him into using his powers last year.

"Emma, a word," Deirdre says, gliding between Emma and Bells.

"I'll see you soon!" Bells says, waving as he goes down the tunnel with Jess and Abby.

"What's up?" It's probably breakfast related, like *you forgot to wash your breakfast bowl properly* or *you put the wrong thing in the compost bin.* She doesn't know Deirdre well, but judging from how things went at breakfast, she seems to have taken on the leadership while Genevieve and the Trans were busy with their rescue missions.

Deirdre smiles at her, and Emma is hit with the scent of cinnamon and vanilla. It's overpowering and too sweet, and she wants to cough.

"Cavern Six is for the training session."

"Yes. I know that," Emma says, blinking at her. "Why do you think I'm going?"

"Why *do* you think you're going? You don't have any powers to develop."

"So?" Emma tries to sidestep around Deirdre, but the woman intercepts her and looks down at her again. "It's training," Emma says. "Everyone needs to be there."

"Right," Deirdre says, eyes narrowing. "But you won't actually be coming along on any of those missions. These are going to be meta-human battles, and you are not meta-human."

Emma's mouth falls open. It's not as though she hasn't thought about this before, working with her friends who all have powers. She's smart and resourceful, the one with the plan, but she's never counted herself *outside* of the plan just because her genes aren't randomly expressing a particular trait. Her friends have never thought less of her or left her out. But Deidre, practically a stranger, is demanding that she *sit out*.

All of Emma's logical arguments go out the window as hot anger rises inside her. Her hands stiffen, and she stands there, frozen, as she struggles to come up with a sound argument.

"Glad you understand," Deirdre says, turning around and marching ahead.

The door slides closed. Emma's still standing in the hallway, fuming. She's got a comeback now, but it's too late to use it. She storms off.

She finds Brendan fiddling with his electronics in Cavern Two. "Did you know everyone's at training and developing their powers for our first battle?"

"Yeah," Brendan says. "Try this, will you? I'm improving the DED replacement and adding more functions, but the strap is bothering me."

Emma puts the device on her wrist; the ends hang awkwardly. There's no buckle or snap. "Uh, is it…"

Brendan scowls. "So, most of the metal here is being used, and I need every little bit for the circuits, so… I could tie it?"

Emma holds still while Brendan ties a clumsy knot. The device hangs loosely on her wrist, and Emma flicks at it. There's a digital display, no holograms, and a single button for navigation. "It'd work," Emma says. "I'm worried about losing it. Where'd you put the battery?"

"It runs off body heat," Brendan says proudly.

"Cool!"

She scans the room. It's filled with workbenches and tech, some familiar and some bulky pre-Collective models all in various stages of assembly or disassembly. There's also a hulking object covered in a sheet and a *Do Not Touch* sign.

"That's Abby's 'secret' project," Brendan says, not looking up from where he's fiddling with a screwdriver. "Won't let anyone near it. I can't even be in the room when she works on it, but it's so obvious what it is."

Emma studies the shape and touches its protruding edge. It's hard, bulky metal, with sharp edges and corners— a mecha-suit?

Something bumps into her foot. "Hi, Chả!" Emma pats Jess' round bot. It beeps at her and zooms around in a circle. "That's new!"

"Abby added some emotes for Jess." Brendan hums to himself.

"When did—"

"My dad did a supply run to Andover and picked up a few essentials."

Emma blinks. "And no one told us?"

"It was a quick fly-by. He wouldn't have been able to stay long anyway," Brendan says, waving her off as if it doesn't matter that another member of the Resistance could have helped them with their missions.

Emma bites her lip and tries to tamp down the hurt she feels. And Jess didn't even mention it! Well, they only did weekly check-ins, and maybe it was before they got the radio up and running.

"No one really ever volunteers to help me with stuff. I'm surprised you're here, actually."

"Deirdre didn't want me in training," Emma says slowly. "She said I wasn't a meta-human and shouldn't be coming along."

"Deirdre couldn't plan her way out of a paper bag," Brendan peers at a circuit and picks at it with his tweezers. "I wouldn't worry about what she thinks." He sets his project down. "Do you really want be over there with everyone while they meditate or do whatever they do to work on their powers?"

"No, not really," Emma admits. "But it's the principle of the thing."

"I know," Brendan says. "Here, hold this in place while I solder it."

EMMA KNOWS THERE'S A PLAN, it's just not *accessible* to her. Every time she goes into the main cavern the adults stop talking, Deidre directs her to help with household chores or to make herself busy somewhere else. Emma's angry; it was her idea, her plan, and she's Mastermind, although Emma is careful not to call herself that here.

Deirdre is the only A-class meta-human here, and she's appointed herself the leader. The other adults seem to accept it, which Emma doesn't understand at all. Even Jess' parents, whom Emma's looked up to and loved forever, seem totally happy to defer to Deidre. Chloe, whom Emma thought *was* in charge, is so busy that she just lets Deirdre walk all over her. Yes, keeping the base running is a priority, but surely the mission itself—the Resistance, taking a public stance against the League—should be the main focus.

The last time they were all here, it seemed pivotal to convince everyone that hiding wasn't sufficient. And Emma and her friends took action: going after the Meta-Human Registry and destroying it, thus protecting meta-humans from both the League and Orion's experiments.

Now, there's a plan, but everyone has duties and a mission except Emma. Jess and Abby are tinkering on Abby's new mecha-suit, which she can use without her powers. Emma almost wants to ask, since they're building one, what if they built one for Emma as well? But Emma isn't sure how coordinated she would be wearing more than fifty pounds of metal.

Emma doesn't really want to wear a mecha-suit. What she *is* good at, seeing the big picture and planning things and executing a vision, she isn't allowed to do.

EMMA PACES IN THE UNDERGROUND tunnel. Finally, headlights appear— Bells on his new Brendan-designed motorcycle, followed by Jess and Abby and Steven in a car.

Bells takes off his helmet and shakes out his hair as the others get out of the car. Bells glares at Jess, who folds her arms and looks at Abby, who just looks at her feet. Steven rushes to the entrance to the hideout as if he's going to be sick. No one says anything as they follow.

Emma falls into step behind them, anxious. "How was it? Did you get on the broadcast?"

"I don't want to talk about it," Abby says, pushing past Emma in the earthen hallway.

"Was it that bad?" Emma asks.

Jess sighs. "You know how Chloe was supposed to lead this mission?"

"Yeah, and?" Emma likes Chloe. She always has something nice to say about everyone.

"Deirdre just kinda steamrolled over her plan, and we almost all got caught by the Authorities," Bells says.

"Great," Emma says flatly. "And I'm not allowed in the planning room while everyone just—"

Jess gives her a sad look. "I'm sorry, Em. You can tell me your ideas and I can bring them up at the—"

Emma sighs just as a voice crackles through the speakers set up in the framework of the caverns. "I need all Leadership Personnel to report to the main cavern immediately." Deirdre's voice echoes.

"Leadership Personnel," Emma repeats, rolling her eyes. "Can't believe she named it that."

Emma's brushed aside as Michael rushes past her, running for the main cavern.

"Sorry!" he calls.

"What's going on?" Emma doesn't remember what Michael's power is—something to do with dreams—but knows he's been acting as the Villain's Guild chief medical officer.

"I don't know," Jess says.

Determination lengthening her stride, Emma walks toward Cavern Six. "I'm not Leadership Personnel, but I say we should crash this party."

"My favorite kind of party," Bells says, winking at her. "Let's go!"

Jess sprints ahead. By the time they all get to the main cavern, it's in an uproar. Genevieve is trying to get attention, and people are clamoring, all gathered around something on the table.

"Why did we even bring it in here?"

"If no one was expecting this package, this means our location is compromised—"

"Just destroy it!"

"Open it!"

Cass hunches his shoulders, trying to appear smaller. He's a broad-shouldered man Emma once thought was terrifying, especially as his villainous alter-ego Plasmaman, but she soon learned he's quite sweet. He looks up at Chloe. "It was with the rest of the supplies in the drop."

"And you didn't think it was suspicious?" Chloe crosses her arms.

"None of our other supplies are ever labeled either! I just thought it might have been more food," Cass protests.

Genevieve frowns. "But we all know exactly where each thing is coming from—any of us who need supplies is cognizant of when to expect them—this box is unaccounted for."

"We should open it," Emma says, but no one can hear her over the commotion. She turns to Jess, who's next to her. "I mean, even if it's a threat we won't know until we know what we're dealing with, right? And we can use precautions in case it's anything explosive." She's already brainstorming the best way to open it remotely.

"We should figure out where it came from first," Jess says.

Abby murmurs in agreement.

Bells shifts, stretching until he's as tall as the cavern ceiling; his head bumps a stalactite. "It just looks like a box," he says. "Made out of... cardboard. Taped closed."

"I vote we open it," Victor says.

"But what if it's rigged to explode?" Emma says, frustrated. The adults are still arguing. Someone suggests taking it outside, and they're bringing up robots when— *Fwip*. Cass is standing next to the open box with scissors dangling from his hand.

Silence.

"Oh. I thought we said we were opening it." Cass looks inside. "Doesn't look like it's doing anything. I actually don't know what that is."

Emma gives up trying to see over everyone and elbows her way to the front. Jess follows while people take turns looking inside.

"It's another box?"

"What is it? A bot?"

"Too small for a chorebot—"

"Not the right size for a DED or a computer—"

"Too big for —"

Jess takes a sharp breath. "I know what it is."

"What?"

She glances at Brendan. "Look."

Brendan looks inside, then looks back at Jess with a strange expression on his face: a mix of hope and revulsion and confusion.

"What is it?" Emma asks.

"It's a twenty-first-century storage device for a computer." Jess looks at her parents. "It can't be read by a DED or any of our devices. It's completely incompatible with datachips."

Abby rolls the small thing between her fingers. It's about two inches long with a metal input port jutting from it.

"Okay, so, someone sent us a bunch of data we can't read?" Chloe asks, frowning.

"I didn't say that," Jess says. She looks at Brendan; her voice drops to a whisper. "The three of us had a twenty-first-century computer because we had a bunch of pre-Collective movies on devices like these."

"The three of you." Deirdre frowns. "Who are you talking about?"

"Brendan, me, and my sister," says Jess.

Abby scowls. "So, these files are from Claudia? What makes you think they're safe? Isn't she working for Orion?"

Jess fiddles with her fingers and exchanges glances with Brendan. "Yeah. I mean, for the longest time Orion was her idol, you know? Mine too, before I knew. But everyone kept saying Claudia was the next Captain Orion, and she modeled so much of herself after her. She dyed her hair, started dressing like her, and even after we told her about Orion and the kidnapping, she didn't seem to care. She really believed that what Orion was doing was right."

Bells coughs. "She's your sister, though. You know her better than Orion." He gently touches her elbow. "Is it okay if—"

Jess nods. "Of course."

Bells clears his throat. "So, last year, Orion captured me to use me in her experiments."

"Something about perfecting her serum for increasing her power level strength?" Brendan says. "Yeah, I remember! We rescued you."

"Yeah, you did, dude," Bells says with a smile and fist-bumps Brendan. "So, I told Jess this, but I haven't told anyone else, 'cause you know, it's her sister..."

Brendan blinks. "What? She's my sister too! You didn't tell me?"

"I didn't want to worry you," Jess says. "You know, in case it turned out to be nothing."

"What is it?" Emma says.

"Claudia helped me escape," Bells says quietly. "She was helping Orion, but I'm not sure she actually was. Orion was taking these supplements to increase her strength, and they tested one on me. It was a breath mint. You know, the kind you used to have, Em."

Emma nods. She loved those little blue minty things and always kept them with her.

"She was lying to Orion. It wasn't a supplement at all. She made Orion think she was getting stronger when she wasn't."

Emma frowns, confused. "So, if Claudia is sabotaging Orion, could she be part of the Resistance? Like, a faction we don't know about?"

Bells lets out a hollow laugh. "Well, she called the Resistance 'losers,' so I don't think so. I don't really know. I mean… Claudia's always been…" He looks at Jess.

Emma never really got to know Jess' older sister; Claudia went off to college and faded into the background of the Trans' family holos and of Jess' stories.

Jess holds up the device. "Claudia's always been on her own side. I think she realized teaming up with Orion wasn't a great idea, and wants to, I don't know, level the playing field."

Abby nods. "There's also… Remember the fallout when Bells was the League's most wanted? I mean, there were security cams all over Orion's base when we rescued my mom, but Bells was the only one recorded. No shots of Jess, no mention of Jess' parents in that confrontation with Orion at my old house. In fact, the whole narrative that came from that, how Smasher and Shockwave attempted to apprehend Orion, was extremely favorable to your parents, Jess. Your whole family could have been blacklisted by the League, or worse."

"Yeah. That would be just like Claudia," Jess muses. "Keeping us safe, even when she was betraying us."

Brendan snatches the thing from Jess' hands. "So what are we waiting for? Let's go see what she sent us." He's already racing down the tunnel.

She sent files— massive amounts of them. Opening them on the twenty-first-century computer takes time. The thing takes at least five minutes to warm up.

It's smaller than the "television" that Jess set up for them in the basement of the Trans' house for their hangouts and sleepovers. A physical keyboard is attached to a large rectangular screen on a hinge, so the whole thing could be closed and carried, Emma supposes.

"Do you know what this is?" Jess tilts the screen. "Anyone?"

Bells shakes his head; Emma squints and peers closer. It looks encoded, but there's a familiar pattern, a cadence to the way the data is structured; if only she could remember where she'd seen this format before. *Headings, subheadings, graphs, charts— a textbook? No, something else...*

Abby raises her hand hesitantly. "I've been practicing connecting with tech again with my powers. I've moved small objects with my telekinesis before; if one power is starting to work, the other should too. I could try—"

"No," Jess says. "We can't risk you getting sick again. Also, we don't know what exposing you to this data would do."

"Yeah, what if there's a virus? We wouldn't know how that would affect your mind, Abby," Emma says.

"You shouldn't risk it," Jess says.

Brendan clicks his tongue and scrolls through the information. "There's a lot here, but it looks like data logs from a programming language. I can figure this out."

"Oh! I *have* seen this before," Emma says. "It's a statistics program, like what I used to use to run my bio experiments for school. This is a form of data output." She claps and point at a jumble of letters. "This looks like genetic code. These letters are all tri-nucleotide sequences."

Abby gasps. "It's her research. Claudia sent us Orion's research on how she made that anti-power serum."

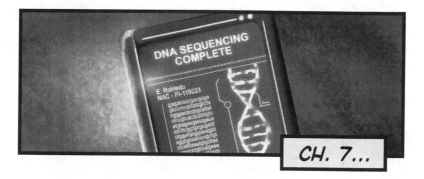

"I've got it covered," Michael says. "What, are you a super-genius too?"

"Just smart." Emma wedges her foot in the door. Behind Michael and his stubbled chin, she can see the twenty-first-century computer next to a modern holoscreen with rapidly scrolling data. It took her some time to figure out that Leadership Personnel moved the files to Michael's medical station and lab. She knows he's been in charge of the health care of the Villain's Guild and remembers from their last visit that he helped monitor everyone's power levels too. She never warmed to him, especially because of the snide way he treated Bells until he realized how powerful Bells was.

"I've already got Brendan and Abby in here with me, not to mention Chloe, who is an actual expert in statistics," Michael says.

"I can help," Emma insists. She was the one who realized it was a report, after all.

Michael sighs. "We're dealing with a lot of sensitive information. Orion's experiments aren't exactly the most detailed or well documented, so getting through this to where we can understand it is a challenge, let alone trying to create an antidote."

Abby, eyes ablaze, is scrolling through several different projections and arguing with Brendan. A hologram rotates next to Chloe as she studies the code.

"Oh, I did my AP Bio project last year on viral vectors. Is that what you're looking at?" Emma asks brightly.

"We've got this covered, Emma, thanks," Michael says.

Emma loses her foothold on the door as Michael gently nudges her out and closes it. She knocks furiously. *Super strength would be very handy right now,* Emma thinks, glaring at the door. She punches it and winces; her very normal fist doesn't make a dent. She winces and shakes her aching hand.

Like frightened birds, a flight of impulsive thoughts races through her. She could find a ventilation shaft and sneak in, but she shouldn't *have* to! Emma has just as much right to be in that room as everyone else. Brendan is a genius, but Emma helped him with algorithms for finding the Resistance, and Abby is great, but her experience is in engineering, not coding.

Emma scowls and shuffles off down the hallway. She passes two people who don't even acknowledge her. She might as well be invisible.

No, if she was invisible, she'd be a meta-human with a power. Then she'd be useful to the Guild and included in plans and not left behind on missions that were her idea in the first place. She was not left behind to oversee or supervise, but as just as the backup that no one ever expected anything from, as if giving her that title was only to make them feel better.

EMMA RARELY SEES HER FRIENDS; everyone is caught up in the action. At meals, she's usually alone because everyone's got their own training schedule, but today Jess and Bells managed to steal away to have lunch with her.

Emma pokes halfheartedly at her corn chowder as Jess plops down next to her, then yawns and rubs her eyes.

"Are you okay? Where's Abby?"

"She stayed up all night doing research," Jess says, her voice thin.

"Again?" Emma asks. She's barely seen Abby aside from a few scattered moments throughout the day.

"She's been doing that a lot." Bells raises an eyebrow. "I mean, I sleep pretty late, and she's usually still in the lab working on her mecha-suit or one of her many secret projects."

Jess crosses her arms. "She and Michael have been talking a lot. I think she's working on a way to get her powers back, but I wish…"

"Is she okay?" Emma asks.

Jess' voice wavers. "I don't know," she says finally. "She's been keeping weird hours."

Bells nods. "She woke me up yesterday at, like, three in the morning, asking if I wanted to go for a run."

"Yesterday?" Yesterday afternoon Abby asked Emma if she wanted to play volleyball in the gym. They tried to set up the net, but, while Emma was still untangling it, Abby ran off to go do something else.

"Yeah, she's been… off. Like, she will talk with Michael for hours and hours about meta-genes, and I don't follow all of it, but Michael doesn't seem to either? And he's an expert." Jess buries her face in her hands.

Emma wonders if Abby is trying find something in those files that could get her powers back, reverse-engineer the serum somehow. Whatever it is, it's keeping her occupied. They finish eating, and Bells pecks her cheek before running off with Jess to training. Emma, hoping that running some laps on the treadmill will help her feel better, finishes her chowder and follows them to the gym, but the training area is filled with people exercising their powers. Tanya and Sasha are popping in and out of thin air all over the cavern, and Ricky, well, Emma can't see him but she assumes he's there.

Bells is practicing rapid shifts, blending into the background of a changing screen. Emma's sure he'd talk to her, but she doesn't want to interrupt his practice; his training is important. Just because Emma doesn't have anything to do doesn't mean she can distract other people from their tasks.

Emma climbs to the lookout platform. She sits alone, swinging her feet over the edge, watching the forest. *Do I even have a place here?*

"Psst," a voice not-so-subtly whispers behind her while Emma's flipping through a book.

"What?" Emma turns around, cross.

Michael waves at her and holds out his tablet.

"What's all this?" Emma looks at the screen.

"Based on your genetic history, the powers you could potentially unlock." Michael waggles his eyebrows. "Remember when I gave everyone physicals? I ran your DNA too. Look!"

Emma takes the list.

Electric manipulation
Super strength
Voltage increase

Emma doesn't realize her fingers are trembling until Michael reaches out to hold the tablet steady. It's true; meta-abilities did run in her family. Tia Rosa could send little zaps of electricity from her fingertips. It had been no more than a curiosity, and she was Registered, but never was a part of any Meta-Human Training program.

"Come with me!" Michael gestures for her to follow.

They walk past all the main large workspaces, past the medical labs, past the halls that lead to the dorms. When they get past the garden caverns, Emma begins to get suspicious. "Where are we going?"

Michael opens a door into another long cavern.

"What is this, the sickbay?" Emma asks, but then she recognizes the space. This is where they had their physicals and tested their power levels. It looks the same, with curtains sectioning off rooms. But behind the curtains, shadows quiver and people moan and groan. She tenses; some of them must be in pain, and the reek of vomit lingers. "Ugh, it smells awful, Michael."

He frowns. "Yeah, I gotta get Deirdre back here to freshen up the scent."

"What's wrong with everyone?" Emma frowns, folding her arms. "Why are so many people sick?" Things like the common cold and most infections have long been dealt with by vaccinations provided to everyone in the Collective. "What happened?"

"Adverse reactions to the new R-31 serum," Michael says.

"The *what?*" Emma stops. "You mean what Orion injected into Abby?"

"This is a different strain I've been developing," Michael says.

"You mean you—" Emma doesn't even know where to start. "You don't know where those files actually came from! What if the information had been incorrect or malicious or—"

Michael twitches. "Look, we don't know why the files are here, but it's definitely Orion's research. We know that the League has all of these resources; why shouldn't we?" He draws a curtain. "This is Nina," he says.

Emma doesn't recognize her; she must be a new recruit.

Nina's face is ashen, she's breathing heavily, and her fevered eyes are glazed over, but she smiles. "Hi, Michael," she says before turning to Emma. "Nice to meet you. Are you going to be invoked as well?"

"Invoked?"

Nina holds her hand out. Very slowly, a pulsing ball of light begins to form. Sweat beads on her brow, and Nina exhales laboriously as the ball of light gets as large as her palm.

"Excellent, Nina!" Michael claps his hands. "Don't strain yourself, you have to preserve your strength. Don't use your powers outside of the testing period! Wait for official measurements."

Emma stops. "So you're helping Nina develop her powers? Why is she sick?"

"Nina previously did not have any meta-human abilities," Michael says, puffing up his chest with pride.

Emma freezes. "What."

Nina beams. "I mean, I was a good candidate, since my cousin could create these balls of light, so there's a foundation for it in the family, at least. I'm so excited! I can finally help out on the missions!"

Emma grabs Michael by the sleeve and drags him out of Nina's curtained cubicle. "What are you doing?"

"Working with the data we have. It's revolutionary." He grins at her. "Want to be next?"

THE BLOOD RUSHES TO HER head as Emma dangles upside down on the lumpy couch to watch yet another episode of *The Gentleman Detective.* She trails her fingers across the floating blue pixels, scattering Styx Kipling's form as he looks for clues. Emma's taken to hiding in the cluttered storage room, away from the business of the Guild. These forgotten boxes and shelves stacked full of memory chips and old paperbound books won't judge her.

"Do I want to be next?" Emma mutters darkly. She throws another handful of popcorn in her mouth and chews angrily. *How dare he assume what I want?*

Maybe he was just trying to be nice, another part of Emma reasons.

Emma sighs. It's not that she hasn't thought about having a power, but it never was a possibility before, so it never went any further than *oh that would be cool.* She thinks about it now, imagining herself hurling lightning bolts at Captain Orion alongside her friends, leading the charge with Deirdre crying out apologies in the background. She has wondered what it would be like to feel what her friends feel, to have that experience. Maybe powers would be nice.

She thinks about the sick people in Michael's lab. He hadn't perfected his own version of the serum and he was already doing patient trials.

If it was ready, would you do it? That voice whispers in her head. Emma scowls and turns up the volume.

This show is a thousand times less fun without Bells and Jess. She misses their tradition of watching the new episodes each week, laughing at Bells' shrieks of delight and Jess' befuddled face as she tried to figure out the clues. Before they got swept up into this mess, Abby would join them too. It had been nice, a piece of soft, mundane quiet they could enjoy even while the rest of their world seemed to spin out of control.

Outside, Emma can hear people moving about, making plans, taking action.

Emma sighs and flicks her hand at the screen with more force than necessary, scattering the words *Next Episode* into pieces. The movement makes her lose her balance, and she topples out of the couch and onto the packed dirt floor. She coughs, spluttering. If she'd been with her friends, she would have made a joke. Jess would offer her a pillow, and Bells would probably tug her into his lap, but she's alone. All her friends have official duties, and Emma is watching reruns.

"I can't just sit here and do nothing," Detective Kipling says, jawline set.

"That's absolutely right," Emma mutters. So she can't help with this part of the plan? *Fine.* She's got other plans she can check on. Emma stands up and dusts off her clothes.

She kicks open the door and strides down the hallway; ignoring others' puzzled looks, she barges into the gym. Bells is throwing kicks at a punching bag. It shakes with the force, rattling the chain. Emma marches right up, grabs the bag, and holds it still.

"Hey, Em," Bells says. "Wanna work out?"

"We have to call your dad," Emma says.

THEY'RE A FEW DAYS AHEAD of Bells' scheduled call, but Emma wants to try anyway. "Sean's bound to be monitoring the transmission at Grassroots headquarters," Bells says. "He and his boyfriend chat all the time."

Emma wonders how that relationship works, since it's long distance. She and Bells have been in the same place but somehow worlds apart. She thought she'd have so much more time here with Bells to talk to him and figure out what they were doing with their whole relationship thing, but he's been so busy, preoccupied with training.

Nick and Collette are travelling again, this time to the South on more Grassroots business. It's frustrating, checking in with Sean to hear from Bells' parents confirming the meeting, but at least it's something. Emma alternates between going with Bells to the radio transmission room and working out in the gym.

"Sean just heard from my dad," Bells says, interrupting Emma's latest round of sit-ups.

"That's great! Are we all set to go to Grassroots? Are they ready to help with the network and everything? This could completely change the tide—"

Bells' eyebrows knit, as if he's about to tell her something she's not going to like. This is exactly the face he made before they had that huge argument about Pluto in seventh grade. "Well, he agreed to convince the plenary board— that's, like, their version of the Council—"

Emma grumbles. "So much bureaucracy."

"Yeah, well they agreed to hear you out at the headquarters in the Louisiana region. The location is secret, but Dad will meet us in New Orleans, and Grassroots will meet with us near there."

Emma's already packed; it feels like she never unpacked to begin with. Her instincts tell her not to split up the Sidekick Squad again, but when would she get another chance to pitch to Grassroots?

"That's a *great* idea!" Jess says, ever-optimistic, when Emma presents her the idea. "Bells, this is amazing! Oh, tell them Chloe says hello! And that the crops are doing better than expected."

"Will do." Bells looks at Emma and gives her a cheeky grin.

"Okay." Emma can't help smiling back at Bells. "We'll be gone for a week. During that time, we'll meet with the leaders of Grassroots and ask about tapping into their communication system. Since they already have one, we won't have to recreate a system from scratch."

"Sounds good," Jess says, sighing.

A note in her voice makes Emma wonder if Jess actually believes it's a good plan. Having a friend who always believes everything will work out can be stressful because Emma doesn't have a scale. Jess is hopeful about *everything*. But she does seem down now.

A door opens and shuts, and Abby flies in. She greets Jess with a wet kiss and turns around, her eyes bright. "Bells! Emma! Hey, sorry I'm late! I was in the lab with Michael. We've got this in the bag, it's gonna be awesome; how are you, Jess told me about the Grassroots plan, that sounds so cool, do you think I could come? Wait, I think Michael needs me here—" Abby is speaking so fast Emma can barely keep track of what's she's saying. She's always known Abby was ambitious. When she was class president and captain of the volleyball team, she was very driven, but this feels different.

Bells' eyebrows seem to jump off his head. Emma glances at him, and he seems to wordlessly agree: *Abby's acting really strange.*

"Hey, Abby," Emma says. "Thanks. We're getting ready to go. How are you?"

"Great!"

Abby does not look great. There are bags under her eyes, and her face is pale and drawn, and she looks much thinner.

"Jess says you haven't been getting a lot of sleep."

"How can I sleep when there's work to do? Come on, this is the Resistance! There aren't enough hours in the day to take care of all the things we need to do! Oh, that reminds me, I gotta see if the results for our latest experiments are done. Bye! Have fun in the South! We'll catch up with you in a week!"

Abby turns around in a whirl of red curls, and the door slams shut behind her.

"So, yeah," Jess mumbles. "I'm worried about her."

"I think she's probably just excited about her research," Bells says. "It's, like, the newness of it all; she'll crash and then sleep for three days, probably. Is she still trying to use her powers?"

"No, she told me— I know, we don't want a repeat of what happened last time."

Rushing Abby to the hospital after she collapsed was terrifying. Emma drums her fingers on the control panel, trying to appease her nerves. "Hey, it'll be okay," she says. "Just tell her to lay off the coffee and get some rest, okay?"

Jess sighs one more time and hugs Emma and Bells. "Be safe. Set up a radio as soon as you can and call me."

"Same frequency, same time," Emma says.

"I'll be there every Wednesday, like clockwork," Jess says. She squeezes them tight.

"Take care of Abby," Emma says. "And say goodbye to your parents and everyone for me."

"I will."

Jess gives them one last glance before shutting the door, and Emma and Bells are alone in the supply room.

"It's going to be fine." Bells steps closer. He picks up a strand of her hair and curls it around his fingers. "You know, we don't leave for another half hour and once we're down South my whole family will be there and we won't have a minute alone together—"

"Oh, you're right," Emma says.

Bells grins at her; his blue hair shifts to purple. "What do you want to do until then?" He leans forward with a mischievous glint in his eyes and then he ducks his head; a small smile starts on his lips.

It's adorable, so very Bells. She's always wondered about moments like these. *People say "attraction" can be those feelings that make you want to kiss someone else, right?*

A surge of affection rushes through her, and, now that they're here, that they're *together,* Emma can try to figure out, yet again, what all of these feelings mean and what she can do about them. When Bells tried to save everyone on that train after they destroyed the Registry, Emma thought she might lose him for real. She knew she needed to tell him how she felt.

Feelings churn inside her now; doubt creeps in. *Did she do the right thing?* She loves him. *What do you know about love, anyway?* A small voice in her head counters.

Emma tells the voice to shut up. This *is* a moment when she wants to kiss him—when the person she cares about is being soft and sweet and cute—and Emma just, Emma wants to show him how she feels, wants to be close to him.

So she does kiss him, pulling him close to catch his lips with hers. Bells makes a surprised, pleased noise, kisses back softly, and tangles his fingers in her hair. When he pulls back, his eyes are bright, his cheeks are flushed. "Hello," he says softly.

"Hello," Emma says, looking into his deep brown eyes. She's hyper-aware that they're alone, sitting together on the couch, and Bells is smiling at her in that incandescent way that makes his whole face shine.

She smiles, starting to relax, when doubt creeps up on her again. She thinks about moments like this one, and how everyone she's dated has eventually expected things from her. *It's the normal process for a relationship, right?*

Emma takes his hand and smiles, despite the nervousness churning in her stomach. "So, do you, uh—" Emma hopes her tone is light and playful. They've kissed before, and she's enjoyed it, but it's probably time for their makeout sessions to progress, especially now that they're in a relationship. She trails off, hoping he understands, and waggles her eyebrows at him just to be sure he does.

Bells laughs, pulling her into a comfortable position with both of them cuddled on the couch. "I'm not ready for sex," he says.

"Oh, me either," Emma says, relieved.

Bells lifts one eyebrow. "Then why did you ask? We had this conversation already, Em!"

"Like a month ago!" Emma throws her hands in the air. "I don't know if you changed your mind and wanted to now or something! You're the one who was, like…" She lowers her voice and attempts a sensual drawl. "...we're all alone and we won't get to have another chance."

"To make out." Bells rolls his eyes. He puts his hands on Emma's shoulders and looks into her eyes intently. "Is that okay? We talked about kissing and cuddling before—"

"Yes." Emma pulls him forward and kisses him again. It's warm and safe and *Bells* and soft and sweet.

Bells hums, drawing patterns on her arm. Emma's feet are propped up in Bells' lap, and she's cozy and comfortable and doesn't ever want to move.

"Hey," she says, suddenly nervous.

"Hm?" Bells has a hand in her hair, stroking it. It feels nice, his fingers massaging her scalp, relieving all the tension she's been feeling this week.

"What if I won't ever be ready? Or don't want to ever?"

Bells' hand keeps stroking her hair, and he presses a soft kiss to her forehead. "That's okay. Just let me know what you want and don't want."

"Isn't sex, like, something you'd want, though? In the future?"

"Hey," he says. "Look at me."

Emma sits up, intending to curl up into a ball, but he's holding her other hand and giving her a soft, focused gaze. "I just— I thought it's something we're supposed to—"

"Hey, hey, c'mon," he says. "Whatever we both put into this, it's gotta be something we both want. And I never want you to feel like you have to or are supposed to do *anything* you don't want to."

"Okay," Emma says quietly.

He leans forward and doesn't kiss her as she's expecting, just presses his forehead against hers. Emma closes her eyes, taking it all in.

She doesn't know how long they sit there. It could be minutes or an hour, just Bells gently stroking her back, Emma breathing slowly and inhaling his scent.

Beep.

"Hang on," Bells says. It's his tablet, forgotten on the floor.

Emma nods. It should be important; the only people who can access their private network and would be within range are members of the Resistance or Bells' family.

"It's Dad," he says. "He's here. You ready to go?"

Emma takes a deep breath. "This is gonna be great. We can do this."

"Me and you, the Sidekick Squad, an unstoppable team," Bells says with an infectious grin.

"I thought you didn't like that name." Emma smirks, holding back a laugh.

"It's growing on me," Bells says, taking her hand and squeezing it, and Emma feels that warm surge of affection again. She squeezes back. This will be great. They're a team, they're *together,* and it's going to work out perfectly.

New New Orleans is bursting with colors and tantalizing smells. After their high-speed train ride, Emma woke to warm sunshine and people everywhere. Striding through the Jackson Square hoverstation, she yawns. She tosses the burner DED with the train ticket information in the trash and jogs after Bells, who's stopped to wait for her by a pillar.

Emma's already lost sight of Nick and Collette, Bells' parents, who've changed disguises subtly at least twice since they met at the station. She spots them wearing different hats, and Bells' brothers Simon and Sean have changed their jackets. Emma's trying her best to stay inconspicuous using her wigs, and Bells— well, Bells has that covered. Emma's proud of him for learning to shift so fast. There used to be a visible difference when he shifted, but now he can change in the time between breaths.

As they pass through the central transit station and away from the train platforms, Emma is overwhelmed with the sheer amount of movement. Emma follows Bells through the square and down the street, through several types of markets: fresh produce, handmade gifts, clothes. People call out prices, beckoning passersby to come look at the wares in their shops. Musicians play lively tunes, drawing crowds who swipe their DEDs at collecting ports. Above them, buildings old and new seem to shine in the summer light, surrounded by monorails and the flow of people in a constant, moving rhythm.

Emma can barely keep up; she wants to see *everything*.

New New Orleans is one of the few cities in the North American Collective that retains much of its rich history from before the Disasters. Emma isn't sure about the "New New" moniker, although Bells assures her it's a thing. The people of New Orleans rebuilt so many times in the face of storms and floods even before the Disasters that rebuilding again after the World War Three didn't faze them. Bells still has family here, descended from those who didn't evacuate with the other Broussards in the post-X29 hurricane that devastated the city.

The plaza is bustling with the morning going-to-work crowd, college kids on their way to class, and street vendors with delicious smelling carts. Any other day Emma would be glad to amble through the city center, but they aren't sightseeing today. Bells eagerly points out art and history museums as they pass, and Emma makes a mental note to try to make some time to do fun things together.

It's hard keeping up the brisk pace, especially when Emma wants to look at everything. The city is so beautiful, and this area is filled with musicians playing merry tunes and the delicious smells of fresh seafood. Bells looks as though he wants to follow his nose, too, and winks at her when she does a double-take at a vendor shaking powdered sugar onto beignets fresh from a fryer. "We'll go later," he mouths at her and takes her hand as they catch up with the rest of his family.

Emma takes in the archways and cast-iron balconies, the mix of ancient brick and gleaming chrome, the walls painted in bright, warm hues. Emma wants to linger, but there's no time.

The monorail train is crowded. Children press their noses to the windows to take in the city and the expansive view of the buildings built high above the older historical districts.

A shrill whistle sounds.

"What?" Emma blinks as no one seems to notice.

"High tide," Bells says. "Come on, you look like a tourist."

Emma feels like one, gasping at how the lower buildings automatically rise up around the square to meet the other buildings on the sky-street platforms as the square fills with the gentle waves of the tide coming in.

Emma gasps, watching avidly as all the people just go about their business as usual, either walking briskly through the knee-high water or taking lifts up to the elevated monorail platforms or the sky-street.

"Does this happen all the time?"

Bells laughs. "Yeah, whenever the tide crosses over the levees. Back when the sea level was lower, I think the original plan was just to keep making the levees higher and higher, but every time it rained the city would have to pump water out. The Historical Preservation Society found a way to preserve these ancient buildings by working with the tide, not against it."

Emma watches the city rise; she remembers reading about the engineering marvel that keeps the city afloat. She peers out the window, trying take in the complicated tech that makes living in this area possible.

The car is filled with conversation; Emma overhears bits of French, Spanish, Japanese, English, and Portuguese throughout the train, and is comforted by the familiar sounds of multiple languages overlapping one another.

Emma reaches for the handhold, but she can't quite reach the bar. Bells gracefully grabs it and smiles at her. He jerks his head at his arm, and Emma takes it. She rolls her eyes at him before he can tease her about her height. They sway with the motion of the train as it curves through the city, and Emma can't keep her eyes off the changing landscape. It's easy to be captivated by the constant flow of energy, the bright columns of the old architecture, the steep roofs and parapets that are dwarfed by the shining glass and chrome steel of the new buildings.

As the train leaves the center of the city, its passengers empty out: children going to school, people on their way to work, people with bags of groceries. After a man holding a chicken delicately in his arms exits the train, the Broussards and Emma are the only ones left in the car.

"This is our stop, come on," Nick says, beckoning them.

Emma squeezes Bells' hand and tries to practice the speech in her head one more time. This is it; they're going to meet the contact waiting to take them to a Grassroots headquarters.

Here on the outskirts of New New Orleans, it's quieter. Emma's footsteps on the cobbled streets seem to echo with uncertainty. She catches her reflection in a shop window and winces. She looks like a child; it's her height, she knows, and her round face. Maybe they won't take her seriously. Maybe she should have worn heels.

Emma grits her teeth; no, that could have gone horribly wrong, too, looking as if she's trying too hard, like a child playing dress-up.

On a nondescript street corner, Collette stops and reads a sign outside a bakery. Emma follows her lead and pretends to be totally immersed in chatting with Bells. Nick steps backward, closer to the corner outside the bakery, and ever so slightly jerks his head. Emma follows his gaze and sees the reflective shine of a small camera that's embedded in the wall.

Bells' parents step out of the frame, and Bells takes Emma's hand, following them. Her heart is thudding with excitement. All the secrecy surrounding Grassroots and how they work is fascinating; she can't wait to learn more and apply that to the Resistance.

A solarcar that's seen better days pulls up. Its panels are worn and scratched, and the paint on the metal is long faded. The window rolls down, and a man with bright, dangling earrings regards them with a bemused look. He nods at the Broussards and gives Emma a quick glance, as if he's sizing her up. It seems like a test; she's not sure if she passed.

"Angel, so good to see you!" Collete says warmly. "Thank you for picking us up!"

"Of course, of course," Angel says. "Bells, you've gotten so tall and handsome!"

"It's a burden I must bear," Bells says, saluting Angel theatrically. "This is Emma, Angel."

"Great, great," Angel says, with barely a nod.

They bustle into the car before Emma can think of a good way to introduce herself. The inside is clean, roomy, and comfortable despite the dilapidated outside appearance, with water and fresh fruit waiting for them in a cooler. Emma is impressed; Grassroots really is a well-run organization.

The Broussards chat with Angel as the car speeds them out of town. Emma leans back, wanting for the right time to say hello. *What if Angel is a senior member of Grassroots?* She doesn't think she's making a good impression. She doesn't want to butt into the conversation, and there never is a good spot for her to jump in. It seems Angel and Bells' parents go way back, and they're already caught up in a complex discussion about Sean and Simon's current Grassroots project.

To her surprise, when they pass a glass storefront, there is no reflection of them or their car. Angel must have activated an advanced camouflage function.

The buildings thin out as they drive through the city, and then they pass familiar-looking signs warning them about the Unmaintained areas. The well-paved road gives way to cracked concrete as they blaze through the bayou, passing over spillways and miles and miles of thick, overgrown wetlands.

They're keeping close to a rushing river; its glimmering waters sparkle in the distance. It's so wide that at first Emma thinks it's the ocean.

Everything is so green and lush with life: cypress trees and swaying willows and trails of moss reaching for the ground. And yet the landscape still echoes that wild feel of the Unmaintained lands back home; it's familiar and unfamiliar all at once. A few times Emma notices more camouflage techniques, such as an entire tree shifting to let them pass and then sliding back into place.

They stop once to recharge the car at a Grassroots charge station cleverly disguised to look like part of the landscape. The adults are caught up in conversation, and Bells has his sketchbook out and is lost in his own world.

Emma goes for a short walk while they wait.

Mesmerized by the relentless flow of the water, she stops just short of the shore of the great river. The wind picks up, whirling around her, and a sudden gust almost knocks her hat off. Emma laughs, clapping her hands to her head. She catches her breath, steps back from the edge, and takes in the massive lifeline in front of her. She inhales and exhales with the rhythm of the river, steady as the beating of her own heart.

"Nice view, isn't it?"

Emma turns; it's Sean, Bells' older brother. "Hey," she says awkwardly remembering Bells' long-ago suggestion they talk. She's been so busy with the Resistance, and Sean's always been away on Broussard business, so she hasn't had a chance. During the car ride, he smiled at her, but there was no way Emma would bring up her personal questions in front of Bells and the rest of his family.

Sean nods, humming to himself with a knowing smile. "Bells mentioned a while ago you might have some questions for me?"

"Yeah," Emma says, relieved he brought it up first. She twirls her fingers in her hair. "Sorry, this is weird."

Sean gives her an amused look. "Is it because you're dating my brother?"

"Yeah."

Sean laughs. "No worries. I mean, I don't really wanna know that stuff either, but be safe, you know? You're being safe?"

Emma turns bright red. "We haven't— We aren't—" she trails off. She *definitely* doesn't want to talk about sex with Bells' brother, but, then again, she doesn't know who else she can talk to.

Sean pats her on the shoulder and laughs. "It's okay, you know. You don't have to tell me."

"Thanks, but I want to talk," Emma insists. She paces, trying to think of what she wants to say and what she wants to know. "So we haven't, and we talked about it, and Bells isn't ready, and I'm not ready and I, I mean, I've done it before…" she trails off.

Sean waits for her to speak.

"I think I might be asexual," Emma blurts out.

Sean nods; his face seems warm and open.

Emma exhales; she knows a few ace people at school: Courtney on the volleyball team, Peter in her history class. But she's never talked to them about it. It would feel strange to reach out to them now, not that she could, now that she's left school.

"I mean, I don't know. I still feel like… sex, it mostly… it was okay? But I didn't think it was a big deal, since it seems like a lot of people do it and especially being in a relationship—"

Emma understood the power of social capital at school. She had it all figured out. She wasn't one of the most popular kids in her class for no reason; she knows she's cute and has a warm and bubbly personality and gets along with people very well, especially with the people she dated. Emma thought sex was supposed to be a huge factor in staying together for many people.

The weight of those expectations seems even heavier now, and Emma wants this relationship with Bells to be perfect. She can't mess this up. He's her best friend. And now he's her boyfriend.

"Okay." Sean gives her a warm smile, turns to look at the river, and waits for her to continue.

"I talked with Bells about it, before, and we're, we're good," Emma says hesitantly. The whole sex conversation actually went really well. It seemed like an open and shut door as far as Emma was concerned. But she still has worries. "I mean, some of the stuff— I don't get either? And I've never really gotten, like, my past relationships, the, like, big stuff with the flowers and the gifts and the... I don't know if..."

Sean listens, letting her ramble on about the gestures and the touches and what they mean and what they could mean, and Emma thinks she's not making sense at all, but he's really easy to talk to, and, after a few minutes, Emma stops, embarrassed.

"Do you want to hear my story?" he asks.

Emma nods.

"For me, I knew way back when, even in high school when people were all about crushes and dating and stuff." Sean grins with his hands in his pockets; he sways a bit as he talks.

"I was more interested in studying agriculture and working on the farm every day. I was asked out a few times, but I didn't really understand how dating was different from friendship, and it got confusing. And then in college, I dated a bit before I met Ryan. I don't really care about sex, but, if my partner is into it, I'm into it, you know."

Sean's voice is soft and contemplative, as if he's thought about this a lot. "I like kissing and cuddling, but my friend Diana doesn't, and a professor I know doesn't like any kind of touch at all. There isn't a right or wrong way to be asexual: some people are touch-averse, some people aren't; there are different levels of attraction and stuff. If you think you're asexual and feel comfortable using it to describe yourself, that's great."

When Sean smiles, the corners of his eyes crinkle just as Bells' do. "Ace, gray-ace, wherever you are on the spectrum, it's okay. There are a lot of people who feel the same way."

Emma learned about asexuality before, but it was just flat words on a screen. What Sean tells her about his life and his feelings, she's felt that too. Not understanding what other people meant when they saw someone pass by and said they were cute— Emma didn't quite get it either. She didn't understand it when her friends imagined whole futures about dating and kissing and having sex with people who were effectively strangers; Emma couldn't imagine it at all, despite what she would say, hoping she'd fit in.

Even when she was dating, kissing was weird. She didn't have another word for it. It seemed too up-front, too physical sometimes, but she tried it. In some of her past relationships— Kyle, Denise, Carlos—she liked kissing them, but how much of that was the kissing itself and how much of it was liking the time spent with them, she wonders.

"Do you, like, find people attractive?" Emma asks. She doesn't know until she says it aloud how much this question has been bouncing about in her head, because everyone always seemed to just automatically *know* if someone is hot.

"What do you mean? Like, I see so-and-so on the street or think some celebrity is hot or pretty or cute or whatever?" Sean strokes his chin, regarding her.

Emma nods. Celebrities and strangers were called pretty for some confusing, pre-determined reason. Emma puzzled over their features and thought about the other students in her grade and she figured it out. There were dimples and colors of eyes and jaws and cheekbones; there was a formula, an algorithm. The same way so many people in her class said, "Oh, Bells is so cute!" in that dreamy way, she could look at him and think *yes, he's wonderful, he's funny and smart and beautiful and I love being his friend.* And then she saw what they saw: his symmetrical face, his smooth skin, the trendy way he styled his hair. He fit into the formula of attractiveness.

"Yeah, I can appreciate people who are pretty." Sean smiles at her. "But they're only aesthetically pleasing. I don't think about wanting to kiss them or have sex with them or anything, but that's part of me not being attracted to people like that, you know? What attracts *you* to people?"

"Uh, if they're interesting," Emma says. Everyone she's dated has always been fascinating, and Emma wanted to be in their orbit and learn more about them. "I mean, I talked a lot about their physical features like their eyes or hair or whatever, but that's because that's what everyone else talked about." It never had anything to do with how they looked, Emma realizes. Dating was just another problem, another formula to solve, and Emma was determined to be good at it.

"My friend Diana did that too," Sean says. "I think a lot of people have that experience. You're not alone, you know."

Emma's thought about this, but it always seemed like a vague theory, far away and untouchable. It didn't feel tangible and certain the way it does now.

"Do you feel comfortable identifying as asexual?" Sean asks, tilting his head. There's no judgment in his tone, and the question is simply open, waiting there for her.

Emma takes a deep breath. She's thought about it often enough, but never felt quite brave enough to claim that word for her own. Emma wished she had an *aha* moment like Jess that time in freshman English. Jess was reading a poem aloud and then, all of a sudden, she stopped, her eyes widening. "Oh. That's me. I'm bisexual," she said, seeming a little stunned.

There were a few amused chuckles in the classroom, and Emma heard a "well, how did you *not* know, I knew, like, *in middle school*" and the little breath of "ooohs" from the kids obsessed with knowing who was crushing on who. While the school's flitting interest in Jess' revelation faded, Emma's own questioning came to the forefront of her mind. When Emma first discovered what asexuality meant, at age eight, she didn't think about applying it to herself. Then, Emma was on a flurry of research binges, figuring out how hovertrains could float in the air and why the sky was blue. Learning that there were people with little to no sexual attraction to other people was another fact of the universe that Emma understood. She moved on to topics that were more interesting at the time, like space, and then that became the focus of her eight-year-old research obsession.

Discussing asexuality in health class freshman year brought the concept back to mind. Emma delved into research, as she does whenever a topic fascinates her. It was like opening a door full of possibilities, and Emma tried to learn as much as she could. But she also thought hard about what other kids at school thought about her. She wanted to succeed so badly. She tried so hard to understand what people were talking about and experiencing that she pushed all of these feelings and questions deep inside her, as if she was afraid of them. Emma thinks if she just learned what asexuality meant now she'd hang on to the word like a lifeline, like the possibility that *this is me*.

Facing the question now, Emma finds that she is brave enough. The word resonates with her, a note falling into tune.

"Yes," she says, relaxing for the first time since this conversation began. "I think— I *am* asexual," she says, settling into the word.

"Cool." Sean gives her an easy smile, and they sit in comfortable silence.

"What about the other stuff? Like how I'm confused about, like, relationship stuff in general?" Emma asks.

"You know that romantic and sexual attraction aren't the same thing, right?"

"Yeah, of course," Emma says. They talked about it in that health class freshman year. Everyone knows this. "I've thought about being aromantic before, but I don't know if it fits exactly. I mean, I thought asexual didn't fit perfectly for me either, since I've liked sex sometimes. But—with the sexual attraction stuff—I mean, it feels the most right."

Sean nods. "Good. That's the most important part. If it feels right to you."

"I've thought a lot about being aromantic, too, but sometimes I'm not sure," Emma admits.

"So there are a lot of arospec people, and everyone has their own experience, you know?" Sean throws his arms out wide as if he's drawing an endless circle. "Like, maybe never having romantic attraction. Some people have a little bit or feel like they can develop romantic relationships after building a bond or getting to know someone." Sean pats Emma on the shoulder. "Anywhere you are is perfectly normal."

Emma exhales. She's read this, but hearing another person say it to her feels good.

"You're asexual and aromantic, right? And you have a boyfriend?"

Sean smiles at her. "What about him?"

"Do you like that— him being your boyfriend?" Emma cringes, asking such a strange question. Emma tries to sum up how *weird* the word feels for her, as if there's a whole new expectation for their relationship. "I don't know if *I* like Bells being my boyfriend," she says, feeling small as she admits it. "I love him, of course, but, like—now that we're— I don't know. I thought I was trying to express something *big,* something like... He gets me. I get him. And we're, like, soulmates, you know? And I thought going from friends to romantic relationship was a good way to show how I feel, but..."

"Hmm..." Sean draws out the sound thoughtfully. "Do you know what a queerplatonic relationship is?"

Another term from that same class so many years ago. Trying to remember the definition is difficult. "Like friendship? That's what we already are, though."

"A queerplatonic relationship can look different for many people, but the important part is that it encompasses that bigness that you were talking about." Sean slows down, speaking with careful consideration. "A queerplatonic relationship can have very close emotional connections and commitment between people and can be a helpful way of saying that you are life partners, but not necessarily romantic."

Oh.

"So I'm comfortable with Ryan being my boyfriend, and he likes it a lot too." Sean chuckles. "Technically, Ryan and I do have a very queerplatonic relationship, but we also like being romantic with each other. I also lean a bit more toward being demiromantic, so it works for us. I think we talked about it about a month into dating. I was a little nervous at first, but it all worked out. I've dated people before who didn't get it, but Ryan is great. We talk a lot about, like, our boundaries and what I'm into and not into."

"Queerplatonic," Emma repeats, as if a weight is being lifted from her shoulders.

"Hey, Em, wake up. We're here."

Emma blinks groggily. The afternoon sun has long faded to dusk; it's nearly dark. *How long have they been driving? Several hours, at least.*

"Where is everyone?" She and Bells are alone in the car. It's parked in a dimly lit tunnel; there's a strange texture to the walls.

"Ma and Dad had some business stuff to work out first, and you were knocked out. I figured it would be better to let you sleep. I mean, you haven't really been getting good rest lately, right?"

It's a thoughtful gesture, but Emma can't help but feel frustrated, as though she missed a chance to meet people and to have these adults to take her seriously. She sits up, rubbing her head; she feels awful. She hates naps. She always wakes up more tired than she was before.

Emma tries to get her bearings. Now, with her eyes adjusted, she can see from the faint glow of the lamps above that the tunnel is made of thickly woven moss and vines grown over a wire framework. *Clever, hiding aboveground like this.* Then, Emma realizes that there weren't many bunkers built below ground in the wetlands.

Splotches of dappled sunlight filter through the greenery, but otherwise Bells' hair seems to be the only color left in the world. The streaks of violet in his dreads glows with vivid intensity. She kisses his cheek. "How long have we been here?"

"Eh, maybe an hour. I don't think Torrance would be ready for a while, so we would have had to wait inside anyway."

Emma peers at the sketchbook in Bells' hands and spots a few unfinished impressions: the city square, musicians in the street, and a beautiful girl Emma doesn't recognize. "These are really good," she says. "You did all these on this trip?"

"Yeah," Bells says. "Some at the beginning of the book are older, though. Wanna see?"

He hands her the book, and it seems to take on a new weight in her hands. She knows how private he is about his art. She's seen his work before, but he's always guarded about his in-process sketches. Emma turns to the beginning of the book and fumbles for the interior light. Brightness floods the vehicle, and Bells' drawings leap into stark contrast.

The first few pages are familiar: the high desert of Nevada, the train track striking a clean line through cacti scattered across the sparse landscape, a closeup study of a cornstalk and then the corncob itself with each kernel detailed in Bells' careful hand, sketches of Jess and Abby. Emma traces her fingers around their faces; she misses them too.

The city of New New Orleans leaps out at her: the lines of the buildings, the city squares, and the girl. Emma flips through the pages, and the lovely stranger keeps reappearing, seeming to look up from the page with a knowing smile. She's beautiful, drawn with a precise hand on some pages, her form appearing amidst scribbles and sketches on others, as if Bells couldn't draw fast enough, as if she was going to escape from the page and leap, demanding and vivacious, into real life.

Emma stops on the last page, where the girl is captured laughing and catching her hat before it's caught by the wind. She's taking in the beautiful river flowing ahead of her; her face seems filled with determination. Emma takes in a sharp breath. The girl is her. She didn't recognize at first the elegant curve of her neck, the confidence in that gaze. *Is this how Bells sees me?* She feels suddenly self-conscious. *What if she's not living up to the girl he thinks she is?*

"What do you think?"

"It's lovely, Bells," Emma says. Now just to channel that confidence.

"THEY'RE READY FOR YOU. GO ON IN."

"You're not coming with me?" Emma is suddenly nervous but doesn't want to admit it. She swallows the bubble of energy and watches Bells shake his head.

"It's your proposal. I can't go in with you, sorry. They have very strict policies and don't want me to bias them. Dad says it was hard enough to get them to bring you here, let alone meet with you."

Emma walks the narrow corridor alone. The enclosed hallway between greenhouses is fogged with condensation, and Emma can barely see the greenery behind the glass. With each step she rehearses her speech, practicing her opening lines over and over until she finally comes to the end of the hallway.

The door creaks open when she pushes it. Inside is a circular room sunk in the ground with many seats around the rim, like a round lecture hall. Most of the seats are equipped with holoprojectors; a few are occupied by people. Nervous energy bubbles over; her hands shake. This is more people than she bargained for.

The two men standing in the center of the room are apparently legends in the guerrilla farming movement: Torrance Whitaker and Skye Coulson. Nick and Collette had talked nonstop about them, mishaps and pranks when they were all in school together, silly things that would in no way help her in this professional meeting.

"Hello," Emma says. It's one thing telling their parents and friends about the truth about the League and asking their support, but it's another thing to talk to complete strangers. She's hoping that they'll be sympathetic, since they've been working their whole lives against the Collective's broken systems.

Emma takes a deep breath and pulls herself to her full height. "I'm here because I want to talk to you about joining the Resistance."

The two men glance at each other and then break into incredulous laughter. "Join the Resistance?" Skye asks between guffaws.

Torrance gives her an amused smile. "Honey, we *are* the Resistance. We've been fighting the Collective since before you were born."

"Right!" Emma says, nodding furiously. "I mean, I know about that. Bells' parents have been part of Grassroots forever…"

Torrance nods. "Yes, the Broussards are wonderful. They've been key to keeping their region well-supplied for the better part of two decades."

"Yes, absolutely!" Emma's thrown a little off guard. In her head, her practiced speech now sounds naïve and redundant, especially with Torrance and Skye looking down at her like every teacher that's underestimated her before. Emma stumbles and speaks quickly, as she does when she's nervous. "So, the entire Heroes' League of Heroes is a scam. The Collective's training process is just a way for them to keep meta-humans in check." She knows she's rambling, but she keeps going anyway, skipping the introduction and going right to the middle.

Torrance and Skye just stand silently in judgment along with the other adults as Emma improvises, trying just to hit the highlights: meta-humans forced to play a role, the villains being kidnapped and experimented on, the entire League doing heinous things in the name of enhancing their powers.

"So... that's why we have to stop the League," Emma concludes awkwardly. It's not the polished speech she meant to give, but she feels so flustered, standing on this platform with so many eyes on her. "That's why we've been going around trying to tell as many people as possible the truth."

Torrance laughs. "Look, we've *been* resisting."

"So..." Emma feels as if she's missing the joke. "Will you help us?"

Skye smiles at her, bemused, as if she's a child with a cute idea. "Well, it looks like you and your friends have uncovered some of the unsavory truths about the Collective."

Torrance looks at his partner and nods. "Yes. It's a noble goal, and I wholeheartedly believe that telling the people of this country the truth about their heroes is good, but it doesn't fix the main problem."

Emma falters. "Right... the system is flawed, but..."

Skye claps his hands, as though he's glad Emma agrees. "The North American Collective has a long way to go in providing adequate infrastructure to support its people. The obsession with superpowers and the amount of energy invested in melodramatics to pacify the public and keep people well-entertained and distracted is something that should have ended a long time ago."

Emma nods, even if she doesn't agree with *everything* Skye is saying. Sure, the country is obsessed. Superheroes are celebrities; everyone wants to know who's dating whom and what they're wearing and stuff, but that comes with being in the public spotlight. That's not going to stop overnight. Emma doesn't want to stop the press coverage, but use it to focus on the real story. She tries to put this into words, but all that comes out is "But…"

Torrance and Skye seem like pillars, with their arms crossed as if they've already made up their minds. "Grassroots has been a vital part of keeping people well-fed when the Collective marks up the price on all fruits and vegetables for shipping them. We commend you and your friends for uncovering this meta-human business, but it doesn't actually concern Grassroots," Torrance says.

"We appreciate you coming all this way to let us know," Skye says. "We support your endeavors."

"Is that a *no?*" Emma says, shocked. She hasn't even made her proposal about why they need Grassroots' communication system.

One of the holos speaks up, a woman with the flag of the Southeast Asian Alliance pinned on her blazer. "The North American Collective is flawed; we support your attempt to reveal those flaws."

"So you say you're supporting me, and that's it? Look, we need access to an efficient communication system, something you already have! So we'll be safe. We've already been attacked, and so many people are in danger. You know that all those MR-D4Rs have military capabilities, right? And with so many of them, it'll be too easy for the Authorities and the League to apprehend anyone they think stands in their way." Emma knows her voice is getting higher and higher, but she feels desperate.

"We are aware of the MR-D4Rs and how the Collective might misuse such a resource," says another holo, a stiff-looking man with the European Union insignia on his coat. "That is why Grassroots members operate in the highest secrecy, and all our communication is encrypted far beyond what you might even imagine."

Emma feels as if she's been talking in circles. *This* is why she came to Grassroots for help in the first place. Bells' idea of using the network seemed so perfect, but she never imagined Grassroots hearing her out and then just saying *Good job on figuring it out! Good luck with that.*

Her frustration turns into anger, even as Skye and Torrance give her polite smiles that can only mean dismissal. "Thank you for your time, Emma. This hallway will lead you to the main annex, and the Broussards should be done with their business by now and be able to escort you out."

Skye and Torrance turn to address the people and holos in the room. "The next order of business..." Torrance begins.

"No!" Emma snaps.

The two leaders stop and look at each other and then at Emma as if to say, *why is she still here?* All the other adults turn their eyes on her.

"Look, I get what you're saying, that you have your own missions and stuff to do, but this is important! In order to change the system we need to, to..." She's grasping at straws here, but she thinks there's an important point she completely forgot to mention. "The system is unfair, yes! But the Council, Kingston, and the government are directly in league with, with the League!" Emma splutters, aware of how ridiculous she sounds, how young she is, how inexperienced she is, but she hates most of all feeling ignored and treated as if she doesn't matter in the slightest.

The Grassroots members look at each other, they murmur, and the scrolling wall of text translates into multiple languages.

She's got their attention now, for better or for worse. Emma tries to pull herself together. This is her last chance. The Resistance is depending on her. "Look. Kingston is *awful*. He's been pushing the League's agenda hardcore, probably ever since he's been elected in 2104, to distract the public from the conflict he's pushed us into overseas with Constavia. And that's about mining tantalum to enforce even more control over meta-humans and keep us all in his control!"

Skye holds up a hand. "I don't disagree. Kingston is a manipulative and opportunistic man with a desire to stay in power. I didn't know about Constavia, but it doesn't surprise me."

"Aren't you worried about him pushing our country to war?" Emma says, throwing up her hands. "We need to remove him from representing the Central Regions as President, from the Council, from any position of power!"

"But how are you doing that?" Torrance points out. "We've seen what you've been doing, trying to spread the word. I've seen the 'The League is a Lie' graffiti all over towns. It's just the topic of the month on the conspiracy boards and it'll be forgotten as soon as the next thing comes along."

"But it's changing," Emma says. "Yes, the graffiti is a start, but we can capitalize on the public questioning the League. My plan is to have meta-humans interrupt battles being broadcast and to tell the public what really is happening, but it's taking some time, especially with the way it's being covered in the press." And, with Deirdre in charge at the Villain's Guild, Emma's not sure how effective all of those missions are.

"You're telling some superpowered people to pick fights with other superpowered people so that the fights will stop being staged," Torrance says. "Do you see how ridiculous that is?"

Emma falters. "There are some people who *are* looking beyond what is scripted and actually reporting what's happening."

"The average person can't tell the difference," Skye says. "If I watch the news and I see two costumed people fighting each other, I'm going to assume things are going on as usual."

Emma is tired of having to explain herself, having to keep proving that her goal is a viable one. Just because they don't have clear results now doesn't mean that they aren't doing something. "Look, the Resistance…" Emma stumbles. "Those meta-humans are stopping the fights and telling the reporters what is happening."

"Right, but if that part gets edited out and no one sees it, all we have are the usual fights. So what if a few people we've seen as heroes before are now villains?"

"That's why I came to ask you about your network, to see if we can broadcast something without someone from the League changing it to suit their narrative." Emma tries to stay calm. "Please," she adds.

Torrance laughs, short and patronizing. "Our network is the *original* network, spun by dreamers and communicators hundreds of years ago, people who were so loathe to be out of touch with one another they would lay miles and miles of underground fibers under their city, across immeasurable distances, under oceans, through mountains. Grassroots is a movement that connects all the Regions. We make food accessible despite a government that is more concerned about appearances than productivity."

"Grassroots communicates using an older network," Emma muses, thinking aloud. "The pre-Collective one with the underground fibers and stuff."

Torrance lifts an eyebrow. "And?"

"All we need is a simultaneous broadcast on everyone's DED that can't be deleted."

"I think you are mistaken in thinking that we can actually connect to the national broadcasting system. That's the point. We don't," Torrance says. "It's how we can communicate privately with one another."

"Oh." The little bubble of hope that was inside Emma pops.

Torrance pats her on the shoulder. "Look, we appreciate you coming here with your findings. I didn't know that business about Kingston and Constavia, but the upcoming election does give us the opportunity to replace him. All the more reason to."

Emma's shoulders slump. She doesn't want to wait until next year for a *maybe*. She wants to take action now.

Maybe the patting is supposed to be a gesture of comfort, but the motion is actually guiding her out the door.

"Don't lose that passion for your goals," Torrance says with a wan smile. "We believe in you!" The endorsement echoes in the long, empty hallway, and then the door closes with a resounding *thud*.

Emma stares glumly into the seemingly endless green of the wetlands and the sparkling beauty of water trickling slowly toward the river. Sitting here, one might never know that the green disguises an entire headquarters for Grassroots: enormous rooms and networks of moss-covered tunnels, all devoted to a secret organization with a vigorous, successful history— an organization that doesn't seem to care that the Resistance needs help.

Emma wipes her tears and sniffs. She barely tasted dinner, as delicious as it was.

Bells' family had been sympathetic, and all Emma could do was nod and say thanks. Inside she had been churning with anger; how dare they not even hear out her entire idea, not see that the Resistance needed *them*? That if they didn't work together, Kingston and the League might stay in power forever?

"I'm sorry it didn't work out, sweetheart," Collete said.

"I can't believe Torrance brought you into the meeting with all the regional and international chapter leaders," Nick said. "That's quite an honor, to be heard out like that."

Emma just nodded; she didn't know what to say.

"Well, I'm glad Grassroots leadership understands the situation now." Collete smiled at her and smoothed her hair, and that only made Emma feel more like a kid. "And asking for help was very brave. It sounds like they didn't have the means for a national broadcast like you wanted anyway, right?"

"I guess," Emma said.

"That's too bad," Bells said. "I totally thought it was gonna work out, that the comm system seemed exactly what we needed."

"It's not connected to the national data system," Emma explained.

Thinking back on the conversation, Emma realizes that that Grassroots could have offered support in another way, such as letting the Resistance piggyback on their existing communication system, eliminating their current unsecured radio communication between hideouts. *I guess I forgot to bring that up too,* she thinks, flustered.

Emma hugs her knees tighter and tries to distract herself by watching the river and appreciating the desolate beauty of the Unmaintained lands.

Behind her, footsteps approach. That must be Bells. He gave her a meaningful look earlier during dinner, right after that awkward conversation. After more than a decade of friendship with Bells, Emma could interpret his looks down to the wire. This one clearly said, *I've got an idea, but I have to wait until we're alone to tell you.*

"Hey," Bells says, sitting down next to her. "You okay?"

"I'm fine," Emma says.

Bells nods, but he doesn't say anything. They watch the water, and Emma thinks back to another time when they sat like this, looking over a forest, and Bells silently offered her support. She's filled with gratitude; for Bells, for his thoughtfulness, his everything.

"I'm not fine," Emma says.

Saying that aloud makes it seem real, and she stands up, says it again. "They heard me out, but they treated me like a child the whole time. Like, 'Oh, it's great you figured this out but hey, we're the ones doing the real fight against the Collective.'"

"No way!" Bells' eyes widen as Emma recounts her experience with Torrance and Skye and the Grassroots leadership. She paces, telling Bells how they disregarded her, and at the end of it she's exhausted. She plops back down on the ground, feeling her anger dissipate into the earth.

"That sucks, the way they talked to you," Bells says. "I'm sorry. You didn't even get to say your whole speech!"

Emma laughs, relieved. "So what's your idea? You have one, right?"

Bells grins at her. "There's a vehicle that the org was gonna scrap that my parents wanted to give to me before the League gave me that solarcycle. It's here, actually, and I know that, now that I don't have the official Chameleon cycle anymore, my parents were gonna give this one to me when I turned eighteen."

"Yeah?" She can see the mischief sparking behind Bells' smile. She loves his way of looking outside the box to getting things done.

"So technically it's already mine, just not yet. I know where the keycard is. We could just take it and go."

The idea lights a fire inside Emma. "We could go anywhere. We could go all the way to the Rockies and get Jess and Abby. We could go off on our own mission."

Bells laughs, affectionately bumping her shoulder. "There's the Mastermind Emma I know and love. All right, let's do it! What do we need?"

Emma sits up, and blood rushes to her head, making her dizzy. "Should we wait until everyone is asleep to sneak out?" Emma doesn't know the routines of this Grassroots hideout, but she's pretty sure that stealing a vehicle—even if it's supposed to Bells'—is sure to cause a ruckus.

"I can leave my parents a note so they don't worry, like we're gonna take the car and go visit my 'art school' friends."

Emma nods. "That's a good idea. That way they won't worry as much as if we just disappeared. Wait, what if we *really did* track them down?"

The idea is taking hold, exploding in a thousand new directions. *Art school.* Emma almost laughs at the euphemism Bells used for the summers he left to go to the Meta-Human Training center before he told them all his shapeshifting secret. Last summer he told them he was going to a special art program in Aerial City.

"What, find the other meta-human trainees?"

"What about Christine?" Emma asks.

Bells' eyes light up. "Yeah! I think she's been working on something, but she definitely wants to take action?" He waits, tracing Emma's fingers with his own playfully. "You know, for your plan, we actually don't need Grassroots or the Villain's Guild."

Emma thinks about this. The communication plan with Grassroots' network? They can't do anything about it right now. But what they can do, what she's wanted to do from the beginning, but thought it was too big, too impossible… She gasps. "Interrupting a live broadcast— we *don't* need the whole Villain's Guild to do it."

Bells makes a drawn-out *mhmhm* noise. "Maybe just a few of us, you know?"

Emma nearly bounces. "We *could* just do it now. We don't need to convince everyone. Sure, the support would have been nice, but we don't need their permission. If we don't move forward, they never will!" She stands up, thinking about Christine's powers. That would be great. She could keep the staged battle restrained while Emma or Bells talks to the camera. Or maybe Bells should shapeshift into someone the public trusted, like a reporter? What about Wilton Lysander?

Emma thinks lightning quick, trying to put a new plan together. They need to find Christine first. "Have you heard from her?" Emma wishes Christine had come to Andover with Ricky and Sasha and Tanya, but she had already left the Villain's Guild, and they didn't know how to contact her.

"She was hiding out in New Bright City the last time we talked," Bells says. "We could all meet up with her there."

"And take matters into our own hands," Emma says. This is what she's talking about. "Yes, let's do it."

THE CAR IS NOT AT all like his motorcycle; it's clunky, seeming to take up all the room in the tunnel. Emma can tell he's not impressed. Bells has a very specific style. He likes his jackets sleek and evoking the old-school leather style, his jeans black, his shoes bright and colorful. Bells' aesthetic is almost effortlessly cool, with a touch of unexpected color.

This car is loud and obnoxious; its lights and the front metal grille seem to give it a face, one that's smiling ironically.

Emma loves it immediately.

Emma runs her hands over the side door. "Hello," she says warmly.

"What are you doing?"

"Saying hi to the car," Emma says, grinning as she admires the beast. And what a beast it is, towering over them as if it's surveying its prey.

There's no keycard. Apparently, this car was rebuilt from twenty-first-century tech, and there's an actual key. Bells hands it to Emma, who traces her fingers over the metal teeth, fascinated. She's only seen these in diagrams, when she was obsessed with engines and projected various twenty-first-century paraphernalia all over the room. Keys disappeared from vehicle design in the early twenty-second century; people favored using either a keycard embedded with a datachip or just syncing directly to their DED.

Bells squints at the door. "Do you know how to—"

Emma pokes the key into the car's side, turns it, and hears the tumblers click. She climbs into the driver's seat and beckons Bells inside.

Key in the ignition and turn.

The car's engine growls. It sounds completely unfamiliar. It's a different kind of engine, Emma realizes. She runs her hand across the dashboard, trying to figure out all the features. The beast is a messy mix of twenty-first-century tech and Grassroots innovation, cobbled together to create a working car.

"This is leather," Bells notes with interest, running his hands along the scratches in the seat fabric. "All right, that's cool. It's like, a hundred years old, though. Is that a fuel engine?"

Emma shakes her head. It must have been rebuilt from one of the first attempts at electric cars: a hybrid engine, designed to run on both fuel and battery. She didn't see solar panels on the roof of the car, but, as she scans the interior, she can see there's a set of them folded neatly in the back.

The interior feels too spacious for the two of them and their backpacks of scant supplies.

Bells hums. "Good, because I have no idea where'd we get fuel. I thought all that stuff was gone already. Used up."

"Grassroots must have some fuel stores," Emma muses. "I bet the car has a battery-only option. I saw solar cells in the back, so we can recharge as we go."

Bells nods. "Ready to go?"

Emma has never been more ready in her life.

She steps on the gas, and the car purrs, heading forward into the dark.

NEW BRIGHT CITY IN THE Hopestar Region is a four-hour high-speed train ride from New New Orleans, but they're definitely not going to be able to go that fast. It will take a week of driving at least, and that's not factoring in how long the solar cells will need to charge.

Bells is fast asleep with drool running down his chin, so it's just her and the wide-open sky and the road ahead of her. She pauses for a quick break to relieve herself outside, wondering if she should turn on the camouflage function. She hasn't figured out all the options and features of the car yet, but that button was easy enough to find. Emma has a sinking suspicion that camouflage will use a lot of battery power, so it's probably best to activate it only if they pass any active Regions.

Emma uses the sun's position to plot a northwest course. Without a map, she can't know for sure if it's the best course, but at least they're headed in the right direction. She thinks fondly of the map in their hideout in Andover, which was marked clearly with all twenty-four Regions. They'll have to be careful to stay in the unplottable Unmaintained lands.

Traveling incognito is not new to Emma; they did this when they drove to the Rockies from Nevada. But this trip is twice as far, and they don't have the benefit of having Jess and her power pointing them in the right direction.

THE SUN IS HIGH IN the sky when Emma notices the battery gauge blinking. She pulls the car to a stop and glances at the odometer before hopping out of the car.

"We're there already?" Bells jokes, rubbing at his eyes. He's still blinking awake, stretching and yawning like a long-limbed cat.

"Oh, yeah, record totally broken for quickest cross-country trip." Emma snorts, pulling water bottles from the back and handing one to Bells.

He's got his sketchbook out, scribbling away. "Know where we're going?"

"I'm no Jess, but I figured out which way is northwest," Emma says. "There's a maglev track I've been following out of the corner of my eye too."

"Good idea. They can't see us from there, right?"

Emma shakes her head. She squints, trying to see as far as she can into the distance: nothing but shimmering heat over miles of wetlands and trees. A looming advertisement proclaiming THE COLLECTIVE WILL PROTECT YOU FROM P019 is just legible enough to be unnerving.

The long billboards were easier to spot than the track itself. The stretched signs, designed to be visible from the high-speed trains, haunt the edge of her vision. With every warning of the P019 event, Emma grows more and more nervous, despite her initial affirmation that everything would be taken care of by then. November is approaching faster than she thought, and the constant barrage of HAVE YOU RESERVED YOUR SPOT IN YOUR REGIONAL SHELTER YET? and PREPARATIONS AND YOU: HOW TO MAKE SURE YOU'RE SAFE DURING THE IMPACT on the signs only unsettles her more.

Emma gets out of the car. She has no idea how far they've gone; she figures they must be well out of the Louisiana Region when the signs become few and far between.

Bells hands her his notebook through the car window; he's drawn a rough map of the North American Collective. The coastlines and the shape of the country itself look good, but he's drawn blobs all over, as if he's guessing where the Regions are.

"We need a real map." Bells shakes his head. "We can't keep following the train tracks forever."

"There's a ton of maps at train stations," Emma muses.

"Hmm, we all know what those maps look like, though," Bells says, hopping out of the car. He picks up a stick and traces in the dirt the stylized hovertrain routes that most people know as a "map" of their country. It's barely a map at all, designed for people who only go from region to region. It has no details about the Unmaintained lands, the roads, or what kind of hazards they'd meet.

Bells helps her set up the solar panels, and they lean against the south side of the car in the scant shade. In the distance, a train zooming along the track is a barely perceptible glimmer cutting across the country.

"We need a pre-Collective map," Emma decides.

Bells nods. "Let's see if we can find one."

It's an eerie drive, weaving their way through the forgotten cities abandoned in the Disasters. Emma and Bells take turns driving long stretches. They fall into a routine: drive, eat, rest, charge the car. They drive past signs for places long since gone, the ghosts of old advertising, signs beckoning to shops, some still filled with wares.

They don't have much luck in the first few towns they come across, but, in a stroke of luck, Bells spots a boarded-up store. The lettering is peeling and faded, but one word is clear: BOOKS.

Sweat drips from Emma's brow as she and Bells push on the crowbar, prying the boards free. Finally, they open up enough room to crawl inside.

Emma coughs, blinking and trying to adjust to the light. It's not quite dark. Sunlight is seeping in from the cracks in the boards; dust motes trail lazily in the air.

"Oh, wow," Emma says, once she can take it all in.

"We can't take everything," Bells says, holding up a hand. "I know that face."

Emma gasps. "So many books. And they're all historical and, like, not vetted by the Collective's Censorship Council. Everything here is precious."

"I know, but—" Bells does a double take as they walk past a display of DVDs.

"Do you think they have the next one in that series Jess likes?" he asks, already picking through the titles.

Emma laughs at him from the next aisle, LITERATURE, and shakes her copies of *A Desperate Arrangement* and *Put Down in Words* at him. "Maybe. What happened to 'we can't take everything?'"

"It's a present! It doesn't count!"

Emma hesitates, about to put the novels back down on the shelf. It would be impractical to bring reading for fun, but if it's a present…

She finds a shopping basket and drops in the novels. She's sure someone will enjoy them when she's finished.

Bells is somewhere deep in the store, whooping about detective novels. Emma laughs, marveling at how, aside from a thick layer of dust, some sections of the store seem new, as if the books are waiting for customers to discover them.

After the Disasters, everyone just fled. People looking for resources sought food and clothing and other supplies first. *Books are heavy*, Emma muses, although, as she runs her hand along an empty shelf, she realizes that people most definitely came here, looking for a distraction, an escape, maybe some love stories or stories about space.

Space.

Emma walks quickly through the store; they must have a science section.

She grabs a fiery red book with *MARS* emblazoned on it and greedily flips through, reading about the missions and NASA and how the journey to get there began. Emma thumbs her finger over the photo of the Opportunity rover drawing pictures in the red soil of Mars and giggles as she reads that Curiosity sang Happy Birthday to itself. She wonders if Curiosity is still beaming data at Earth with no one to receive it.

When the North American Collective was formed, the space program was deemed an unnecessary expense, and the government focused on rebuilding the country and on food production in what few areas were still arable. They still benefit from the space program every day; its tech is in every aspect of their lives, from communication to travel.

"Hey, I found a book on hybrid cars! It says our model is a 2027. Exactly one year before the X29 flare. It must have been parked in a bunker to avoid getting fried." Bells grins, holding a book aloft at her. "Whatcha got there?"

"Mars," Emma says, tracing her fingers over the red planet.

"You'll get there," Bells says. "We just gotta fix the government first."

Emma laughs. It seems so simple when he says it.

"We can always come back here another day to get these books," Bells says.

Right. They came for maps. "Did you find a travel section?"

Bells holds a large book aloft. *North America Road Atlas 2027.*

"Perfect!" Emma flips through the pages, looks at all the roads and interstate highways. She's seen these: in some places, they're big enough for four cars to drive next to each other. She thinks about the millions and millions of people who used to live in this country and the massive structures they built, the roads on which they traveled. Surely they didn't need a road this wide only within a city?

It's so strange, the rigidly defined lines separating "Canada" and "United States" and "Mexico" and all the states and provinces within them. The interstates are identified with a numbering system Emma doesn't quite understand, but she finds New Orleans and a familiar river. They must be close to this *10* that goes east through the wasteland. They can take that and connect to this other network of roads and go northeast from there.

Bells peers over her shoulder, touching several bodies of water at the top of the page. "Oh, are those the Dead Lakes? Hopestar is north of that. You can see the lakes from the train."

"Great Lakes," Emma reads from the map, looking at the bodies of water. She shakes her head. The lands and cities around them were among the first to be evacuated after X29; several nuclear plants failed there, and radiation seeped into the water. It would affect the area for a long while. They should avoid driving through there, too, on their way to New Bright City.

Bells takes out a pencil and traces a route. Emma squints, trying to follow along, but it's getting harder to see in the fading light.

"Should we keep moving? It's getting dark." Emma glances outside. "Our panels should be charged enough to get us through sunrise."

Bells yawns, nodding blearily. "Let's get this stuff back to the car and do one more quick scan in case we see anything we want."

They load the books into the car and pack up the solar panels. Emma winces; her neck aches when she crawls inside the store. They've been trying to push as far as they can, charging the solar panels at least twice a day, especially right before dark so they can push through the night. Emma's tired, and she can see Bells is, even if he hasn't said anything. The adventure is getting old very fast: bumpy roads and a dwindling supply of instafood and protein packs, sleeping in the car, and getting barely any rest.

At the back of the store, a door has a sign above it that reads EMPLOYEES ONLY. "Let's check in here," Emma says, pushing it open.

It's a small but cozy room, stuffed with couches and soft armchairs and decorated with still 2D photos. One side of the room has a kitchenette with a sink and a strange-looking stove.

Bells whistles, plopping right into one of the armchairs. "Look at this, Em!" He grins as he leans back, and a panel pops out so he can put his feet up.

Emma laughs, sitting down on the couch. It's soft and comfortable despite the dust, and she sinks into it, closing her eyes.

"Hey," Bells says. "How about we take a break? I think we're making good time."

"Let's just stay here the whole night. I don't think either of us have gotten more than a few hours' sleep."

Bells kisses her forehead. "Sounds good. I'll go get the blanket!"

THEY EAT HOT SOUP AT an actual table, laughing over a picture book about cats Bells found. Warmth fills Emma's stomach. It's the same calories they've been eating every meal, but somehow, the food is more filling this way instead of eating in the car. It's a small luxury, but sitting here and resting is just what Emma needed.

The couch folds down, too, and the cushions make decent pillows. With the blanket it almost feels like a real bed.

Bells has already taken off his binder and tossed it on another of the armchairs. "I want to be the little spoon," he announces, crawling under the blanket next to her.

"You're taller! It's not optimal for me to be the big spoon."

Bells sticks his tongue out at her. "You're the little spoon in the car because there isn't enough room for you to cuddle me properly, but now we do have enough room."

Emma laughs. "Okay, okay, come here." She throws her arm over him and then a leg for good measure. "Nice?"

"Yes. I feel very safe and protected."

Emma closes her eyes and snuggles closer. She feels safe, too.

TURNER CITY IS WILDLY DISORIENTING. After so long in the Unmaintained lands, setting up camp on dirt roads and broken concrete paths, it's strange to be in a city, however small. They need supplies, though, so it's a necessary detour.

Emma pulls the hat down over her curls and adjusts her sunglasses. Bells painted flowers and designs on her face, enough to confuse any facial recognition software. It's not quite as dramatic as the punk look with geometric shapes, but the flower aesthetic is common enough so that someone passing her by would merely think she's following the trend.

Bells shifted to a taller version of himself; his face is more angular and a bit wider. It's somewhat similar to his "Barry" persona, the face he used for so long at the Meta-Human Training center. Taking this form is second nature to him, and Emma spots him smiling at a reflection in a storefront. It's not exactly like Barry, Bells told her, since he was sure Barry's face was wanted. This guy is more freckled, with bright fiery orange-red hair, almost like Abby's. It looks great contrasted with his dark skin.

"Cute. Who are you supposed to be?"

Bells winks at her. "Styx Kipling, gentleman detective. Now let's go get ourselves some radio equipment so we can call Jess and Abby."

After buying more food and water with their burner DEDs, they locate a hobby shop on the outskirts of town that sells electronic "junk." It's seen better days. The shelves overflow with glittering tech: holoprojectors and MonRobot parts and commtech and more.

"You sure they would have it here?"

"Let's just keep browsing," Emma says. "If they do have it, it wouldn't be out," she mutters. "Radios are pre-Collective tech, so the sale and distribution of them is illegal."

"You kids need help finding anything?" An older man with thick glasses approaches, peering at them curiously. His nametag reads JORDAN and PRONOUNS: HE/HIS. Emma wonders if he lived through the time of the Disasters to see the country fall apart and a new one come together.

Bells shakes his head.

"Well, I'm Jordan, just give me a holler if you need me."

Emma glances about the store and tries to get a quick sense of who Jordan is. Glasses mean he never opted for corrective surgery even when it was accessible through the North American Collective healthcare system. He runs this shop despite the more lucrative career options he could have taken, so clearly he's passionate about electronic junk.

A few posters catch Emma's eye. "Are these for sale?" Emma asks. The pre-Collective one with the laser swords was one of Jess' favorites. A huge symbol is displayed over the door too; it looks handmade, but it's familiar: red, almost a circle, but the arc has been cut into three distinct whorls.

"Not for sale." Jordan folds his arms and follows her gaze to the symbol. "You a fan?"

"Yes," Emma blurts out. There was a password among nerds like this. That's how they found the first "Resistance." "We're—" she glances at Bells and jerks her head.

"Han shot first!" Bells announces brightly.

"Yes," Emma says quickly. She hopes that's right.

Jordan's eyes crinkle up as he laughs. "Always good to meet more members of the Rebel Alliance!" he snorts. His demeanor goes from suspicious to friendly in an instant. "You all from outta town? Never seen you before in our bunker."

Bells nods. "Yes, just traveling and visiting family, but, uh, I just miss it, you know?"

Emma tries for what she hopes is a conspiratorial eyebrow waggle. "I know there's a vetting system—we have a very extensive one back home in our group—but you wouldn't happen to have anything you can share?"

Jordan beckons her to the back of the shop. "C'mon, over here." He pushes aside a circuit board on a shelf; behind it, there's a disguised keypad. He taps out a code, and there's a telltale click as the shelf swivels forward to reveal a flight of stairs. "Follow me!"

Emma raises her eyebrows. "What's with all the hideouts underground?"

"Better than way, way above ground," Bells mutters.

Emma pats him gingerly on the back; he's probably thinking of the swaying walkways hundreds of feet up in the trees at the Meta-Human Training center.

They follow Jordan downstairs into another living space. It's decorated with all sorts of paraphernalia: a broomstick hanging on a wall, elaborately painted and polished wooden sticks, a statue of a person in a strange black uniform, and a cape holding a laser sword.

"This is great," Emma says, looking around. Jess would probably get a kick out of this. "You ever talk to other chapters?"

"Yeah, occasionally, to trade DVDs and such. Mark over in New Bright City is the only one with a Blu-Ray player, though."

"Do you have a radio?" Bells asks.

"Yeah," Jordan says proudly. "We're piggybacking on several towers, got a really strong signal. Mark's just barely in range."

Emma whistles. If they can reach New Bright City in the Hopestar region, the Rockies are definitely within range. "Mind if we make a transmission?"

"Always happy to help a fellow geek," Jordan says.

He gets them set up, and Emma scans the channels, looking for the familiar background music of *The Gentleman Detective*.

"You think they'll be there?" Bells seems nervous. He grabs a chair and spins it around to sit in it backward. He runs his hands through his hair; Emma can tell he's anxious. He's losing some of his shift; his nose looks like his own now, and his freckles have disappeared.

"Wasn't your hair red?" Jordan asks, narrowing his eyes. "Might be my old age, but I could have sworn…"

Bells shrugs, letting Jordan second-guess himself. Emma taps the microphone. "Hello? Anyone there? This is Emma. Bells and I are talking to you from Turner City."

The episode keeps playing, and Bells frowns. "They might be out."

Emma glances at Jordan. "What's the date? Day of the week? And the time?"

Jordan looks even more curious, but he just tilts his head. "It's two thirty-ish Friday..." he glances at his DED. "October second, 2124."

Two-thirty every Wednesday was their usual call time. If anything, Emma knows Jess, and Jess would never break that habit, even if she hadn't heard from Emma and Bells—especially since she hasn't heard from them. Jess and Abby are probably worried sick. Emma imagines them camping out by the radio every week at the designated time, maybe more often.

Styx Kipling's deep voice is their only company. "I'm on the case!"

"Soon everyone will know the truth," Bells echoes. He gives Emma a look that says everything is going to be okay.

Jordan's face scrunches up. "Okay, not to be rude, but actually, I am. I thought you said you were with the Resistance? And contacting the rest of your group? So this is a good show, don't get me wrong, but you know it's not illegal, not really grounds for good Rebel Alliance-type media." He huffs. "I can't believe I brought you kids into my secret lair and let you use my radio!"

He grabs the microphone, turns it away, and reaches to turn the radio off.

"Hey!" Emma says, more loudly than she meant to. They've come so far, and now to be pulled away at the last moment just isn't fair. "We are just need to talk to the rest of our group!" Emma pleads. "It's important!"

"*The Gentleman Detective* is standard for us to play on this channel when we're using it," Bells says, shrugging with an air of too-easy casualness. He gives Jordan a conspiratorial grin, as if he's letting him in on a secret.

"Oh." Jordan relaxes. He turns the microphone toward Bells.

Emma gives Bells a look. She's seen him charm people before; she just doesn't understand how he does it. He's basically said the same thing she said, but what, nicer?

Bells shrugs, patting Jordan on the shoulder. "Thanks, man." He turns the microphone, listening intently. "Hello?"

Nothing but the episode. Another minute goes by, and Emma gets more and more nervous. She listens as Kipling carries out his investigation; she's heard the opening lines in his office multiple times, but they've never gotten past that part. Kipling leaves his office on a fast pursuit. Now there are the sounds of wheels speeding off and shouts as Kipling chases his suspects.

"Hello?" Emma says into the microphone. "Jess? Are you there?"

The sound of an explosion makes her jump, but Bells puts a steadying hand on her shoulder. "It's just the show."

Right. There's nothing to worry about. Bells knows this episode inside and out.

Emma tries to keep her breath even as more explosions and loud clangs echo, somehow growing louder in the small space.

Bells sits up, startling her. "Wait a minute—"

"What? I thought you said it was part of the show!" Emma grabs Bells' hand.

"The first explosion, yes. But…" Bells frowns.

Static crackles. And there's the sound of another explosion and screams.

"So that's—" Realization sinks in immediately. Emma gasps. "No! Jess! Abby! Mrs. Tran? *Anyone?*" Emma shouts over the line.

Jordan blinks. "What's happening?"

Bells grabs the microphone and speaks quickly. "If anyone can hear this, please let us know you're okay!"

There's more noise, as if a cavern is collapsing. Emma imagines her friends struggling in the dirt and she hates feeling useless, hates not knowing what is happening.

Something clangs. A door, maybe?

"Emma!" Abby's shout is a mixture of relief and panic. "Where are you?"

"What's happening? Are you okay?"

"The Villain's Guild is being attacked!"

Bells grips the microphone with his hands tightly. "By who—" he starts, but Abby just keeps talking.

"I think the Trans are handling it. I can't tell who is attacking us, but it looks like new meta-humans in new costumes, or maybe the League added a bunch of heroes we haven't heard of? But I could have sworn someone had Bellevue's powers. But didn't she pass away two years ago?" Abby's words flow so breathlessly that Emma barely can parse what she's saying.

"Slow down!" Emma finally manages to get a word in. She glances at Bells, who is wide-eyed. Abby seemed scattered before, and now, even during an attack, she's rambling. "What's going on? Are you okay?"

"Jess and I were packing some stuff and were on our way out before the cavern collapsed, but I heard you, so I came in!" There's shouting and the sound of muffled thuds, as if everything is falling apart. Despite all this, Abby starts chitchatting. "How are you? Where did you go? We couldn't get any info out of Jess' parents. They said they talked to Bells' parents, and that you all just went off on a romantic road trip to visit his *art school friends*. Did you go find Christine? Where are you?"

Emma tries to gather her thoughts, if they have limited time, if everyone is evacuating before the entire headquarters collapses, she needs to convey all the vital information. *Who knows when they'll be able to connect again?* "We're safe. Bells and I are on our way to New Bright City. Can you meet us there?"

"New Bright City! Got it!" Abby confirms in a bright voice. "Jess! Hey, Jess!"

"Abby, what are you doing? This whole place is gonna blow we have to go!"

"It's Emma and Bells!"

"What are you talking about? Why are you here anyway? We have to go, Abby, come on—"

"I heard—"

"Jess!" Emma cuts in.

"Emma?"

"Hey, we're calling from Turner City," Bells says.

Emma can picture the mixture of relief, panic, and confusion on Jess' face. "Wow— you actually— hi— so good to hear from you, but we can't stay, the whole cavern is gonna blow."

"Got it," Bells says. "Stay safe, meet us in—"

"—I don't know where or how we'll catch up, but my instinct says east, but I can—"

"That's right," Emma exhales. Jess will always know where they are, and she'll be able to find them, no matter what. "We'll be in the Hopestar region in three days—"

There's another explosion and then only static.

THREE DAYS SEEM LIKE AN eternity. Bells is on edge; Emma is filled with pent-up frustration, anger, worry. They started this trip to New Bright City full of hope and the promise of adventure, now, they're speeding there as quickly as they can, hoping for some news—any news—of their friends.

Part of her wants to throw caution to the wind and turn back to the Rockies and find them immediately, but without a reliable way to communicate they could be heading into a trap or miss meeting them entirely.

"If we only had just a few more seconds on that call," Emma mutters, kicking over a rock while they wait for the car to charge. "Exact coordinates, or a meetup time, anything!"

Staring at the ground, Bells clenches and unclenches his fists.

"Jess and Abby and Brendan and, like, *everybody*—"

"Jess will be able to find us," Bells says, looking into the distance, as if their friends might pop into view at any moment.

"I hate waiting," Emma mutters. "I want to find *them*."

"I know," Bells says.

The safest bet is to keep to the plan, even if Emma hates how it makes her feel. They follow the pre-Collective map, charting a safe course past the Dead Lakes. The air is crisp and cold, and occasionally soft flurries of snow fall. The clothes they brought are suited to the Nevada desert, and the warm coats they wore in the Rockies are barely enough for the Northern regions in late fall. They spend the time waiting for the car to charge either cuddled up with each other or running laps around the car trying to coax warmth back into their limbs.

They cross into Hopestar abruptly, going from cold forests and rocky terrain to paved roads and brightly lit towns. They pause at a charging station, using the last of their burner DEDs to fuel the car.

Bells walks out of the convenience store, clutching his jacket to himself. He looks unusually solemn.

"Any news?" Emma asks.

Bells shakes his head. "You think they're okay?"

"No news is good news," Emma says, more to reassure herself than anything. "The League would have boasted about catching anyone from the Guild—"

"Most Wanted," Bells offers. "Heinous supervillains."

Emma snorts; they climb back in the car just as another vehicle pulls in. They'll have to be careful now and use disguises.

"They'll be fine," Emma says. "Jess knows where she's going, and Abby is super resourceful, and Brendan—"

Bells laughs. "Yeah, they're okay— I just—" he glances at Emma, taking her hand.

"Yeah," Emma agrees. They don't have to say anything; the unspoken fear hangs in the air, heavy and growing by the minute. It's not knowing that's the worst.

New Bright City is visible long before they get close. Its chrome skyscrapers, monorails, advertisements, and huge holograms dwarf the surrounding forest and the scattered towns of Hopestar. One billboard illustrates the skyline of New Bright City under a repulsion shield and carries the words THE COLLECTIVE HARD AT WORK: PROTECTING YOU FROM P091; it flashes again, showing a brand-new MR-D4R model buzzing around a house. A huge holo is projected over the entire city: a loop of Starscream punching Dynamite in broad color as the giant holograms fight around the top spire of the COFAX building, the tallest building in the country.

Silence is long left behind. Emma doesn't know where the music is coming from but it's constant, multiple layers of sound layered atop one another: cars and people laughing and talking and colorful advertisements projected in the air, in streets, in walkways, outside of stores. Everything is moving fast: the people, the buses, the trains. Emma's been here before, but the city never fails to overwhelm her.

Bells slams on the brakes, nearly hitting the car in front of them. "Sorry," he says. "That holo jumped out into the street! Is that normal?"

"For here," Emma says, glancing at the disappearing blue pixels of the person running with the slogan SNEAKERS BY STARSCREAM.

It's too bright, too intense. Everything is gleaming white and silver-chrome; blue pixels swirl and holos leap from everyone's devices. Emma has to shield her eyes from the reflection of the hot sunlight on the immaculate stone pavement. The buildings rise like monoliths in massive columns, disappearing into the clouds, and multiple layers of streets and greenways rise into the atmosphere.

The other cars seem to be driving in sync, merging and changing lanes and stopping in rhythm as the people inside them chat effortlessly or look out the windows. It seems Emma and Bells are the only ones with a driver-operated car.

Emma always thought the process to get a license was made incredibly difficult and expensive so that it was a luxury to be able to drive your own car. She had always felt proud of passing the complicated Manual Driving Authority test. In Nevada, it wasn't uncommon to see a few people driving manually, although most people preferred the convenience of the automated vehicles or taking the bus.

There's a brilliant flash of light overhead and Emma gasps. "Bells, did you see that?"

"Starscream," Bells offers. "This is his town. Or, well, it is now."

The hero had never been one of Emma's favorites, and since they uncovered the conspiracy Emma doesn't know where he stands. It sounds from Bells' tone as if Starscream is well in the pocket of the League, if he's still playing hero for this town. With Captain Orion out of the picture, he's been elevated to her previous position as the country's darling, the most famous and revered hero.

Starscream is followed by two camera drones; a few people look up and point, gasping.

"Look! It's Starscream!"

"Wow! What a fight!"

Emma's been so out of touch; she's forgotten this farce is still happening. It seems so contrived now, watching Starscream shoot blasts of light and "apprehend" Dynamite.

"Come on, move!" Bells blurts, but traffic is still ambling at a very slow pace. Everyone's automatic cars inch them forward.

"Here, switch with me," Emma says.

Bells nods and scoots out of the driver's seat, and Emma climbs over him. He smiles at her as she goes and his hand is warm, gently squeezing her arm. Emma smiles and impulsively kisses him.

"What was that for?" Bells asks.

"Nothing," she says. "Just you were being cute."

Bells gives her a small smile. "Come on, hotshot. You gonna get us out of here?"

Emma laughs. "Am I ever."

She takes a deep breath and then presses on the acceleration pedal. The car speeds forward, zooming between lanes, narrowly avoiding the other cars. Emma weaves in and out of traffic, heading north through the city toward Christine's rendezvous point.

Bells grips the dashboard, grinning with delight. He whoops with joy as they pass another group of slow cars and then whips his head around.

"You see something?" Emma asks.

"Just a feeling. Duck into this alleyway here."

Emma does as he says, waiting in the darkness. Around them, everyone tunes into the fight between Starscream and Dynamite. Emma can see it, too, projected above them. Starscream is punching Dynamite dramatically; his cape sweeps with every move.

A gray car speeds past the alley, horn blaring. "This is the North American Collective Authority. You are operating a driver-operated vehicle in a restricted area. Please exit the vehicle immediately."

Emma exhales. "I didn't know it was illegal to drive your own car in this city!"

Bells narrows his eyes. "We'll have to drive slow. Blend in."

After waiting a tense moment, they return to the street and drive achingly slow, too slowly. Emma parks the car in an immaculately clean, multi-level carport, ignoring the curious looks several people give her as she hops out of the driver's seat. They adjust their disguises and then take an elevator up to one of the many greenways, which is lush with trees and flowers and pathways and fountains.

They're only a few minutes late at the rendezvous point under the clock tower, but they don't see any sign of Christine.

Another five minutes go by. Bells frowns. "She's not here."

"Maybe she's late?"

"It's not like her."

"Do we have another plan? Another location to meet her at if she doesn't make this one?"

Bells shakes his head. "Let's wait a bit longer."

Emma waits, watching the clock tick, growing more and more impatient. The broadcast in the sky is now livestreaming Starscream recapping his battle with Dynamite to reporter Wilton Lysander. The pixels blur behind Starscream, and he brushes the back of his head, as if there's an annoying fly.

Lysander laughs. "Now tell me about this new look of yours! Updated colors and a new cape! Very sleek—"

"Hey, I was talking to you!"

Starscream turns around, and so does Lysander. The camera zooms in on a smaller masked figure: a girl with flowing blonde-brown curls wearing a bodice and flowing skirt. "Yeah, that's right!" she says. "You're a fake and a liar and just doing exactly what the League tells you to!"

Starscream scoffs at her. "Who are you? Some sad excuse for a villain?"

Lysander laughs. "And your outfit! It's several centuries old."

Emma gasps. "Isn't that Christine?"

Bells' mouth falls open. "What is she doing? Confronting Starscream on her own?"

"She's doing my plan," Emma says, awed. "I love it!"

Bells grabs her hand and runs. "Come on! That's in Postonwish Square!"

Emma runs alongside him for a few breathless moments until she stops to catch her breath. "Wait—"

Bells stops a few paces ahead of her; his eyes dart frantically. "Should we stop her? Join her? I don't even have a supersuit anymore!"

"Does that matter?" Emma responds.

"Oh, right—"

Bells closes his eyes, and his clothes barely flicker as he shifts his clothing. The leather-look jacket he's wearing over his T-shirt and jeans gives way to a very familiar, rainbow-hued green supersuit, complete with mask.

"What's the plan?"

"Uh…"

"You always have a plan!"

Right, right. If Christine is confronting Starscream, it'll be a battle, right? So that's best suited for Bells and his powers. Then they'll need to get away before the League or the Authorities show up. "Okay, I have a plan!" *Christine is incredibly powerful, right? But she can probably only use her powers for a few minutes? Ten?*

The people they're running past are focused on the projected livestreams on their own devices and also the huge projection in the sky, all showing the same thing: Starscream and Christine are facing off.

At the scene, a crowd of laughing people clustered around Starscream and Christine is visible in all the live feeds.

"Is this the new villain?"

"I can't believe the losers that the Villain's Guild is putting out nowadays. She barely even has a costume together!"

"What is that, a bodice?"

"My name is *Crinoline!*" Christine does a dramatic twirl; her skirts flutter around her.

"What's your power? Anachronism?"

Even more laughter. Bells' fists clench. "How dare they…"

Emma grabs Bells by the shoulder. "I'm gonna run back to the car. You go get Christine, and, whatever she's doing, make sure that it keeps going. The broadcast, it's live, so whatever you both say, it's unedited, right? Go for it and make sure to mention that the League is a lie!"

"What are you—"

"You and Christine are gonna need a getaway plan!"

Emma turns around and runs in the opposite direction as fast as she can. She speeds past people completely absorbed in the ongoing fight. Emma tries not to pay attention to it, but she can hear Starscream taunting Christine in every DED she runs past and even see their conversation larger than life above her.

"You're too late, kid. I've already stopped Dynamite's bank robbery. You can go home now."

"Not until you admit that you and Dynamite were *faking* the whole fight and the robbery! For the League!"

Starscream scoffs. "And what are you gonna do about it? Do you even have any powers? You look pretty useless to me."

"Useless?" Christine's eyes narrow. "I'll show you how useless I am," she mutters, raising her hands.

Starscream laughs, raises his arms as if he's gonna shoot a burst of sound at her, but, as he rushes forward, his supersuit comes to life. Threads blooming wildly out of control, spinning wildly and wildly; the arms of his jacket completely come undone, rushing around and around, binding him in a circle.

"Hey! What's going on?"

Jackets stitch themselves to pants and shirts as both Starscream and Wilton Lysander slump forward, falling down as they're rolled in their own clothing.

"Hello! I just wanted to say to you all who have been following Starscream's adventures: They're all fake; he's picking battles with Dynamite because the League told him to, and the so-called villains that they say are bad only pull those pranks because—"

"That's right," another voice behind her says, and it's Dynamite, even though Emma saw Dynamite led away earlier in tantalum cuffs.

Bells. This must be Bells, shifted.

"I am a villain in name only," Bells-as-Dynamite announces. "I was directed to go into the villain path right after Meta-Human Training…"

The sound of a siren comes over the video: the Authorities.

Emma curses at herself for getting distracted and darts up the stairs, two at a time, ignoring the broadcast until she finds the car.

Keys. Engine. Go.

Emma races through the streets, weaving in and out of traffic lanes, and drives right into the main square, then honks her horn as people jump out of her way. She knows if she keeps this up that the Authorities will be after her, but she just has to keep going and not get caught.

Bells and Christine are talking right into a cameradrone when Emma pulls up, even as sirens wail and get closer.

"Get in!" Emma shouts.

Bells and Christine clamber into the backseat, and there's an awkward side-hug from Christine. "Perfect timing!" Christine giggles.

"Come on, we gotta go!" Emma says.

Bells shuts the door, and then Emma speeds them away from the still-twitching Lysander and Starscream on the pavement.

Emma tries to concentrate on getting them out of there; Bells and Christine are hugging and are already catching up, laughing with excitement. Emma concentrates as she swerves into an alleyway and listens for the sirens of the Authority.

Christine claps her on the shoulder. "Great to see you, Em! Where are we going?"

"Glad we found you," Emma says. "First step is away from here, and then I gotta double back and lay a false trail in case anyone is watching."

"Thanks for getting me. I was excited to see you today but then I got sidetracked when I saw that hack Starscream and I knew I had to try—"

Bells jumps in immediately to reassure her. "No, it was great! I love your new outfit, by the way! Did you make this supersuit? Or is it still called a supersuit if it's a... I don't actually know what it is, but you look awesome!"

Christine laughs. "This is a bodice over a dress. So, outfit works!"

"You look great, Christine," Emma says, still watching for danger. "So, the plan: We've been hiding the car in the woodland just outside the city. We could—"

"Oh!" Christine says brightly. "I've got a safehouse!"

Christine guides her through the city, pointing out sidestreets and alleyways, but they do occasionally have to drive on the main streets, where they must pretend to be in an inconspicuous automated car. They manage to get out of downtown, far too slowly for Emma's liking, but at least they aren't being actively pursued. The tinted windows do help.

Emma drives to a suburb where a number of pretty, multi-storied houses are spread out on a hill. "Go right," Christine says. "This whole street is monitored for security purposes. The Authorities, too."

Emma follows Christine's directions to a hill overgrown with vines. Christine waves her hands at it, and they lift to reveal a dark tunnel. As Emma drives through, she realizes the "vines" are actually knit from green yarn and fabric. *Clever,* Emma thinks.

The motion turns on a number of lights. "So who all is at your safehouse?" Emma asks.

"Oh, just me. When I left ages ago, I tried to convince Jess and Abby to come with me, but they were set on staying with their folks, you know. And I even asked Steven, light-spot guy. But he thought staying in hiding with the Villain's Guild would be better."

"We were there just a while ago," Bells says.

Christine laughs. "Yeah. Did they ever figure out an action plan? It was all research and discussion. I was bored, so I left. What were they up to?"

"They just got attacked," Emma says. "That whole hideout in the mountains is compromised. I don't know where they all are now." She bites her lip. It is the third day; they should be here by now.

"Have you seen Jess or anyone?" Bells asks.

Christine shakes her head. "I haven't heard. I didn't even know there was an attack. That's the kind of thing the League loves to boast about, though, shutting down Villain's Guild headquarters."

Emma's gone through many possibilities, each one of them more troubling than the next.

"Here we are," Christine says when the tunnel slopes upward. "You might as well make yourselves at home and wait in comfort."

The driveway lights up, welcoming them as they enter a cavernous garage. They join a sleek blue solarcar and a few other vehicles waiting quietly in the dark.

Christine gestures them forward. "Got any bags? Need any help?"

"Oh, we got it—" Emma starts, but Christine is already waving her hand.

Something touches her foot as it slithers past her, and Emma recoils in disgust. In the dim light she can barely make out the thick ropes coiled on the ground flicking to life. The ropes slink toward Emma and Bells' bags in the trunk, tie themselves neatly around them, and move toward the house like giant, floppy snakes.

"Neat!" Bells says, stepping over the rope and reaching down as if he wants to pet it.

"Very cool," Emma says, stepping over the rope and trying not to let the snakelike movement bother her. *It's just a rope; it's not alive.* Emma rushes ahead so she doesn't have to see it.

Christine keys in a complicated code on a datapad, and then a door swivels open, revealing a brightly lit hallway.

The house is bright, airy, and spacious, filled with modern effects and a few anachronistic touches that Emma takes as Christine's personal style. A tall, polished-walnut grandfather clock stands in the corner; the hallway is lined with a number of dress forms with half-finished dresses, ornate with ruffles and lace.

Bells lets out a low whistle and taps his feet on the tiled floor. "Nice. This feels more you than the Vegas place."

"Yeah, I didn't stay there that often," Christine admits. "One of my dads used it whenever he had work stuff. I like this house best out of all of them."

On the mantle a number of holos loop, showing a series of moments frozen in time, using the most advanced holotech, showing the images in full color. They could be any three attractive and capable-looking adults holding a baby in a ruffled dress, but Emma nearly trips when she recognizes three of the most prominent figures in maglev tech and aerospace engineering: Frankie Taylor, Carolina de Sandoval, and Joshua Ibarra. The holo loops between all three of them taking turns holding baby Christine and various shots of them kissing each other in easy, casual affection.

"Aw," Bells says. "Your parents look cool!"

Cool is an understatement. Cool is the very least of what Emma feels right now. "Your parents," Emma says, breathless. "Are they— are they here?"

Christine gives her an amused look. "They're all traveling right now." She considers, ticking her fingers thoughtfully. "Abroad in the European Union doing work with the United Federation, at the mine in Argentina, and, oh, back in Nevada right now."

"They've got style," Bells says, looking around the house.

"Yeah," Christine says with a note of sadness in her voice. "Anyway! You all hungry?" She turns brusquely, gesturing them forward to follow her. They walk through two expansive living rooms, what looks like a doorway to a home theater, and several hallways lined with doors before entering a kitchen. It's spacious and modern without being cold and austere; Emma can easily imagine it filled with laughter and the sounds of family.

"Siblings?" Emma asks.

"Nope, just me," Christine says. "I think they were too busy, plus it took forever for them to get to the top of the queue at GenTech, so they didn't wanna bother with another one," she says, grinning at them.

"Oh, yeah," Emma says, recognizing the genetic recombination company. "My moms waited like, twenty years; that's why there's such an age gap between me and my brother."

Christine nods in solidarity, then presses what Emma thought was just a wooden panel in the wall, but which swivels to reveal a refrigerator. "Allergic to anything? There's lots, what do you want?" Christine pulls out container after container from the fridge, gestures at all of it, and then proceeds to pull items from a pantry.

Bells whoops, popping open a bag of chips and crunching noisily. Emma laughs when he passes her the bag and watches Christine gesture toward a classic-looking MonRobot to heat food. Soon the two of them are eating a savory stew.

"This is from my mom's hometown in Mazatenango. It's kak'ik," Christine says.

"It's great," Emma says, taking another spoonful. It's delicious, warm, and spicy and fills her with warmth.

"Reminds me of a sopa your mom made once," Bells says thoughtfully. "Hey, do you remember that weird protein stuff they had at Meta-Human Training?"

"Ha! The one in Baja?"

The conversation quickly drifts to summers spent at mysterious, secret training locales. As Christine and Bells catch up, Emma turns her focus to the tasks at hand: regroup, gather their resources for the next step. She wonders if Christine has any burner DEDs or if they could make some.

Emma finishes her kak'ik, and, as soon as she sets her empty bowl down the MonRobot picks it up and takes it away.

"Thanks, Christine for having us," Emma says. . "I think the next step is to set up lookouts for Jess and—"

"Whoa," Christine says. "You know there's a curfew after dark, right? They wouldn't be able to move around without getting the Authorities on their tail. There's no point in going outside now. We'll have to wait until morning."

More waiting. Great.

EMMA WAKES UP TO THE scent of coffee and Christine loudly singing in Portuguese. Bells is already in the kitchen when Emma gets downstairs. He's humming along and has a half-eaten omelet in front of him. "Hey, Em! Did you sleep well?"

"It was okay," Emma mutters.

It was not okay. She couldn't get comfortable in the soft bed with fluffy pillows. She's fallen asleep wedged up against the cold metal door with the sharp corner of Bells' elbow digging into her and even on the ground with the wind howling over them and dust blowing so severely that they'd wake up covered in sand. Maybe Emma just missed Bells: the constant comfort of his presence, the soft intimacy of having his arms slung around her, the little hitching breaths, even the little soft snores.

"I slept great; those sheets are so soft," Bells says happily.

Guess he didn't have the same problem.

Christine grins at Emma. "I've got mushrooms, onions, tomato, avocado, four different kinds of cheese, what do you want in your omelet?"

"Uh, everything, sure, thanks," Emma says.

Emma watches Christine deftly toss the ingredients in a pan, shaking them as she hums.

Emma takes deep a draw of the rich caffeine. She immediately feels more alert, ready for the day. "Hey, do you have any unmonitored way of making holocalls?"

"Not really," Christine says. "I've got the house connected for incoming data, sure, for the newsfeeds and stuff, but it's definitely not secure. I've got a few unregistered DEDs that will bounce your location, so this house is safe, but—"

"Speak in code," Emma says, nodding. "I got it."

EMMA SIGHS, HOLDING CHRISTINE'S DED away from her. Her mothers' voices echo from it, and she winces as they ignore all of Emma's security warnings about speaking vaguely and in code. She just wanted to reassure them she was okay, but hearing from her was enough to set off a worried frenzy. It's as if the conversation she had with them before leaving to work with the Villain's Guild and build up the Resistance hadn't happened at all.

Emma brings the device back to her ear. "Mom, look—"

"You need to come home right now!"

"You and Bells *stole a car* and left in the middle of the night—"

"It was his car!" Emma protests. "And don't use names. This isn't a secure channel—"

"You are grounded!"

"You can't ground me; the Resistance needs me!"

"We *need* you. Do you know how terrifying it is, not knowing where you are and if you're safe, and with the incoming meteor storm— you need to be in a Collective-sanctioned shelter, not gallivanting about the country!" Samantha Robledo's voice takes on the sharp, determined cadence she uses in her Council speeches. "It's time you stopped playing these games and causing trouble."

Emma frowns. Parts of this doesn't make sense at all— didn't her mother warn her that the shelters might not be safe?

Josephine's firm voice doesn't waver. "We're coming right to Nuevo Los Angeles and picking you up right away."

What?

"You're lucky that I've got a Council meeting there this week. We'll bring you right home."

Realization dawns on Emma. Her moms are playing to the monitored channel. It was a code after all. She exhales in relief, wondering what's going on back home, why her parents felt the need to throw a false trail.

"Thank you, I love you. I'll see you soon," Emma says.

"I love you! This will all be over soon."

Emma ends the call and sits, hanging on to her love and her hope.

"ALL RIGHT, IF JESS IS looking for us, we should get somewhere she could find—"

"We can go back to the park," Bells suggests.

"That's a great idea. We can go out in different disguises every day and wait for them to find us." Emma nods at Bells.

"Is that the plan? Just waiting for all of them right now?" Christine asks. "If Jess can find us, we should be doing something in the meantime." She sets a perfect omelet on Emma's plate, smiling at her. "New Bright City is not only the capitol, but also the center of the Collective's media and entertainment. As you saw yesterday, I've been pretty good about tracking down where they stream Starscream's interviews—"

"I actually had an idea about doing this on a larger scale," Emma says. "I agree, being here and getting broadcast in newsholos goes a long way toward changing public opinion—"

"That's not the first time I did it," Christine says, her mouth flattening into a thin line. "I know you all have been super busy out west with your Resistance recruiting campaign and stuff, but I've been getting broadcast at least once a week."

Bells whistles, flicks through a holo-display, and gestures at the myriad results. "You've got a lot of hits for Crinoline," he says proudly. He peers closer, reading a few of the headlines. "They're all about how you're an inept villain with strange fashion sense but it's a good start!"

"Clearly, I'm no match for the Heinous Chameleon." Christine giggles.

Emma gives Bells a jaunty thumbs up. "You'll always be the number one most wanted."

"It's kind of difficult with all of this, come on." He gestures at himself, smirking, until Emma tosses a pillow at him. He catches it; his smile broadens.

Emma enlarges the projections; the holos expand as she reads the articles. "None of these say anything about the truth about the League," she says. "Look, it's great that you're getting yourself out there, but they're just spinning you as another villain."

Christine sighs. "Yeah, I've crashed livestreams before, but they usually cut it right after I start talking. And any recordings they scrub clean."

Emma nods. "Right. But that's just you as Crinoline, right? Now what if we had someone, live on a broadcast, who could talk to the public, someone they know and trust?"

"Like talk to a reporter directly?" Christine tilts her head. "So many are in the League's pocket."

Bells taps his chin; his hair shifts longer and curls.

Emma gestures at Bells.

He raises an eyebrow at her. "Me? Public enemy number one?"

Emma rolls her eyes and makes a wavy motion with her hands.

"What's that supposed to be?" Bells teases.

"You know!"

"*Oh!* Haha, okay, someone like—" Bells' face completely rearranges, his shoulders broaden, and then, sitting at the table with them, is Lowell Kingston, complete with immaculately coiffed, ash-blond hair. Bells adjusts his shirt collar and straightens his charcoal-gray suit with the seal of the Collective pinned to the lapel. "Citizens of the Collective, I implore you…"

Emma shakes her head. "No, that would get scrubbed too fast. Kingston would definitely notice that we were impersonating him."

"Yeah, but he's the most politically powerful person in the country, so…"

"A reporter," Emma says. "A specific reporter who only talks about superheroes, who everyone loves."

Bells winks at her and snaps his fingers. "Why didn't you say so?"

He shifts again. His hair elongates into a sparkling pompadour and his jawline squares. Wilton Lysander, the Collective's most famous superhero reporter, trusted for the latest in gossip, news, and every salacious detail. People would snap up his segments immediately.

Christine raises her eyebrow. "Wouldn't we have the same problem? What if the real Lysander notices and shuts it down?"

Bells points his fingers at Christine in Lysander's trademark posturing. "Good point."

"Okay, but Lysander prides himself on being the first to know what's happening," Emma says. "He wants, above all else, for people to watch his show and to share it."

"Yeah, he definitely did a number on me with the whole 'Chameleon is the world's greatest villain' thing," Bells says. He shifts back into himself, shrugging. "But I would say, he definitely has his self-interest first."

"He probably already knows the truth," Christine says. "He must suspect, at least, having covered superheroes for so long, and helping the League spin stories. I mean, unless they're feeding it to him, and he's just regurgitating it."

Emma takes a deep breath. "We don't know his motives. If a broadcast of Bells as Lysander goes viral, Lysander won't deny it. He wants those ratings, those views, those clicks. And who knows? Maybe we'll convince him."

Christine nods. "I think it's a good idea, Em! You know, there are a few reporters I've noticed who have been questioning some of the weirdness, you know? Like how a bunch of villains disappeared last year, and some heroes too, and then all of a sudden we've got new people."

"New people?"

Christine manipulates the holos on the table, scatters them, and pulls out files and expands them; the light dances in her fingertips as she goes. "I saved some livestreams about it. Hang on, here we go."

Emma recognizes the reporter in downtown New Bright City: Farha Rao, wearing a pink dress and a matching headscarf, smiling at the camera. "And we return to the scene where the new hero Sublimate has just recovered a stolen painting from the Museum of Modern Art. I wonder if Sublimate is any relation to the now retired Aerodraft? They do seem to have the same powers. The Collective has been very secretive about anything to do with the meta-gene and how it manifests, but we do know that these powers tend to be passed down genetically. I wonder, if Aerodraft and Sublimate are siblings, then why have we never seen Sublimate until now? And why did Aerodraft retire so suddenly at the age of thirty-six? I'm Farha Rao, back to you at BNN."

It's a lot to take in. "So was this scrubbed?"

"Yeah. It's not on the Net anymore. But it was definitely broadcast."

Bells studies the holo and Farha's intent expression. "She's great. She was the one who covered our train heist in Middleton."

Christine smiles. "That was you? I thought it seemed very specific, targeting those MR-D4Rs."

Emma chuckles. "Yeah. We destroyed a good number of them. Farha's the only one who picked up on the fact that it wasn't some new villain, that maybe we were trying to say something."

"She covers Middleton, mostly, and a few smaller beats in New Bright City, but she asks a lot of good questions." Christine expands the holo until Farha's face is life-size; her curious eyes look right back at them with a piercing gaze. "Can we trust her? What if she sends us to the Authorities?"

"There's a chance of that, but I have a feeling she's been looking for answers, and we have them." Emma hopes this is going to work. It's the last plan she's got.

"She looks nervous," Bells says, peering through the binoculars. He hands them to Emma. "What did you say?"

The intrepid reporter is at least twenty minutes early to their meeting. Farha adjusts her headscarf, looking around. Taking everything in, her eyes dart to the top of the roller coasters, then to the snack carts. Two small cameradrones buzz about her head while Farha speaks into her DED as if she's recording notes for herself.

Emma likes her immediately. She's smart, planning for a meeting with an anonymous source, looking for all the potential ways to escape should the meeting go wrong. It's what Emma would do.

"Maybe I was a bit too cryptic," Emma says. "But she's here!"

It was easy enough to find Farha's direct line; her citizen ID number was listed on the Broadcast News Network holopage. She's scheduled today to livestream the opening of a new ride at Roaring City Adventures, one of the many theme parks in New Bright City. Emma wasn't sure Farha would even respond to her message, but she agreed to the meeting.

Now to just talk to her.

"Should we go over there?" Christine asks.

"Let's stick to the exact time, otherwise she might mistake us for someone else," Emma says, handing the binoculars to Christine.

Christine hums in agreement, watching through the binoculars.

With Christine's generous wardrobe and Bells' shapeshifting skills, it's easy for them to adopt any number of disguises. Today Emma is wearing a long, flowing, blonde wig, over-sized sunglasses, and a bright yellow dress Christine designed. It was fun, at first, having long hair to throw around, but the wig is itchy, and she keeps wanting to scratch her head.

"Here, lemme fix that," Christine says, tucking one of Emma's escaping curls under the wig cap. She also opted for a more modern look today, nixing the petticoats in favor of a long tunic and leggings.

"Thanks," Emma says. She glances at the time on Christine's watch; they're still early. She adjusts her earpiece. They probably won't need the short-range radios, but it's always good to be prepared.

Bells pulls out his sketchbook and doodles as they wait. He's shifted into a boy with a wide nose, an easy smile, and sandy brown hair that falls in waves across his eyes. It's another one of the faces he's been using, and Emma almost has to smile because, despite whatever shift he's using, he's still so clearly Bells. Maybe it's the way his eyes squint in concentration or his slow, easy smirk when he realizes she's watching him.

Emma peers over Bells' shoulder, and he shuffles over to make more room and flips the pages for her to see.

There's Jess' face, her broad smile emerging from the smudged lines of Bells' sketches, and Abby tilting her head with her eyebrows lifted at a calculating angle. The page is wrinkled and a bit torn from erasures, as if Bells has been drawing and drawing, trying to remember their faces.

"I miss them," Bells says.

"Me too," Emma says. "I hope they're okay." She looks up at the sky, at the city, and beyond. It's strange how distinct the difference is between New Bright City and the forest that surrounds it. In the Nevada region, the desert had been a constant. The cities themselves were pockets of light and metal and people, and the wild scrub of the Joshua trees and creosote bushes and the deep reds of the canyons dominated the landscape. The countryside had been sparsely populated, even before the cities themselves were built.

But New Bright City seems surrounded by ghosts. Just outside the city, there's another skyline of towering skyscrapers, some still standing, some crumbling and falling apart, their metal bones long picked over by recycling crews. The skeletons of the buildings remain, rising out of the new-growth forests, only memories now of the cities that were here hundreds of years ago. They're barely visible outside of the glimmering protective shield that has been raised around New Bright City in preparation for the impending P019 impact. The projected date is still more than a month away, but the shield is activated today to show to the citizens of New Bright City the strength of its protection.

Emma wonders where Jess and Abby are, if they're getting closer, if Brendan went with them, if the Trans and Genevieve and the other adults are okay, or if they were all captured in that attack.

"They're gonna be fine," Emma says, maybe more to herself than anything, as if saying the words will help make it true. "I only wish they would get here sooner, I hate this waiting."

"Speaking of waiting, it looks like Farha isn't," Bells says, peering over the bush.

"What?"

Farha is running off, her cameradrones following right behind her, buzzing.

"She must have seen something!" Emma gets to her feet. "Come on!"

Christine sprints ahead, dodging through the crowd. Bells hastily shoves his sketchbook and pens and colored pencils into his bag before following suit.

Emma can barely see Farha ahead of them; her pink dress is a blur as she runs as fast as she can, dodging people left and right.

"Move, people!" Emma curses, halting in her tracks, nearly bumping into a group of people stopped in the middle of the sidewalk. "What are you all staring at!"

"Oh, no, that's so awful!"

"Where's Starscream! Somebody call for help!"

"No, Starscream can't fly, we need…"

"Captain Orion?"

"No, Captain Orion is a villain…"

"Those poor people!"

"What other heroes can fly?"

Emma follows their gaze and stops just short of Bells and Christine, who are also frozen, watching the sky with horror.

"Up there!" Bells points at the tallest roller coaster, where a set of cars is stalled at the top of one of the loops. Everyone has stopped to stare and hold up their DEDs.

"Oh, no," mutters Emma, looking at the top of the roller coaster. There are people waving from the track and shouting. "We should—"

She blanks. *They should do something to help, but what can they do?* She racks her brain, scanning the surroundings. Bells is frozen, looking at the height. Maybe Bells could shift the nature of the track back to functional? But they don't know what's wrong with it, what if there's a virus in the tech or something, what if it *hurts Bells*—

Bells pushes forward, and Emma follows, grabbing his hand. "What are you doing? We need a plan!"

"I can fix the track. It's magnetic, right? Same concept. I've done the opposite before, so, in theory, I just need to get close enough to touch it."

"Yes, but—"

Terrifying, high-pitched screams echo from above.

"Okay, go!" Emma says, rushing forward. They pass Farha, who is surrounded by cameradrones and a knot of anxious people.

"I'm here at Roaring City Adventures, where an electronic malfunction has stalled a car full of park-goers at the top of the COFAX Scream'N'Dream ride," Farha says into her microphone, facing one cameradrone hovering right in front of her. The other tiny drone is speeding to record the people stuck at the top of the track.

"What went wrong?" Emma wonders as she brainstorms for potential solutions. "Maybe if we get to the control room, we could figure out how to fix it."

"Control room is that way—"

Farha continues, her voice grim. "I'm hearing now from the technicians that there is no way to fix the Scream'N'Dream until the power comes back on. A generator was destroyed by the surge of power from the shield demonstration."

Christine twitches. "If someone falls, I could try to catch them, but—"

"How much time do you have before you're tapped out?"

"Five minutes," Christine says, counting the number of people trapped. "And falling at that speed, I don't think— I don't know, I have to be able to see what I'm moving to concentrate, and if everyone falls, I can't—"

Emma touches her arm. "It's okay; hopefully it won't come to that. Bells is almost to the track. He's got this—"

Emma looks at the base of the roller coaster, but she doesn't see Bells climbing it. He's in the crowd of people behind held back by the Authorities.

"Great," Christine mutters. "What are we going to do?"

"We need to cause a distraction," Emma says. "Get the Authorities away."

"Please do not exit the ride until we can get it working again," an official shouts into a megaphone.

The crowd gasps and points, shoving closer.

"No!"

A little boy has climbed out of his seat; Emma can barely see the toddler, scrambling for a platform a few feet away, climbing along the rickety metal railing, and trying to reach for an emergency panel.

The crowd stills, and then seems to erupt in panic.

"Watch out!"

"No!"

"Now, Bells!" Emma whispers through the small headset radios. She's glad she brought them.

Bells catches her eye and nods as he slips through the crowd and past the distracted Authorities.

Something speeds across the sky, heading right for the track.

"Oh, could that be Shockwave? He can fly!"

"No, it's clearly a mecha-suit!"

Emma follows the pointed fingers and sees the plume of smoke trailing from a mecha-suit flying toward the roller coaster. Mecha-suits, typically used by the military or for construction, all have similar clunky designs sprawled with advertisements. Two known meta-humans wear mecha-suits, Swift Emblem and Master Mischief, and Emma knows immediately this is neither of them, or anyone else from the League, for that matter.

This particular mecha-suit has strange, colored patterns, too small to make out. A mecha-suit is prime advertisement real estate, and a corporation would make its ads splashy and large.

Christine stops and blinks. "Do those metal pieces look like they were once a…"

"Washing machine," Emma says, recognizing the brand. The entire mecha-suit is built from different pieces of tech. Wait a minute, she's seen this before, half-built in a cavern—

"It's *Abby!*" Emma exclaims.

The boy loses his grip on the track and screams, falling toward the ground below—

Abby sweeps by, plucking him out of the air as the crowd cheers. She descends, setting the boy down on the ground just as a treacherous creak sounds from above.

Farha steps forward with her microphone. "Amazing! A child who might have plummeted to death from the malfunctioning roller coaster has just been saved by— What's your name, hero?"

Abby doesn't say anything, just gives the camera a jaunty salute before flying back to the top of the track.

"Emma, I need your help." Bells' panicked voice crackles in her earpiece. "I can't see once I…" he trails off; the trepidation is apparent in his voice.

"I got you," Emma says. "There's a hold just above you. Shift and stretch your left arm two feet."

The crowd is so intent on the mysterious hero in the mecha-suit now flying back and forth from the top of the track carrying one person down at a time that they don't notice another figure slowly climbing up the track. Emma guides Bells until he finally reaches the top.

He's not quite fast enough.

The track suddenly rumbles back to life as the power surges on. Lights crackle as the car plummets forward to the drop going ten times faster than it should.

Bells grabs the track and disappears.

"Please work; please work," Emma mutters to herself.

Abby grabs the end of the cars just as they start to screech and pulls forward.

"And we see our new mysterious hero grabbing the end of the Scream'N'Dream cars and attempting to prevent the passengers from plummeting to doom! Our brave hero just moments before had been ferrying people safety— three passengers have been rescued, and the lives of twelve still hang in the hands of our unknown rescuer, who is losing their grip—"

The crowd gasps as the car screeches forward and Abby falls backward, but there's no plummeting. Instead, the car slowly glides down the precariously steep slope and down the track to the roller coaster starting platform, where it's greeted by park officials.

"Oh wow, good job, Bells," Christine says, impressed.

Emma's whole body slumps forward as some of her tension disappears. She hopes Bells will be in a safe spot when he lets go of the shift, which might be soon. Emma turns her binoculars on Abby at the top of the track, who is looking around as if she's putting the pieces together.

Bells appears, lying prone on the track, and then he's falling.

Abby catches him and then flies off; her rocket boosters pulse before they disappear from sight in the city skyline.

The crowd disperses; some of them trail off in that direction, where they hope to get a glimpse of the new hero. Farha is surrounded, speaking nonstop into her microphone; her eyes glitter.

"I'm Farha Rao, reporting live from Roaring City Adventures, and that was your first look at a brand-new hero who prevented what would have been a tragic disaster here in the park. Apparently New Bright City's own Starscream was spotted golfing at the East Hopestar Resort and declined questions from my colleague at BNN. Now that brings up the question: Why wasn't the hero tasked with protection of this city here today? Why didn't he leave as soon as he heard about the accident and the people in danger?"

Farha tilts her head and cocks her eyebrow at the murmuring crowd around her. "It's curious that the Heroes' League of Heroes has not yet stepped in to comment on the nature of this new hero and where they hail from. Is the League falling behind in their social media or is this a sign of something else?"

Farha eyes the camera and grins, as if she's putting together a piece of the puzzle. "Most similar in style and power type to our mysterious new hero is Master Mischief from the Nevada region! Master Mischief was a technopath who often wore a mecha-suit when he was orchestrating elaborate pranks. Master Mischief has not been seen since 2123—"

A man in an Authority uniform pushes past Emma, followed by another, and another.

"Hey! Excuse you!" Emma scowls up at them.

One of the Authorities snatches Farha's cameradrone and smashes it to the ground. "You're done here."

"Hey!" Farha glares at them as they surround her. "You can't— I have a BNN license."

Oh, no. They're closing in on her, and this can't be good at all.

"Christine, can you change the colors of fabric or just move it—"

"Color, form, texture, anything."

"Make me look like Chameleon!"

Christine snaps her fingers, and Emma's dress transforms into a super-sleek, rainbow-hued supersuit. The fabric stretches up and over her head like a mask; it's not a perfect copy, but she just needs the color.

"Hey, losers!" Emma taunts.

The Authorities whip around, staring at her.

Emma doesn't wait for them to process what's happening, she just bolts in the opposite direction. She can hear them shout as they follow her when she weaves around people in the park.

Christine huffs, running right behind her. "You know you're almost out of time, right? I'm almost—"

"It's been more than enough." Emma exhales as her outfit returns to normal.

The Authorities run past them, shouting earnestly.

"Chameleon is worth twenty-thousand credits!"

"No way, that reward is mine!"

Christine watches them go. "Well, that was pretty brilliant," she says.

"Thanks." Emma glances toward the crowd at the roller coaster, but Farha is gone. Emma sighs. She's glad Farha got away, but they missed their chance to talk to her.

"Hey," Christine says, putting a hand on her shoulder. "Things didn't go according to plan, but—"

Emma shakes free of the gesture and looks up at Christine.

Christine pushes her hat up on her head and gives her a reassuring smile.

"Okay." Emma pushes her feelings and frustrations away. She doesn't want to talk about the plan that spiraled out of control and Bells narrowly escaping injury. She's just glad Abby was here to help.

Emma squints at the sky. Now, which direction did Abby go? She and Bells must be hiding somewhere or meeting Jess—

"Hey! Miss me?"

Emma whirls around, and there's Jess, grinning at her. She's adopted the makeup and aesthetic of the punk movement; her hair has been chopped into asymmetrical lengths, her bright brown eyes peek out from behind orange geometric patterns painted on her face, and she's even wearing a long trench coat with the designs and logos of popular alternative bands. Behind her, three

MonRobots cheep. Emma recognizes Chả, Jess's LR-DR model, and the other two KR-D4Rs from Abby's house.

"Jess!" Emma shrieks. She throws herself at her friend, and Jess laughs and picks her up and spins her in a delighted circle. "I'm so glad to see you! I was so worried, did you…" she trails off, careful of where they are in the crowded park. Emma itches to know everything, but this probably isn't the best place to talk.

"Good to see you," Christine says. "Uh—"

Abby's two MonRobots spin around her in circles, beeping. Chả is scanning her face and trilling in a deeper tone.

"Aw, did you get an upgrade?" Emma can't help reaching down to pat Chả on its little round dome, and it cheeps at her. Emma laughs, looks up at her friends, and then notices that they're drawing a few curious looks. "We should go," she mutters, before people ask about the strange MonRobots or anything else.

"Good plan." Jess turning around and strides forward. "Come on, I set up a meeting point with Abby. Brendan is with the van—"

"Please tell me he didn't drive," Emma says.

Jess snorts. "He's gotten a lot better; Abby and I couldn't do all the driving."

They talk in sparse details, not giving too much away for fear of being overheard, but Emma gleans the basics: Jess, Abby, and Brendan escaped with what tech they could salvage, including Abby's mecha-suit, and made their way to New Bright City. The rest of the Villain's Guild is scattered. Emma wants to know more about where they went and what they're doing, but that'll have to wait.

Emma and Christine follow Jess and her billowing coat as she leads them through the extensive park and then down another skybridge, and then they get in a clanking lift that descends to ground level. The light completely disappears as they continue below ground level, and the noise of people and cars and monorails fades away.

Christine scoots closer to Emma and Jess; her eyes are wide. "We're meeting them in the Underbright?"

"The what?" Emma blinks, trying to take in Christine's reaction.

Jess shrugs. "I thought it was just abandoned pre-Collective transportation tunnels and stuff. Didn't they have a bunch of primitive underground trains?"

"Yeah, but—" Christine's voice drops to a whisper. "The place is overrun with criminals and giant mutated rats!"

Jess grins. "Well, I haven't seen any rodents of unusual size yet, so I think we'll be okay."

The tunnels are lit with flickering lights, set there by whom, Emma doesn't know. Occasionally she hears footsteps and faint conversations or sees flashes of light from side tunnels, but they fade away immediately.

"So does the Collective know about the Underbright?" Emma asks curiously. It seems like an endless labyrinth of tunnels, lined with pipes and tracks and wires and signs that no longer make any sense. It's different from any of the clean, well-kept Resistance bases built from the ancient bunkers. Those had been prepared to shelter people during the Disasters; this place may have once had a purpose, but now it's nothing but dripping water and echoes.

Christine shrugs. "I mean, the Hopestar region pretends anything below ground doesn't exist, and for good reason. The Authorities would never come down here; they couldn't possibly drag everyone to Corrections." She glances around as they approach a five-way junction. "And they'd get lost."

Jess turns back to throw a smile at them without breaking stride. "That's not a problem if you have Compass with you!"

"Compass?" Emma can barely see Jess in the dim light of the tunnel, but the confident expression on her face, that's new. "You're using the name!" She smiles, remembering those meetings they had in Jess' basement. Emma had been so enthusiastic about the Sidekick Squad, creating agendas and plans and banging that gavel.

"I am," Jess says, blushing slightly. She's backlit against the soft lights in the tunnel, and the geometric patterns on her face give her a commanding aura.

She looks at her friend; Jess seems taller, somehow, or maybe Emma got shorter. It seems like years when it's only been weeks, but there's a different air to her, a hardened one that speaks of a similar path that Emma and Bells had out there in the desolate wilds, traversing from city to city through the Unmaintained lands.

"Good," Emma says, nearly bursting with pride for Jess, who was always timid, always careful, always too nice, too afraid to take up space. "Being a hero looks good on you."

Now that they're out of immediate danger, Emma's hypervigilance fades as they walk. They're safe and secure; despite Christine's claims of giant rats, the tunnels are mostly deserted. Any other people down here are taking care to avoid them.

"My mom and dad are a few days behind; they've been helping Genevieve set up safe houses for those who didn't want to take an active part of the Resistance," Jess says.

"I'm so glad no one was hurt," Emma says. "Did you figure out who was behind the attack?"

Jess shakes her head. "We were all so careful with the location of the base. No one outside the Villain's Guild knew where it was."

Christine frowns. "So it was someone from the inside."

"I don't— but—" Jess falters and looks at Emma. "No, someone must have been followed somehow, and the location was compromised."

"What about Claudia?" Emma asks. "She knew where it was."

Jess doesn't say anything, just bites her lip. "Come on, we're almost there."

"Oh, you can tell how close you are now?" Christine asks eagerly. "That's so cool!"

Emma wonders if Jess knows anything more, if she's thinking the same thing Emma is now: that Claudia didn't have a change of heart after all.

She studies Jess and the animated way she's talking about her powers with Christine, the way she's talking about her time at the Villain's Guild and how amazing it was to work on her powers with other meta-humans. *It suits her*, Emma thinks. Jess might say otherwise, but Emma can see how other people look up to her.

"There it is!" Jess says proudly as they turn the corner.

Sitting in the dark tunnel is the most derelict van Emma has ever seen. It's dented and scratched and, like Abby's mecha-suit, looks as if it's been made out of parts. "I bet you've been turning heads," Emma says.

Jess shrugs. "We were planning on ditching it soon or reupping the camfoil when we get to your hideout."

The van door slides open to reveal Bells waving a slice of pizza at them. "What took you so long? We had time to get pizza and get here way before you!"

Emma laughs and gets inside the van with Jess and Christine following behind her.

Abby's still wearing the mecha-suit but has removed the helmet. She gives them all a half-hearted wave. Up close Emma can see the true scattered nature of her suit. The chest plate is made from a washing machine, the gauntlets from the old computers at the Villain's Guild, and the shin guards and hip plates are from what might have been a stove.

Emma tries to hug her and laughs when she meets mostly metal. She breathes in the smell of ozone and burnt fuel and looks more closely at Abby. It might be the light, but she looks thin and drawn; her cheeks are hollowed out in a sickly way. Emma pats the arm of the mecha-suit, and it echoes. "I'm so glad you're here," Emma says softly. She doesn't know what else to say. "That was amazing, what you did at the park. When did you finish this?"

"The first prototype was finished in the Rockies," Abby yawns. "I'm still, I'm still perfecting it..." she trails off, blinking slowly.

"It's okay, get some rest." Jess fluffs a pillow behind Abby. She flips open the pizza box and frowns as she hands Christine a slice. "Bells, how much did you eat? We only got one pizza."

"There are two boxes though!"

"That bottom one's from last week!"

"Oh! I thought there was enough!" Bells says, frowning. "Em, you can have this one. I only took one bite."

"Sure," Emma laughs as Bells hands her the slice of pizza, dripping through a greasy napkin. It's hot and cheesy; she'd forgotten she hadn't eaten all day.

Emma munches happily as she takes in the cluttered, homey mess. The back of the van is an eclectic mix: jumbled tech and wires, open duffel bags with clothes spilling out of them, bins filled with protein packs and water, a jumbled set of sleeping bags and pillows right next to a charging dock. Emma can see Abby's AHHS volleyball sweatshirt, a bunch of colorful hair ties strung up on the dashboard, toothbrushes sticking out of the door pocket.

Outside the van, Chả meeps a pitiful noise, and Jess obligingly picks it up and sets it inside the van on the charging dock. "Can you get Jacks and Jills?"

Emma starts to get up, but Christine is already bounding out of the van with her pizza hanging from her mouth. She carries each MonRobot inside, huffing with effort. She clambers in, and suddenly Emma's hyper-aware of how cramped they are with all of them and the bots.

Jess pulls the door shut behind them with a clang, and then all the natural light disappears.

"Hey! We got everyone! Can we go now?"

Emma recognizes Brendan's voice but can't help but break into uncontrollable giggles when he leans around the front passenger seat to face all of them. While Jess' disguise is just enough to disarm facial recognition software, the boy has gone so above and beyond the punk aesthetic that Emma thinks it's not even a disguise anymore, but an attention catcher. His hair has been gelled in thick spikes, and one of them hangs directly in front of his face. Many blocks and squares are painted on his face, and one eyebrow has been shaved off. He looks like an abstract painting and is very, very conspicuous.

"Hey, Brendan," Bells says, catching Emma's eye with amusement. "Nice outfit. Very punk."

Brendan preens. "I know, right? I said they weren't doing enough."

Jess rolls her eyes. "You look like the very first image search result for 'punk' on the Net. Like, the most extreme version." She turns to everyone else in the van. "This is why he didn't come with me to the park."

"Hey!"

Emma giggles.

Brendan snorts. "Whatever. You wouldn't last a day without me. Who else could have engineered this van out of scraps and kept us all hidden on our cross-country fugitive road trip?"

Emma laughs. "Didn't A—"

Jess puts her hand on Emma's arm and gives her a warning look, shaking her head.

Did Abby not help them engineer the van? Emma watches her friends and notes the careful way Jess and her brother are speaking around the mecha-suit in the room. Abby's fallen asleep now; her head bobs forward.

"Fine, Shortstack, you're a real genius; here's a cookie," Jess says in a light tone.

"We're out of cookies because *someone*—"

Jess rolls her eyes. "Please tell me your hideout is big enough that I can get away from Brendan. He smells."

Brendan scowls. "Well it wasn't a picnic sharing such cramped space with you, either! We could have gotten here earlier if your stupid powers weren't taking us in so many different directions! But no, we always have to listen to Jess' gut."

Jess scrounges around under a seat and then throws a bag of cookies at Brendan. "My gut is *always* right, and I may not always know what question I want to ask but I certainly always get us where we *need* to go," she says.

Christine takes a bite of her pizza. "Is it always like this?" she asks.

"Oh, worse," Bells says happily. "Jess and Brendan once flooded the Tran's basement with pudding."

"That was your fault!" Jess and Brendan accuse each other.

"Whatever," Jess huffs. "We did take a roundabout route, but we didn't get caught. We rushed here as fast as we could. I mean, every day we've been trying to push for as many miles as we can, but you know, the Unmaintained roads aren't exactly..."

Jess gives the sleeping Abby a look that speaks multitudes, and Emma wonders what they faced along the way.

Bells laughs. "If you had Emma driving you would have gotten here sooner! I think I lost a few eyebrows just from the speed."

Emma nudges him playfully. It does feel good, having everyone together again. There will be no more waiting. It's time for action.

ABBY'S THE FIRST ONE OUT of the car when they arrive in Christine's underground port, startling Emma.

"I call dibs on the shower!" Abby's high-pitched laugh echoes from outside the van.

"Where did— what— I thought she was asleep," Emma says.

Jess looks at Brendan. "What was that, twenty minutes?"

"Eighteen minutes, twenty seconds," Brendan says. "Looks like it's going to be that kind of day."

They share a long look. *What's been going on?*

"There are several showers; don't worry," Christine says as they walk to where Abby is bouncing by the door.

Christine enters her keycode, and, as soon as the door opens, Abby zooms off, whooping in delight as she discards pieces of the mecha-suit.

"Uh, welcome, bathrooms are down the hallway," Christine calls out.

Brendan bows his head to her in his formal way before disappearing down the hallway.

"Are you hungry?" Christine asks. "Of course, you probably are, that wasn't enough pizza…" she trails off, watching Jess' heavy expression. "I'll go make some dinner. Make yourself at home!" Christine says before heading off to the kitchen.

Jess sighs, picks up the metal armor pieces, and huffs as she drags them out of the way. Emma picks up the heavy chest plate. Bells grabs the other side, and the two of them crab-walk to the corner.

"Is Abby okay?" Bells asks.

Emma was just wondering the same thing.

"I don't know," Jess says, biting her lip. "She won't talk to me about it, whenever I say I'm worried about her. She hasn't been sleeping much, but she has so much energy, it's hard to keep up with her. And sometimes, like, her ideas, I don't really follow them. I dunno. Maybe it was just me. Brendan's almost always in his own world, so this past week I haven't really had a good scale to judge by." Jess sighs. "Or maybe I'm changing."

"Are you two okay?" Emma asks.

Jess wipes her hands on her shirt. "I think so, but sometimes she just gets mad at me for no reason, or sometimes she'll be really—" Jess blushes, pushing her hand into her hair. "I just— I hope she gets some rest. I think she's just been really stressed out and, like, with Michael's experiments and the possibility of getting her powers back and building this mecha-suit, she's been doing so much." Jess stretches, trying to hide a yawn.

Emma nods, feeling the urge to yawn herself. "You should get some rest too, you and Bells, you worked really hard this afternoon."

"Good plan," Jess says wearily. She gives Emma one last hug before shuffling down the hallway.

Bells flops onto the couch and flings his arms open as he pats the spot next to him.

Emma sinks into the fluffy pillows and into Bells' arms as he wraps himself around her like an octopus. He shuts his eyes, sighing contentedly.

"Are you really gonna sleep like this?" Emma asks in mock indignation. "This can't be comfortable."

"I know, but it made you laugh," Bells says, smirking at her. He waggles his eyebrows at her before sitting normally on the couch.

Emma closes her eyes, but she can practically see the thoughts spinning frantically behind her lids. She's got too much to do, too much to plan, now that everyone is here. They can't waste any time.

The couch is comfortable, and Bells is humming to himself, tracing patterns on her hands, and Emma thinks, *just five minutes*.

EMMA WAKES UP TO SHOUTS and laughter. Bells is still on the couch next to her, but he's wide awake, clapping and laughing uproariously. Brendan, Christine, and Abby are wearing VR headsets and sensorsuits and are playing a complicated game that involves swift kicks and punches.

"Behind you!" Brendan shrieks.

"Not on my watch!" Abby says, grabbing Christine by the waist and spinning her around as Christine delivers another flying kick to an invisible enemy.

"How long was I out?" Emma asks.

"Eh, like an hour," Bells says.

"That's too long!" Emma cries, springing up from the couch. "I should have been planning immediately!"

"It's okay," Bells says. "You needed the rest."

"Yeah," Jess says, plopping down next to her. She's changed into a fresh T-shirt and pair of pants and scrubbed the punk makeup from her face.

Emma pulls up her intricate plans on Christine's console, manipulating the pixels deftly until she has all her files drawn up. It's a poor replication, in her opinion, of the elaborate planning board they had in Nevada, but it's a good start.

"Okay, this meeting of the Sidekick Squad is coming to order," she says, tapping the console. It barely makes a sound; she misses her gavel.

"Aw," Christine says, pulling off her headset. "Do we really need to do this now?"

"Yes," Emma says. "We need to debrief with Jess, Abby, and Brendan—"

Abby yanks her headset off and tosses it onto the couch; her eyes glint with fierce energy. "What's there to debrief? We weren't ever going to convince them about anything."

Jess sighs. "She's right. The more the adults talked about it, the more they disagreed. A bunch of people just wanted to hide. After being experimented on by Captain Orion or having been rescued from being kidnapped, they just wanted to live in peace. And then those who wanted to fight couldn't agree on a way to do it."

Bells shakes his head. "Did you figure out what happened? Who attacked you?"

Brendan looks sadly at the headset in his hands. "We still don't know. Someone had set explosives all around the base like— I think they didn't know where exactly everything was, but they had a general idea. Enough to cause significant damage, at least. The Rockies base of operations is now completely destroyed. A few people were hurt— broken legs, sprained ankles. Michael is taking care of them."

Emma nods. "Where are they now?"

Jess frowns, glancing at Abby, who is now pacing in front of the VR sensors. "Everyone basically scattered. We didn't have a real plan on where and when to meet up; everyone was just trying to leave. I know that Michael and Deirdre and the injured meta-humans were headed to Port Clarion; there's an unused bunker there they want to convert into another headquarters."

Emma sighs. "So the focus would be on rebuilding another safe place, a shelter. Abby, your mom is building safe houses?"

Abby taps her fingers. "Yeah! She and the Trans were headed this way; I know they did like your plan, Emma, so they want to come help, but they needed to get other folks to safety first. Did you know Steven is from Middleton? There's another spot-on-the-wall meta-human there too, but they aren't related."

Emma has no idea what this has to do with the conversation. "Uh, thanks."

Abby squints, reading Emma's projected plans to confront Starscream in New Bright City. She flashes Emma a wide, gleaming smile as she traces the ideas with her fingers. "This is an awesome plan! Yes! We should totally confront Starscream. I need to upgrade the mecha-suit, and find another fuel source. We should get started with this right away, and actually, Christine, I was wondering if you had any tech you weren't using, I could see if I could get some supplies together and repair my mecha-suit."

"How are you powering that thing, anyway?" Emma asks.

Abby's face turns guilty. "We used the last of the fuel for that roller coaster rescue."

Emma blinks. "Fossil fuel. You used *fossil fuel?* Where did you even get it?"

"We tapped an old launch site," Abby says, looking as if she's about to begin another mile-a-minute speech.

"It was not easy to find," Jess says. She looks at Emma and Bells, and something about this makes Emma think this isn't the first time Jess has had to rein Abby back.

Emma thought Abby seemed more energetic than usual before they left for Grassroots; this is a different kind of energy— one that's taking a toll. Abby's face looks thinner, almost gaunt, as if she hasn't been eating, and there are deep circles under her eyes.

"I think we can wait to build stuff, Abby; we just got here," Jess says.

Abby peers closer at Emma's plans. "Were you just planning to wait around Starscream's local hangouts? The League probably has specific algorithms. Brendan, we can definitely plot this out and anticipate his next appearance—"

"Ooh, for sure!" Brendan says, yawning. "But first, sleep. Maybe after one more game."

Abby shrugs. "We gotta get started, right, Emma? Got any coffee? Oh! I can do the algorithm and start on the mecha-suit upgrade."

Jess' eyes widen. "Abby, are you sure? You were driving the last leg. You can start that tomorrow."

Abby is swaying, as though she can't seem to stop moving. "Nope! We've got too much to get done and too little time."

"Coffee is over there," Christine says, raising an eyebrow. "You're welcome to look through the work rooms. I've got a lot of old parts. My dad would stockpile stuff for design, so I'm sure you can cobble together something. And tools are down in the east wing. I can show you if you want."

"Yes! Let's go!"

Abby taps on Christine's shoulder until Christine gets up from her lounge chair and leads her off.

Emma catches Bells' eye, and they both turn, concerned, toward Jess.

Jess draws her knees up to her chest. "I don't know what to do. I mean, I feel like she's okay, but maybe this is just the way she is, and I didn't know her very well before—"

"Uh, no," Emma says. "I was in volleyball with her three years and she's never been like this."

"Maybe," Jess says. She flicks through Emma's saved files listlessly, pauses on a saved holovid of Farha Rao, and presses play.

Farha gives the camera a steely-eyed glare. "If Aerodraft and Sublimate are siblings, then why have we never seen Sublimate until now? And where did Aerodraft go? I'm Farha Rao, back to you."

"What's this?" Jess asks. "I've seen this reporter before."

Emma nods, expanding the folder. "Christine started saving all her broadcasts because the network deletes them almost immediately, especially if she's asking questions about meta-humans."

"I wonder what's happening. Do you think it's Orion?" Bells muses. "I know she's still at large, and she mentioned wanting to kidnap people for her experiments. But without the Registry…"

"Well, you got rid of the master list," Brendan says. "But the League still has people they were keeping tabs on, right? Like all their official heroes and stuff in their cities. I mean, it's not just villains anymore. Some people have gotten upset that their favorite hero disappeared too. Retired, some of them. But it's highly suspicious."

"Yeah, especially since someone else with their exact same powers has popped up." Emma says.

"No way," Bells says. "I mean, if they were in Meta-Human Training, I would have seen them in the last five years, you know!"

Jess reads Christine's notes; her eyes narrow. "These powers…" She glances at them, frowning. "These are exactly the same powers of people who've disappeared in the last five years. It can't just be a coincidence."

Emma nods. She glances at the notes Christine has made about the new meta-humans.

Sublimate, wind manipulation (Aerodraft, wind manipulation)
Medusa, motion stabilizer (Bellevue, motion stabilizer)
Chillout, ice manipulation
Sonic, super hearing and voice projection

"Aerodraft, she's, like, thirty, isn't she?" Emma tries to remember the facts on the trading card holos she had. And Chillout's powers sound awfully like Icebolt, who had the ability to manipulate snow and ice. And she had definitely heard of someone with Sonic's powers before. Didn't the hero from Turner City have super-hearing and voice projection, too? Echo, that was it.

"Yeah." Bells peers over her shoulder. "And she didn't have any kids."

"Secret baby?" Brendan asks.

"But look at this," Bells says. He's on the holopage for the Heroes' League of Heroes. There's a whole new detailed section on quite a few new people. "Sublimate, aged forty-five."

"I mean, it could be siblings, like Rao said," Christine says. "But yeah, that is weird. And with that kinda power, they would have showed up before now."

Emma doesn't like it. She doesn't like it one bit.

CHRISTINE'S EXPANSIVE HOUSE HAS MANY guest bedrooms, but everything feels so vast and empty, even with Jess and Abby and Brendan joining them. There are wings full of empty rooms and Emma hasn't even explored the whole thing. Her room's tiled floors are too cold, the bed is too big, and once again, Emma can't fall asleep. Her thoughts are a whirlwind of worry, not only about the Resistance and their plans, but also coming back to Bells and their relationship. She got used to falling asleep next to him and to the comfortable rhythm of their conversations on the trip; having everyone back has thrown her out of balance just when she found it. It's nice to see the easy familiarity between Bells and Christine. She knows they've been friends for years, all those summers when Bells was away at Meta-Human Training. She knows they didn't really date— that time Christine showed up at that disaster triple-date was just a ruse.

Some ruse, Emma thinks. She was dating Carlos, perfect Carlos, who, by all rights was a perfect boyfriend, but Emma never understood how or why or what she was doing with him. Sure, he was interesting, and they had a good time together. But he was so sincere and serious about dates and anniversaries and he projected this whole future that Emma just couldn't see herself doing. When she'd dated others, she'd break it off when she realized the romance was wearing on her, when dates became a chore, when kissing itself lost its shine. Dating Carlos, she struggled, trying to find conversation topics and ignoring the growing dread of the sense of wrongness. She thought she could tough it out. After all, dating was part of her plan for school's complicated social game. Breaking up with Carlos was a relief, but also disappointing. Emma was disappointed in herself; she thought it would work out this time.

Emma remembers that awkward bowling date. *Would it have been just as awkward if it had been her and Bells on a date?*

Emma groans into the pillow. *Maybe.* Maybe it's only awkward because it's a date and there are specific romantic implications to do with that.

While they've talked about sex, they haven't talked about romance; they haven't had the time, what with all the missions and the trainings, and then on the road Emma was just enjoying being together. Now that she is alone with her thoughts, trying to sleep and missing Bells, it's come to the forefront of her mind again.

Emma stares at the ceiling and finally decides to get out of bed. She might as well, since she can't sleep.

She hustles outside, her bare feet cold on the tiled hallway, and makes her way to the kitchen.

At first, Emma thinks she imagines Christine's silhouette on the couch in front of the fireplace. Christine hair seems to glow, lit by the fire. Her skin glistens in the low light; the flames flickering in the grate. A book is open in her lap, and her head nods forward.

Emma tries to step as quietly as she can, so she doesn't wake her up, but the living room is unfamiliar and dim.

"Oof!" Emma trips over an ottoman and falls to the floor.

Christine startles awake. "Wha— what?"

"Sorry," Emma says sheepishly, pulling herself up. "I couldn't sleep."

"Oh, is everything okay?" Christine says. "Need any more pillows or anything?

"The bedroom is great. Thank you."

Emma lingers, not sure why. Christine stretches, catlike, moving with a feline grace. "You wanna sit?"

"Sure," Emma says. "Thanks for having us here in your house and everything."

"No problem." Christine yawns.

The couch is elaborately ornate, like everything in this house. Everything seems to scream of wealth and opulence: every piece of furniture; the thick, expensive drapes, the cool marble tile beneath their feet.

"It's a lot, isn't it," Christine says dryly. "Mother always did like to make a statement." She runs a finger along a sculpture. "Loved filling her homes with beautiful pieces." Her voice is bitter. "Myself included," she says, glancing at the holos gracing the mantelpiece.

There are trophies and mementos, awards and accolades for Christine, and many holos of her, looking elegant and poised, wearing beautiful, sleek, modern dresses and accepting awards. The polished, demure Christine posing in the holos with her smile not quite reaching her eyes seems like a shadow of herself. Emma doesn't know Christine well, but what she does know of her—colorful outfits, outgoing, wild ideas—seemed very much as though she was on the same wavelength, a kindred soul. It's funny, how similar they were and how different.

"I'm sorry," Emma says.

Christine is still somewhat of a mystery to her: the way she holds herself, always elegant, always observant, eyes glittering, watching and planning. Emma knows she comes from old money; each of her parents comes from a legacy more ancient than the Collective. She moves in a society Emma doesn't understand. Her own family is well off, comfortable, for their region. But there are so many customs in Christine's life: the way she comes and goes about her various homes and estates, the way she's gotten herself involved with the Resistance and then uninvolved and then involved again, as if it's merely a passing interest. Because ultimately, whether or not the Resistance succeeds or fails, it seems as though it won't much matter in Christine's life— or maybe it will.

"Your parents push you to be different from who you are?" Christine asks.

"Sometimes," Emma says. "I mean, they want me to be my best. But it's more like be neater, don't rush into things, do the dishes more often, don't leave your books and research lying around." She hesitates. "I love my moms, but sometimes I think they do want me to be like them. Go to medical school or get into politics or something."

"And you don't want to do that?"

Emma shrugs. "I mean, it's interesting, but I don't really care about that."

"What do you want to do?"

Emma glances up. Through the skylight, the barest glimmer of stars is visible. She knows there's another world out there in the stars; she's read the books and seen the photos of people going beyond the world they've always known. Somewhere out there, millions of miles away, is a red planet that's waiting for her.

"Mars," Emma says finally. "I want to go to Mars."

Christine lets out a low whistle. "That's cool. Too bad the Collective never started a space program, and everything we know about pre-Collective space programs has been, well, lost."

Emma nods. Research is so difficult. It's not banned, precisely, but in the same manner that much pre-Collective media is banned—old books and movies and the way people thought, the way they thought then, the way they wanted to move forward, their dreams of the future, the way they looked toward the stars—it's not gone, but it's not available either. No one talks about it or cares about it. They've got everything they need, apparently: beautiful sparkling cities with a flourishing economy and people thriving in a once devastated land.

Christine knocks her shoulder against Emma's. It's a familiar gesture, and Emma smiles. Despite her misgivings about where she is and how she feels about her place in the Resistance, it's nice, to have a friend like her, who can appreciate her dreams. Emma can definitely see what drew Bells to her; they could rival each other in snark, Emma decides.

"Emma Robledo, first girl in space," Christine says.

"Oh, I won't be the first," Emma says. "I know there have been many." She wishes their names and stories hadn't been lost to time. There are entire laboratories hidden in the Unmaintained lands; who knows what stories they could tell.

"You'll be up there." Christine smiles at her. It's a real smile, unlike the ones gracing all the holograms flickering on the mantel. "I believe in you. Just like how I believe in your plan."

Emma exhales. "Thanks. I appreciate that."

"I appreciate you," Christine says, the corner of her mouth quirking up.

And here is the moment, a moment that Emma recognizes after years of looking for patterns, looking for understanding how people interacted with one another and realized when and how they would know, *oh yes, I like this person.* Because she does like Christine, and something like this—how she feels right now—it's something Emma would have clung to, wanted to label immediately, even if she didn't understand how she felt. And maybe the Emma of last year, the Emma of two years ago, who wanted to fit in, who eagerly sprang to announce her latest crush, would wax poetic about Christine, about her sparkling wit and her hair and her eyes.

Emma doesn't need to name those feelings anymore.

It feels freeing, to know what she's feeling doesn't have to be romantic to be valid, that this easy, growing affection is something precious and beautiful in its own way.

Christine tilts her head, as if she's considering the moment as well, and then— "Do you want some hot chocolate?"

"Sure," Emma says.

Christine goes to the kitchen with her shawl trailing behind her like a cape, and Emma follows, grateful for the time to think.

"How are you and Bells doing? I'm so happy that worked out, by the way." She winks at Emma. "How was your *long* road trip? Lots of fun, right?"

Emma blinks. "I guess?" She watches Christine fuss, boiling water and pulling several metal tins and a spoon from a cupboard. "Weren't *you* interested in Bells?"

Christine shrugs. "I was," she says, as if it's that simple and easy, as though she knows her own feelings with a surety Emma has never had. "We figured we're better off as friends. Besides, I think he was so in love with you it would have never worked out."

Ah. Right. Guilt floods Emma again.

Christine gives her a small smile. "When we pretended to date, you know that was all for you, right? He wanted you to be jealous." She blinks at Emma. "Were you?"

"I don't know," Emma says. It feels awful to admit that. It's the first time the words have taken flight, and it's strange how with Jess, who knows her so well, or even Abby, that she can't even broach this.

"I mean, I do, but—" Emma sighs. "It's complicated. I don't know where I'm at. I love him, but I… romance, I'm not really sure if I can do that." She repeats Christine's hand gesture and gives her a watery smile.

Emma thinks about last year. It was easy, once you gained a reputation at school for being an incorrigible flirt. She bounced in and out of relationships, constantly talking about who she was crushing on at the time. Maybe she overdid it. *Was she interested in those people?* She never could figure out why getting serious scared her, and she always ended those relationships before they got to that point.

Christine hands her the hot chocolate, and Emma lets the steam rise and surround her face. She inhales its rich, deep, scent, and takes a sip.

"Relationships are complicated," Christine agrees. "But figuring it out can be worth it."

They sit in comfortable silence, drinking their chocolate. Emma's nerves settle with the sweet warmth of the chocolate and Christine's company, her steady acceptance and acknowledgment.

"You're right," Emma says. "It is worth it."

She offers her half-empty mug to Christine, who clinks it against her own. Her head swims with too many thoughts, too many emotions and feelings, so she changes the subject. "How are you doing?"

"Relationship-wise?"

"Uh, yeah."

"I mean, I haven't seen anyone seriously since Ricky. He really did a number on me."

Emma nods; she heard the story from Bells: Christine-and-Ricky, inseparable at training, and then after the summer was over went back to their homes, and Ricky found another girl despite being long-distance with Christine. She gives Christine a sympathetic look and raises her cup of chocolate.

Christine laughs, clinking her cup against hers. "How is he doing, anyhow? I heard he joined up with your merry band of misfits in Nevada."

"Oh, yeah, Bells recruited him and the twins," Emma says. "I mean, he's..." she shrugs. "Ricky. Annoying, enthusiastic, occasionally invisible. I guess he got better at it? Bells helped him with his control."

"That's good," Christine says.

Emma misses that dynamic, how easy it was to work as a team, how all their goals seemed within reach. "That's it. We need them here. What we've been trying to do, we need to do more of that, at a broader level, to get notice. What's more noticeable than even more meta-humans?"

Christine raises her eyebrows. "Are you getting the band together again?"

"The Sidekick Squad, back in full force, all right!" Emma pumps her fist in the air.

The radio crackles. "Hello, this is Mastermind for the Sidekick Squad, over." Emma says. "Do you hear me, Squad Base?"

There's nothing but static. She's been trying to catch someone at base the past few days, but so far hasn't had any luck. Emma sighs. Maybe no one at base has turned on the radio. She should have left better instructions. She wonders if the new members of the Resistance have been spreading the word in their own way, if they've made progress. She wonders if Ricky has managed to stay invisible for longer than ten minutes. She wonders if Sasha and Tanya ever were able to succeed in their teleportation experiments; the last she'd heard, they were still working up in size and quantity.

"I thought you wanted the other members to concentrate on your original plan of spreading stories by word of mouth?" Bells asks.

"Yes, I want that to keep going, but we don't need everyone to be on that," Emma says. She takes a deep breath. "My plan— we can do it. But we need more of the Sidekick Squad and a few of our new members."

"Okay," Bells says, twirling the microphone cord around with his fingers. "I think we've been doing pretty well."

Emma scowls. They've tried again to get on the air, but it was too dangerous, trying to interrupt another battle; either the Authorities would show up immediately or Starscream and the staged villain would get away after their quick battle. It's as if the League caught on and now each staged battle is done under the full watch of the Authorities. Since the plan requires Bells to play the part of Lysander, Emma can't figure out a good plan for in which the rest of them fight Starscream *and* another meta-human without getting caught by the Authorities. Even with special earplugs, Starscream's soundblasts are too powerful, and none of them can stand up to them.

At least Farha Rao is on board.

The meeting did go well. She was suspicious at first, but she remembered seeing Emma and Christine at the park.

"I saw you. You used your powers to help me escape," Farha said.

"Well, my idea, Christine's powers," Emma said. "But you understand, right? Why people like Christine aren't allowed in the League and why the League tells other people to be villains?"

Farha steepled her fingers; her eyes glittered. "Oh, yeah, I'm going to try my best to help you kids blow the lid off this conspiracy." She narrowed her eyes. "But you'll need more than just Crinoline shouting at the camera. It's old news, the public's already tired of you. Look, if you all come up with different outfits and actually pose a threat, that's when everyone's going to pay attention."

Right. They need to actually stop the battle, not just interrupt it.

Emma sighs, listening to the static, thinking about the plan. Maybe they should just go back to training and working out and call it for today—

"Squad Base, I hear you!"

"Sasha!" Emma shrieks, relieved. "Is Tanya there with you?"

"Yeah, I'm gonna get her—"

"Hi!"

"We're so excited to hear from you!" the twins chorus. "How are things going? Is the Resistance totally massive now? Is the League about to learn what's coming to them?"

"Uh, it's a work in progress," Emma says, stumbling over the words. She feels guilty about not having more done at this point. She thought by now everything would be over; they'd reveal the League as corrupt and everything would be perfect again, and she and her friends could go back to their lives. Go back to school. Go pursue their dreams.

Bells speaks into the microphone, snapping Emma out of her reverie. "How are things back at base?"

"Good. The new recruits have been really excited about spreading the word. Michelle is in Middleton and Bobby's in Port Clarion now. I think just from word of mouth we've got a lot of people in town aware and convinced of the truth."

"That's good," Emma says, relieved. It seems like a drop in the bucket, a single drop in the tide that they need to turn, but any news is good news. "Sasha, Tanya, have you ever been to New Bright City?"

"Yeah, went there on a school trip once. Why?"

"That's where we are now. Can you get to the city, and we'll pick you up and get you to our new headquarters?"

There's silence across the line, and muddled voices that Emma can't quite hear, but it sounds like Sasha and Tanya conferring in hushed, interested whispers.

"I think so, but we'll have to do several jumps. Doing a few hundred miles will knock Sasha out for a day, so we'll need to stop to rest," Tanya says. "We did figure out how to bring bulky items with us. That'll slow us down a bit more, but if that will help, we can do it."

"How long do you think it'll take?"

"Not sure… two weeks, maybe?"

Emma looks at Bells, who nods back. She wants to start right away, but she can wait two weeks, especially if it means safe travel for the rest of the Sidekick Squad. Using Sasha and Tanya's powers, they won't need to worry about finding a safe route or staying hidden from the Authorities.

Bells leans forward. "Okay, question. If you teleport the car, will it teleport everything inside it?"

"Yes," Tanya says. "I mean, as long as it's touching the car; the ground doesn't count. You know, the same way I can teleport a person and, you know, all their inside organs and whatever they're wearing."

Bells laughs. "Ha, ha! Remember Chrono? The meta-human that could time travel, but only for five seconds, and clothes didn't count. Christine couldn't figure out any fabric that they could take with them."

Emma blinks. She's never heard of any such meta-human. They've never been introduced to the public.

Tanya and Sasha laugh over the line. "Oh, man, that summer. They never wanted to use their powers because it meant showing up in their birthday suit whenever they did."

Emma snaps her fingers. "Focus, come on."

"Right, right. Okay. Could you get a van?" Bells asks.

"Hm, I think so. Ricky's dad has one for his shop. We can get it here from Vegas. Why? Do you want us to fill it with supplies and stuff?"

"Can you bring my motorcycle?"

BELLS IS BEYOND EXCITED ABOUT his bike, humming to himself and smiling as he does chores about the house.

"You don't need to do that," Christine says dryly, watching him do the dishes.

"It's relaxing; I like it," Bells says. "It reminds me of my routine at the restaurant."

"I thought you had MonRobots for that. I saw a KR-D2 yesterday," Emma says, not looking up from her tablet.

"Oh, we had two, but not the K series, the old versions. They'd only have so much battery life before they needed to charge, so we would need to wash 'em manually every now and then," Christine says.

"It's cool, I like keeping busy," Bells says.

Emma agrees; keeping to a routine while they're here has helped ease the anxiety of waiting.

"You don't have any MR-D4Rs, right?" Emma asks, looking around. Christine has the highest tech of everything, so if she has the latest MonRobot for chores…

"Oh, absolutely not," Christine says. "I mean, after those models chased you out of Andover? And you had them attack you up in Aerial City, right?"

Emma shudders; the memory is fresh in her mind.

"Yeah, not having those murder bots in my house," Christine says. "Isn't Phillip Monroe, like, totally working for the League? He made those things!"

"He's being forced to," Bells says. "Orion mentioned it too. He thinks that the League has his wife and Abby and that they'll be hurt if he doesn't comply."

Emma nods. "I think that's what Kingston wanted to do with me, why he wanted to kidnap me."

"But Abby's here," Christine says, confused. She jerks her head toward the loud music echoing down the hallway from the room Abby's claimed for her workspace. "And Genevieve is on the run."

"Yeah, but Phillip doesn't know that. Plus, with holotech I'm sure they've convinced him what he sees is real. And there's torture." Emma grimaces. She's read about the inhumane things people used to do to manipulate others, to draw information from them.

Bells shakes his head, frowning. "I mean, he seemed healthy, but I don't know. We've only seen him a few times when they've trotted him out for press for Monroe Industries, which is run by Stone now, who's in Kingston's pocket."

"And he was wearing tantalum cuffs," Emma remembers.

"So whatever Phillip is designing now, it's tech for the League, right?"

"Or Kingston," Bells says. "Emma wasn't an enemy of the League, but Kingston definitely logged her as a threat."

"Do you think Abby's dad is designing more…"

"I think he's stalling," Emma says. "If they're keeping him alive to design more things… I mean, they could have experimented on him, the way they did on Abby's mom and all the other meta-humans, but they kept him."

Jess nods. "Like there's only one version of the MR-D4Rs."

"That we've seen," Emma mutters.

She vividly remembers the electric crackle of the arms of the one that pursued her, the one that had been living in her house, just waiting to be activated. And then there are the ones with guns. Bells protected them then, but they haven't figured a way to be safe. Guns have been gone for so long that there's not a lot of information on how to protect themselves from them. Emma knows from some of the old pre-Collective movies that there are special vests, but they haven't figured out how to make them. Christine says she could replicate them, if they could get their hands on one.

They try several reconnaissance missions under heavy disguises, but asking at the malls and department stores draws only confused looks. No one has ever heard of such a fabric or such a vest. It makes sense, Emma thinks, since no one has any firearms, either.

But the MR-D4Rs do.

"I don't know about this," Christine says, looking around them in the dark.

"You said it yourself, the Underbright is filled with criminals," Emma says, brandishing the flashlight.

Bells holds his hand up at the light, squinting. "I mean, if Jess says we'll find one here..."

"Well, it's not an exact science but I did lead us down here so..." Jess shrugs, leading the way.

"I'm great at haggling! I got this. Whoever we're dealing with is going to deal with me!" Abby says, walking behind Jess.

Christine's loaded several datachips with credits; they weren't sure how much they would need, so there's a different amount on each card. Bells also has a backpack filled with fresh vegetables, courtesy of a Hopestar Grassroots contact.

Emma can hear other people in the abandoned tunnels and a few times she can see people disappearing into the shadows from the lit platforms. Before they were trying to avoid others; now Jess is leading them directly toward one of the bustling platforms where people have set up shops in a riot of color and chaos. They weave around the crowds and the stalls and tents filled with wares, trying to blend in. Despite carefully choosing their and disguises, Emma still feels as if they're drawing suspicious looks from everyone.

"Stick together," Christine says.

Abby zooms off toward a stall at the end.

"That's not it. Abby!" Jess calls after her, and then sighs. She turns around, her shoulders slumped, and gestures to the rest of them to follow her. "I think we're here." Jess jerks her head at a tent. "I'm going after Abby. I'll meet you back here."

Emma steps inside the shop warily; the walls are made from pieces of once-colorful fabric, stitched together in a motley way. Piles of clothes, mannequins, and fabrics clutter the store. Everything looks well-made. Emma drags her hand down the sleeve of a coat.

"Hello," says a soft voice. "Can I help you?"

A reedy-looking man looks at them and taps his fingers together.

"Hi," Brendan says. "We are in need of a vest."

"What kind of vest? Something bespoke, perhaps?"

There's a commotion outside; voices scream and yell.

Emma pops out of the tent and looks around. People scurry down a ladder into the Underbright from an open grate, as if they're running away from something.

"That's all right; you're safe down here," an old man in the stall next to her mutters.

"Safe from what?" Emma asks.

"Superheroes," the man says, going back to his book without looking up.

The light from the grate disappears as the last person closes it, but Emma can still hear the terrified people on the street.

Bells, Brendan, and Christine exit the clothes tent. Brendan wears a puffy vest and looks very proud of himself.

"What is it?" Bells asks.

"There's a battle going on right above us," Emma says.

"What?" Jess says, holding hands with a sheepish-looking Abby.

"Let's go!" Emma's already striding toward the wall and the ladder.

"Emma, we're not prepared," Christine says.

Bells tilts his head. "I thought you wanted to wait to do a confrontation once the supersuits are done and the others get here?"

"We can't pass up this opportunity!" Emma says, already pulling herself up. It's time for action! She's been itching for this. And even if they can't take on Starscream, they can at least do some reconnaissance and see what's going on. Besides, Farha promised she would give them interview time.

That's if you got your act together, a small voice says inside her head.

Too late. Emma's already pushing the grate open.

From her hiding place under the street, Emma can see people run off in every direction and hear people screaming.

"Someone get the Authorities!"

"Where did Starscream go? He's the hero! He's supposed to protect us!"

Emma wedges herself forward, pushes the heavy sewer cover aside, grips the edge of the opening, and pulls herself up through up onto the street.

Emma dusts herself off, standing up tall, trying to see through the chaos. People are screaming and running away, running past her, shrieking in terror, but from *what*?

Emma pushes forward, and she can hear her friends right behind her as they press through the street. No one is paying the fugitives any attention, they're all trying to get away from—

Captain Orion stands before them, a grin spreading on her face. Her eyes gleam as she steps forward, her ragged cape fluttering in the wind. Her hair, once featured in many shampoo and styling commercials as thick and luscious and flowing, is now tangled and matted. She's not doing anything other than standing ominously on the street and gleefully watching people scatter.

Bells is frozen. He's still shifted, wearing another boy's face, and Emma can see that he's thinking: if he shifts now, he'll reveal his identity as Bells and make himself a target. They don't know what Orion wants.

"That's right, run, you fools," Orion declares. "I'll show you. I'll show everyone!" She raises her hands, throwing lightning into the air, and then turns around and blasts at the people on the street.

"Should we go back into the Underbright?" Christine asks.

"No, Orion would see us," Emma says. "And then all those other people would be in danger."

"This way!" Jess says, turning left and running down a side street. "This way to safety!"

"It's a dead end, Jess!" Emma can barely see the end of the street. Maybe there's something she doesn't know, something Jess' power is telling her, maybe they can just hide there. Christine is right behind her, and Emma takes Bells' hand, pulling him forward into the alley right behind Jess.

"Orion is as good as a meta-human as any to take on." Abby stops where she stands. She opens her backpack. "My new mecha-suit isn't complete, but I know it's got enough power to give her a good fight."

"Do you see cameradrones? No one is watching. No one is going to know what happened here. What we have to do is get out alive!" Jess reaches for the backpack, but Abby shakes her head.

Abby presses a button, and a chest plate and gauntlets clank and unfold. She puts them on and runs away, shouting loudly. "Hey! Orion! You fake excuse of a hero. Come at me!"

"What the—"

"Abby, no—"

Orion turns around from observing the chaos. She grins, slow and wide. "Abby Jones. I thought you were dead."

Orion cracks her knuckles, walking forward. "Well. A good thing you're not, because I could use another one to power me up. Claudia told me your powers were nullified, but you would still be of *much* use to me." Orion turns her head and raises her eyebrows.

"Tran," Orion says suddenly, her eyes taking on a wicked gleam. "I know you." She stalks forward, advancing on all of them, who are now trapped at the end of the alleyway with nowhere to go.

Jess' eyes go wide and she reaches for her scar where she was shot with Orion's lightning.

Orion raises her hands, fingers sparkling with electricity. "You ruined my plans back in Nevada. You too, baby Tran." Orion raises her eyebrows at Christine. "You're the most pathetic attempt at being a villain I've ever seen. I'm going to enjoy putting you out of your misery." She looks at Bells. "You. I don't know who you are."

Orion turns to Emma and squints. "And you threw a table at me, if I recall."

"I'd throw it again!" Emma snaps.

Orion laughs now. "Oh honey, look around. You've got nowhere to go."

Emma's throat goes dry. There's nowhere to run, nowhere to go. There's just this corridor and her and her friends with their backs to the wall.

Abby's eyes are wide with fear. "You, you…" she raises her hands and the gauntlets, closes her eyes.

Nothing happens.

Orion laughs. "Built yourself another suit, huh? Oh, please. Give up. You're nothing without your powers."

She punches Abby right in the chest. There's a sickening *crunch* as the metal is crushed, and Abby lets out a cry of pain as she flies backward.

"Abby!" Jess cradles her head and looks up at Orion. "Stop, please!"

Christine is shaking. "Look, why are you doing this? You clearly just need some food and a good rest," she pleads.

Orion laughs, high and shrill. She's a shadow of her former self, or maybe, Emma thinks, this is who she's always been: power-hungry and desperate and willing to hurt to get what she wants. For the first time Emma thinks about Michael's offer. If she had powers, if she was strong like her friends, they could get out of this situation. Abby's twitching, and Emma wonders if she's thinking the same thing about her own powers.

Orion raises her hands, and lightning crackles between her fingers. "I'm going to enjoy this," she says. "It's your fault. I was the most respected hero of the Collective," she sniffs. "I had a fan club and people screaming my name and worshipping me, and now I'm nothing. Reduced to a laughingstock. I'm not even a villain anymore, no one ever talks about *me* on the news. I didn't even make a complete round on the news cycle as Orion the villain. They couldn't even afford me that?" She shakes her head. "I'm going to get it all back, and you're all going to pay." She glances at Jess, at the scar on her neck. "I should have killed you when I had the chance. And now I'm going to kill all of you right here."

Orion cocks her head. The lightning crackles and bursts, and she watches them quiver, as though she's enjoying teasing them.

There's a rush of wind and a flash of color from above and a loud *crack* as Orion is punched in the face.

"Claudia?" Jess' voice quavers.

Claudia tosses her hair over her shoulder and looks at the straggling crowd still in the street, who stop, stunned. A few people clap, and several people start to cheer.

"Who is that? Is that Echo?"

"Thank you! She was so terrifying!"

"My name is Powerstorm," Claudia says, smiling at the crowd outside the alley. "And I am here to rescue you."

A single cameradrone flies out and starts recording.

The wind picks up, blowing Claudia's hair. Her hair and her cape flutter heroically in the wind, both of them raven dark and shiny. Claudia's hair is fluttering in elaborate waves, loose and flowing in the wind. Did Powerstorm have a cape? Emma doesn't remember exactly, but she doesn't think so. No, Emma remembers, her uniform echoed Captain Orion's colors, like a weak shadow. Where Orion's was stark white with blue detailing and a blue cape, Powerstorm's was gray and mottled blue, apparently to assemble a storm. Her hair was curled then, set in large ringlets that would fall about her face, reminiscent of Orion's own abundant blonde curls. Wasn't Claudia blonde, too, back then? They were going for a coordinated look when they started fighting crime together.

Claudia's new outfit is black, with gold striations. The bold look is completely stripped of any echoes of Orion but has no less sense of grandeur. It's just as gaudy, as if announcing: HELLO, I AM HERE. LOOK AT ME.

Claudia picks up Orion's twitching figure and flies with her to the crowd and drops her onto the street.

"Claudia, why—"

"Shut up," Claudia says, stepping on Orion's chest. "Your reign of terror is over."

And then she *waves*.

The applause is thundering.

"A real hero!"

"Finally!"

The chants start to merge, and then begin to take rhythm. "Powerstorm! Powerstorm! Powerstorm!"

Emma can see Jess where she's frozen with her mouth open. Myriad emotions flicker across her face: hurt, relief, confusion, betrayal, all forming and then disappearing as if Jess is struggling with what to feel, how to feel.

"Is that Claudia?" Bells asks from behind her, his voice aghast.

"The one and only," Emma mutters. "Powerstorm here to save the day." She'd been a fan, when the Heroes' League of Heroes topped Emma's list of people to obsess over. She remembers the stats: Powerstorm, youngest hero inducted into the League—until Chameleon, of course—slated to follow Orion in her footsteps as one of the most powerful meta-humans. She was Crystal Spring's hero in the Nevada region for a while and Emma wondered why she didn't move to a bigger city. Then again, most of the large cities already had their share of heroes, so she was probably biding her time.

Jess is frozen still, shell-shocked.

"Come on, Jess, we have to go!" Emma grabs her hand and pushes forward now that the exit is clear. They can head back to the Underbright and where the car is parked now.

"I went here because I knew this was the way to get help but I didn't, I didn't know she'd be the answer," Jess mumbles. "Should we, should we say hi? I mean, she knows it's us, right, she knows we're right here—" she looks at her brother, who's standing with his mouth wide open.

Emma glances back at where Claudia—Powerstorm—is surrounded by well-wishers and admirers. The camera drones have turned their sights on her. They could have been hurt or taken by Orion for her experiments. So, Claudia did save them. But why?

Claudia tosses her hair back, striking a pose as people wave their DEDs erratically, taking pictures. A few people are already asking to take pictures with her.

"I don't think now is a good time," Bells says, raising his eyebrows. "Authorities would be on their way, anyhow. We gotta get out of here."

"We should say thank you?" Jess blinks, confused. "I— she's my sister!"

"Come on," Emma says, taking Jess' hand and leading her out of the crowd. The Authorities are already buzzing around, heading right for Claudia and the crowd.

Emma halts them, ducks into an alcove, and watches the crowd avidly. People scatter with the onset of the gray-suited officials, and then, just as they enter the thick of the crowd, Powerstorm, fist held high, cape flapping majestically, shoots into the air.

"Now that's a real hero," a man says, watching her ascend.

"Yeah, right," Emma mutters under her breath.

"But Clau—"

The Authorities have tantalum cuffs on Orion and are leading her toward an unmarked van as she struggles.

"You can't take me!" Orion cries out. "You don't know what they'll do! Please!"

Emma watches, wondering what Orion is afraid of, but she can't wait for the Authorities to find them next. She hustles her friends along the street and finds the hidden entrance to the Underbright. There's no time to linger.

Jess paces at Christine's. "We should reach out to her. To join the Resistance."

Bells raises his eyebrows so high they almost disappear into his hair. "Haven't you forgotten who gave you that scar?"

"Orion did," Jess says petulantly.

"Yeah, and who was helping Orion? Who attacked us at the base outside of Andover?"

Jess waves her hands dismissively. "Claudia was just following Orion's orders."

"She tried to get *you* to join her!" Emma remembers this story well.

"Exactly. You know she, you know, didn't want to hurt us."

"Oh, you know, aside from taking my powers away," Abby bites out sarcastically.

Jess stops where she stands, and an awkward silence fills the air. "I didn't mean— I wasn't thinking—"

"That's right, you weren't thinking," Abby says coldly, getting up. She brushes past Jess roughly, shouldering her as she passes by.

The door slams shut.

"I just— you know that I know what Claudia did to Abby was wrong, so wrong." Jess says, looking beseechingly at Emma and Bells.

"Yeah, I don't know that Abby knows that—"

"She does know!" Jess cries out in frustration. "Who's been behind her every step of the way as she's been making herself sick trying to get her powers back? Who's been supporting her through all the weird— I don't even know what's going on with her right now, but I know it isn't normal!"

"It's just stress," Emma says. "We're all stressed."

"Okay," Jess says, seemingly mollified. "I just— you know where I'm coming from, right? Claudia's smart. She has to be doing this for a reason. I just want to know why."

Brendan coughs. "I think I may have a way."

"I'm sorry, you did *what*?" Jess' eyes blaze with anger.

"Went back to our old house before we left Nevada last year," Brendan says sheepishly.

"You mean the house that was under surveillance?" Bells asks.

"I wanted to see if she'd go back, you know." Brendan shrugs. "It's what I would do. Anyway, I went through the whole house, all the hiding places, and found this."

Brendan holds up a small, slim device; it looks awfully similar to the pre-Collective datachip that was mailed to them at the Villain's

Guild. He takes a deep breath. "I haven't shared it yet because we weren't in New Bright City and it wouldn't have mattered, but I feel like this is a good time as any." He's already got the primitive machine booted up; he plugs the device in. It looks as though there's only one file on the drive.

"Well?" Emma asks.

Brendan bites his lip, glancing at Jess. "Okay. But maybe you all should sit."

It's a shoddy, pixelated video that looks strangely flat on the screen. Emma is about to ask what kind of weird joke this is and why Jess would go to the trouble to record this video when she realizes it's not Jess.

It's Claudia.

Without the glamorous makeup and dramatic hairstyle, she looks like Jess: same brown skin, wide nose, and dark eyes. She looks behind her, then turns to face the camera. Her image seems small; her two-dimensional form wrings her hands. "So I have no idea if you're going to receive this message or not, but if you aren't, I might be next. I think— I think Cindy is— she's actually gone and did it, and I don't— I'm not about to kill anyone. And if I don't leave, I'm next."

Jess has gone unnaturally still; her gaze is focused on her sister.

Claudia sighs and looks up. "Jess, Brendan, Sidekick Squad, I still can't believe that's what you named yourselves, seriously, and you do need to hide your digital footprint better. At least you stopped transmitting data from our old house; you know anyone with the genetic keycode, people like me, could still access that."

Claudia shrugs. "You're just lucky I think it's in your best interest that Cindy doesn't know where you are or what you're up to. But, here goes. Sidekick Squad, you're my only hope."

Jess claps her hands to her mouth; a near-hysterical laugh bubbles out of her.

Emma raises her eyebrows. "What just happened?"

Bells snorts. "It's a joke. I think."

Jess waves her hands on. "Is there more?"

Brendan shakes his head. "A little bit, but it's all garbled. I reconstructed it as best I could, but it boils down to coordinates within New Bright City. She's been wanting to meet."

"For how long?"

Brendan shrugs. "It's hard to tell. At any time after we left Nevada, that's when she left this for us. Which means she's been looking for us—"

"To save us and get on our good side," Bells says. "I see what she's playing at."

"Do you think she tracked us to the Rockies?" Emma wonders. "The files—"

"Yeah, they were in the same format," Brendan says. "I mean, I suspected it was her, but now we know for sure."

"Do we trust her?" Christine blinks, looking between Brendan and Jess.

Emma shakes her head. Her first instinct is a hard no. She remembers Claudia well; remembers the way she treated Jess like an afterthought. Jess and Brendan are too easily swayed; they *want* to trust her. Emma understands; Claudia's family. But she's already betrayed them; she could very well do it again.

"Look. Claudia's always been dramatic," Emma says carefully.

"Yeah, this fits well with her." Jess still looks hopeful, though.

"This? It looks rehearsed."

Jess frowns. "Are you sure? She's obviously in the middle of something, sneaking away so Orion doesn't catch her sending this message."

"Right, some of it definitely feels authentic, but this whole bit here—" Bells rewinds the speech, the long bit about the Sidekick Squad being her only hope. "—this bit looks practiced. See how easily it rolls off the tongue. I mean, it's what I would do if I was lying through my teeth and wanted to get my story straight."

"But—"

"I mean, she does genuinely look terrified. Whatever Orion was doing, it scared her. Enough to leave, enough to take a stand."

ALL ATTEMPTS TO AGREE ON a next step with Claudia come to a standstill. They argue for hours, and Jess stubbornly refuses to believe that it's anything but a good idea, while everyone else— even Brendan, however curious—thinks it's a trap.

The next few days are tense; Christine busies herself with making the new supersuits and Brendan helps her. The awkward silence between Abby and Jess grows until it becomes nearly tangible, and everyone else in the house avoids talking about the Claudia situation.

Abby's taken to shutting herself in her workroom for long hours at a time, and, Emma isn't sure, but one time when she woke in the middle of the night, she heard loud, wracked sobs from inside.

Any questions as to whether Abby was okay would be met with stubborn silence or her retreat into the room, so they've all been treading carefully around her.

It's not the best solution, but Emma isn't sure what else to do. The timing of the return of the rest of the Sidekick Squad couldn't be more perfect, and Emma busies herself coordinating their arrival.

BELLS PEERS THROUGH THE BINOCULARS. "They said just behind the bathrooms at the square, right?"

Emma nods, takes the offered binoculars from Bells, and focuses on the bathroom door and the "All Genders" sign on its front. She turns her head slightly, to watch the bushes right next to the bathroom. It's the best spot they were able to come up with: a known location that shouldn't have changed much, a particular patch of concrete next to these bushes. Tanya and Sasha both have been there before, and it's large enough for the vehicle they're teleporting. It's also a good space because there's a supply road right behind it, so it won't be inconspicuous when they drive out of here. They debated with someplace more surreptitious, but the it was unlikely they'd find something better that hadn't changed since Tanya's last visit.

She hands the binoculars back to Bells, watching the shrubbery carefully when it shakes; there's a soft *whoosh* of displaced air and the sound of several somethings hitting the ground.

"Ow. Are you sure these are the right coordinates?"

"Yes, I'm sure!"

"Ugh! Can you guys, like, make sure that you don't poof me right onto the boxes? Those corners hurt!"

"I don't have control over that!"

"I told you to tighten up in a ball!"

"That's not a superhero entrance!"

"I don't know why you insist on posing like that; no one's here to see, and you always end up toppling over anyway."

"What if someone were to see?"

"The whole point of this is that *no one sees,* now get off me—"

"Stop, shut up, I hear someone outside the bushes."

Emma knocks on the van door, grinning. "Hello! What's this I hear about a superhero pose?"

NEW ENERGY TAKES HOLD OF Emma, and she goes back to her plans with renewed vigor. This time she's going to make it right. They get to work right away, with Brendan plotting out when Starscream would appear next, and Jess and Emma pinpointing locations while Sasha and Tanya rest from their long journey. Ricky disappears almost immediately, sheepishly avoiding Christine, but then Emma spots them talking casually in the hallway, going from stiff hellos to conversing about their upcoming mission.

The first task in confronting Starscream and the League is actually looking like a team. Christine's job is to make supersuits for everyone, transforming fabric using the bulletproof vest as a guide. She's already come up with a much more energy-efficient material.

"This is amazing," Ricky's voice says. A bag of chips floats, held by an invisible hand, and a chip floats out of the bag and disappears. "I've been invisible for *twenty minutes.* Do you know how cool that is?"

Bells laughs. "It's pretty brilliant. Christine, what'd you do—"

Christine high-fives Brendan. "So, we've reverse-engineered tantalum—"

"What?" Emma gasps. "I didn't even know you had any!"

Christine beams. "It was challenging, but fun! Anyway, Abby was the one who came up with the compound. I just made it wearable."

"That's amazing, Abby," Emma says.

"Yeah," Jess says, weakly. "You worked really hard—"

"Uh huh," Abby says, rolling her eyes. "Don't ever say I was doing stuff for no point again."

"I never said—"

"Uh huh, but you thought it, you made that face—"

Christine coughs. "Anyway, Emma, do you have any specifications for yours?"

"Me?" Emma blinks. "I don't need one! I don't have super-powers!"

Christine narrows her eyes. "You need one. You're part of the team. Come on, you're the one that said we had to look good."

"I meant you all!" Emma glances around at everyone. "The whole point is to look like a superhero team, someone who could take on a major League hero and win. Jess?"

"Uh," Jess glances at Christine. "Yeah, Emma's the brains here."

"You didn't give me any specifications for your suit either," Christine says, tsking at her.

"I don't really need a suit," Jess says. "My powers aren't very impressive."

Christine glances at everyone, and Emma suddenly feels very self-conscious. "I thought that was the plan? Confront the League as a team? How can we do that if don't have the best tools?"

Bells laughs, falling off the couch, and continues shaking on the floor. "I'm just imagining all of us in matching outfits. It's too much. What are we gonna—"

Christine giggles. "Didn't you guys give yourselves a name?"

"The Sidekick Squad," Emma says. She came up with the name back when having secret meetings in Jess' basement and trying to look for the Resistance was the biggest part of their plans. She doesn't know how she feels about it now that it has grown beyond her and her friends.

"Yes! Matching supersuits!" Brendan says, pumping his fist in the air. "Mine should be super-stealthy and have lots of pockets!"

"I don't think I want mine to be shiny this time, although that was cool. I did like the green, but maybe more rainbow-y? Or more blue? Add some purples? Ohhh, what if I had all the colors?" Bells muses, drifting off into a daydream about the colors of his suit.

"Christine, do you have fabric that would breathe well under my new mecha-suit?"

"You're still building a new one? We don't have access to any more fuel, though!" Jess looks shocked.

"Not yet," Abby says, raising her eyebrows.

The room goes quiet. Emma doesn't know what to say, after all. Jess has been so worried, and Emma is more than a little concerned. She remembers Abby's feverish energy when she was running for student body president and the endless drills for the volleyball championships, that constant focus. But this feels different.

"We already went through this; trying to use your powers makes you sick," Jess says. "I don't want you to get hurt again."

Abby shakes her head. "Who said I'm going to use my powers for this new mecha-suit? Look, I'm building one that'll run with—"

"Ooh, a nuclear reactor?" Brendan says, his eyes lighting up.

"No," Abby says. "But there are other alternatives, and I don't have to fly. I mean, just change the capabilities, and I'd have armor and could hold my own against Starscream, for example, or withstand one of those blasts—"

"Okay," Christine says, taking notes.

Jess is looking worried again, and Emma doesn't want to start another conversation about this, so she changes the subject, diving right back into the plan. "All right, we need to find out when there will be another staged battle. Bells, how did it work? When you were with the League? They gave you assignments—"

"There would be a dead drop with a data chip, so it'd be random, keyed to Starscream and his usual route. We can't know for sure unless we hack his DED directly," Bells says.

"No, no, I've got an algorithm down," Brendan cuts in. "We can predict when and where they'll strike next. I can even cross-reference the villains that he's been 'fighting' and make sure we go up against someone we can handle." Brendan scrunches up his face before scooting backward and out the door. "I'm gonna go check!"

"Good, because we might have to fight both of them at once if they're really confused." Emma nods. "Okay, I'm here as getaway driver, and Sasha and Tanya, once they're rested up can help move you away from blasts. Ricky, you attack while invisible. Christine, you can use your powers to restrain them while we explain, right?"

"Yup," Christine says. "But you have to tell me exactly when. I've only got about a five-minute window here and then I'm done for the day."

Bells spins the chair he's sitting in and crosses his legs. "So last time it was Dynamite, then Fireheart, and then Jetstream. Who do you think would be the easiest to persuade to join the Resistance?"

"Hmm," Emma thinks. "Dynamite is the main villain here in the east. And remember, he doesn't care about our goals. He's the

League's lapdog, and he actually might try to hurt people. What about Swift Emblem and Aerodraft?"

"Oh, we've been trying to contact them for forever," Jess says. "My mom said Swift Emblem would be open to it, but they're not good at confrontation. Getting them to leave their comfortable spot where the League takes care of them would be hard."

"Isn't Aerodraft missing? We haven't heard from her in a while."

Emma shakes her head. There's so much to consider. Since New Bright City is the capital of the Collective, it's always swarming with Authorities. It would be only moments before they'd be surrounded. The escape plan is crucial. This would be about making a big, splashy statement. And then finding a way to chat with the villain and maybe even Starscream. If they got Starscream, then they'd have most of the top-listed heroes on their side.

"It's done; it's done!" Brendan says, running into the living room and promptly tripping over his own feet. The tablet he's carrying flies out of his hands and skids onto the rug, thumping. "Er. Maybe not."

Abby picks up the tablet and fiddles with the projections. She whistles, handing it to Brendan. "Can't believe you haven't broken all your tech yet."

"I make all mine to be durable! I know that I tend to drop stuff." Brendan grins, flicking his fingers at the tablet.

"When can we expect to see Starscream next?" Jess asks.

"Every eight days we have a high-profile crime stop: a bank robbery, a car chase, something like that. Then every three days we have a smaller profile event, like boosting public morale—"

"Does he rescue cats?" Bells asks.

"About once a month I've logged a domestic cat rescue," Brendan says. "This is based on data from the last ten years." He presses the tablet, and a new projection flits into the air, a neatly organized spreadsheet.

Christine reads the data. "So we can expect another high-profile event in two days. Probably on the south side of the city."

Brendan nods. "They try not to do an event in the same area twice, keep the pattern going. It's actually very consistent." He presses the tablet again, and it turns into a map. "This is where we need to be tomorrow."

EMMA TUGS AT THE FORMFITTING supersuit. It feels weird, especially because it's the same fabric Christine and Abby made to help focus meta-abilities. *Is it wasteful that she's wearing it?*

She taps the steering wheel; Bells is sitting next to her, ready to shift into Lysander and approach the scene.

Starscream hasn't been spotted yet. They're across the street from a jewelry store and arrived just in time: Echo is stealing jewels; gleaming necklaces bounce at his neck as he laughs and sweeps jewelry into his bag.

"I kinda want to jump in and stop this robbery," Bells says, shaking his head.

"Just wait," Emma says. "Test, test, this is Mastermind, over."

"Compass here."

"And Abby!"

"Do we have to do this?"

"Sound off," Emma repeats.

"Here and There are here— c'mon, I love our code names but seriously, roll call?"

"Invisible Boy— okay, can we change this? Can I be Invisible *Man*?"

"Crinoline here. Invisible Boy is Invisible Boy because that's what you requested when—"

"Okay, stop right there!" Ricky yelps.

"Starscream still isn't here yet," Emma says. "Isn't that weird?"

Bells nods. "Yeah. Usually the League likes to have someone on the scene immediately. And look, there are already cameradrones."

Echo cackles, holding two bags full of jewelry and dashing into the street with two cameradrones recording him.

People gasp, backing up.

"Where's Starscream?" Tanya asks. "This plan doesn't really work if we don't have a staged battle to stop."

"Uh—" Emma thinks quickly. "Maybe he isn't going to show up. Maybe Echo is actually robbing this store and—"

"YES! Invisible Boy to the scene! Tanya! Teleport me!"

"You're fifty feet away. You can walk."

"But the element of surprise!"

"Go ahead," Emma says.

Echo stops halfway down the street, wincing in pain. "What? Who's there?"

Christine appears next to him as Tanya snaps her fingers. She gestures at Echo's bags, unraveling them with her power. All the jewelry clatters onto the street.

Echo's mouth falls open. "What? Who are you? This isn't in the—"

"In the what?" Christine asks, grinning.

Echo gulps, looking at the cameradrone. "You cannot stop me! I am Echo!" He doubles over, grabbing his stomach. "Ow!"

He glances up, looking from Christine to the other people on the street. "Is this a test?"

"Yup! And you're failing!" Christine waves her hand.

Echo's sleeves stitch themselves to his torso, and his pants legs stitch themselves together. He falls over. "What even is— wait, I know you! You're that second-rate villain that's always going around after—"

His sleeve unravels and reforms around his mouth, muffling him.

"Okay, cue Lysander," Emma says. "Everyone else, stay put. Ricky, you can stop, Christine's got him trapped already."

Bells steps out of the car, adjusts his bowtie, and pats his coiffed hair. People seem to relax after spotting him.

"Good evening," Bells says in Wilton's oily tone.

One of the cameradrones points toward him.

Emma exhales. *Okay. Step one. Now to—*

Something flashes in the sky. Lightning? The sky was clear; there shouldn't be any chance of a storm.

Lightning flashes again, and Emma sees a flash of red and another crackle of white-hot light. The whole street echoes with the booming sound of someone landing right in front of Echo.

"You're not getting away, Echo!" booms a deep voice. It's familiar, but Emma can't place it.

Christine freezes. "What— who are you?"

The drones immediately start buzzing around the new meta-human.

The man stands tall; he's wearing a bright red supersuit with a flowing gold cape and a red facemask and is *definitely* not Starscream. "My name is Vindication." He punches the ground;

his fists glow red with energy. The asphalt cracks and melts, turning into a puddle.

"Hey!" Echo says, twitching as he sinks into the melted asphalt.

Vindication turns his gaze on Christine, who takes a step back.

A cold chill runs down Emma's spine; whoever this is, the look on his face is pure venom. *Is he Starscream's replacement? Why does he look so angry?*

"You," he says, advancing on Christine. "You've been a thorn in my side." He opens his palm; lightning crackles in his fingers.

Sasha and Tanya pop into the car and then Ricky. They need to leave *now.* Emma waves frantically at Sasha. "Get Christine!"

"I'm trying!" Sasha says, scrunching her face.

"Get out of there!" Emma shouts into the radio. Christine's five minutes are up, she can't—

Christine pops into the car just as they see lightning race down the street, right to where Christine was standing.

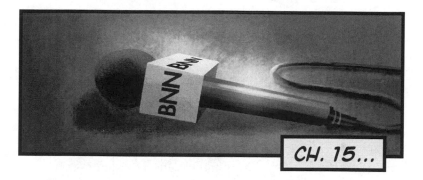

"That was close." Christine exhales. "What about Bells?"

"He thinks, he thinks Bells is Lysander," Emma says weakly. "It would be suspicious if he just disappeared too."

Vindication roars, shaking his fist at the sky. "You— you're early," he says, noticing Bells for the first time.

Bells nods, playing along. "I thought it would be prudent to be here," he says.

"Fine, let's do it now," Vindication says, gruffly. He kicks at the still-struggling Echo, who is stuck in the pavement. "How do I look? Hair?"

"Perfect," Bells says, snapping his fingers. The cameradrones point toward them.

"You can edit out the part with that kid," Vindication says. "Meddling pest."

Emma watches, gripping the wheel tightly. *Who is this guy?*

"Of course," Bells says, bowing his head a little.

"You're laying it on a little thick," Emma whispers over the radio. "Lysander doesn't bow!"

Bells wobbles and does a curtsey.

"Are you okay there, Wilton?" Vindication asks, narrowing his eyes.

"Never better. Shall we?"

Vindication coughs and turns toward the camera. "Greetings, people of the North American Collective. I am Vindication, the newest member of the Heroes' League of Heroes, and I have a special message for you tonight. Anyone who would oppose the League and their mission is against the Collective itself. And rest assured, this evil will be stopped." He gives the camera one final look of smug satisfaction before flying into the sky with his cape fluttering dramatically.

The people on the street whoop and applaud.

"Is it just me or were Vindication's powers…"

"Exactly like Captain Orion's," Emma says.

"WHERE DID HE COME FROM?"

"Who is he?"

"Those are *definitely* Captain Orion's powers."

Emma paces, tuning out the worried conversation of her friends. "What was Orion saying when the Authorities were taking her away?" she wonders aloud.

"Something about not knowing what they'll do," Jess offers. "She sounded scared."

"What would *Orion* be afraid of? She's the most powerful meta-human in the country," Christine says, worrying a piece of fabric in her hands.

"Well, technically that's not true," Emma says. "If we're going by power rating, that is."

"Huh," Bells says, flopping upside down on the couch with his hair dragging on the floor. "So who is the most powerful in the country?"

"You are," Emma says with a broad grin.

Giggling, Jess elbows Bells playfully. "That's right! Bells had the highest rating when we tested in the Rockies."

Abby crosses her arms. "Well, we don't know anything about this Vindication and how powerful he might be."

"That's true," Emma says, remembering their problem.

Christine flicks the projections above her console. "Well, it looks like the League updated their page. Vindication definitely outranks Orion in power."

Emma shakes her head. *Where have all these new meta-humans come from? They certainly haven't been in training, according to Bells, and all their powers seem awfully like—*

Emma gasps. "The powers," she says. "These new meta-humans in the League, they're *new meta-humans.*"

Christine frowns. "What do you mean?"

"You know how Michael was testing power capabilities back at the Rockies?" Emma asks.

"Yeah, he's a nurse. And a scientist," Jess says.

"He was working on Orion's research and trying to find a way to invoke powers in people," Emma says.

"He what?" Abby's mouth falls open. "I thought we— he was supposed to be helping me! We worked so much together decoding that research, and he never told me what it was for— I just assumed that he was working on reversing the effects of the serum for me!"

"I think he was doing that, but he definitely prioritized this other project," Emma says. "He showed me, back at the base. He was already at human trials. I don't know how far he got; it didn't look like it was going that well." She remembers the sickly way that woman looked, even as she proudly made a ball of light.

"Human trials?" Abby gasps. "Michael said he was *months* away— ugh! I'm going to call him right now. Jess, what's the Port Clarion frequency?" She stalks off, all scarlet curls and fury.

Jess gives the rest of them an apologetic look before following Abby down the hall.

"If Michael only had part of the research and he was working on duplicating it, that means the League's had this tech for a while already," Bells says. "Why haven't they used it before?"

"Maybe they didn't have it before," Emma muses. "Maybe when they made Orion their scapegoat, they found out exactly what she was doing and took her research."

"I thought she was working on power enhancers," Jess says.

Bells shakes his head. "She thought she was. Claudia made her think she was getting stronger when she wasn't. Placebo effect."

Emma waves her hands. "Well, I don't know what exactly power transference entails. In any case, she's in the hands of the League now." She bangs a book on the table; it's not quite the same as the gavel, but it still makes a nice, commanding sound. "Let's get back to the plan. Brendan, when do you think we would see Starscream or Vindication—"

Jess walks back into the living room, wringing her hands.

"What is it? What's wrong?" Bells asks. "Is everyone okay?"

"Oh yeah," Jess says. "But they said the Port Clarion is compromised."

Christine's mouth falls open. "I thought that was where they were going to rebuild the headquarters after the destruction of the Rockies base!"

"Where are they going now?" Tanya asks.

Jess takes a deep breath. "Deirdre and all the meta-humans, they're all coming here."

"DON'T WORRY, KIDS. WE'LL HANDLE it from here on out," Deirdre says, her hands on her hips as she oversees people unloading luggage and equipment into Christine's home.

It's chaos: unpacking and commands and all the meta-humans from the Villain's Guild bustling about.

"Plasmaman just found a spider and asked me if I had a cup and a piece of paper," Christine whispers to Emma.

"Sounds like Cass," Emma says. "Did he ask you to trap the spider?"

"Yeah, he wouldn't go near it." Christina shakes her head. "One of the most terrifying villains in the Collective is here in my house and afraid of spiders. I mean, I know he's not a real villain, but…"

"I get it, though. Spiders do that leg thing," Emma says, wiggling her fingers and laughing.

Deirdre has found a chair to stand on. "Most excellent. We'll use this as the communications annex."

Cass is barely visible over a huge box, wobbling down the hallway and tracking mud everywhere. "Be careful! Those are antique rugs," Christine says.

Every inch of Christine's expansive home has been taken over by the thirty-seven odd meta-humans who have gathered inside: the remnants of the Villain's Guild and what Emma once thought would be the driving force of the Resistance. She's not sure what it is now. She heaves, setting the last box in one of the spare bedrooms.

"Perfect, thanks," Michael says, dusting his hands off and smiling at her. "It's good to see you again, Emma."

"Yeah," Emma says. "Glad you're all here safe." That's true, at least. Maybe *more* true for the Trans and Abby's mom. She's not sure how she feels about all the people who kept her out of plans in the Rockies. But this time she's not going to stand for it.

"The Resistance is looking good these days," he says, setting up his computer console.

"Oh, you're part of the Resistance now?" Emma cocks an eyebrow.

"Of course, we are," Michael says, chuckling. "We're fighting back against the League!"

"Hey, you know your research that you were doing with invoking powers?" Emma asks.

Michael's face falls, and he looks at the floor with an ashen, guilty look. "Ah. Yes. That. I mean, I had most of Orion's notes, and I didn't know what the consequences. I was swept away by the possibilities! You can't— I'm sorry if I made you think I could—"

Emma holds up her hands. "Wait, what?"

Michael sits on one of his boxes and buries his face in his hands.

Cold horror sweeps over Emma. "What happened? Is everyone okay? Uh— Nina?" Emma doesn't know how many other people Michael had in his trials.

"She's fine. I realized why it wasn't going to work with the methods I was using; that's why everyone was getting sick." Michael sighs.

"So you stopped the treatment and everyone's better?" Emma asks.

"Yeah. They don't have powers anymore either, that's for sure," Michael says.

"Huh." Emma sits down next to Michael, thinking about all the new meta-humans on the scene. If the League is behind their powers, they must have used this same research. "Do you think there's a way to make it work?"

Michael gives her a grim smile and doesn't answer the question. "I was going about it all wrong, but I'm glad I did."

Emma raises her eyebrow. "You're glad you messed up and did the experiment wrong?"

Michael laughs, a mirthless, hollow sound. "If I had just decoded everything from the start and tried to replicate everything— I—" he shakes his head. "It's awful. I can't believe what it takes. I don't even want to tell you. It's so gross."

"Well, now you can't *not* tell me," Emma says.

Deirdre's grating voice echoes from the living room. "Resistance meeting!"

Michael sighs and gives Emma a small smile. "Back to work, eh?"

"THE FIRST PLAN OF ACTION is direct confrontation, right in the middle of Starscream's next planned battle with Icebolt." Deirdre sets down her megaphone to give Brendan a smile. "Thank you, Brendan, for this handy algorithm." She turns to the crowd with an eager smile. "Now, it's key that we are recorded. Once we have Starscream and Fireheart apprehended, we'll redirect the cameras, where Chameleon as Wilton Lysander will explain to the public the truth."

The room echoes with applause.

"Genius!"

"Fantastic!"

"That was my idea!" Emma gasps, elbowing Bells next to her. "Did you hear that? She's using my idea!"

"Yeah! Isn't it great? I finally got her to listen," Bells says, grinning at her. "Now we can move forward with the plan. That's what you wanted, right? For all of us to take action?"

Emma falters. "Well, yes. She didn't give me any credit though."

Bells frowns. "Yeah, Deirdre is like that."

Emma clenches her fists. "I'm not even going to ask if I can go. I'm just gonna do it."

EMMA PARKS THE CAR, IDLING in an alleyway in clear view of the town square. "Hey, Mastermind here. Over?"

Static crackles; most of her friends are out of range. Abby, Sasha, Tanya, and Ricky are off with Tree Frog and Arête in Shinewright, another Hopestar town, where they're hoping to interfere with a battle between Sublimate and Swift Emblem. Emma looks for any sight of Jess, her mom, or Bells.

She has to admit, Deirdre's simultaneous three-city battle interference is actually pretty cool, even if it is based on Emma's plan.

"The Heinous Chameleon, reading you loud and clear, over." Bells turns and gives her a little wave as he dismounts from his motorcycle. He glances around the empty street, and then his dreadlocks melt into coiffed hair, his face elongates, and his leather-look jacket transforms into a glimmering, sparkling suit. "Anyone see you leave Christine's?"

"Nope," Emma says proudly.

She watches Bells leave the side street and enter the square; it's crowded already with people and a news crew. This must be a big battle; there are multiple drones buzzing around and also camera people hefting large cams for broadcasting live in high definition. Farha Rao is looking furtively over her shoulder, pretending to adjust the pin in her headscarf. She spots Bells and gives him a nod of acknowledgment.

Down the street, Starscream and Icebolt are trading blows; Emma can hear the echo of Starscream's shrill energy bursts, and she can see slivers of ice slicing through the air. The camera people follow their moves diligently; drones catch multiple angles as another follows Farha as she narrates. Emma looks through the binoculars and squints as she studies Icebolt's face. He definitely is pulling his punches as the villain, stopping every few minutes to hurl a practiced quip at Starscream.

A shadow falls from above, and Emma grins. She always loved seeing Jess' mom in action.

Li Hua lands fist-first, punching the street, and the asphalt buckles and shatters as she stands up and marches forward.

"Farha Rao on the scene here in New Bright City, where Starscream has apprehended Icebolt in the middle of an alleged robbery. Smasher, retired hero from Andover, Nevada has just approached and is walking toward us," Farha announces, gripping her microphone tightly.

Li Hua strides down the street in her supersuit with regal strength in every step as she approaches the center of the square.

Emma's not annoyed at how well it's going; she's not. It's not as though they had an established hero like Smasher with them; they couldn't have pulled off this plan.

Bells coughs, stepping toward Farha.

"What an honor! New Bright City, I'm being joined tonight by one of the most famous reporters in all the Collective! Wilton Lysander, thank you for joining me tonight."

"Thank *you*," Bells says with a grin. "I'm only too happy to mentor a young reporter. Oh my! What is happening back there? It appears Smasher is fighting our hero Starscream. Why?"

"Icebolt is innocent!" Smasher shouts, standing between the two meta-humans.

"He very clearly just stole from that bank; look at that pile of money!" Starscream says, gesturing from the money to the camera.

"What are you doing?" Icebolt hisses.

"You don't have to do this," Smasher says. "The entire system is a lie!" She picks a streetlamp off the sidewalk with little effort, easily bends the metal device, wraps it around Starscream's arms, and continues to bend it around his mouth so he can't shout any sound blasts.

Icebolt wavers, as if he's unsure what to do. Emma watches avidly, hoping that he'll join the Resistance. *It just takes a little nudge, that's all.*

Li Hua steadies him by the shoulder and nods at him.

Bells strolls over to them, ever so casually. "Smasher, can you tell me what is a lie? Why did you trap Starscream? He clearly was apprehending Icebolt for robbing that bank."

Li Hua levels Icebolt with a look. "You're new, aren't you? Fresh out of Meta-Human Training? Did they promise you everything? And this was the only way to do it?"

"I don't know what you're talking about," Icebolt says. "I'm a villain. I just robbed that bank."

"But why?"

"I'm evil?" Icebolt glances at her and then the camera and gives Farha and the crowd in the square a pleading look. "This is a test, isn't it? I am so sorry! I forgot my backstory! Please let me try again; I'll do better this time!"

Starscream, behind his metal cage, blinks.

A shadow falls upon them, and Mistress Mischief is floating down, her cape fluttering elegantly around her. "I can definitely explain."

"Mistress Mischief!" Farha gasps, gesturing at her crew, but they're already filming.

Mistress Mischief stands next to Smasher and gives her a cordial nod. "It's a familiar script, at least to the villains. You are blissfully unaware, locked into your role as this town's hero, but when the previous villain stopped doing anything for you to stop or fight, they had to bring in someone new." She jerks her head at Icebolt.

Emma notices the slight bit of recognition on Bells' face, but as Lysander he can't break the act. Bells knows who Icebolt is.

"So tell me, Mistress Mischief, aren't you and Smasher sworn enemies? Nemeses?" Bells tilts his head.

"That's what the League would have you believe. We're actually great friends now, but for the longest time, I, as a hero, thought that my job was to protect my city from villains like Mistress Mischief and Master Mischief." Smasher looks squarely in the camera. "But the Mischiefs both were assigned to Andover to wreak havoc in order to provide the public with engaging superhero drama."

"What do you mean, assigned?" Farha asks.

"It is a way of keeping meta-humans in check," Mistress Mischief says. "To keep us occupied with our roles."

Icebolt looks from Smasher to Mistress Mischief and then back to Farha and the camera. "So this isn't a test. Wait, Harris isn't here?"

"Your handler isn't here," Mistress Mischief says gently.

"But he—" Icebolt looks about, frantic.

Farha swoops in, standing next to Icebolt and grinning at the camera. "Do you mean Charles Harris?"

"Y— yes?"

"I'm Farha Rao, reporting live from New Bright City, where Icebolt and Mistress Mischief are talking about their experience as *assigned villains*. Icebolt, how long have you been working with Charles Harris?"

"Uh— three months?" Icebolt speaks into the microphone, blinking awkwardly.

"And can you tell me more about what that entails?"

"Well, uh— sometimes he calls me, but they leave me assignments through a dead drop—"

Jess' voice crackles over the line. "Bells, you gotta wrap it up; Authorities are coming."

Emma starts the engine.

Smasher and Mistress Mischief exchange a glance. "Well, thank you for hearing us out today," Mistress Mischief says, nodding at Farha as she levitates herself away.

"We'll be going now!" Smasher says, picking up Icebolt and Starscream before running off down the street.

"I'm Wilton Lysander, always the first on the scene with breaking news!" Bells winks at the camera. "A shocking reveal! Meta-humans forced to stage fights as heroes and villains for public consumption! Back to you, Farha!" He bobs his head and bows to her before rushing off.

Farha gives him a look that makes Emma chuckle; Bells is being over-the-top again.

Farha turns back to the camera to finish her broadcast. "You might know Charles Harris from the few statements he's given as a representative of the Department of Meta-Human Affairs and also as a faculty member at the Meta-Human Training Center, but here we have it: Icebolt was *assigned* to fight Starscream today."

"Heading to my motorcycle now," Bells mutters over the radio as he runs. "Clear?"

"Head east before ducking into the Underbright entrance off Fourth street," Jess says. "My dad is supposed to pick me up."

"I haven't seen him," Emma says. "He didn't come with us today! Isn't he in Herndan with Deirdre?" Emma spots Jess on the corner waving frantically. She revs the engine, zooms over, and stops in front of her.

"Come on!" Emma flings open the car door just as the gray-clad uniformed figures of the Authorities rush around the corner.

"Stop that broadcast right now!" an official shouts.

Farha Rao draws a circle in the air, gesturing quickly to her crew. "What seemed to be at first a straightforward robbery from the meta-human Icebolt is actually a scripted attempt! What a scandal! You heard it here first from Farha Rao!"

A van pulls right in front of Emma's car, and all of Farha's crew piles in with Farha last. She catches Emma's eye and grins, waving her microphone.

Emma waves back.

"Stop right there! You are under arrest for violating the terms of your broadcast license." They stop short, staring at Jess and Emma. "Wait a minute—"

Jess climbs in and slams the door shut. "Go!"

"My turn," Emma says, gripping the wheel with exhilaration.

She leads them on a merry chase through town and then races into the Unmaintained lands.

"They'll run out of charge in a few miles," Emma says confidently.

"Turn right up ahead!" Jess announces.

Emma swerves to the right, speeding down a cracked street flanked by derelict buildings. She keeps driving, pressing forward, always staying ahead. The Authority vehicles are top-of-the-line, but no cars are made to travel this fast and this far when there's no need to leave the city.

"There aren't any charging stations ahead, and they know that," Jess muses. "Just keep going."

Sure enough, the other vehicles fall back, and it's just Emma and Jess whooping triumphantly in the Unmaintained lands.

CH. 16...

Emma's good mood deflates as soon as they get back to Christine's.

Deirdre stalks toward them before they even open the doors. She purses her lips into a thin line and narrows her eyes.

"Good job, Compass," Deirdre says as Jess hops out of the car.

"Uh, thanks." Jess reaches over and squeezes Emma's hand. "Don't let her get you down," she whispers.

Emma smiles at her in appreciation. "Thanks."

"Your parents want to see you in the communication annex," Deirdre says to Jess.

"Oh, okay—" Jess glances at Emma.

"Go ahead," Emma says.

Jess gives Emma one last look before dashing out of the carport.

Deirdre turns on Emma, straightening her spine as she looks down her nose. "What were you doing on the mission?" Deirdre demands.

"Helping." Emma crosses her arms.

"You could have gotten hurt. You distracted the others from their tasks."

"I was an integral part of the escape," Emma snaps.

"Stay out of it," Deirdre says. "For the last time. Go help Chloe set up a chore wheel or something. This is meta-human business only."

"Meta-human business only," Emma mutters to herself, flicking through the computer console. "The Resistance is *my* business," she says, kicking a file cabinet. She glances at her ear-set radio on the table. It'd be pointless putting it on; everyone is too far away anyway, gone on a mission, carrying out the plans; Emma's plans.

She scrolls aimlessly through the decoded notes from the data recovered from Orion's research, flicking through incoherent ramblings. It seems as though all of this wasn't even decoded; Brendan must have looked at it and just decided they were useless, random phrases floating ominously through the void.

Emma sighs. The past few days have been a whirlwind of activity; every single day, a team goes out to interfere with a battle, often coming back with another meta-human. Among the new recruits are Icebolt and Fireheart; everyone is thrilled, but Emma can't find it in herself to care.

She should be excited, she should be thrilled, but every time she tries to get involved, Deirdre suggests tasks like filing, and she keeps everyone so busy that no one notices that Emma's being left behind. Emma doesn't have the heart to tell them either. Brendan's busy developing new communication tech, Abby's off working on her mecha-suit again, and Bells and Jess are leading most of the teams taking on the League.

It seems as if it's going well until Vindication shows up. He ruins everything; he's too powerful, and somehow the Authorities always aren't too far behind him. He's only appeared a few times, but no one has been able to challenge him. Even Mistress Mischief, who's been able to hold her own against Captain Orion, had to retreat because Vindication would just *keep attacking,* often without regard for the safety of onlookers. It would take several people just to get people out of the way of his lightning blasts.

Vindication is also unpredictable; no algorithm can predict where or when he will appear.

"He can fly; he's got lightning and energy blasts," Emma mutters to herself. "He's stronger than Orion." She sighs. *What is she even doing? Is this pointless, continuing to plan?*

No.

Emma is *Mastermind.*

They need someone who could defeat Vindication. Bells is their strongest, but his abilities aren't geared toward direct attack. They need someone whose destructive power could actually take him out. Even Smasher's super strength and Mistress Mischief's levitation powers aren't a match; they run out of power too soon, and somehow Vindication only appears at the end of a battle when Smasher and Mistress are already tapped out. The few times they've tried to save their strength, Vindication never showed.

Emma paces, thinking about the origin of meta-abilities themselves. They need someone who is powerful *and* has stamina, like someone directly descended from one of the original meta-humans on the SS *Intrepid* who were exposed to the brunt of the X29 flare.

Or maybe one of the originals themselves.

But they're all dead.

Wait! Are they?

There's a knock on the door. Jess leans against it with a concerned look on her face. "Hey, have you been here the whole time?"

"Yeah, I was just looking through the data Claudia sent to us." Emma yawns.

"Cool," Jess says. "Hey, I know we haven't been able to hang out since the missions really started taking off, but you know that everyone appreciates you, right?"

Emma pats Jess' hand and attempts to smile at her. "Thanks."

Jess sits down next to her, squinting at the screen. "Did you find anything interesting?"

Emma shrugs, scrolling through her notes, lingering on Orion's thoughts about destroying the League. "Hey, do you have a copy of your old history textbook somewhere?"

"I think so," Jess says, pulling up her tablet and flicking through it. "Yeah, there's a bunch of books I threw on here so I could study while at the Rockies." She pulls up the history book, chuckling as she hands it to Emma. "I meant to, but never got around to it."

Emma takes the tablet, searching for information on the Intrepid. "You know all the meta-humans your parents have been recruiting? You've been looking for people on the Registry, people Orion was targeting for experiments. What about people who have been forgotten, people incredibly powerful, people who were on the Intrepid?"

Jess tilts her head, taking this information in. "Gravitus is dead. I don't think anyone else on that ship became a hero." She frowns. "One became a professor? And one— oh! Do you remember the Mountain?"

"No?" Emma's never heard the name.

Jess nods, tapping a name on tablet. "That's her: Patricia Southard. She was one of the astronauts on the Intrepid. She was powerful, too, but disappeared after the League was formed. Abby had this comic of the Mountain and Gravitus fighting crime together. They had similar powers, I think."

Emma reads the passage.

During the X29 solar flare, cosmic radiation catalyzed the latent meta-gene in 0.0001% of the population, resulting in the first wave of meta-humans. The types of abilities and the level of intensity varied in genetic expression, and it was clear that this was not a mere fluke in human history, but a milestone in the evolution of the human genome. The meta-gene is still under close study as monitored by the Department of Meta-Human Affairs, but the effects of X29 will be seen for generations to come.

The astronauts on the SS Intrepid during the incident were exposed to a significantly higher amount of cosmic radiation, resulting in four of the crew exhibiting extremely heightened meta-abilities. Lieutenant James Oliphaous, who later became known as Lieutenant Orion, was one of the first A-class heroes in history. His superstrength, speed, flight, and manipulation of heat were among the most powerful abilities ever recorded in both intensity and class level. Dr. Olivia Tham's precognition and fortitude were the driving force behind the success of the formation of the North American Collective in the wake of the disasters. Vance Stackson's ability to manipulate soil, earth, and the force of gravity itself and Dr. Patricia Southard's ability to transform bedrock made them a formidable team as Gravitus and Mountain.

"Tham was a key part in creating the Collective and probably the League itself," Emma mutters. "It would be hard to convince her that the League is wrong. What if she came up with some of the staged battle ideas?"

Jess shrugs. "In any case, she's a retired professor at Port Clarion University. I'm not sure she'd be able to take on Vindication in a fight, though."

"Yeah," Emma agrees. "They'd be like, over a hundred years old, all of them, if they went through X29 as adults."

"You still think Southard would be a good idea?"

"Hey, my abuela Claudia can totally handle herself," Emma says. "I think Southard is a *great* idea." She scans the rest of the page and does a quick search through the book, but Southard's name never comes up again. "That's all it says about her. What happened?"

"The League did," Jess says. "I mean, the whole fight between Lieutenant Orion and Gravitus was about the formation of the League and the purpose of it. I'm guessing Mountain wanted to stay out of it. There aren't any mentions of her aside from that one old comic; it's like she disappeared."

Emma snaps her fingers. "That's it. We need to get her."

"Absolutely not," Deirdre says. "Look, it's great that you found this information, but no one has heard from Southard in over fifty years."

"Right, so not even the League remembers her or cares," Emma says. "But if we got her on our side, told her about the League— I mean, she was there when it formed! She could tell us all sorts of inside information."

"It would be a pointless mission," Deirdre says. "We do not have the time or resources to devote to looking for a woman who doesn't want to be found."

"I could start."

"You do not have the authority to lead any missions," Deirdre sniffs dismissively, handing her a datachip. "Now these are reports that need to be sorted."

EMMA IS DONE. SHE'S DONE playing nice, done asking for permission, and done with people judging her value. She knows what she's worth and she's going to prove it. She throws the duffel bag of clothes into the car and double-checks her provisions: the solar panel for the car, protein packs, and other dried foods. She's ready. They don't need her here. She's better off going and getting information, being useful in the ways she knows she can be.

Instead of doing Deirdre's filing, Emma put on a disguise and headed right to the New Bright City Library, where she dove into research about Patricia Southard. She found archives about the crew of the *Intrepid* that said Southard was born in Havenstown in pre-Collective Canada. The North, now. With the map she and Bells found on their trip, Emma pinpointed exactly where it is. It should only take her a few days to get there. She also found a number of unexplained incidents through the years that sound exactly like Southard's powers. Three years ago, a man fell through an icy lake, but a column of earth rose up under him, carrying him to safety. Another family was rescued on the road when a mudslide mysteriously moved itself out of the way so they could pass through. It's clear that Southard is still in that area, hiding somewhere.

Emma shuts the trunk.

I'm not running away, she tells herself.

Footsteps sound behind her.

"Emma," Bells says softly. In the soft light of the tunnel, the worried set of his jaw almost seems to speak for him.

Emma sighs. She should have known he would put the pieces together and figure out she was leaving. She should have been more secretive; but Bells knows her, knows her patterns; he would have noticed something was wrong the minute he spotted missing food provisions.

"Where are we going?" he asks, all casual.

"We aren't going anywhere," Emma says.

"I know you've got a plan." Bells steps forward. "And now you've all packed up and you're raring to go. I'm ready, whatever it is."

Emma shuts the trunk, and it clicks with a resolute finality.

"The Resistance needs you here," she says, biting her lip to keep it from wobbling. Her voice quavers and, if she doesn't finish this and finish this fast, she's going to cry. "You're important to the plan. It's started already, people are questioning the League. You, you need to stay."

"What?"

"I need to go." The words seem to grow in the air as she speaks, getting heavier and heavier, as if they're tangible.

"Emma, you don't have to go alone," Bells says. "Here, just let me go get Jess and—"

"No!" Emma snaps, louder than she means to, but it feels good to say *no.* After all this time doing what other people want, going along with the plan because it's good for the Resistance, she's tired.

"Em—"

The nickname irritates her, and Emma tosses her bag into the car, slamming it shut.

"No. I don't want you to come with me, I don't want Jess or Abby or Brendan or Christine or *anyone*. I don't need you!" Emma says, her voice getting louder with every word. "You all can stay here with your powers and going on missions and being *super* together! You're just wasting your time, you know that? The plan is great, but no one accounted for Vindication, and even with all these meta-humans, you can't figure out a way to keep doing the broadcasts without anyone getting hurt."

The car trembles as if it's going to break. It just might. Or maybe that's Emma.

"I'm going to go make things right," Emma says. "Don't follow me." She's tired, so tired of being taken for granted and not being good enough. "Goodbye," she says, without even a backward glance.

She drives down the tunnel with Bells' stunned form standing still in her rearview mirror. He gets smaller and smaller as she goes, and every so often Emma glances back to see if he follows her, but he doesn't. He just watches her go.

Emma tries to shake Bells' hurt, stricken look from her mind. He'll be fine. She knows he'll be fine. He's got plenty of missions to lead and the Resistance isn't even going to miss her. Her friends all have better things to worry about than the fact that Emma doesn't get to go on the missions.

The tears come hot and fast, blurring her vision. The night air whistles past her, and snow starts to fall around her, and she can't see past the flurry of white, so she slows down while she tries to figure out how to turn on the windshield wipers.

Emma jabs furiously at the car's control screen; her fingerprints smudge the oils already there. A fat teardrop lands next to her hand, and another, and another.

EMMA WAKES UP COLD AND stiff. At least it's not snowing anymore. She drives carefully, watching for people, but it's all empty, crumbling highways and rusted signs, including one she passes reading *Welcome to Canada.*

There'd been a border here once, just as there once was a border between the United States and Mexico; both had been long forgotten once the Collective came together, but that sign was still here, a reminder of old borders that no longer matter, cities that barely exist. The roads are all that's left, crackling and crumbling as the force of nature reclaims them.

It's just a chance, driving out here on a hunch, but Emma knows how strongly *home* resonates. Southard's got to be out here.

Emma thinks of the home where she grew up with her mothers doting on her, her friends nearby, when her biggest dreams and worries had to do with school and space. Would she go back? Emma thinks of the house in the canyons, the one built by Abby and her mom, the one where her moms are now— *is that home?* She's lived in so many places this year, they're all blending together.

She shakes herself as she parks and exits the old, creaking vehicle, imagining herself triumphantly coming with Southard to New Bright City. She sets up the solar panel, heaves it and grunts, and thinks of defeating Vindication and not of how difficult this is by herself.

Emma sighs. This whole plan seemed a lot more glamorous when she first thought of it when she left. "I'm not useless," Emma says to the empty road and field.

She's going to find Southard, and then Deirdre and everyone will eat their words. Emma is a valuable member of the team despite what others may think. She doesn't need to be on missions with everyone; she just wants them to *see* her.

Don't you want powers? You could be a hero like your friends, a small voice inside her says.

Emma pushes the voice aside, trying not to think about what that would entail. She clears a flat area to lay her sleeping mat down. She's got wood to gather for a fire and dinner to make. She doesn't have time to worry about her abilities. She's got this.

EMMA SLEEPS WHEN SHE'S TIRED, eats when she's hungry, and is at the whim of no one. If she wants to drive recklessly and all over the road, she can. She makes her own schedule, is the boss of her own mission.

It's only fun for a short while. Soon loneliness and guilt eat at her, and Emma keeps seeing Bells' stricken face over and over again. For the first time in a long time, she's truly and utterly alone, with the whole of the world in front of her and a mission of her own to pursue. Emma thought it would mean freedom, but she misses everyone.

At every spectacular view she thinks of Bells and how he'd love it; Abby would love the strangeness and stillness of the abandoned factories and would want to explore them; Jess would squeal about how cute those rabbits are. Emma misses Bells elbowing her when she sleeps, the way they chatted about anything and nothing, even the way he snored.

Emma hefts the solar panel back into the trunk one morning and it *clunks* loudly, as if it's hitting another piece of metal. She fumbles around in the trunk until she finds a small case. Inside is a cracked tablet. She didn't pack it; Bells must have snuck it in, hoping she'd find a way to message him on the encrypted channel. Or maybe he left a message for her. Either way, it's broken now. There's no point in wondering why he left it for her.

Emma takes a deep breath, focusing on the road and pushing those thoughts away. *They're better off without her, anyway.*

A COLD, SWEEPING WIND RUSHES across the valley. The sky is clear for now; clouds are forming in the distance. It's a good thing she's charging the solar panels; it looks as though there's another storm coming.

Havenstown is empty, and her arrival is anticlimactic. It's filled with nothing but desolate buildings half-covered in snow. Emma tries hard to ignore her disappointment; it's not over, not yet. Southard was definitely spotted near here. All Emma has to do is thoroughly search the surrounding area.

The back of her neck prickles. She should get going. Every instinct is telling her to leave, get out of the open, but not committing to a full charge could very well mean getting stuck in the storm.

"Hello?" Emma calls out.

Out of the corner of her eye, she sees something move. "Is someone there?"

Emma shakes herself, trying not to jump at shadows on the deserted street. Maybe it's coming from a vantage point. Havenstown's buildings sprawl as far as she can see, climbing even onto the high slopes of the mountain. Emma can see homes built *on* those steep slopes and even higher, accessible only by a winding road. She shakes her head. *Ridiculous.*

Snow is starting to come down now, and she wonders how the people would deal with it, whether they'd be able to access the town for food and supplies. She gets dizzy, trying to trace the road hugging the side of the cliff and almost misses the flicker of light.

Emma watches it carefully. *Is that a cloud or a plume of smoke?*

There's that flicker again, almost like the gleam of cam-foil. Emma looks closer; there's a perfect mirror of that exact tree line, just like at the Broussard's secret farm. Someone is hiding here, in this ghost town in the middle of nowhere.

Emma continues on foot, trudging toward where she saw the light. If Jess were here, she'd know immediately where she was going, and if Bells... well, he'd do something amazing. He's always got something up his sleeve. And Abby would have plotted the trajectory or pinpointed exactly where Southard's hideout was based on the glimmer of the reflection of that holo.

Powers aren't everything, Emma tells herself. The logical part of her says she's being childish, that of course her friends love and appreciate her, but she's tired, tired of being excluded, tired of being looked over, of being asked to stand back.

"No more," Emma mutters angrily, and then promptly trips and falls face first into a snowbank. She dusts herself off and keeps going.

She has no idea how far she has to go. She should probably get back to the car and change out of these wet clothes before she's too tired, but it's not as if the car has any charge to run a heater anyway. As long as she keeps moving, she'll be fine.

She hears something ahead.

"Patricia Southard?" Emma calls. "Is that you? My name's Emma. I'm a friend. I'm not with the League," she announces. Her breath blossoms into little clouds in front of her as she pants with effort, hustling up the hill.

As she gets closer, she can see a person's shadow at the top of the hill. Emma waves, picks up the pace until she gets a little closer, and then stops.

It's not a person.

A *howl* echoes in the air.

Emma freezes. She knows the stories of the wild animals that roam the Unmaintained lands, of the hordes of previously domesticated animals, dogs and cats and who knows what else, left to themselves to forage and hunt, gone feral over a hundred years. There are also animals that were always wild in this country: bison and wolves and bears and mountain lions and coyotes. *But they all went extinct, right?*

Another howl.

"No one knows for sure," Emma tells herself. "The Collective tells everyone that the Unmaintained lands are unsafe, that there are creatures out here, but they're just stories, lies from the Collective."

More howls this time; whatever it is, there's more than one.

Emma spots movement above her on the far snowbank: something that moves quickly, something that is decidedly not human or robot, an animal on four legs, with pointed ears and a tail pointed up. It raises its great head and howls again. Another beast joins it, and another, and they stalk forward.

"Wolf," Emma says, laughing in spite of her fear. "Hi," she says. "There are a lot of you, aren't there?" Had they been following her? How long have they been watching her?

The largest wolf's eyes are ice blue and gleam with intelligence. They all look hungry, snarling at her, and Emma shakes when she spots the teeth.

Teeth. Long and sharp and so many of them.

Emma stands tall, shaking, and she tries not to let them know she's afraid. She has no idea what to do. Her mind spins in all different directions about how this is it, and she didn't even get to say goodbye...

The largest one howls again and yips loudly.

"Heel, Star! You too, Baby!" calls a gruff voice behind her.

The wolves—dogs?—wag their tails, and they sprint to a bundled-up figure behind them. Their demeanors immediately become playful.

"Oh, come on now, you can't have forgotten what a person looks like; they're clearly not a rabbit, you silly fools," the person says fondly to the wolves, patting them on their heads. The largest one stands to greet the person. On its hind legs, it's as tall as the person is. It should be frightening, but Emma wants to laugh at the eager animal.

"You," the person says. "Who are you, and why are you here? How'd you find me?" The wolves turn to look at Emma with a wary eye, and one of them starts snarling again.

Emma holds her hands up. "I'm not with the League! My name is Emma," she says, and then fatigue and exhaustion take over and she loses her balance, falling forward.

EMMA STIRS. THERE'S A WARM heavy weight on her, something fluffy like fur that's moving rhythmically, and then something rough and wet drags across her face. "Eurgh," she says.

"Eurgh is right," says the voice next to her.

She opens her eyes wearily, one at a time. There's a crackling fire and the smell of something savory and delicious coming from somewhere, and an old woman is regarding her curiously.

On top of Emma is one of the wolves, no, two of them. The wolf—or dog?—beams at her, tongue lolling out of its mouth and panting, and then licks her face again. It's so strange that Emma just accepts it, as if she's in a dream.

"You've been out of it the whole ride back. You don't hardly weigh a thing," the woman says gruffly. "You'll need to change out of your wet clothes or you'll get hypothermia. These are clean. There's a bathroom in there." She jerks her head at a small door. "Do you need help? Star, Yeti, come over here."

The furry weights move off her, and Emma just stares, not really believing what she's seeing. It feels as though she's moving underwater, and she's so cold and tired, and her mind is hazy. She moves on autopilot to the small cramped bathroom. The sweater and sweatpants are clean and dry, and a bit too big for her, but Emma is grateful to be out of her wet clothes.

She is immediately greeted by wet noses and eager dogs when she exits the bathroom. "Thanks," she says hesitantly. Is she dreaming? That would make much more sense. She's freezing to death out in the cold on a pointless mission gone wrong, and her mind is playing tricks on her.

"Rest." The voice is gentle and firm.

Emma is gently bundled up in a blanket and tucked in and then she drifts off to sleep.

EMMA WAKES UP AGAIN, UNFATHOMABLY warm, but with a much clearer head. She jolts upright with alarm, the details of the foolhardy mission and nearly freezing to death in the search for Southard.

There's a confused whimper next to her, and Emma almost startles again, seeing the wolf-like creature eye her curiously. She remembers them surrounding her, and Emma thought it was going to be like the stories of the wild creatures roaming the Unmaintained lands, tearing and ripping her to pieces. This one's mouth is open, with the tongue lolling out in a comical way.

"You're a dangerous predator," Emma says. Saying what she knows calms her down, but the wolf's tail begins to wag with so much enthusiasm that his entire body shakes. "You're a wolf? A dog?"

Emma remembers that dogs had been kept as pets before the Disasters. Like cats, there are plenty of historical holovids of them floating around the Net, but unlike cats, who occasionally were still kept as luxury pets, there are only stories about dogs.

The wolfdog is making a sad, whining noise now and noses at her face. It's soft and wet, and Emma laughs despite herself, throwing her hands in her face to stop it. Her hands touch the soft, warm fur, and there's a happy rumbling noise of approval.

"Okay," Emma says, patting the creature on the head again, and he seems to smile, panting excitedly, and she keeps up the motion.

Emma sits back, petting the wolfdog and taking in her surroundings. She's in a one-room cabin dominated by a wood-burning stove in the center. There's a bed filled with quilts, a desk cluttered with strange items Emma has no name for, and what looks like a bulky piece of tech, possibly a pre-Collective computer. A fire crackles merrily in the stove, lighting the place with a soft, amber light. A delicious smell wafts from a pot, and Emma's stomach growls.

How long was she out? She vaguely remembers being found, waking up in the cabin, and changing into dry clothes, but barely remembers anything else, aside from an old woman and an improbable number of wolfdogs. Emma pulls the blankets around her and spots her clothes drying on a rack near the fire and the contents of her pockets carefully laid out on a side table.

The door opens, and with it a gust of howling cold wind rushes inside, along with a figure wrapped head to toe in a puffy coat and even more wolfdogs. It's a chaos of noise and furry bodies and noses as they bound inside the cabin.

The one by Emma's side lets out a joyful bark, and the others answer, excitedly dancing about the figure as layers are removed to reveal an old woman. Emma watches as she pulls a scarf from her face. Her glittering eyes regard Emma.

"You need to eat," she says, stepping closer. Up close, Emma can see her face is gnarled with wrinkles. Wisps of flyaway hair frame her face. Across her face runs a wicked looking scar, branched and forked like lightning, so faded it's almost imperceptible.

Oh. She's encountered Captain Orion, or someone with that very same lightning power.

Emma straightens up, brimming with questions.

"Eat," the woman says, ladling the contents of the pot into a bowl and pressing it and a spoon into her hands.

"Oh, I didn't—" Emma struggles. She isn't sure of her place here, doesn't want to assume anything. She feels strange, lightheaded, but takes a mouthful, hesitantly, and then almost groans in relief. It's a thick, hearty stew flavored with spices, with chunks of vegetables and meat. She eats ravenously, finishing the bowl before she even knows it.

"Eat more; you're too skinny," the woman says, refilling her bowl and handing it back to her.

Emma smiles at her, feeling warm and content, not just with the food; the gesture is so reminiscent of her abuela. She feels safe and protected, and, despite the strangeness of the situation, thinks everything is going to be okay. She pats the dog next to her and watches the others, fascinated. Every inch of floor is covered with dogs; there are seven, all looking at her and her bowl with various amounts of interest.

"Oh, they won't bother you. They just like the chase, and you gave them quite the chase. Yeti, quit it," the woman says to the dog trying to nudge under her shoulder. "That one is Star, you've already petted him once, and now he's going to be badgering you all night to be in your lap." She jerks her head, pointing out each dog in turn. "Yeti and Bigfoot and Sasquatch and Baby and Pluto and Neptune."

The dogs grow bolder and bolder, licking her face and demanding more attention. Emma is more curious about this woman who is introducing all her dogs before herself. She jumps up, remembering the car still sitting on the outskirts of town. The movement startles Star, who makes a sad noise as he topples to the floor.

"My car, I need to—"

"Your car will be covered in a foot of snow in an hour. Don't worry about it."

Emma sinks back onto the couch, and Star and Yeti clamber into her lap and lick her face as her host gives her a calculating look.

"And who are you, and why are you wandering around the Unmaintained lands by yourself?"

"My name is Emma. I'm not—"

"With the League. Like you said." The woman snorts, handing her a cup of something hot. "You can call me…" she frowns, as if she's forgotten her own name. "My friends called me Trish."

"Nice to meet you. I'm Emma." Emma looks at Trish, taking her in, noting the ominous past tense. Maybe all her friends are gone now. She looks as though she could be Emma's abuela's age, maybe older. "Thank you for helping me," she says. "I was looking for…" Emma shrugs and sighs. "Well, I'm not sure if you know anything about them. It was a while ago."

"Must be someone important," Trish says. "For you to risk your life coming out here."

Emma shrugs. "It had to be done. We're going to need all the help we can get to bring down the League."

Trish snorts. "The League!" She places her hand on Emma's forehead. "Well, you're not feverish, that's good."

Emma gestures out the window. "That's Havenstown, right?"

"It once was, yeah. People are long gone, aside from me."

"Do you know Patricia Southard? She was one of the astronauts on the Intrepid. Did she ever come back to this town? It would have been after 2035. I was researching the original meta-humans, and I think she must be the only one unaccounted for from that first wave of people who got powers."

Trish stares her down and then tosses another log in the fire, which pops and crackles. "You finish eating that. I've got work to do."

TRISH IS A VERY GRUFF and barely talkative host. She ignores all of Emma's questions about Southard, seems to have very little interest in the League and the Resistance. For all her taciturn and grumpy manner, she makes Emma take the bed, despite Emma's protests that she can take the couch.

On the next day, Emma starts packing up to go, but Trish takes one look at her zipping up her thin jacket and sits her down. "Look, a storm like this, you'll never get enough sun to recharge your panels, and, even if you did, you won't make it far before you run out of juice again." Trish shakes her head. "I'm surprised you made it all the way out here. You're tough. But it would be pointless for you to die in the storm. Better to stay here, at least till the storm's over."

"And how long will that be?"

An indifferent shrug is the answer. "Days. A week, maybe. Maybe longer. It's a long way to spring just yet."

Emma's too weak to argue on the first day. Besides, the dogs are good company. Star's taken to following her around, curling up at her feet and sitting in her lap as she peruses Trish's bookshelf full of dusty romance novels. Emma can begin to see why people loved having these companions.

Trish disappears for hours at a time, bundled up in layers. Sometimes she brings the dogs with her; sometimes she goes alone.

"Can I help you do anything while I'm here?" Emma asks on the second day.

Trish gives her a calculating look. "You look like the wind could knock you over, but, by all means, if you want to help, I've got a million chores to do."

She leads Emma down a packed snow tunnel outside the cabin; it's surprisingly warm inside, and Emma marvels at how thick the snow is. There's a neat little enclosed trail that goes to another shed, where an axe is resting in next to a pile of logs.

"Can you chop wood?"

"I can try," Emma says.

A few minutes later her arms and shoulders are sore, but she doesn't want to give up. Besides, Trish, despite her gruffness, or maybe because of it, really does remind Emma of her abuela, and she thinks about how she would feel, living all the way out here alone.

There is wood to chop and the dogs to feed and traps to check and fish to catch and it seems Emma is terrible at all of it, aside from petting the dogs, but she tries her best. She can do this.

The mornings have a serene beauty, all icy frost and trees glistening gently. There's a silence that Emma has never known before, deeper, as if the world is waiting, listening.

Emma thinks about the world beyond this little icy haven, about the Council and the League and the battles raging on.

I could stay here, Emma thinks. Trish seems in no way wanting to kick her out. Emma thinks she might be lonely.

Emma could stay here and hide forever. She would miss Bells and Jess and Abby and her parents but surely the Resistance will go on without her; it's not as though her plans have been very useful lately, anyway.

BEFORE EMMA KNOWS IT, A week has passed. It's hard to tell, the way the days and the routines blur together.

Trish taps her spoon on her oatmeal bowl and eyes Emma. "So what are you hiding from?"

Emma scowls at her breakfast. "I'm not hiding from anything. I'm here on a mission, I told you."

Trish waves her spoon at Emma. "There's no one here. Storm's over. You can go home now, you know." She takes a bite of oatmeal. "It's no problem if you want to stay, though. It's been nice having the help. And you're not so bad to talk to."

Emma huffs. "I can leave at any time I want."

Trish gestures toward the door.

Emma takes another bite of oatmeal. She can't leave empty-handed, and she doesn't know what the next step in looking for Southard is either.

"You are running away!" Trish guffaws at her. "Don't worry. I ran away too. We can be two outcasts together."

Emma scowls. "You don't understand! I'm not— I'm not a meta-human, and Deirdre said I couldn't come on any of the missions, and I just felt so useless I had to go do *something*."

Trish takes a long sip from her coffee. "You talk a big talk about making change and doing stuff, but it sounds like you left your friends to do the work."

"That's not true," Emma says angrily, setting down the bowl. "I can do work. I'm gonna do some right now."

EMMA HEAVES THE AXE, MUTTERING angrily to herself as it lands solidly in the thick trunk of the tree, wedging a sharp cut in the wood. She steps back, ready for the tree to fall. She *didn't* leave the work to her friends. She wasn't even allowed to go on missions. Trish is just trying to rile her up. *It must be living out here alone for so long.*

The tree creaks again, and a clump of snow falls as it shudders and then topples to the right, hitting another tree. The trajectory changes dramatically, and then both trees topple toward Emma. She takes a step back, eyes widening, and then glances up at the swaying branches and towering trunks of the trees. She turns around to run, get out of the way, but it's already falling.

Suddenly a huge pillar of earth shoots up, scattering snow and debris everywhere, building a wall between Emma and the falling trees, swooping up and over her head and hardening, like an earthen cave. Emma can hear the thunderous creaks as the trees crash down upon her, but she's safe in her little cave. She touches the wall; it's solid. She traces her fingers across the grains and finds the water bottle she was drinking from. It's frozen, stuck inside the earth.

Something shifts outside, and she hears more creaks and noises.

Then the cave dissolves into fine grains, and Emma's bottle clatters to the ground.

Trish is standing there, her eyebrows scrunched up in concern. "Are you okay?"

"I'm fine!" Emma says, standing up and brushing off dirt. "That was amazing— you're— you're—" *a meta-human*, Emma's brain helpfully supplies, but, as the shock fades, she realizes it's not just that. "You're Patricia Southard."

Trish sighs. "Yes. That was me, a long time ago. It feels like another life. Sometimes I wonder, if I hadn't been on that spaceship, if I wasn't on that mission, if I could have just lived a nice, normal life, married the woman I loved, had some kids, and then died when I should have." Trish turns, jerking her head back down the mountain.

Emma grabs her water bottle and the axe, and follows, her head spinning with questions. She's wasted so much time, just hanging out at the cabin with the dogs and helping Trish with her chores. If she had known she had actually succeeded in finding Southard, the one meta-human who could tip the scales in their favor, she would have already been on her way to New Bright City by now, ready to save the day.

Trish doesn't answer any of the questions that Emma peppers her with on the way to the cabin. "Why didn't you say anything? You knew that I was part of the Resistance and we need your help. Don't you care?"

Trish doesn't answer, just busies herself with making tea. She hands Emma a mug, then stares into her own cup.

Emma takes a sip, savoring the invigorating tea while watching Trish. All this time this centenarian has been taking care of her; Emma's come to think of them as friends.

"When you first showed up, I panicked," Trish says. "I didn't want to tell you who I was, especially if you were looking for me. I'm still surprised you managed to get here in the first place."

Emma grins. "I knew that you grew up here, and I figured you were attached to this town before it was leveled by the Disasters."

Trish sighs. "It's beautiful here. It still is. It's not the same, after the eruption, but it's my home. It's always been. I mean, it was enough that the government trotted me around like their prize pony from city to city that sprung up in this newfangled alliance—"

"The Collective."

Trish snorts. "Right. Three countries— one country now, with one goal: survival. And survive we did. We dismantled the space program, dedicated everything toward clean energy and rebuilding our cities and our heroes, who led the way." She sighs, looking out the window.

"It was really hard to find anything about you," Emma says. "Other than the fact you were on the Intrepid."

Trish shakes her head. "I stopped playing the part. Left before it all blew up, before Vance started demanding and arguing with James about his League, about its goals—"

"Look, Vance. Gravitus knew it was wrong, creating this system," Emma says. "It's gotten out of control now. People are getting hurt."

"Vance is dead," Trish says heavily. "Look, Emma, I appreciate everything you've done, but I just want to live out here. On my own. With my dogs. I'd rather just not be involved with what the League gets up to, and how they use my name. I'd rather just be forgotten and I'm fine with how all that played out. Last I heard of the world, James' grandkid was running the show."

Emma bristles. "That kid, Captain Orion—"

Trish laughs. "She ain't a Captain of anything, didn't serve our nation in any way other than to fight in staged shows all across the nation. Keeps the public mollified, you see."

"I know all that. Look, I told you—" Emma swallows. "My friends and I, we found out about all that. That's why we started the Resistance. We're going to stop everything."

"Stop what, the League?" Trish laughs again. "Good luck with that. They're the most powerful organization in the country."

"But the Collective—"

"You think that the League and the Collective are two different organizations? Come on now. The leaders of our great nation have always been working with James and his little band of so-called heroes. It's built into the foundation of this country. The heroes protect. Or rather, distract."

"The Council—"

"A bunch of figureheads. The Three run the whole show."

Emma bristles. "The Councilmembers do good. They work hard. My mom has been on the Council for ten years; she's served Nevada well."

Trish eyes her. "I'm not saying that the Councilmembers don't do a good job of running their little Regions and helping their constituents. But how much power do they have to really create change? How much change is possible?"

"I know that the Council, once they learn about the League, they'll want to change it. They won't want to be part of a lie."

Trish stands up, shaking her head. "What if the lie is too great? That people will lose faith in how their country is run, that they've been lied to this whole time? Widespread panic. Chaos. Maybe we'll return to the time of the Disasters."

"The people deserve to know!" Emma can't believe she's gotten this far, actually found the famous Patricia Southard, and she just wants to hide here in her cabin?

Trish eyes her. "You are tired. You need to get some rest."

Emma wakes up to a loud noise she can't place. It's a constant roar, persistent and never-ending. At first, she thinks it's from her dream, but she blinks awake, rubbing her eyes. The dogs are all outside, barking aggressively, and Trish is nowhere to be found. Emma pads to the window; it's not unusual for Trish to be gone, but she almost always heats water for Emma.

Outside the window is a metal monstrosity Emma's only seen in history books— a helicopter.

"What in the world?" Emma opens the door, and her heart leaps into her throat.

Trish, her jaw set in a grim line, is shaking hands with Lowell Kingston.

"No, no, *no!*" Emma shrieks. "How could you?!"

"Sorry, kid," Trish says, barely audible over the roar of the helicopter. "You can't beat them, you know. I might as well get something out of this." She glances up at Kingston. "And from here on out, my home, the location, all of it— wiped from the map?"

"Rest assured, Ms. Southard, no one will ever bother you again," Kingston says. He turns to Emma, smiling his odious grin at her.

Behind Kingston, the familiar hard edges of the MR-D4R MonRobots advance upon her, hovering right for her.

Emma runs. She knows it's pointless, knows there's nowhere she can go in this open, sunlit plain of snow, but she runs anyway, tripping over snow and ice and rock. A sharp pain blooms in her left shoulder, and then Emma's vision blurs, and she knows nothing else.

EMMA EXPECTS RESTRAINTS WHEN SHE comes to consciousness, but when she shifts in her chair she can't feel anything. She can't hear anything either. Cautiously, Emma opens her eyes.

She's in an office, clean and neat, with a full bookshelf of well-loved books, worn and carefully read. There's plush carpet under her feet.

Emma is immediately suspicious. She jumps to her feet, wincing at the pain in her shoulder— a bot must have shocked her. Emma paces the office and tries the door; to her surprise, it's unlocked.

She wanders down a carpeted hallway, also tastefully decorated; she's growing more and more suspicious by the minute. There— a window.

Emma opens it and then gasps.

They're incredibly high up, too high. The building is all chrome and glass, and below Emma can spot moving cars on a greenway; she must be in one of the higher levels of New Bright City.

"Lovely view, isn't it?"

Emma whirls around.

Kingston smiles at her, looking just like his campaign poster. "I'm afraid I have to apologize for the rude method of transportation; a few of those bots still have you programmed as a Class Five Threat. I hope you aren't in pain? I can have a doctor check you if you like."

"Where am I?" Emma demands.

"COFAX, of course," Kingston says with a sharp smile.

He took her to the heart of political headquarters, to the most important building in New Bright City. Emma doesn't understand.

She can't take her eyes off his shiny, white teeth; they seem to gleam unnaturally. Emma thinks about the warm grandfatherly persona he presents: his suit offset with a cardigan and a clever lapel pin. It's all a carefully constructed persona, this quiet, befuddled veneer that belays a cold and calculating interior.

He pulls something from his pocket, a cellophane wrapped sweet. "Do you still like caramels, dear?"

Emma stares at the offered candy; a distinct memory comes back to her. She's six, hiding behind her mother's skirts, following Mama's sleek pantsuit closely. Mama had just been elected to the Council then, and it had been the first time the three of them had gone to New Bright City together to celebrate Mama's journey toward making a difference.

It was Kingston, she's sure; back then he hadn't started wearing suits, just a cardigan and pressed trousers and glasses.

"Ah, yes, you must be Samantha Robledo, our new representative for the Nevada region," Kingston said, taking Mama's hand and shaking it solicitously.

"Serving on the Council is such an honor. But I imagine you'll be wanting to do a single term, just to try it? And then get back to your family?"

"My wife, Josephine, and our daughter, Emma," Mama said, introducing them.

"Hello, little lady," Kingston said, crouching down to her height. "Would you like a caramel?"

Emma had been on a train all day, tired and hungry, and she remembered seeing the candy and grabbing it with delight.

"Say thank you," Mom whispered.

"Thank you," Emma said.

"Such a polite child," Kingston said. "I imagine you'll be a wonderful citizen one day. A great asset to our flourishing country."

Emma barely remembers the rest of the visit; she mostly remembers tagging along with Mom to the zoo and the Museum of Select Pre-Collective History, marveling at the ancient types of transportation. She met Kingston twice more during that trip, and then forgot the strange old man.

She wishes she remembers now. Was he dead set on the presidency so early on? Had he already formulated a plan that would involve allying with a corrupt League of Heroes and resort to kidnapping and blackmail to get his way?

"Come along. We've much to discuss." Kingston doesn't wait for her, just starts walking down the hallway. He presses his hand to the wall. A disguised lockpad glows and something whirrs behind the wall.

Kingston turns and smiles and jerks his head at the opening doors. "After you."

Emma steps forward. She's got nowhere else to go; she might as well see what Kingston has to say. She tries to remember everything about the elevator and what she sees so she can use it for an escape later.

The elevator is all glass with a view of the sky outside. In the reflection, she notices how strange she looks, in her dirty and weatherworn clothing. Next to Kingston, polished in his suit and tie, she looks like a scared child.

Emma is determined to be anything but that.

She touches the glass; it's cold beneath her hands. Outside, small fragments of ice streak across the glass. The atmosphere is thinner, Emma remembers. She looks up, and is it her imagination or does the bright blue of the sky look deeper, darker, suggesting the edge of space beyond? *No, there's something else, something shimmering—*

"Ah, it's quite impressive, isn't it? New Bright City's impact shield. The P019 event will feel like nothing more than a light rain." Kingston smiles at her as if he expects her to be impressed.

Emma doesn't say anything; it's cool, sure, but all the major cities in the impact zone have been working on their own shields and preparations for the upcoming meteor event. New Bright City's isn't more impressive just because it's taller.

Emma startles and almost loses her balance when the floor almost seems to drop below her as the elevator descends at a brisk speed.

Kingston gives her a patronizing smile. "Don't be nervous, dear. We're quite safe. I imagine it can be quite overwhelming, if you're afraid of heights."

"I'm not," Emma says, resisting the urge to roll her eyes. She wasn't lying, she isn't afraid of heights at all, unlike Bells, who gets nervous standing on a balcony. She stands her ground firmly and watches as they plunge through cloud layers. Why bring her to the top of COFAX only to take her back down?

"It's quite a view, isn't it?" Kingston muses casually. "Three hundred and seventeen floors, in case you were wondering. I take this elevator from my office and living quarters to the lower levels of COFAX every day. It's humbling, to be able to see the country and the people I am responsible for."

Emma doesn't think humble is living hundreds of floors above your constituents, but she keeps her mouth shut.

"You were the top in your science class back at Andover Heights High School," Kingston muses. "And you were in an accelerated college preparatory class as well, with a noted interest in aerospace."

"So?" Emma turns her wary gaze up at Kingston. *What's he getting at?*

"Even though aerospace engineering pursuits haven't been active since the days before our great nation was formed? Such a unique passion," Kingston says, stroking his beard. "One might say that it goes against the ideals of the Collective." He chuckles, shaking his head. "Space travel."

Kingston steps up to the glass and looks at the sky. "Our forebearers wasted so much money trying to find the stars when we had enough trouble brewing on the ground."

Emma glares at him. "That *unique passion* developed most of the technology we use and enjoy every day. And space travel is *inspiring.* That's why I want to do it. To go to Mars. To learn and discover new things. And to recover the knowledge we lost. It's *useful,* okay?"

"Oh, I never said that research wasn't useful, dear. Just all those spaceships, those rocket fuels. You know we don't have the capacity to spend so much of our resources on such fruitless endeavors that don't benefit the public."

Emma scoffs. "And you think our current endeavors do? I know about Constavia."

Kingston doesn't deny it. He merely continues gazing out the window. "Tantalum is a valuable resource, and it's my responsibility to secure it."

"That tantalum belongs to the people of Constavia. Just because you're waging a war there and distracting everyone with—"

"I'd be careful with what you're accusing me of," Kingston says, his eyes flashing. "You don't know what it takes to keep this great country going."

"I know exactly what you're doing," Emma mutters. "The League is just a coverup."

"Don't be so naïve. Everything has its place. Even you."

Kingston puts his hands in his pockets and looks out to the view as they descend into the city itself. The elevator slows as it continues past many tiers of streets with people driving and walking and enjoying their day, and then a greenway with its swaying trees rustling in the wind.

The shifting holograms bear the news of the day: Starscream punching Dynamite over and over and Sublimate flashing his shiny white teeth for toothpaste.

"Such a beautiful city," Kingston says. "I've been all over the Collective, and I can say that this one is the most efficient. You can't even see the clutter of the Unmaintained lands."

Emma looks where the buildings end and sees the massive billboards and more glowing advertisements among the solar fields. So it's true; people in New Bright City can't see beyond the shine of their own world.

"You know, growing up with all these heroes, I've always wanted to be one. To get a taste of the power, the recognition. What would it be like to fly, I wonder?"

Emma bites back the sharp comment on the tip of her tongue. Kingston is one of the most powerful men in the Collective, what does he want superpowers for? But she can see it in his eyes, the hunger.

"Do you?"

Emma narrows her eyes. "Do I what?"

"If you had the chance, would you want to fly?"

Emma stares at him. He already knows her interests; he's researched her. Sure, she loves the thrill of moving so fast it'd be impossible to measure, but even more she wants to discover the unknown. "I'm not a meta-human, there's no point in even asking," Emma says, her voice flat.

Kingston waves his hand theatrically. "Flying isn't for everyone, of course. What about super-strength? Night vision? Any ability you can think of." He drops his voice to a whisper; the corner of his mouth quirks up as if he's dropping a salacious secret. "It's possible. I can make it happen." He taps his DED, and a hologram projects into the air between them. A man wearing a hospital gown nods at the camera, holds his arms out, and a great gust of wind blows about the room, knocking over the bed and other medical equipment. "You may know this man as Sublimate."

Emma watches the holovid; a strange feeling wells up inside her. It's one thing to suspect Kingston and the League had been creating new meta-humans and another to see proof.

"Like you said, science is progress. And I have the key. It's quite simple to use a viral vector to change the contents of your genetic makeup. We've been doing it forever; just look at all the successful cancer treatments."

"Yes, but—"

"And you know that space travel isn't completely extinct. Why, I myself own a shuttle with several other wealthy entrepreneurs who do leisure flights occasionally, just a hobby, you know. We could take you up to one of the remaining stations, if you like."

Emma gasps. "You have a shuttle?"

"Indeed, I do. The ISS *Indomitable.* We have a team of privately funded researchers and technicians, of course. You could be one of them, you know. Or even on the team itself; we're always looking for smart, like-minded people."

"I—" Emma doesn't know what to think. The space program seemed so far away, a distant fantasy, and now it's here within her reach.

"Sleep on it tonight. Tomorrow I can even take you on a tour of the station."

The elevator doors sweep open, and Kingston nods to an Authority officer in the hallway.

"This way, Miss Robledo," the officer says.

"I'll see you tomorrow," Kingston says, before she has a chance to respond.

Emma follows the officer down the hallway. He leads her to a guest bedroom; it's clean and modern, with a window looking up toward the stars.

He locks her in.

EMMA PACES THE ROOM, LOOKING for any weaknesses she can exploit for an escape. She has bobby pins in her hair, but the door is locked from the outside, and there's no handle. The bed is bolted to the floor, not that Emma could lift it, anyway. She tries ripping the sheets and blanket, but the fabric won't tear. Not that it would help; the window opens just enough for her to reach an arm out, so that's not a viable way of escape.

A rap on the door startles her, and Emma drops the blanket.

"Hi! I'm Tony. I've brought you breakfast!"

"Uh, thanks."

Tony enters the room, smiling at her and bearing a tray with scrambled eggs, toast, and fruit.

She takes the tray, eating quietly. She's got nothing to lose here; besides, if Kingston wanted to poison her, he would have already.

Tony stands at attention while she eats, looking out the window. "It's pretty cool, huh?"

"It's already started?" Emma was at Trish's longer than she thought. She watches the glowing streaks of light outside the shield, sparking and glowing as they enter the atmosphere, burning up.

"Don't worry. You'll be safe here. We take care of all the assets," Tony assures her.

"Right," Emma says, pushing the plate away from her.

"I'm so excited you'll be joining us. You're interested in the space program too?"

"I never said I was—"

Tony continues as if he hadn't heard her. "The other assets aren't so lucky, I mean, they were really rude to Kingston—"

Emma's heart skips a beat. "What other assets?" she asks, pretending the answer isn't important to her.

Tony laughs. "Eh, you know, it's just League business. We've been pretty busy trying to keep up with all the procedures, and it sounds like we won't have to waste time convincing them to join the League. It's fine, more resources for us anyway."

"Right," Emma says, smiling awkwardly. She needs to get more information. "I can't believe they were rude! Kingston is so— so— cool," she manages. "Such a great leader."

Tony adjusts his hat, grinning. "I know, right? I hope I can get powers too."

As he's lost in his daydream and rambling, Emma shoves her entire breakfast tray under her bed.

"I'm aiming for, like, superspeed. What do you think?" He strikes a pose, as if he's frozen in the middle of running fast.

"Very heroic," Emma says, giving him her most flattering smile. "So what did these rude assets say?"

"Nothing very creative," Tony says. "You know, back in my day, coming up with great insults was a testament to good character; you can't just curse at someone in another language and have it stick, you know, that's just cheating."

"Uh huh."

Tony's DED chirps. "All right, I've got to get back to my post." He squints. "I feel like I'm forgetting something."

"I know, right? I forget stuff all the time, especially when I'm talking with cool people," Emma says. She's probably laying it on a little thick, but Tony doesn't seem to notice. "Don't even worry about it. It was super nice to meet you, Tony, future speedster."

Tony laughs and gestures back at her. "Kingston's got plenty of meetings today, but I know he made room on his schedule to talk with you." He walks to the door and turns around, grinning. "Don't go anywhere!"

"I won't," Emma says, lying through her teeth.

THE UTENSILS AND PLATE ARE all light plastic, but the tray, the tray is heavy, made from metal. She can use this; she just needs the right moment.

The door opens again, startling her. Emma shoves the tray under the bed and stands up.

"Miss Robledo, I hope you've considered my proposition."

"You never really said what you wanted, so I didn't have anything to consider," Emma says. "Are you always this vague?"

Kingston laughs; he's wearing a silver-striped suit today with a blue pocket square. "Joining the Heroes' League of Heroes of course," he says. "As a meta-human."

"I—"

"I know, I know, it's a lot to take in." Kingston smiles at her. "Come. Walk with me."

Emma follows him out into the hallway as more guards join them, flanking them on either side. Even if she isn't restrained, even if she isn't being kept in a cell, she's still a prisoner here.

Emma counts how many hallways they pass, how many guards are stationed at each door, making a metal map of her room and the floorplan. She watches as a guard swipes their DED at a keypad and a hidden door opens up in the wall to reveal the elevator.

"And if superpowers aren't your speed, I know the crew of the *Indomitable* is always looking for new recruits," Kingston says, leading her into the elevator. It descends into a carport filled with gleaming vehicles. Emma tries to memorize as much information as possible as she and the guards follow Kingston into a sleek, gray vehicle.

They drive down a long, dark tunnel as Kingston busies himself with his DED. News stories and messages fly past too fast for

Emma to read, but she catches a glimpse of Vindication and— *is that Jess' parents?*

She gulps, trying not to reveal her anxiety over not knowing what's happening outside these walls. Someone was captured, and she wants to know who.

"Here we are," Kingston announces. "After you."

Emma gets out of the car and looks up. And up. And up.

It's a space shuttle, as tall as the eye can see, and it's surrounded by bustling people, driving about on smaller vehicles, working on computer consoles.

Emma imagines herself on that shuttle, wearing a spacesuit, meeting with other scientists, bringing back the space program, going to *Mars*.

The picture fades, and Emma can see only Kingston grinning at her in the shuttle bay.

"What do you think?"

"It's nice, I guess," Emma says.

"Mr. President, the main impact will start in less than an hour; you need to be in the safe house," one of the officials says, tipping his hat.

"Thank you. All the assets have been transferred inside the COFAX facility?"

"Yes, sir."

They get back in the car, sitting in silence. Emma can feel Kingston staring at her, studying her. "You know, there's no rule about being a meta-human *and* joining the space program."

Emma thinks about it; he wants her to join him, join the League, go against everything she's been fighting for.

What if she *had* powers? She could fight from within, right? She could take him down from the inside. Even find Abby's dad! She'd be a hero.

Emma shivers. *Maybe that's what you've always wanted,* a small voice says inside her. *You could do it. Become a meta-human, be the hero you knew you always were— and everyone else would be able to see too.*

Kingston hasn't said what he wanted from her; it's probably what he's wanted since he sent that MonRobot last year. He wants Samantha Robledo out of the race.

Mama wouldn't be President, but she'd still be on the Council. And she'd be alive and safe. Emma's whole family would be safe. She wouldn't have to be a fugitive anymore, eating on the run, sleeping in cars, always watching her back. She thinks of all her aunties and uncles and small cousins and everyone getting to live out their lives in peace.

And then Emma thinks about Kingston and his rows of MR-D4Rs and their ever-blinking lights. He won't stop until he gets what he wants, which is to stay in power, and to keep using the system to distract from his own corrupt goals.

His offer makes her uneasy, even trying to fight from the inside; how easy would it be to leave once she's in? Once she says yes, there's no going back.

Emma closes her eyes. She can't do it.

She opens her eyes to see Kingston giving her a steely glare.

"I just need one thing from you. Where is the rest of the Resistance?"

"What?"

Kingston laughs. "Look, it's cute, your little organization. But the League and the Collective itself are far more intertwined than anyone knows. And there's nothing a group of C-list meta-humans can do about it." He grins, leaning forward as if he's telling her a secret. "In fact, in the League's last confrontation, we've arrested several fugitives. It's only a matter of time before we catch the rest."

He projects several images from his DED and expands them with his hands, drawing them life-size, until the car is filled with glowing images of Emma's friends.

Jess.

Christine.

Abby.

Ricky.

Tanya.

Sasha.

Bells.

EMMA'S TOO SHOCKED TO PROTEST as the guards lead her to her room. She sits on her bed, staring at the wall, stunned. *Her friends. How did they get caught? Was it Vindication? Was it because they were looking for her?*

She shakes herself out of her stupor and grabs the tray from under the bed. She bought a little time, giving him false coordinates. He won't be able to check them, anyway, as they're outside of the city and the shield. No one will be leaving once P019 begins.

Emma needs to get out of here.

She grabs the tray and the blanket, braces herself behind the door, and waits.

"Hey! It's Tony again. I brought dinner."

"Come on in," Emma announces.

Tony opens the door, and Emma slams the tray on his head.

"Ow! What the—"

She wastes no time, hitting him again and then throwing the blanket over his head.

"Hey!"

Emma swings the metal tray at his knees, taking him out. Tony falls to the ground in a crumple of blanket. Emma wraps the sheet around him, tying it tightly around his chest. He struggles, wobbling around helplessly as Emma grabs his wrist and takes his DED.

"Hey! I thought we were cool!"

Emma doesn't waste time, just speeds down the hallway.

She ducks into an alcove in the hallway, cursing. Tony's DED won't access the elevator that goes to the carport.

"Level Three Clearance required," states a cool computer voice.

"Tony, Tony, gotta work on those promotions," Emma mutters to herself as she races down the hall, looking for a stairwell. Her plan is out the window, unless she gets another DED. She flicks through Tony's messages, searching for any information about her friends. *Captives* and *assets* brings up nothing, neither does *intake* or *meta-humans*. Emma wracks her brain.

Well, Kingston classified her as a Class 5 Threat, right? So her friends must also be.

There are a number of messages related to "threats."

Before Tony was assigned to her, he was guarding Assets 21, 50, and 39. Emma can't find any information on them, but she does see dates for intake: no, that was way before, and she was talking to Jess and Abby on that day, she was with Bells on that day.

There. Seven new assets taken in and brought to facility 039. The ages match up, as does the "M" tag, which Emma takes to mean meta-human.

Great. Now where is this facility?

She hears footsteps and voices at the end of the hall, so Emma quickly minimizes the projection on the DED. She waits for the guards to pass, catching snippets of their conversation.

"Where's Kingston this morning?"

"On a mission. That's so cool, man. I can't wait until we all get powers."

"I can't wait for the impact to be over. Hate commuting through that shield."

"You live outside the city too?"

"Yeah, rent's ridiculous inside the city. I'm over in Shinewright."

"Cool. I'm just glad we didn't get stuck at any of the outer facilities. That would suck."

"Nah, no one's at any of those. Everyone got evacuated before the impact."

"What about the assets?"

"Moved as of this morning."

There's a pause as one of the guards stops walking.

"Did you relocate the newest set? Thirty-nine?"

"I thought you did."

"Probably. I moved like three facilities full of assets, okay; we moved everyone."

"Are you sure?"

"Whatever. It's almost time for me to clock out; it's not my job to worry about it. Let beta shift deal with it."

Emma flinches. Are the outer facilities in the impact zone? If her friends are out there, they'd be inside a building, sure, but Emma has no idea what the structural integrity of the building would be. But wouldn't they want to protect the assets? Surely Kingston wanted to question them or use them for leverage. *The point would be to keep them alive, right?*

The voices fade, and Emma's panic escalates as she pulls up Tony's dashboard again. There. A map of Hopestar with all the local facilities on it. 36... 37... 38... 39!

Directly in the impact zone.

Emma curses.

"Hey! You aren't supposed to be out of your room!"

Emma doesn't turn back; she just runs.

"Asset out of bounds! Asset out of bounds!"

Alarms blare and sirens blast. Emma runs as fast as she can, dodging the guards' attempt to grab her. For once, being vertically challenged is helpful; she skids right under their arms and avoids their hands. This won't work for long, though; she saw weapons on quite a few of them. But they want to detain her, not to hurt her; she can use her asset status.

This hallway dead-ends. She needs to hide.

The guards are coming her way.

Emma tries each door and fumbles down the hallway with door after locked door until she finds an open one. She shuts it behind her.

THE ROOM IS SOFTLY LIT by rows and rows of tanks bubbling along the wall. Emma can hear the guards shouting outside; she ducks under the table, waiting for them to pass. The door opens and a light shines inside. Emma shuffles backward, right up to a tank.

"Come on, check the next floor, what are you doing in the lab!?"

"I thought— never mind. Let's go!"

The door shuts again, and Emma is alone.

She turns around, shaking her borrowed DED for a little light. It illuminates, casting a faint glow on the tanks behind her. Emma does not scream. She wants to but doesn't.

Inside the tank—and each of the other tanks along the wall—is a *brain*.

Horrified, Emma looks all the brains. Some are whole, some of them have been cut into or sliced into pieces, but they're all clearly human brains. She peers closer, trying to read the labels.

FLIGHT
WIND MANIPULATION
SUPER HEARING
VOICE PROJECTION

They're all meta-abilities, which means these brains…

"No," Emma gasps. No wonder Michael was so horrified. To give someone else powers requires using a meta-human brain. This is how Vindication and all those other "new" meta-humans got their power.

Emma wants to throw up.

SHE FINDS THE STAIRWELL, SCRAMBLING down as many flights as she can. *This should open to the carport, right?*

A door opens, and two guards burst into the stairwell.

"There she is!"

Emma catches the open door and runs out onto the floor, barging into every single room, looking for something, anything— finally the third door yields a breakroom with a coffee station. Emma ducks inside and grabs the steaming coffeepot and empties it onto the slick, tiled floor.

As expected, the guards bumble in, slipping and falling on the hot coffee. Emma grabs a DED from one of them and races out the door before they can get up after her.

Hopefully this one works.

She makes it to the elevator— *yes!* Level Five Clearance.

Emma jabs the button for carport, and the door closes just as the two guards rush down the hallway. She can't help waving cheekily as the doors shut.

The elevator descends and then stops at the next floor. The interior is braced with steel panels on each side. *Each of those might make for a good footrest, and the width of the elevator is pretty small.*

Emma goes for it, jumps up and braces herself between the elevator walls with her hands and feet. She heaves, trying to walk herself up, higher and higher, right above the door.

The door swivels open.

"All right, the game is over, stop—"

"Where'd she go?"

A bead of sweat gathers on Emma's forehead and drops to the elevator floor. She holds her breath.

The guards turn around, the elevator doors close, and she lets herself down slowly. She lies on the cool, metal floor of the elevator, and tries to catch her breath. Her heart is pounding erratically; her arms and legs keep shaking.

The elevator dings once more and opens onto the carport. It's dark, but a light flickers on as Emma walks out. She slinks to the ground, out of sight of the guards patrolling the area, and she ducks behind the cars. She peers at the vehicles; they all look good, capable, sturdy.

"Oh, *hello,*" Emma purrs softly.

The sleek, red convertible seems to be calling her name like a beautiful siren just sitting there in the carport, waiting for her: red trim, leather seats, bright red steering wheel, manual drive.

The license plate reads KING.

It's utterly impractical for her mission. It's an antique model, and one look at the dashboard says it still runs on gas. *And, look at the color.* It'd be visible from just about anywhere.

It's perfect.

Emma crawls over to the car and surreptitiously makes her way to the door. *Hah.* She figured Kingston would be nostalgic. It's not opened by a keycard or by his DED, but with an old-fashioned lock and key. She pulls a pin out of her hair, wedges it in the lock, pulls another one, and waits to hear the tumblers click. It's a slow process, and she's done this before, practiced in Nevada with the others. She remembers Ricky complaining they would ever need to know this, no one used a lock.

At the satisfying click of the tumbler, she pulls the door open as silently as she can, still crouched on the ground. The guards aren't paying attention, but Emma can't trust that they won't look this way, and starting the car and driving it out of here is going to be extremely noticeable. *Best to do it in one go.*

Emma opens the glove compartment and finds a spare set of keys. One of the buttons on the keyfob reads "Start Engine." *Remote activation. Nice.*

She shuts the door as quietly as she can and turns the key. The car purrs to life, a deep mechanical rumble that's all twenty-first-century. It's a gas engine, running solely on fossil fuels. *An ancient vehicle. Fueling it up must cost a fortune.*

Emma can appreciate it, though. She runs her hands along the chrome edge of the dashboard and the leather seats and inhales deeply. The cherry red color continues on the inside in several accents complemented by the walnut wood paneling along the doors.

What a beautiful car!

Emma grins wildly. She's gonna *wreck* it.

"Hey, what's going—"

Emma steps on the gas. The car accelerates like a dream, more powerful than anything she's ever driven, and she nearly loses control as it starts going backward. She careens out of the turn; shifts into forward.

"*Stop*! Stop, that's Kingston's favorite car!"

Emma laughs, waving out the window. She scrapes past another car. "Whoops! Sorry! Actually, I'm not sorry at all! Bye!" she screams gleefully, leaving dents and scratches everywhere as she races out of the garage and into the night.

The night sky is aglow from the bright orange debris falling from space. The impact countdown has already started. The guards don't pursue her, and Emma picks up speed, driving as fast as she can toward the location she memorized on the map.

Outside the shield, Emma sees the glow of fires spreading from the fallen meteors and other debris. When she opens the window, she's hit with the smell of charred wood; the forests surrounding the city must be catching fire. The streets are empty; everyone in New Bright City is already hunkered down in their shelters. Wind whips through Emma's short hair, and with the wind, glowing embers and bits of ash are flying everywhere.

Emma breathes in the hot air as she speeds through the empty streets, racing out of the city in record time. She shudders as she drives through the shield; it feels gross, like wading through pudding, but it's over in a second.

She plows through the Unmaintained lands; the streets here are pockmarked with small craters; a few are still aflame. Emma can see the traces of what once was a satellite: a chrome piece that could be a solar panel, a huge chunk of metal that could be a radio antenna. The sky is filled with white-hot streaks as the meteors continue to fall, bringing with them hundreds of years of humanity's space debris. These pieces—some as small as her fist, some as big as the car she's driving—are causing spectacular damage falling to Earth.

Emma shakes her head, driving as fast as she can out of the city.

A huge, flaming mass comes hurtling toward her, and Emma screams, jerking the car wildly to the right, narrowly avoiding it. She turns to see the mass hit the road behind her.

Emma keeps going.

OUTSIDE THE CITY, THE EFFECTS of the impact are worse. Here in the open fields and the Unmaintained lands it's been dry for ages, creating the perfect tinder for even a stray spark. An entire field is ablaze, and what looks like an official North American Collective farm, entire fields of wheat and corn and soybeans, all gone in an instant.

She heads north, following the old, cracked road, that is repaired just enough to be drivable, but still looks as if it's unmaintained. It must be maintained only enough for Kingston's people to drive out here.

Streaks of blazing fire rain down upon the forest and the mountains surrounding them. The world is on fire. She can hear shouting in the distance, but the flames are taller than she is. The entire field ahead of her is ablaze; the grass is long gone, smoking and charred pieces float about, and she can't tell where the ground ends and the sky begins. She doesn't have Abby's armor or Bells' shapeshifting ability or Jess' ability to find a safe route; she doesn't have any powers at *all*. But she can do this. She can find her friends.

Emma coughs, exhaling smoke as she sees a shape in the fire. That must be it; it's the only building for miles, an ugly squat square thing with a reinforced door. The facility looks flimsy, made from plywood and scrap in a clumsy attempt to blend in with the rest of the pre-Collective buildings that were gutted by the Disasters but still stand. It's clearly an outlier, something built recently for a sinister purpose.

Emma shakes; her hands drum on the wheel as she recognizes her friends' voices. Abby's cries out in a hoarse voice. Bells shouts as if he's struggling with a heavy weight. Jess gives steady assurances even as her voice wavers.

Emma looks up at the sky, unsure how much time she has. An unnaturally bright star seems to be growing exponentially, and Emma gulps. *This must be it.*

It's one thing to calculate a trajectory and see the solution in numbers and coordinates on a screen, and another to see the result of countless calculations and predictions in person: meteors hurling toward Earth. The damage from the first wave of debris is already evident in the pockmarked field, huge craters in the earth, the entire field gone up in flames. Emma can feel the heat in the air, and it seems to pulsate, thicken, take on a life of its own.

The building is still standing, but it seems to be locked.

Crash. Another piece of debris takes off the entire roof of the building, and now the whole thing is on fire.

Screams.

Flames grow taller and taller, lick the edge of the building.

Emma takes a deep breath. She has no one to help her, no one behind her, no powers to think of, but she's not going to let that stand in the way of helping her friends.

"I just have to cross the field," Emma mutters.

A few seconds are all she needs. She spots a path; bare bits smolder where the flames aren't as intense. She can avoid the fires; it'll be like a game, except this is very real and losing would mean certain death.

On the other side are her friends. They need her help. They need *her*.

"I'm on my way." Emma jams her foot on the pedal, going at full speed.

The little convertible launches forward. It's just momentum and wheels and determination now, and Emma and the car fly through the fire, past the flames and the danger and toward the waiting darkness.

She pushes open the door and jumps out of the car, tumbling forward into the smoldering grass. She can smell burnt hair—her own—and singed rubber and fabric. She rolls into a little ball, watching the vehicle gain mass and momentum.

The car charges through the doors of the facility and bursts through the metal like a hot knife through butter. The building never stood a chance.

The wind picks up, and Emma knows there are hot embers landing in her hair, on her shoulders. She runs forward, right into the open gap in the burning building.

She takes off her jacket, uses it to cover her mouth and nose, but still coughs as she pushes through the smoke. It's hard to see, but there's a glimmer of metal and chains somewhere through the flames.

Fire. Fire all around her, blazing unnaturally in all sorts of colors. Metals in the air, corroded paint in the buildings burning; this facility is filled with toxins that give the fire new life, the flames taking on colors. Most prominent is dark violet. Purple has always been her favorite color; it's alarming now to see it so menacing, so ready to destroy. Emma remembers the properties of tantalum; it burns purple. It must be everywhere here at this compound. Tantalum suppresses powers. So, if it's everywhere, her friends won't be able to do anything to get out.

Emma charges forward.

The air is heavy, and the fire outside seems distant, just background noise. But the fire is the least of their worries; P019 isn't over, and there are more meteors to come. Emma looks up, and the night sky is unnaturally bright as the star that isn't a star hurtles toward them. "Bells! Abby! Jess!" Emma yells.

"Em!" Bells sounds both relieved and terrified.

"How did you know we were here?" Jess coughs.

Emma waves the heavy smoke away and finally can see them all clearly; they're all standing; a set of heavy chains is wrapped around the seven of them. "It's a long story," Emma says, grabbing the chain and yanking.

"We've tried that," Bells says. "There's tantalum in these chains, tantalum all over the building— I can't shift—"

"Okay, okay, I'll figure out a way." Emma exhales, shaking her head at all of them. "I can't believe you got caught!"

"It was Abby's fault," Ricky says.

"Not my fault," Abby snaps. "Look, we had to go after you—"

"And then Vindication—"

"I told you not to follow," Emma says, looking for something, anything to break the chains with.

"You told *me* not to follow," Bells says smugly. His expression changes into worry. "Did you— are you okay?"

"Is *she* okay!" Ricky shrieks. "She's not the one chained up in a burning building!"

Emma grabs the first thing she sees; a long, heavy hunk of metal that probably belonged to a sign or a pole. She drags it forward, being careful of the jagged edges of broken steel, and steps around the smoldering wooden beams.

She walks around her friends and the heavy chains binding them to the pole and picks out a wide swath of chain links between Jess and Bells. She heaves the jagged metal, silently thanking all the hours and hours she spent with Southard cutting logs.

Emma swings.

The sound of the steel hitting the links clanks, and beads of sweat drip down Emma's forehead. She swings again, gritting her teeth at the jarring sound, and then there's a satisfying *clink* and the sound of a link dropping to the ground. Emma grabs at the chains, pulling the first layer free.

Christine kicks the chain, forcing another layer down.

"What are you doing?" Sasha elbows her sister, pushing at the chain.

"Trying to teleport!"

Jess and Abby kick and push and finally all the chains are on the ground.

Ricky whoops just as another beam falls from the collapsing building.

Emma coughs. "Come on, let's get out of here!"

The sky is now almost as bright as day, lit by blazing fire.

"We're not gonna make it," Abby mutters.

"We're going to make it!" Jess affirms, pumping her fist. "Just run!"

Bells cracks his neck; his body extends as he grows, his arms and legs grow longer and longer. "I've got this," he says. He picks them all up and strides through the falling beams and fire as Jess frantically shouts directions.

"Left! Now, right! And jump!"

Fresh air meets them just as the sky blazes with another meteor, which crashes into the building. The ground shakes and buckles, but they're all safe, lying in the parched dirt. Even Kingston's beautiful car survived. The paint is scratched, and the front is dented beyond belief, but it looks mostly intact even crashed into a wall.

Ricky coughs. "You can still use your powers? How come I can't?"

"The tantalum," Jess says. "We were in there for hours; it affects us differently, I guess."

Sasha whistles. "Bells, you're something else."

"I know," Bells says proudly, exhaling.

Emma doesn't know who bursts into laughter first, but it's infectious, and soon all seven of them are giggling and laughing.

Jess grabs Emma in a hug. "Thank you so much; we thought— I didn't think we'd ever see you again."

"Yeah, it was a good plan. I mean, leaving us here chained up in tantalum," Abby says, heaving. "We couldn't get out and—"

Emma doesn't know why, but she lets out a short burst of hysterical laughter. "No one with powers would be able to."

She turns; Bells is lying in the dirt next to her, and now face-to-face with him, she's overcome with emotion: affection, relief, hope, all bundled together in a tumultuous mix.

"Oh, Em—" Bells says, eyes brimming with tears. "Is a hug okay?"

"Yeah, of course," Emma says, exhaling.

Bells wraps her up in his arms, and then it's just her and Bells and how much she's missed him.

Emma looks up and smiles at him. She has so much she wants to say, starting with how sorry she is for leaving but it all disappears with that smile. Everything she was afraid of, not being good enough for the Resistance, being worried about Bells— it all seems so small now.

Bells smiles at her, and Emma can see five-year-old Bells telling her, "friends forever no matter what," and Bells telling her months ago that he would always love her, and it all will be okay.

THROUGH THE BILLOWING SMOKE BEHIND them, the trailing embers glowing against the dark, wasted landscape, a figure steps strides toward them— a masked man wearing a supersuit in red, a V emblazoned on his chest. His cape flaps majestically in the wind.

Vindication.

Emma sits up. Her friends do too, sharing a terrified look; Emma can only wonder about their last interaction.

Bells is shaking. Jess grips Abby's hand. Ricky cowers behind Christine. Sasha and Tanya close their eyes, as if they're trying to use their powers.

Emma's mind spins. *A plan.* She needs a plan.

Vindication laughs. "Well, Miss Robledo, how commendable. You've found my assets." he says. His voice is familiar, the way he says *Miss Robledo*—

Bells squares his jaw, stepping forward. "If you wanted to kill us—"

"Just frighten," he says coldly. "You weren't in any real danger from the impact; I just wanted to show you what happens when you cross me."

"We could have died!" Tanya snaps.

"Perhaps," Vindication replies. "In any case, it wouldn't have been a huge loss. There are plenty of other meta-humans I can work with."

It's the voice—the tone—the practiced way he's shaping his words: camera ready, as if he's leading a show.

"Lowell Kingston," Emma says suddenly.

"What?' Jess turns sharply to look at her. "You're sure?"

Vindication doesn't say anything, but Emma knows she's right. Vindication is Kingston. Kingston is Vindication. The very same man who sits as one of the scions of leadership on the Council, the man the country trusts most, he's been gallivanting around as a masked vigilante.

Abby whips her head toward him, and, behind her, Emma can hear her friends take the image in. The man and his fluttering cape, the way he's hovering in the air, the glowing embers of the burnt hills behind him, the smoke slowly rising. He's all coiled anger and power in front of them, the same man who's graced the news with promises and comfort guiding the Collective toward a bright, shining future.

"That's who you are," Emma says. "Those experiments, you had Orion's research, too. Except you had all of it, and you perfected it. That's what you were offering. Powers. Activating the meta-gene. Except you can't fully activate a gene that isn't expressed in someone. But you can, literally, inject powers into someone, and it would take, if you had enough of their brain tissue."

"Very astute, Miss Robledo." Vindication—Kingston—laughs, pulling off the mask. "I clearly won't be needing this anymore; this was all part of the plan, anyway."

"And what plan is that?" Jess demands.

"You think I'll tell you everything?"

He glances up, his eyes cold and triumphant, and then effortlessly floats into the air.

He's flying. Lowell Kingston is *flying*. Emma knew Vindication could fly, had seen it recorded; but it's something else, something utterly and terrifyingly *real*, seeing it happen before her.

Emma is frozen in shock, in fear.

Through the smoke, more figures are approaching: two, three, five, seven. Emma can't count them, there are too many. Some of them are distinctly human, but many of them are the square, hovering robots that haunt her nightmares. They're getting closer.

The first to join Kingston's side is Dynamite.

Kingston paces, as if he'd timed this for extra drama. "You know, your little Resistance efforts are sad, really. I've come across your messages, trying to warn people. Oh, so easy to find, to erase."

Abby's hands ball into fists, and she tenses as if she's going to charge forward, but Jess holds her back. Jess looks at Emma, her eyes questioning.

Emma's thinking. If he has Orion's powers—controlled lightning blasts and flight—he should also have her power level. Orion was a Class C, despite all the supplmenets and attempts to be stronger.

"We need to run," Jess whispers. "I don't know why my instinct says backward—"

"There's too many of them, they'd surround us," Emma says. "And the bots—"

"I've got an EMP in my pocket," Abby whispers.

"Okay. Keep him talking," Emma says; a plan is forming in her head. "Abby, wait until the right moment."

"He just said he wasn't going to monologue," Ricky mutters.

"Oh, yeah?" Bells says, with exaggerated cheekiness. He gives Emma a sidelong glance and a wink; he knows what he's doing.

Bells calls out to Vindication, challenging him. "What makes you think you could use those powers better than Orion? It's all for show, anyhow."

"Yeah," Sasha taunts. "Like, flight? That cape?

Christine scoffs. "You look ridiculous. What cheap fabric! Couldn't you have used something that isn't polyester?"

Kingston's eyebrows twitch.

"And what's up with that color scheme?" Tanya adds. "So gaudy."

"It's *dramatic,*" Kingston says, testily. "I am power, I am influence, I am— VINDICATION!"

Emma yawns. "You're quite boring as a hero. I'm actually disappointed."

Kingston's face turns red. "How dare you? I am the best meta-human this country has ever seen! Better than Orion, better than the original wave really. I'm going to revolutionize the way we use powers. No more of this silly farce." He grins, every one of his gleaming white teeth sparkling with menace. "The only people who'll have powers are the ones I decide are worthy. No more Heroes' League of Heroes, no more Villain's Guild. It'll be a new era!"

Kingston laughs, stepping forward, holding his hands out and watching the lightning crackle between his fingertips. "You know, when I first started in Meta-Human Affairs, we talked about so much about meta-humans, especially the truly powerful ones. The idea of the League itself, a group of heroes founded to help people and inspire others, well, after the Disasters, they needed something to focus on. A villain." He smiles. "Everyone needs a good villain, you know?"

Emma makes a gesture behind her back, encouraging her friends to follow her. *How much longer will they need?* She steps backward, a few steps at first, then faster. She hopes it seems they're afraid. Yes, Jess is backing up with her, and Bells, and Abby.

Kingston is still talking. Behind him, other meta-humans approach, and the MR-D4Rs rise up behind them, flanking them like a small army. "Gravitus was an easy scapegoat for the early stages of the League, but it's really only in the last decade that we really came across a great system. Meta-Human Training, to find the perfect people to cast as villains. Interesting powers, of course, low enough level that they weren't a danger, and of course finding the right leverage." Kingston looks to his side, where Dynamite is grinning maniacally. "And of course, sometimes we happen upon individuals that have just the right temperament."

"Is that why you kidnapped us? Locked us up in tantalum— you were going to take our powers too?" Bells glares at Kingston, and then makes a gesture behind his back. A thumbs up. It's simple, clear. He trusts her. He trusts Emma's plan. He has no idea what it is, but he's going with it. Bells glances at Emma and mouths the words, *I got you.*

Emma wants to smile back, to repeat it to him, and the tension, the fear, the worry she's carrying eases. Oh, yes, they could all very well die in the next moment. But right now, she feels invincible.

Emma reaches in her pocket and presses a button on the car keys and behind them she can hear its engine purr.

Kingston shrugs. "Take your powers," he scoffs. "Nothing so dramatic. It's quite a lot of work, the power-transfer process. And you're all quite useless, aside from the shapeshifter."

Bells tenses.

"Don't you dare touch him. Stay away from my friends. All of them," Emma says, her voice hardening with anger. "You think this makes you stronger? It doesn't."

Kingston holds up a finger and wags it at her. "You know, despite all her incredible powers, Orion was weak. Gave in to monologuing, which is how I know you children recorded all that incriminating footage in the first place. Unlike her, I am quite aware of the power of image. And I am above monologuing."

"You killed Orion," Emma says. There's a part of her that's shocked, angry, even sad; she didn't deserve that.

Kingston gives them a smug grin. "You're right. And you know, we were right, to rein her in. All she ever wanted was fame and fortune and to be the face of the North American Collective. We gave her all that and more. Why, with her powers, she could have easily been the most dangerous and lethal…"

How long has he been talking? How strong had Orion been? Bells said she'd clocked in at four hours, and that was with supplements. Kingston had another mission this morning, and if he flew here, he must be almost tapped out. They're so close. They just need the right moment to make a break for it.

"When I say *now*," Emma whispers to Abby.

She probably dared too much. She shouldn't have risked the movement; it's drawn Kingston's attention. But Emma had to take that chance.

Kingston's eyes narrow. "You're fools, all of you. And don't you—" he laughs suddenly. "Why, you almost had me. I almost started telling you everything, but I can see right what you're doing; you think you're so smart."

He laughs again. "All this time I've been working with the League I thought it was about control. But this? This is unparalleled." He flies in the air, zooming directly at them. "It turns out that all I needed was some perspective."

Oh, no. Oh, no. The monologue is over. "NOW!" Emma screams. "Run!"

She whirls around and dashes for the car; behind her, Abby activates the EMP and throws it at Kingston's supporters and the bots. It goes off in a silent thump, and then the first row of MR-D4Rs powers down.

It's a mad scramble. Emma's heart pounds, and she makes sure her friends are right behind her as they rush into the car.

Emma presses on the gas and doesn't look back.

Emma just drives, not even looking for the road. She needs to gain as much speed as she can. Her friends are shouting something, encouragement or fear or both, and then Bells' hands come to rest on her shoulders, squeezing her in affirmation. The meteors are still incoming, and huge pieces of debris crash about them, all fire and flame and destruction raining down around them. The ground is quaking; every bit of flaming shard thunders as it crunches into the earth.

Emma swerves to avoid a huge piece, and everything turns to hyperfocus. There's nothing but her beating heart and her hands on the wheel and concentration on getting them out of here. She jerks the wheel to avoid another flaming piece of debris, but she keeps going, keeps pushing forward into the night.

They've got to get out of the blast zone. Emma looks at her options: the bare fields ahead of her and the road and the gentle slope.

She turns sharp right toward the hill and lets gravity pull them forward, and then momentum takes the lead and they're still going, going.

Finally, the car rolls to a stop, and Emma blinks and the world comes back to focus.

"It's stopped," Jess says. "The worst is over."

There are still a few small bits raining down, floating embers falling behind them, but the sky is dark again and the stars shine, glimmering billions of miles away in their distant homes.

Emma turns around and, in the distance, where the building once stood is nothing but a crater reaching out to just a few feet behind them, pocked with huge pieces of a satellite. Shards of metal, twisted and burned beyond recognition, lie scattered across the ground, but everything seems unnaturally cool now. Kingston and the other meta-humans are gone; they must have fled to avoid the impact.

She takes a deep breath, taking in the scent of ozone, and thinks of the dream she had as a child of going to see the stars. The stars had come down to them tonight, but they lived.

EMMA'S TEMPTED TO KEEP THE car and drive right to Christine's, but she admits Abby's paranoia is right; it probably is bugged. It wouldn't be worth it to escape from Kingston's clutches only to lead him right to their hideout. They drive to the city and hide the car in one of the ramps leading to the Underbright for future debugging. From there, it's just a matter of walking through the network of tunnels until they reach the other side of the city.

"Hey," Emma says. She and Bells have fallen behind on the walk; their hands brush. She can sense his hesitation, the question in his eyes; it's probably time. "I'm sorry about leaving like that."

Bells shakes his head. "I'm sorry if I— I don't know if it was me, if I ever said anything to make you feel like you weren't useful—"

"No, no—" Emma sighs. "I let Deirdre get to me."

"I could have said something."

"You did."

"Yeah, once, and then I got caught up in the missions. I'm sorry, Em."

Emma sniffs. "Can I hug you?"

"Of course— I only asked earlier because I thought you didn't— you didn't want—" Bells sighs. "Well, I thought you wanted to break up or something."

"I…" Emma presses into his chest; Bells rests his chin on her head; his arms pull her close. She sighs, closing her eyes, and then opens them, pulling out of the hug. "I think I've been stressing out about the relationship thing too. Honestly, I don't think I can do the romantic relationship, Bells. Being boyfriend-girlfriend, it's weird. I don't think it's really something I could do."

Bells nods, looking at her sincerely. "Okay. You know that I'll always love and support you, right?"

Emma bites her lip and smiles at him. "Me too. And I've been really happy being *together* with you too. I just— I think I jumped into labeling it something that I wasn't comfortable with, or maybe built up all these expectations in my head." She takes a deep breath and looks in his brown eyes, taking in the soft way he looks at her, the way he's holding her, the way he's always had her back. "You're really important to me. I want to be with you and have a relationship and I think— I think what I want is a queerplatonic relationship." Emma's nervous, but she knows it's what she wants, knows that whatever happens now, at least she was honest about that.

Bells nods once more, smiling. He wipes the tear threatening to fall down her cheek. "I think that would be great."

"Really?"

He pulls her back into the hug and kisses her forehead. "Yes. Absolutely."

"And you're happy?"

"Em, we've talked about this— this relationship is what we make it. I'm happy to be with you. Romance isn't the only kind of love." He smiles at her, pressing his forehead to hers.

Emma can feel him breathing, can feel his heartbeat pounding in a steady rhythm in his chest. Those fears and worries she's been carrying in her heart fade away, and she feels a fervent hope blossoming inside her, growing stronger and stronger. They've got this. They've got everything to look forward to and can develop this relationship together.

"So HE HAD A SPACE shuttle?" Brendan exclaims, stunned. "That's impossible; how could he have hidden it?"

"Maybe it's in that massive abandoned building just east of the city," Sasha muses.

"I still can't believe you all got caught," Brendan mutters. "I was so worried when you didn't come back, and then Mom and Dad—"

Jess chuckles, elbowing her brother. "You were too busy anyway helping Michael destroy all his research."

"Did you really see brains?" Brendan asks, practically bouncing.

"Yeah," Emma says.

"I'm glad you came and rescued us," Bells says, "but I'm just thinking of all the possibilities if you wanted to play as a double-agent."

Emma scoffs.

"Come on, you could have gone to space!"

It's not a dream that's gone entirely; Emma thinks of school and a future in the stars and looks up at the sky. "It'll still be there," Emma says. "When I'm ready." For now, the fight is what's important. Without changing the corruption in the Collective, there won't be a future—a good one, for anyone.

They turn the corner, running into a group of teens wearing similar punk makeup and clothes. "Hey!" one says, waving at them. "Are you going to the speech?"

"Yeah," Jess says.

"You know that League is a lie, right?"

Emma blinks. "What did you say?"

"The League! The whole system is messed up, like how we watch all these heroes and villains fight one another—"

Emma and Bells trade stunned glances. "Yeah! The League is a lie!"

The punks and their friends nod at them before continuing on their walk.

"I can't believe it," Emma says. "The word-of-mouth movement. It worked."

"See, your plans are great," Bells says, nudging her.

THE SQUARE IS CROWDED, FILLED with people avidly waiting for news. From the back, Emma can barely see Kingston approach the podium, but she can see his smug countenance projected above the square.

"Citizens of the Collective," Kingston says, gripping the edges of the podium. "It is a time of great turmoil and confusion. I understand the recent events and skirmishes between meta-humans, especially this new crop of villains, associated and unassociated with the Villain's Guild, have left many of you afraid for your safety."

There's a murmur growing in the crowd.

"Now, various reports about the nature of the League have been broadcast about over the Net. I urge you not to listen to these reports, as they are wildly inaccurate. Trust in the Collective. Trust in the Heroes' League of Heroes. We are here to protect you from all the new vigilantes out there. You may think our country is going wild and out of control, but it's more important than ever before to obey the Authorities and the Council that protects you. Many of you have upgraded your MonRobots and your home security, with good reason. This is a good first step. But the next step is electing officials who can properly protect you."

He steps back from the podium, and the curtain rises to reveal a number of meta-humans standing shoulder to shoulder next to him. Aside from a few familiar faces, everyone looks brand new. "I stand with the League, and we are here to protect you. The so-called Resistance are nothing but rabble-rousers and dissidents who seek to destroy the unity of our great nation. You may know that the Central Regions are to vote soon on a new leader to represent them for the North American Collective. Who better to lead you than a man who has led you through the most prosperous era of peace and safety these past few years? Who has stepped up to protect you in this time of new fear and turmoil?

"Citizens, I have an announcement. Our heroes have often protected their identities behind masks and alter egos, but I see no need for this. In my support for the League and out of respect for my fellow meta-humans—"

Emma hears gasps.

Kingston holds out his hands and floats above the podium, and then lightning crackles in his left hand, and his right hand glows with red-hot power, and then he brings it down onto the podium, which explodes into splinters.

"I have no need for a hero name; I *am* a hero. You may have seen me a few times these past few months, masked, as I joined my fellow meta-humans in the League in your protection. I was masked then because I didn't want to overshadow the hardworking heroes in the League. But rest assured, I am stepping forward now into the light, so all know the truth. I will use my powers to protect you from this imminent threat."

"Kingston! Kingston! Kingston!" The shouts grow louder and louder until Kingston's name is indistinguishable from the roars of cheers and applause.

"Why are they clapping? He's the one who's been causing all the 'turmoil and confusion,'" Jess says, her mouth set in a grim, flat line.

"They don't know any better," Bells says.

"Maybe they do," Emma says, looking through the crowd. There are a number of people whispering to each other, not participating in the mob of applause; a few pull up their DEDs. She can see in the projected holos the last battle with Captain Orion and Orion clearly advancing upon innocent bystanders in the street, lightning sparking from her fists. Another holo of Vindication pushing aside citizens as he stalks toward Smasher and Shockwave, Starscream ignoring citizens crying for help, hero after hero showing their true nature.

Something crackles behind her, and Emma watches, stunned, as the holodisplays advertising Starscream's shaving cream and

Sublimate's hair gel disappear; the pixels rearrange themselves until the two displays read MISCHIEF LIVES and the LEAGUE IS A LIE.

People turn and point, and someone shouts, "The League is a lie!"

Another sign appears, this time projected by a DED, and another, and another.

Yes, the crowd was awed and stunned by Kingston's display of power, but the chorus of Kingston's name dies down. A few people still shout for Kingston. They don't know the truth.

But Emma does. And so do her friends. And all the Resistance. And many of the people in this crowd. She thought they were a fledgling group, but the numbers prove that they aren't. Everywhere, all over the Collective, people are asking the right questions and looking at the evidence before them.

Emma smiles.

"What?"

"Look, a "The League Is a Lie" shirt," Emma muses.

"Excellent," Jess says.

Emma squeezes Bells' hand. He squeezes back, and Emma's heart soars. She knows where they stand, knows where they stand together.

She looks at her friends, all here despite everything, despite everyone that's come against them: the League and Kingston and Orion and even those in their own Resistance, the differences they've had, the struggle to move forward. Despite everything, they have. And it's clear now that the fight is in the open, and there's nothing that Kingston and the League can do to stop it now that it's started. Every person in every region has the opportunity to question Kingston's word now.

"Change is coming," Emma says. "I promise."

In the face of corruption and lies, they stand together, ready for everything to come.

THE END... FOR NOW!

**ABBY JONES
AND THE SIDEKICK SQUAD
WILL RETURN IN
NOT YOUR HERO**

ACKNOWLEDGMENTS...

It seems like quite a long while ago when I first started on this journey with the *Sidekick Squad*—I remember wanting to tell a superhero story with LGBTQ+ protagonists, and it's become so much more. The books I did not have when I was a teen—I wanted them to exist for teens now, especially those in this community who have not have the opportunity to see themselves in fiction, as heroes, as valid.

For Emma's story, I wanted there to be room in the novel for multiple characters who were at different stages, from characters who were confident and had settled into their identity to characters who were just figuring it out, because people are at different stages in their lives. Emma's questioning arc, especially where she is on the aromantic spectrum, closely mirrors my own, and in writing this I hope to show a questioning character's journey who had the opportunity to learn and grow in this way. It took me a long time to understand where I was on the spectrum, and reading characters who were a-spec and questioning helped me understand more my own identity and being demiromantic. I wanted to have a character that could exist in this space for those who were questioning and also to show this journey as a normal experience.

Thank you to the incredible team at Interlude Press: Candy, Annie, and Choi, who from the very beginning believed in this story and gave it a home. The *Sidekick Squad* would not be here today if it weren't for that first enthusiastic yes back when I first submitted my first manuscript. Thank you for your endless work and dedication toward nurturing and publishing LGBTQ+ stories. To Annie and everyone on the editorial team, thank you for being such an integral part of this journey. Thank you, Choi, for bringing Emma and the world of the *Sidekick Squad* to life in such vivid color and design and for all the spectacular details and touches. Thank you to Candy for the incredible support and outreach for these stories and helping them get in the hands of readers everywhere, from libraries to booksellers to reviewers. It truly is an honor to be a part of the IP family and work with so many amazing and passionate people.

Thank you to my agent Thao Le and the team at the Sandra Dijkstra Literary Agency for all your support and optimism, for your inspiration and enthusiasm for my ideas; working together is a dream come true.

For early readers, cheerleaders, and writing partners, whose feedback on this journey has been unmeasurable, I cannot thank you all enough: Claudie Arseneault, Ashley Poston, Karuna Riazi, Erica Cameron, Michelle Pierce, Erica Robledo, Joseph Jess Rey, Nilah Magruder, Amy Spalding, and Jenn Polish. Thank you for your thoughtfulness and bringing multiple perspectives to the table, for your time and support.

To Emma and Bells' namesakes, thank you for being an inspiration, for all the joyous ins and outs of reading and writing and chatrooms, for your friendship and love. Thank you to Michelle, Katrina, and Em, for all the endless scrolling of love and support and friendship, here's to what sparks joy. Angie, Becky, Mai, Cal, Beth, Michael, Sylvia, Freck, KT, Leda, Tay, Karen, Mel— thank you so much for all the encouragement, the positivity, and the memes. To Lingfei, the best of friends and best of late-night food runs and movie marathons, thank you for being there. To my LA wolf pack, Chloe and Kate, to old shenanigans and new. Thank you to Diane, Serena, Jeremy, Silas, Rae, and Evelyn for all the wonderful adventures from this year and for your support. Thank you to all the fantastic folks at Inkwell, the Procrastinators, the Sprinters, and the Yellow Gardens: to the endless group chats and love and support of friends, named and unnamed, thank you for being there for me, for sharing your time and energy.

Thank you to the Lambda Literary Foundation and the Writers' Retreat for Emerging LGBTQ+ Voices, Malinda Lo and all the wonderful 2017 YA cohort: Sun, Kate, Ash, Melissa, Tom, Charlie, Al, Nita, Laura, Miranda, and Joanna. Thank you for such a wonderful and inspiring and creative workshop, and I'm looking forward to seeing all of your published works.

To librarians, educators, and booksellers, thank you for your endless devotion and work and creating opportunities for books like mine to thrive. Thank you to the incredible team at the Ripped Bodice, to Bea and Leah Koch for creating such a creative and nurturing space, and for my fellow writers who made this space a home: Sarah Kuhn, Rebekah Weatherspoon, Jenn LeBlanc, Janet Eckford, and Diya Mishra. Thank you Maryelizabeth Yturralde and Jackie Joe at Mysterious Galaxy for your passion and fostering such amazing events and panels. Thank you Missy Fuego, Kay Ulunday Barrett, Crystal Perkins, Zoraida Cordova, Emily Kate Johnson, Margaret Stohl, Paul Krueger, Angel Cruz, Charlie Jane Anders, Dahlia Adler, Marissa Minna Lee, Osric Chau, Andrea Walter, and Jes Vu for believing in the *Sidekick Squad* series.

Thank you so much to Julia Ember, Lissa Reed, Rachel Davidson Leigh, Taylor Brooke, Julian Winters, FT Lukens, and Zane Riley for all our journeys and adventures at book festivals and conventions together; thank you for your support, time, and travel. Thank you Rose and Jordan for the incredible creativity and collaboration for FanMailBox; I'm so honored to have the *Sidekick Squad* featured.

Thank you to all the bloggers and reviewers: You're so wonderful and dedicated, whether you're creating websites, organizing bingos and chats, reviewing, creating reclists, or providing thoughtful insight and meaning to books and characters, sharing so much love. I want to shout out to Cece, CW, Corey, Mish, and Kav for all their insight and inspiration. Thank you to all the amazing people out there; your work as a blogger is so appreciated.

To my parents and my brother, thank you for your support, thank you to all my family, blood and found. Writing these books has been a journey, and I could not have done it without so many amazing people to support me. Thank you to the NaNoWrimo writing community, NaNo Los Angeles Coffee House, new friends, and to those who've been with me from the very beginning; you are my anchor.

And above all else, thank *you*—to the readers. For picking up the book and giving it a chance, for reading, for sharing, for gifting it to others—any and all of these—and for being patient and waiting for this book, for the encouraging messages and the tweets and the reclists and the bookstagram shots and the aesthetics and the fanart and the reviews and videos, *everything*. Thank you so much for being here for the *Sidekick Squad*. I'm so thankful you're here on this journey with me and I look forward to sharing the next adventure with you.

ABOUT THE AUTHOR...

C.B. Lee is a Lambda Literary Award-nominated writer of young adult science fiction and fantasy. Her works include the Sidekick Squad series (Duet Books) and Ben 10 (Boom!). C.B. loves to write about queer teens, magic, superheroes, and the power of friendship. When not nationally touring as an educator, writer, and activist, C.B. lives in Los Angeles, where she can neither confirm nor deny being a superhero. You can learn more about her and her adventures as a bisexual disaster across social media.

CONNECT WITH C.B. ONLINE

🌐 cb-lee.com
🐦 @author_cblee
📘 authorcblee
📷 cblee_cblee

For a reader's guide to **Not Your Backup** and
book club prompts, please visit duetbooks.com.

duet.

an imprint of interlude**press**

🌐 duetbooks.com
🐦 @DuetBooks
t duetbooks
🛒 store.interludepress.com

Content Advisory:

Some internalized shame throughout an aromantic and
asexual questioning arc (examined), some sci-fi violence
and offscreen non-graphic minor character deaths.

also from duet.

Not Your Sidekick by C.B. Lee
Sidekick Squad, Book One
Lambda Literary Award Finalist

Welcome to Andover, where superpowers are common—but not for Jessica Tran. Despite her heroic lineage, Jess is resigned to a life without superpowers when an internship for Andover's resident supervillain allows her to work alongside her longtime crush Abby and helps her unravel a plot larger than heroes and villains altogether.

ISBN (print) 978-1-945053-03-0 | (eBook) 978-1-945053-04-7

Not Your Villain by C.B. Lee
Sidekick Squad, Book Two
American Library Association GLBT Rainbow Book List

Being a shapeshifter is awesome. That is, until Bells inadvertently becomes the country's most wanted villain. He's discovered a massive government cover-up, and now it's up to him and his friends to find the Resistance. Sometimes, to do a hero's job, you need to be a villain.

ISBN (print) 978-1-945053-25-2 | (eBook) 978-1-945053-43-6

Seven Tears at High Tide by C.B. Lee

Kevin Luong walks to the ocean's edge with a broken heart. Remembering a legend his mother told him, he lets seven tears fall into the sea. "I just want one summer—one summer to be happy and in love." Instead, he finds himself saving a mysterious boy from the Pacific—a boy who later shows up on his doorstep professing his love. What he doesn't know is that Morgan is a selkie, drawn to answer Kevin's wish. As they grow close, Morgan is caught between the dangers of the human world and his legacy in the selkie community to which he must return at summer's end.

ISBN (print) 978-1-941530-47-4 | (eBook) 978-1-941530-48-1